3 COMPLETE NOVELS

AN

Eva Ibbotson

COLLECTION

Which Witch?

The Secret of Platform 13

Island of the Aunts

DUTTON CHILDREN'S BOOKS ☉ NEW YORK

Which Witch?
Copyright © 1979, 2001 by Eva Ibbotson

The Secret of Platform 13
Copyright © 1994, 2001 by Eva Ibbotson

Island of the Aunts
Text copyright © 1999, 2001 by Eva Ibbotson
Illustrations copyright © 2000, 2001 by Kevin Hawkes

This collection copyright © 2001 by Dutton Children's Books

CIP Data is available.

Published in the United States by Dutton Children's Books,
a division of Penguin Putnam Books for Young Readers
345 Hudson Street, New York, New York 10014
www.penguinputnam.com

Printed in USA
ISBN 0-525-46776-9
1 3 5 7 9 10 8 6 4 2

Which Witch?

Also by Eva Ibbotson
The Secret of Platform 13

Which Witch?

Eva Ibbotson

illustrated by Annabel Large

DUTTON CHILDREN'S BOOKS

New York

For Alan

Library of Congress Cataloging-in-Publication Data

Ibbotson, Eva.
Which witch? / Eva Ibbotson; illustrated by Annabel Large.—1st ed.
p.   cm.
Summary: Deciding that he must sire a child to carry on his
tradition of Loathing Light and Blighting the Beautiful,
the Great Wizard Arriman announces a competition
among the witches of Todcaster, one of whom will marry him.
ISBN 0-525-46164-7 (hc)
[1. Witches—Fiction. 2. Wizards—Fiction. 3. Magic—Fiction.
4. Contest—Fiction.]
I. Large, Annabel, ill.   II. Title.
PZ7.I11555Wh   1999   [Fic]—dc21   99-10199   CIP   AC

Published in the United States 1999 by Dutton Children's Books,
a division of Penguin Putnam Books for Young Readers
345 Hudson Street, New York, New York 10014
http://www.penguinputnam.com/yreaders/index.htm

Originally published in Great Britain 1979 by
Macmillan Children's Books, London
Typography by Richard Amari
Printed in USA
First American Edition
6   8   10   9   7

Which Witch?

Public Library and began to read. He read and he read and he read, and what he read most about was black magic and sorcery and how to tell from a very early age whether someone is going to be a wizard or a witch. After which, he went home and broke the news to Mrs. Canker.

It was a shock, of course. No one *likes* to think that their baby is going to grow up to be a wizard, and a black one at that. But the Cankers were sensible people. They changed the baby's name from George to Arriman (after a famous and very wicked Persian sorcerer), painted a frieze of vampire bats and newts' tongues on his nursery wall, and decided that if he had to grow up to be a wizard they would see to it he was a good one.

It wasn't easy. Todcaster, where they lived, was an ordinary town full of ordinary people. Though they encouraged little Arriman to practice as much as possible, it was embarrassing to have their birdbath full of gloomy and lopsided vultures and to have to explain to their neighbors why their apple tree had turned overnight into a blackened stump shaped like a dead man's hand.

Fortunately, wizards grow up quickly. By the time he was fifteen, Arriman could take a bus to Todcaster Common and raise a whirlwind that had every pair of knickers on every washing line in the area flying

CHAPTER 1

*A*S SOON AS he was born, Mr. and Mrs. Canker knew that their baby was not like other people's children.

For one thing, he was born with a full set of teeth and would lie in his pram for hours, chewing huge mutton bones to shreds or snapping at the noses of old ladies fool enough to kiss him. For another, though he screamed with temper when they changed his nappies, his eyes never actually filled with tears. Also—and perhaps this was the strangest of all—as soon as they brought him home from the hospital and lit a nice, bright fire in the sitting room, the smoke from their chimney began to blow *against* the wind.

For a while the Cankers were puzzled. But as Mr. Canker said, there is a book about *everything* if you only know where to look, and one day he went to Todcaster

3

halfway to Jericho, and soon afterward he decided to leave home and set up on his own.

The search for a new house took many months. Arriman didn't want a place that was sunny and cheerful or a place that was near a town, and though he wanted somewhere ruined and desolate, he was fussy

about the kind of ghost it had. Never having had a sister, Arriman was a little shy with women, and he didn't fancy the idea of a wailing gray lady walking back and forth across his breakfast table while he ate his kippers, or a headless nun catching him in his bath.

But at last he found Darkington Hall. It was a gray, gloomy, sprawling building about thirty miles from Todcaster. To the west of the hall was a sinister forest, to the north were bleak and windswept moors, and to the east, the gray, relentlessly pounding sea. What's more, the Darkington ghost was a gentleman, and the sort that Arriman thought he could well get on with: Sir Simon Montpelier who, in the sixteenth century, had murdered all seven of his wives and now wandered about groaning with guilt, moaning with misery, and striking his forehead with a plashing sound.

And here Arriman lived for many years, blighting and smiting, blasting and wuthering, and doing everything he could to keep darkness and sorcery alive in the land. He filled his battlements with screech owls and his cellars with salamanders. He lined the avenue with scorched tree stumps like gallows, and he dug a well in his courtyard from which brimstone and sulfur oozed horribly. He planted a yew-tree maze so complicated and devilish that no one had a hope of coming out alive, and he made the fountains on the terrace run with blood. There was only one thing he couldn't do— he couldn't raise the ghost of Sir Simon Montpelier. He would have *liked* to do this; Sir Simon would have been company. But bringing ghosts back to life is the blackest and most difficult magic of all, and even Arriman couldn't manage it.

The years passed. Though he seldom left the hall, Arriman's fame was spreading. People called him Arriman the Awful. Loather of Light, and Wizard of the North. Stories began to be told about him: how he could make the thunder come before the lightning, that he was friends with Beelzebub himself. But Arriman just went on working. He had grown to be a tall and handsome man with dark, flashing eyes, a curved nose like the prow of a Viking ship, and a flourishing mustache, but despite his fine looks, he was not at all conceited.

In the years that followed, Arriman set up a private zoo in which he kept all the nastiest and ugliest animals he could find: monkeys with bald faces and blue behinds, camels with sneering lips and lumpy knees, wallabies with feet like railway sleepers that kicked everything in sight. He turned the billiard room into a laboratory in which fiendish things bubbled all day long, giving off appalling smells, and he called in rain clouds from the sea to drip relentlessly onto his roof.

Then one day he woke feeling completely miserable. He knew he ought to get up and throw someone into his well or order a stinking emu for the zoo or mix something poisonous in his laboratory, but he just couldn't face it.

"Lester," he said to the servant who brought him his breakfast. "I feel tired. Weary. Bored."

Lester was an ogre, a huge, slow-moving man with muscles like footballs. Like most ogres, he had only one eye in the middle of his forehead, but so as not to upset people he wore a black eye patch above it to make people think he had two. Before he came to be Arriman's servant, Lester had been a sword swallower in a fair, and he still liked to gulp down the odd saber or fencing foil. It soothed him.

Now he looked anxiously at his master. "Do you, sir?" he said.

"Yes, I do. In fact, I don't know if I can go on much longer. I thought I might go away somewhere, Lester. Take a little room in some pretty market town perhaps and write a book."

The ogre was shocked. "But what would happen to blackness and evil, sir?"

Arriman frowned. "I know, I know. I have a duty, I see that. But how long am I supposed to go on like this? How long, Lester?" The frown deepened and he waved his arms in desperation. "How *long*?"

Lester wasn't the stupid kind of ogre who goes around saying "Fe Fi Fo Fum" all the time. So now he looked at his master and said, "Well, I wouldn't know, sir. Ogres can't tell the future, you know. Gypsies can, though. Why don't you go and have your fortune told? There was a gypsy where I worked. Esmeralda, they called her. Knew her stuff, she did."

So the following week, Arriman and Lester drove into Todcaster to find the fair.

They found Esmeralda's caravan quite easily. You could tell it from the other gypsy caravans because the people who came out of it looked as though they didn't know what had hit them.

"She tells the truth," explained Lester, sniffing happily at the remembered fairground smells: fried onions from the hamburger stall, hot engine oil from the bumper cars. . . . "None of that garbage about dark strangers and journeys across the sea."

Esmeralda was a frizzy-haired lady in a pink satin blouse. Arriman had left off his magician's cloak and changed into a gray pinstripe, but the look she gave him was very sharp indeed.

"For you it'll be a fiver," she said. "Sit down."

She pocketed the money, took a swig from a bottle labeled Gordon's Gin, and began to stare into her crystal ball.

She stared for a long time. Then she pushed the ball away and lit a cigarette. "It's all right," she said. "He's coming."

"Who?" said Arriman eagerly. "Who's coming?"

"The new bloke," said Esmeralda. "The one that's going to take over from you."

Arriman looked bewildered. "What new bloke?"

Esmeralda closed her eyes wearily. "Do you want me to spell it out for you?" She put on a posh voice and droned: "Soon there cometh a great new wizard whose power shall be mightier and darker even than your own. When this great new wizard cometh, you, Arriman the Awful, will be able to lay down the burden of darkness and evil which you have carried for so long." She opened her eyes. "Got it?" she said nastily.

"Oh, yes, yes!" said Arriman happily. "I suppose you don't know *when* he cometh?"

"No," snapped Esmeralda, "I don't. Next customer, please."

After his visit to Esmeralda, Arriman was a happy man. Just to fill in time he planted a brier hedge whose thorns oozed blood, ran an oil tanker aground on the cliffs nearby, and invented a new spell for making people's hair fall out. But most of the time he spent by the main gate, watching and waiting for the new wizard to come.

It was cold work. Darkington Hall was as far north as you could get without bumping into Scotland, and when, after a week, Arriman found a chilblain on his left toe, he very sensibly decided to make a Wizard Watcher.

For the Wizard Watcher's body he used a sea lion shape, but larger and furrier with a sloping and rather cuddly chest. The Watcher had four feet and one tail, but it had three heads with keen-sighted and beautiful eyes set on short stalks. And every day at sunrise this gentle and very useful monster would waddle down the avenue, past the blackened trees shaped like gallows, past the oozing well and the devilish maze, and sit in the gateway watching for the wizard.

It watched in this way day after day, month after month, year after year, the Middle Head looking north over the moors, the Left Head looking west across the forest, and the Right Head looking east toward the sea. Then, on the nine hundred and nintieth day of just sitting there, the Wizard Watcher lost heart and became gloomy and annoyed.

"He cometh not from the north," said the Middle Head, as it had done every day for nine hundred and eighty-nine days.

"He cometh not from the west neither," said the Left Head.

"Nor from the east doesn't he cometh," said the Right Head. "And our feet are *freezing*."

"Our feet are blinking dropping *off*," said the Left Head.

There was a pause.

"Know what I think?" said the Middle Head. "I think the old man's been had."

"You mean there ain't going to *be* no new wizard?" said the Left Head.

The Middle Head nodded.

This time the pause was a long one.

"Don't fancy telling him," said the Right Head at last.

"Someone's got to," said the Middle Head.

So the monster turned and lumbered back to the hall, where it found Arriman in his bedroom dressing for dinner.

"Well?" he said eagerly. "What's the news?"

"The new wizard cometh not from the north," began the Middle Head patiently.

"Nor from the west he doesn't cometh," said the Left Head.

"And you can forget the east," said the Right Head, "because the new wizard doesn't cometh from there neither."

Then, speaking all together, the three heads said bravely: "We think you have been taken for a ride."

Arriman stared at them, aghast. "You can't mean it! It isn't possible!" He turned to Lester, who was getting ready to trim his master's mustache. "What do you think?"

The ogre rubbed his forehead under the eye patch and looked worried. "I've never known Esmeralda to make a mistake, sir. But it's been a long—"

He was interrupted by a terrible shriek from Arriman, who was peering forward into the mirror and clutching his head.

"A white hair!" yelled the magician. "A white hair in my curse curl! Oh, shades of darkness and perdition, this is the END!"

His shriek brought Mr. Leadbetter, his secretary, hurrying into the room. Mr. Leadbetter had been born with a small tail, which had made him think he was a demon. This was a silly thing to think because quite a lot of people have small tails. The Duke of Wellington had one and had to have a special hole made in his saddle when he rode to battle at Waterloo. But Mr. Leadbetter hadn't known about the Duke of Wellington and had wasted a lot of time trying to rob banks and so on, until he realized that crime didn't suit him and he became Arriman's secretary instead.

"Are you all right, sir?" he asked anxiously. "You seem upset."

"Upset? I'm finished! *Devastated.* Don't you know what a white hair means? It means old age, it means death. It means the end of wizardry and darkness and doom at Darkington. And where is the new wizard, where, where, *where?*"

The monster sighed. "He cometh not from the north," began the Middle Head wearily.

"I know he cometh not from the north, you dolt," snapped the Great Man. "That's exactly what I'm complaining about. What am I going to *do?* I can't wait forever."

Mr. Leadbetter coughed. "Have you ever, sir, considered marriage?"

There was a sudden flash of fire from Arriman's

nostrils, and from behind the paneling, Sir Simon gave a gurgling groan.

"Marriage! Me marry! Are you out of your *mind*?"

"If you were to marry, sir, it would ensure the succession," said Mr. Leadbetter calmly.

"What on earth are you talking about?" snapped Arriman, who was feeling thoroughly miserable and therefore cross.

"He means you could have a wizard baby, sir. Then it could take over from you. A son, you know," said Lester.

Arriman was silent. A son. For a moment he imagined the baby sitting in his pram, a dear little fellow tearing a marrow bone to shreds. Then he flinched.

"Who would I marry?" he muttered miserably.

But of course he knew. All of them knew. There is only one kind of person a wizard can marry, and that is a witch.

"It wouldn't be so bad, maybe?" said the Left Head encouragingly.

"Wouldn't be so *bad*!" yelled Arriman. "Are you out of your *mind*? A great black crone with warts and blisters in unmentionable places from crashing about on her broom! You want me to sit opposite one of *those* every morning eating my cornflakes?"

"I believe witches have changed since—" began Mr. Leadbetter.

But Arriman wouldn't listen. "Running along the corridors in her horrible nightgown, shrieking and flapping. Getting egg on her whiskers. Expecting her pussycat to sleep on the bed, no doubt!"

"She might not—"

"Every time I went to the kitchen for a snack she'd be there, stirring things in her filthy pot—rubbishy frogs' tongues and newts' eyes and all that balderdash. Never a decent bit of steak in the place, I expect, once she came."

"But—"

"Cleaning her foul yellow teeth in my washbasin," raged Arriman, getting more and more hysterical. "Or worse still, *not* cleaning her foul yellow teeth in my washbasin."

"She could have her own bathroom," said the Middle Head sensibly.

But nothing could stop Arriman, who stormed and ranted for another ten minutes. Then, turning suddenly very calm and pale, he said: "Very well, I see that it is my duty."

"A wise decision, sir," said his secretary.

"How shall I choose?" said Arriman. His voice was a mere thread. "It'll have to be a Todcaster witch, I suppose. Otherwise there's bound to be bad feeling. But how do we decide which witch?"

"As to that, sir," said Mr. Leadbetter, "I have an idea."

CHAPTER 2

*T*HE WITCHES OF TODCASTER were preparing for a coven and they were very much excited. Covens are to witches what the Wolf Cubs or the Brownies are to people: a way of getting together and doing the things that interest them. And this one wasn't to be just an ordinary coven with feasting and dancing and wickedness. Rumors were going around that a most important announcement would be made.

"I wonder what it'll be," said Mabel Wrack. "Some new members, perhaps. We could do with them."

This was very true. Todcaster now had only seven proper witches. If Arriman had known what a state witchcraft had got to in the town of his birth he'd have been even more miserable than he was, but fortunately he didn't.

By day, Ms. Wrack kept a wet fish shop not far from

Todcaster Pier. She was a sea witch and never liked to be too far from the water. Ms. Wrack's mother, Mrs. Wrack, had been a mermaid: a proper one who lived on a rock and combed her hair and sang. But sailors had never been lured to their doom by her, partly because she looked like the back of a bus and partly because modern ships are so high out of the water that they never even saw her. So one day she had simply waddled out onto the beach at Todcaster Head with some sovereigns from a sunken galleon and persuaded a plastic surgeon who was on holiday there to operate on her tail and turn it into two legs.

It was from her mother that Mabel Wrack had her magic powers. From her father, Mr. Wrack, she had the shop.

Today she closed the shutters early, put a couple of cods' heads into a paper bag, and set off for her seaside bungalow. She was just turning into her road when she saw a group of children paddling happily in the surf.

"Tut!" said Ms. Wrack, pursing her lips. She closed her eyes, waved her paper bag with the cods' heads, and said some poetry. Almost at once a shoal of stinging jellyfish appeared in the water and the children ran screaming to their mothers.

"That's better," said Ms. Wrack. Like most witches, she hated happiness.

When she got home she went straight into her bedroom to change. Covens are like parties; what you wear is important. For this one, Ms. Wrack slipped into a purple robe embroidered all over in yellow cross-stitch haddocks, and fastened her best brooch—a single sea slug mounted in plastic—onto the band which kept her frizzy hair in place. Then she went into the bathroom.

"Come on, dear," she said, bending over the bath. "Time to get ready!"

What lived in Ms. Wrack's bath was, of course, her familiar. Familiars are the animals that help witches with their magic and are *exceedingly* important. Ms. Wrack's familiar was an octopus: a large animal with pale tentacles, suckers which left rings of blood where they had been, and vile red eyes. It was a girl octopus and its name was Doris.

"Now don't keep me waiting, dear," said Ms. Wrack. She had fetched a polyethylene bucket from the bathroom cupboard and was trying to stuff Doris inside. "Tonight's going to be an important night."

But Doris was in a playful mood. As soon as one tentacle was in, another was out, and it was a rather bedraggled Ms. Wrack who at last fixed on the lid, loaded the bucket onto an old perambulator, and set off for the coven bus.

Ethel Feedbag's familiar was not an octopus; it was a pig.

Ethel was a country witch who lived in a tumbledown cottage in a village to the west of Todcaster. She was a round-faced, rather simple person who liked to hack at rutabagas with her spade, make parsnip wine, and shovel manure over absolutely everything, and just as people often grow to look like their dogs (or, the other way around), Ethel had grown to look very like her pig. Both of them had round, pink cheeks and very large behinds. Both of them moved slowly on short hairy legs and grunted as they went along, and both of them had dun-colored, sleepy little eyes.

Ethel had a job at the egg packing station. It was a boring job because the eggs she packed were mostly rotten anyway so there was nothing for her to do, but she filled in by giving the sheep husk and turning the cows dry as she bicycled home of an evening. As for the plants in the hedgerow between the egg packing station and Ethel's cottage, there was scarcely one that wasn't covered in mold or rust or hadn't clusters of greedy aphids sucking at its juices.

But tonight she rode straight home. Ethel was not a snappy dresser, but to make herself smart for the coven she rubbed down her Wellington boots with a handful of straw and changed her pinafore for a clean one with felt tomatoes (showing felt tomato blight) stitched to the pocket. Then she started looking for something she could take to eat. There didn't seem to be anything in the kitchen, but on the hearth rug in the living room she found a dead jackdaw which had fallen down the chimney.

"That'll roast a treat!" said Ethel, scooping it up. Then she went down to the shed at the bottom of her garden to fetch her pig.

Nancy and Nora Shouter were twin witches who worked at Todcaster Central Station. They were an unusually disagreeable pair who hated passengers, hated each other, and hated trains. As soon as Nancy went to the loudspeaker and announced that the seven fifty-two to Edinburgh was approaching platform nine, Nora rushed to *her* loudspeaker and cackled into it that the seven fifty-two had engine trouble and would be ninety minutes late and then it wouldn't approach platform nine at all but would come in at platform five, *if* they were lucky.

So now, when they should have been getting ready for the coven, they were standing in their underclothes in the bedroom of their flat in Station Road, arguing about which of their familiars was which.

"That is *so* my chicken!" shouted Nora, tugging at the tail feathers of the unfortunate bird.

"That is *not* your chicken," shrieked Nora. "*That* is your chicken over there!"

It was a most ridiculous argument. The Shouter girls were identical, with dyed red hair, long noses, and smoke-stained fingertips. They dressed alike and slept in twin beds and they both had chickens for familiars, which lived in wicker crates beneath their beds. And, of course, the chickens, too, were very much alike. Chickens often are—fidgety brown birds who would peck your fingers as soon as look at you. But none of this made any difference to the Shouter twins, who went on bickering so long that they were very nearly late for the most important coven of their lives.

For many years now, the witches of Todcaster had met on Windylow Heath, a wild, wuthering sort of place with a few stunted thorn trees, a pond in which a gloomy lady had drowned herself on her wedding eve, and a single rock on which the ancient druids had done some dreadful deeds.

To get there, the witches hired a bus—the Coven Special—which left the bus depot at seven P.M. (No one had flown on a broomstick since a witch called Mrs. Hockeridge had been sucked down the ventilation shaft of a Boeing 707 from Heathrow to Istanbul and nearly caused a very nasty mess indeed.)

The Shouter twins were still quarreling when they got to the depot, but they stopped when they saw, standing on the pavement beside the bus, a small brown coffee table.

"It's her again," said Nancy.

"Silly old crone," said Nora.

"I've a good mind to stub out my cigarette on her," said Nancy, who as usual had one dangling from her lips.

They glared at the squat, round table, which seemed to be swaying a little from side to side.

" 'Tis a pity when they go simple like that," said Ethel Feedbag. She had loaded her pig onto the trailer and now came over and prodded the table leg with her Wellington boot.

The coffee table was in fact a very old witch called Mother Bloodwort, who lived in a tumbledown shack near a disused quarry in the poorest part of town.

When she was young, Mother Bloodwort had been a

formidable witch of the old school, bringing people out in boils, putting the evil eye on butchers who sold her gristly chops, and casting spells on babies in perambulators so that their own mothers didn't know them.

But now she was old. Her memory had gone, and like many old people she got fancies. One of her fancies was to turn herself into a coffee table. There was no point in her being a coffee table: Mother Bloodwort did not drink coffee, which was far too expensive, and since she lived alone there was no one who might have wanted to put a cup and saucer down on her. But she was a cranky old witch and every so often she remembered the spell that changed her from a white-haired, whiskery old woman into a low, oak table with carved legs and a glass top, and then there was no stopping her. What she did *not* often remember was how to turn herself back again.

"Oh, come along," called Mabel Wrack from inside the bus. "Leave the silly old thing where she is."

From her mermaid mother Mabel had inherited rather scaly legs that dried out easily and itched, so she wanted to get to Windylow Heath where the air was damp and cool.

But just then something happened. Two sparrows who'd been squabbling in the gutter lifted their heads and began to sing like nightingales. A flock of golden butterflies appeared from nowhere, and drifting through the grimy bus station came the scent of primroses with morning dew on them.

"Ugh! It's her!" said Nancy Shouter. "I'm off." And she threw her chicken into the trailer and climbed into the bus.

"Me too," said her twin. "I can't *stand* her. I don't know why they allow her in the coven. Really I don't."

Belladonna came slowly around the corner. She was a very young witch with thick, golden hair in which a short-eared bat hung like a little wrinkled prune. There was usually *something* in Belladonna's hair: a fledgling blackbird parked there by its mother while she went to hunt for worms, a baby squirrel wanting somewhere safe to eat its hazelnuts, or a butterfly who thought she was a lily or a rose. Belladonna's nose turned up at the end, making a ledge for tired ladybirds to rest on; she had a high, clear forehead and eyes as blue as periwinkles. But as she came up to the bus she hesitated and looked troubled and sad, for she had learned to expect only unkindness from the other witches.

Then she saw the coffee table and forgot her own troubles at once.

"Oh, *poor* Mother Bloodwort! Have you forgotten the undoing spell again?"

The table began to rock and Belladonna put her arms around it. "Try to think," she said. "I'm sure you can remember. Was it a rhyming spell?"

The table rocked harder.

"It was? Well, I'm *sure* it'll come back in a minute." She leaned her cheek against the glass top, sending healing thoughts into the old witch's tired brain. "It's coming back, I can *feel* it coming back. . . ."

There was a swishing noise, Belladonna tumbled backward, and there, standing before her, was an old woman in a long mouse-bitten cloak and felt bedroom slippers with the sides cut out.

"Thank you, my dear," croaked Mother Bloodwort. "You're a kind girl even if you are—"

But she couldn't bring herself to say the dreadful word—no black witch can. So she hobbled to the bus and began to heave herself aboard, clutching to her chest a large, square tin showing a picture of King George VI's coronation on the lid. The tin *should* have gone in the trailer—there was a rule that all familiars traveled separately—but Mother Bloodwort never let it out of her sight. Inside it were hundreds of large white maggots which, when you blew on them, turned into a cloud of flies. *One* fly is no good for magic, but a cloud of flies—flies in your hair, your eyes, your nose—that makes a very good familiar indeed.

Belladonna was the last to get into the bus. She alone of all the witches had no familiar. For white magic you do not need one. It was another thing that made her feel so very much alone.

CHAPTER 3

*B*ELLADONNA HAD ALWAYS been a white witch. Even as a tiny baby she had used her teeth only to bite the tops off milk bottles so that the bluetits could get at the cream, and as she grew older her whiteness grew steadily worse. Flowers sprang up where she walked, bursts of glorious music fell from the air, and when she smiled, old gentlemen remembered the Christmases they had had when they were children. As for her hair—from the age of six or so when it had reached her waist, there had always been *someone* resting in Belladonna's golden hair.

Belladonna herself longed for blackness—to smite and blast and wreck and wither seemed to her the most wonderful thing in the world. But though she could heal people and charm the flowers out of the ground and speak the language of the animals, even the simplest bit of evil, like, say, turning a pale green cucumber into a greasy black pudding with bits of fat in it, was more than she could manage. Not that she didn't try. Every morning before she went to work (she was an assistant in a flower shop), Belladonna would stand by the open window and say: "Every day and in every way I am getting blacker and blacker."

But she wasn't, and the worst thing she had to bear was the scorn and spite of the other witches. Belladonna really dreaded coven days when she was ignored and despised and had to huddle by herself out of the warm circle of firelight and feasting with only the familiars for company. The only reason she went was that she hoped, one day, some of the blackness might rub off on her.

The bus had left Todcaster now. There was one more witch to pick up on the way. She was a thin, pale witch whom the others called Monalot after a lady on a radio program who was always complaining. Monalot's real name was Gwendolyn Swamp and she played the harp in the Todcaster Palm Orchestra. Ms. Swamp came from a family of banshees, who are the kind of witch who wails and sighs about the place and tells people when something awful is going to happen. Banshees have never been a healthy bunch, and Monalot was so often ill that to get her to the coven at all they usually stopped the bus specially by her house.

"She's not at the gate," said Mabel Wrack impatiently. The air-conditioning in the Coven Special was making her legs itch unbearably.

So Belladonna, who always took the messages and ran the errands for the others, climbed out of the bus and walked through the garden of Monalot's little villa with the name Creepy Corner written on the gate.

The door was open. Belladonna ran up to the bedroom, knocked on the door—and saw at once that Monalot would not be coming to the coven. The poor witch was completely covered in small red spots.

"It's the measles," she moaned. "All over me. Percy, too." She waved a limp hand to the corner of the room where her familiar, a large, sad-looking sheep, was lying. A sheep with measles is unusual, but where there is witchcraft anything is possible.

Belladonna was very upset.

"Couldn't I help?" she began.

But like most witches, Monalot hated the word "help." "No," she moaned. "Just go and leave me. No one wants me anyway, nobody cares."

So Belladonna poured her a drink, plumped up her pillows, and went out, passing, on Monalot's dressing table, wax images of her doctor and the district nurse, both stuck full of pins.

"I'm afraid it's hopeless," she reported, back in the bus. "Ms. Swamp has the measles."

"Stupid old banshee," snapped Nora Shouter.

"They were always delicate, the Swamps," said Mother Bloodwort. She had opened her tin with the coronation on the lid and was stirring her maggots with a long and bony finger. She was still stirring and muttering when the bus got to Windylow Heath.

Two hours later the coven was in full swing. In the middle of the heath, the bonfire roared and crackled, lighting up the Great Rock on which the ancient druids had done their dreadful deeds. The smell of burnt feathers from Ethel Feedbag's roasted jackdaw rose hideously on the night air; clouds passed to and fro across the fitful moon. The witches had finished feasting and singing rude songs (the kind where "owl" doesn't just rhyme with "howl," but with things like "bowel" or "foul") and were dancing back to back, or trying to. Ethel Feedbag's Wellingtons did not help, nor the size of her behind as she lurched round with Mabel Wrack.

"You're going the wrong way, you stupid stick," yelled Nancy over her shoulder to her twin. "It's widdershins we should be going."

"This *is* widdershins, you half-witted cowpat," Nora screamed back.

Mother Bloodwort did not dance anymore. She sat as close to the fire as she could get, her mouse-bitten robe turned back so that the heat could get at her gnarled old legs. Every so often a handful of the flies that buzzed drunkenly round her head fell into the flames and vanished.

As for Belladonna, as usual she was left out in the cold. No one wanted to dance with her, and anyway, like mothers who hand their children over to nannies and nursemaids, the witches had told Belladonna to take their familiars away to a little clump of thorn trees and keep them quiet.

This was easier said than done. As soon as the familiars saw Belladonna they always went to pieces. Ethel Feedbag's enormous pig had collapsed like a felled tree and was lying on its back, its legs in the air, squealing for her to scratch its stomach. The Shouter chickens, who hadn't laid anything in years, began to puff out their feathers and squawk, trying to please her with an egg. And Doris the octopus stuck a tentacle out of her plastic bucket and laid it softly on Belladonna's knee.

Meanwhile, over by the fire, the witches grew wilder and wilder. Mother Bloodwort was knocking back a bottle of black liquid labeled Furniture Polish: Not for Human Consumption. Mabel Wrack was kicking her scaly legs higher and higher, showing off her garters of lungfish skin. The Shouter twins were hacking at each other's shins.

And then, suddenly, something happened.

First there came—from the very depths of the earth it seemed—a low and sinister rumbling. Then the ground began to shake and shiver and a dreadful crack appeared beneath the Great Rock of the druids.

"It's an earthquake," yelled Mabel Wrack, and the witches threw themselves on the ground, gibbering with fear.

Next came a thunderclap, louder than any they had ever heard, followed by a streak of forked lightning so brilliant that it turned night to day.

"The thunder before the lightning!" wailed Mother Bloodwort, and began to beat her white old head against the ground.

After that came the fog, a great, yellow, choking, blinding fog which rolled across the heath, enveloping everything in its cold and smothering darkness.

"It be t'end of the world," wailed Ethel Feedbag.

"It's the Creeping Death," shrieked Nora Shouter.

Only Belladonna was still on her feet, trying to comfort the terrified familiars.

Then, as suddenly as it had come, the great fog rolled away, there was a last clap of thunder—and the witches gasped.

31

For there, standing astride the Great Rock of the druids, was a figure so splendid, so magnificent, that it quite took their breath away.

Arriman had taken a lot of trouble with his clothes. He wore a flowing mantle embroidered with the constellations of the planets, his trousers were of gold lamé, and he wore not just horns but antlers, which Lester had fastened most cunningly behind his ears. With his devilish eyebrows, his soaring mustache, and the sulfurous glow that surrounded him, he presented a vision from which one simply could not tear one's eyes.

"Greetings, ye foulmouthed hags and lovers of darkness!" boomed the great magician.

"Greetings!" croaked the witches, rising slowly to their feet.

Arriman could not see Belladonna, who was hidden behind a thorn tree, but he could see Mabel Wrack, whose sea slug had fallen over one eye, and Ethel Feedbag, a burnt jackdaw feather sticking to her chin. He could see Mother Bloodwort and he could see the Shouter twins, and when he'd seen them he turned and tried to scramble down the rock.

"Steady, sir," said Mr. Leadbetter, who was standing behind the rock with a sheaf of papers.

"The Cankers have never been quitters, sir," said Lester, placing a huge hand on his master's shoulder.

Seeing his retreat cut off, Arriman reluctantly climbed up the rock again. The witches meanwhile were getting dreadfully excited. They had begun to realize that they were in the presence of the Great Wizard of the North, whom nobody had seen for years and years and years and whose power was the greatest in the land.

"Know ye," Arriman went on bravely, "that I am Arriman the Awful, Loather of Light and Blighter of the Beautiful."

"Know we. I mean, we know," croaked the witches.

"Know ye also that, obedient to the prophecy of the gypsy Esmeralda, I have waited nine hundred and ninety days for the coming of the new wizard to Darkington Hall." He caught a whiff of manure from Ethel Feedbag's Wellingtons and staggered backward.

"Bear up, sir," came Lester's voice from the darkness behind him, and with a great effort, Arriman pulled himself together and went on.

"Know ye also that the aforesaid wizard not having turned up, I, Arriman Frederick Canker, have decided to take a wife."

The excitement of the witches grew to a frenzy. They began to mutter and nudge each other and to cackle fiendishly because it was known that Arriman had sworn never to marry. Only Belladonna went on standing quietly in the shelter of the trees, her periwinkle eyes fixed wonderingly on the great magician.

"Know ye," Arriman went on, bracing himself, "that for my bride I have decided to choose a witch of Todcaster and that whichever witch I choose shall reign—" His voice broke. "I can't do it," he murmured, passing a hand across his eyes. He had just caught sight of Mother Bloodwort's fly-covered whiskers in a sudden spurt of firelight.

"No use turning back now, sir," came Mr. Leadbetter's quiet voice. But both the secretary and the ogre, peering out behind the rock, were very much upset. They had had no idea that things had got so bad in Todcaster.

So Arriman made a last desperate effort. "Know ye," he went on, "that to choose which witch shall be my bride, I have arranged a great competition on the grounds of my estate at Darkington during the fearful week of Halloween. And know ye that whichever witch does there the vilest, darkest, and most powerful piece of magic shall be my wife!"

Pandemonium now broke out. Arriman waited for the lurching, cackling, and hiccuping to die down and then he said: "Mr. Leadbetter, my secretary, will stay behind to give you your instructions for the contest. And remember," he said, throwing out his arms, "that what I am looking for is power, wickedness, and evil. Darkness is All!"

And with a sigh of relief, Arriman vanished.

35

When the witches had calmed down again, Mr. Leadbetter stepped out from behind the rock and handed everyone an entry form for the contest. Mother Bloodwort, who couldn't read, held hers upside down, and the Shouter twins immediately began arguing about how many days there were to Halloween.

"What about that lady over there?" said Mr. Leadbetter. He had caught sight of the pale glimmer of Belladonna's hair between the trees.

"Oh, you don't want to bother with *her*," said Nancy Shouter.

"She's not one of us," said her twin.

"Still, she is a witch," said Mother Bloodwort, spitting out a couple of flies. She was the only one who sometimes had a kind word for Belladonna. So Mr. Leadbetter walked over to the clump of trees where Belladonna was still trying to calm the familiars.

"Oh, dear," he said when he had introduced himself. "How *very* unfortunate."

For he realized as soon as he saw her what was wrong. The little, short-eared bat hanging so tenderly in her hair, the chickens roosting on her feet, the scent of primroses with morning dew on them. "Have you . . . er . . . always been . . . ?"

"White?" said Belladonna sadly. "Yes. From birth."

"Nothing can be done, I suppose?"

Belladonna shook her head. "I've tried everything."

"You won't be going in for the contest, then?"

Belladonna shook her head. "What would be the use? You heard him. 'Darkness is All,' he said." Witches cannot cry any more than wizards can, but her eyes were wide with sorrow. "Tell me, is he really . . . as marvelous as he looks?"

Mr. Leadbetter thought. Pictures came into his mind. Arriman shrieking with rage when he lost his suspenders. Arriman filling the bath with electric eels and giggling. Arriman ordering twelve stinking emus for the zoo and leaving his secretary to unpack them . . . But there was nothing mean or small-spirited about Arriman, and it was very sincerely that Mr. Leadbetter said: "He is a gentleman. Most truly a gentleman."

"I thought he must be," said Belladonna, sighing.

"Well, I'll leave you one of these anyway, in case you change your mind," he said. "And perhaps you'd be kind enough to see that—Ms. Swamp, is it—gets hers, too?" He had turned away when he remembered something. "I'm going to vanish in a minute," he said. "At least I hope I am. I don't have any magic powers myself so I hope the great man will remember. But when I do there'll be some presents on the rock—one for each witch. Make sure you get yours."

"Oh, thank you, I will," said Belladonna. Then she added shyly: "I hope you don't mind my saying so, but when you walked away just now I thought how *very* good-looking it was. Your tail, I mean. Mostly the backs of gentlemen are so flat and dull."

Mr. Leadbetter was very much moved. "Thank you, my dear; you've made me very happy. Of course the moonlight is flattering. By daylight it can look a little crude."

He pressed her hand gratefully. It was on the tip of his tongue to tell her about his childhood and the shock of finding that he was not like other boys, but just then Arriman found he needed his secretary. There was a little puff of smoke and Mr. Leadbetter vanished.

Almost at once, the other witches began to shriek and yammer.

"Look! Over there, on the rock!"

"Something glittering!"

The next second they were all scrambling at a pile of oval hand mirrors, very beautiful ones, set in frames of precious stones. But when they looked into the mirrors' shining surfaces they did not see their own ugly faces. They saw the face of the great Arriman with his flashing eyes and curving nose and magnificent mustache. What was more, the mirror showed the witches what Arriman was doing at any moment in time so that they could get to know him and his habits and know what awaited them at Darkington if they should win.

"What a smasher!" said Nora Shouter.

"Well, you're not going to win, *I'm* going to win!"

"Cor, I wouldn't mind being married to 'im," said Ethel Feedbag. "Give the sheep the staggers, I will, when I get up there—an' the cows the bloat."

Mabel Wrack smiled pityingly. The daughter of Mrs. Wrack, who'd been a mermaid, was such an obvious winner that she had nothing at all to worry about. "Mabel Canker, Wizardess of the North." It sounded good.

"I never thought I'd be glad I buried poor Mr. Bloodwort," said Mother Bloodwort. "But I am because now I can go in for the competition."

"You!" shrieked the Shouter twins. "You're far too old!"

"I am now," said Mother Bloodwort, "though there's a lot of men as likes an older woman. But I've got a turning-myself-young-again spell. It's on the tip of my tongue, and when I remember it I won't half make things hum!"

Belladonna had crept shyly forward and picked up one of the two mirrors that still glittered on the rock. Arriman was taking off his antlers—she could just see Lester's huge hand undoing the tape. The great man looked tired and discouraged. Oh, if only she could be there to stroke his forehead and comfort him!

"What are *you* hanging round for?" said Mabel

Wrack. "*You* won't be going in for the competition."

"That'd be a joke. Blossoming roses in the snow! Golden singing birds! *Yak!*" said Nora Shouter.

Belladonna said nothing. In silence, she helped the other witches pack up their picnics, lifted Doris into the trailer, soothed Ethel Feedbag's pig. But when the bus was ready to leave, she did not join the others. It was a long walk back to Todcaster in the darkness, but she welcomed the idea of it. More than anything, she wanted to be alone.

She was sitting quietly on the rock where he had stood, gazing into the mirror, when a high and irritable voice said: "Well, I think you're just being wet. Wet and feeble."

Belladonna sat up, startled. Then she realized that the voice had spoken not "human" but "bat" and had come from her own hair.

"Not to say spineless," the little bat went on. "Why don't you at least have a *try*?"

"Don't be silly," said Belladonna. "You know perfectly well that I can't even make a toad come out of someone's mouth, and that's the corniest piece of blackness there is."

"People change," said the bat. "Take my Aunt Screwtooth. She was the most useless old bat you can imagine—couldn't suck juice out of an overripe pear without her husband to hold her claw. Then they took a holiday in some place abroad. Transylvania or some such name. She fell in with a family of vampires and settled over there. You should see her now, sucking blood as if it were mother's milk. Fairly sozzled with the stuff she is. And if my Aunt Screwtooth, why not you?"

Belladonna was bending over the mirror again. Arriman was in his pajamas now. Yellow silk, they were, edged with black braid.

"Is that really true? About your Aunt Screwtooth?"

The little bat blushed in the darkness. He had made the whole thing up because he loved Belladonna.

But Belladonna did not see. She was thinking. If she went in for the contest she could at least *see* him again. He'd be one of the judges for sure. And once she was there, maybe she'd find *some* way to help and comfort him.

She stood up. "All right," she said, "I'll do it. I'll have a try."

CHAPTER 4

*M*R. LEADBETTER WAS very fond of watching television. In spite of his little stump of a tail he was a very ordinary person, and when the magic and goings-on at Darkington were too much for him, he liked to go quietly to his room and watch the box.

One of Mr. Leadbetter's favorite programs was the Miss World competition. Mr. Leadbetter knew, of course, that it was silly for girls to let themselves be prodded and measured like cows or turnips at an agricultural show, but all the same he very much liked all the contestants coming from different countries and staying together at a hotel and appearing first in their national costumes and then in their evening dresses and then in their swimsuits, and when the most beautiful one climbed onto the platform and had a crown put on her head, Mr. Leadbetter always felt a lump come to his throat.

So when it was decided to hold a competition for the blackest witch of Todcaster, Mr. Leadbetter decided to organize it rather in the way that the Miss World contest was organized. Not, of course, that he thought of making the witches parade in their swimsuits. Even before he saw Mother Bloodwort and Mabel Wrack and Ethel Feedbag he had not thought of *that*. But it seemed to him a good idea that the witches should be brought together in a hotel first and get their clothes and their table manners sorted out before they got to Darkington. Above all, he wanted to make sure that they knew the rules and that no hanky-panky went on between them. Any witch casting a spell on another witch was to be disqualified *immediately*.

So he rented the Grand Spa Hotel on the outskirts of Todcaster. It was a very grand hotel with a cocktail lounge and a ballroom and a terrace with stripy deck chairs, and the manager, who was quite used to conferences of politicians and schoolteachers and clergymen, rather welcomed the idea of a conference of witches.

But after his first day there, Mr. Leadbetter began to feel that he had made a terrible mistake. Mother Bloodwort and the Shouter twins and Ethel Feedbag just did not *behave* like Miss Kenya and Miss Belgium and Miss U.S.A. In fact, as Mr. Leadbetter said to Lester, who had come to help him, if it wasn't for Belladonna he'd have had a good mind to chuck the whole thing and let Arriman get on with choosing his own wife.

Belladonna, who had arrived earlier carrying a straw basket with her toothbrush, her nightdress, and the magic mirror, had been wonderful. It was Belladonna who had tactfully removed Ethel Feedbag's Wellies and hosed them down in the pantry when the manager complained about manure on his carpet. It was Belladonna who had taped up Mother Bloodwort's tin with the coronation on the lid and persuaded the old woman that at the best hotels one did not come down to dinner in a cloud of flies. And when Mabel Wrack got into the bath fully clothed because her legs were drying out, causing Doris (who liked to be alone) to squirt her all over with inky fluid, it was Belladonna who cleaned up the mess and carried the irritated animal to her own bathroom and quieted her.

Not that she got any thanks for it. "It makes my blood boil," said Lester, "the way those witches talk to you."

"Oh, well," said Belladonna. "It's hard for them, me being . . . you know . . ."

44

They were in the office, which the manager had kindly lent to Mr. Leadbetter, snatching a quick cup of tea. Lester, who'd been badly hit by the sight of the witches in daylight, was prowling around looking for a sword to swallow. Mr. Leadbetter, like everyone who organizes things, was shuffling his papers and worrying.

"Maybe you're just *fancying* yourself white," Lester went on. He found the manager's umbrella, looked at it, and put it down again. There wasn't any real skill in swallowing umbrellas, and if they came unfurled inside it could be messy.

"I'm afraid not," said Belladonna. As usual she was looking into the magic mirror, which she carried with her everywhere. Arriman was sitting hunched up in what seemed to be a broom cupboard.

"Try!" said Lester, who'd set his heart on Belladonna as mistress of Darkington Hall. "Look, see that typewriter on the desk? Bet if you really put your mind to it you could turn it into a nest of vipers or something. I mean, you've got to *believe* in yourself."

Belladonna sighed. She knew it was useless but she hated disappointing people, so she got up and felt in the pocket of her skirt for a magic wand or something of the sort. There wasn't anything, of course—only a handful of healing herbs, the identity disk of a carrier

45

pigeon who was playing truant from his loft, and a baby field mouse. So she put everything back and just closed her eyes, waved her arms over the typewriter, and thought of the blackest things she could think of, such as uncooked liver and shoelaces and open graves. Then she stepped back.

"Oh, dear!" said Mr. Leadbetter.

The typewriter had not turned into a nest of vipers. It had turned into a pot of pink begonias; charming, sweetly scented flowers, each cradling a golden bee.

"Pretty," said the ogre gloomily.

"I told you," said Belladonna, very much embarrassed. She turned the typewriter back again and picked up the magic mirror. How dreadfully the great man would despise her if he knew!

"Still sulking, is he?" said Lester.

"Oh, no, he could never *sulk*," said Belladonna. "But he hasn't perhaps been very . . . *cheerful* lately."

"You can say that again," said the ogre.

And indeed, ever since he had seen his choice of future brides at the coven, Arriman had been in a terrible state. He woke screaming from dreadful nightmares, babbling of fly-covered whiskers chasing him down corridors. He was off his food, his mustache had begun to molt, and he hounded the Wizard Watcher unmercifully, sending the poor beast out to the gate long before daybreak in a last, desperate hope that the new wizard might still come and he could cancel the competition.

"I can't help wondering why he is sitting in a *broom* cupboard," said Belladonna.

"I'll tell you why," said Lester frowning. "Because he's waiting for Sir Simon, that's why. Favorite spot of Sir Simon's, the broom cupboard."

"Is that the rather dead-looking gentleman he speaks to sometimes?" inquired Belladonna.

Lester nodded. "Very dead-looking. Died in 1583," he said. "Murdered all seven of his wives."

Mr. Leadbetter put down his papers and came over, and together the ogre and the secretary looked over Belladonna's shoulder at their employer. Sure enough, a wavering shadow appeared on the surface of the mirror and Arriman rose eagerly to his feet.

"I don't like it," said Lester, shaking his enormous head. "He's been trying to bring Sir Simon back to life for years, but since the coven he's been at it all the time. When I brought him his egg this morning, he was sitting up in bed with this huge book—*Necromancy*, it was called. Nasty."

"I wouldn't worry," said Mr. Leadbetter. "I believe it's two hundred years since anyone managed to raise a ghost."

But he was a little more anxious than he admitted. Suppose Arriman *did* manage it? A man who had murdered all seven of his wives did not seem to be a good person to have around in a house where there was soon to be a wedding.

An hour later the witches were all assembled in the cocktail lounge of the hotel waiting for Mr. Leadbetter to tell them the rules of the contest. They had taken a lot of trouble to make themselves smart. Mabel Wrack had plaited her frizzy hair with a string of dogfish egg cases, Mother Bloodwort's chin sprouted a brand-new bandage, and Ethel Feedbag had nobly left her Wellies upstairs and was in slippers.

"Are we all here?" asked Mr. Leadbetter, letting his eyes rest for a moment on Belladonna, sitting quietly apart from the others on a stool.

"No," said Nancy Shouter, jangling her knuckle-bone earrings. "Silly old Monalot's not here."

Mr. Leadbetter sighed. Ms. Swamp had sent in her entrance form, but so far there had been no sign of her, and he was a person who hated muddle.

"No point in her going in for the competition any-way," said Mabel Wrack. "A flabby old banshee like that."

"And that sheep of hers. Gives me the bots!" said Ethel Feedbag.

The others nodded. It was true that Percy really was a most depressing animal: the kind that always thinks other sheep are having a better life than he is, and eating greener grass, and *doing* more.

"Well, we shall have to begin without her," said Mr. Leadbetter.

But just then the hotel porter came in and whispered something to Mr. Leadbetter, whose face brightened. "Show her in, please," he said. "We're expecting another lady."

But the new witch didn't seem to be someone one showed in. The new witch came striding in like a queen, and as she came the other witches shrank back in their chairs and Belladonna drew in her breath.

Because the new witch was not Monalot. Nothing less like the pale, sickly Ms. Swamp could be imagined. The new witch was very tall, with black hair piled high on her head. She had long, bloodred fingernails, and round her shoulders she wore a cape of puppy skin. Her fingers and wrists sparkled with jewels, but the necklace wound round her throat was, unexpectedly, not of pearls or diamonds but of human teeth. But what startled the others most was the new witch's familiar. Dragging behind her on a rhinestone-studded lead there came a gray, lumbering animal with a snout like a Hoover and wicked-looking claws.

"What is it?" whispered Mother Bloodwort, who could never scrape up enough money to go to the zoo.

49

"I think it's an aardvark," Belladonna whispered back.

"Good evening," said the new witch. "I am Madame Olympia. I have come to take part in the competition."

"I'm afraid there's been some mistake," said Mr. Leadbetter. "The competition is limited to the witches of Todcaster."

Madame Olympia smiled—a smile that sent shivers down one's spine.

"I *am* a witch of Todcaster," she said.

"How can that be?" began Mr. Leadbetter. "We—"

"I have bought Ms. Gwendolyn Swamp's house, Creepy Corner," interrupted the newcomer, dropping the rhinestone lead carelessly onto a chair. "Too small for me, of course, but not without charm. Miss Swamp found she wanted to travel."

"Monalot *never* wanted to travel," said Mother Bloodwort stoutly. "Travel brought her out in spots an' all sorts. It was all you could do to get Monalot down the road for a bag of bulls' eyes."

"She is traveling now, however," said Madame Olympia with another of her sinister smiles. "Oh, yes, she is definitely traveling now. Somewhere around Turkey, I would guess."

She opened her crocodile-skin handbag and began to powder her nose. And when she saw the vain, proud look that Madame Olympia threw at herself in the mirror, Belladonna suddenly understood what kind of a person the new witch was. She was an enchantress, one of the oldest and most evil kinds of witch there is. Morgan le Fay, the one who caused the death of the great King Arthur, was one, and Circe, who turned brave Ulysses' men to swine. Enchantresses are beautiful, but it is an evil beauty. They use it to snare men and make them helpless and tear from them the secrets of their power. And when they have got all they want from them, they destroy them.

"Well, madame, I suppose you had better let me have your entrance form," said Mr. Leadbetter. Fair was fair, and if the new witch now lived in Todcaster she was eligible to join. But he felt very unhappy as he wrote her name down on the register. Mr. Leadbetter didn't know much about enchantresses, but there was something about Madame Olympia that made his blood run cold.

Not only was Madame Olympia not a witch of Todcaster, she wasn't a Witch of the North at all. She lived in London, where she kept a beauty parlor. It was a wicked place. Stupid women were lured into it and assured they would become young and beautiful if they let themselves be pummeled and pounded and smeared with sticky creams, and have their faces lifted and their stomachs flattened. They paid a lot of money to Madame Olympia, who would put a little bit of magic into the creams and ointments that she used so that at first they did look marvelous. But it was the kind of magic that wore off very quickly, leaving the women even uglier than before so that they would rush back to her and pay her more money and the whole thing would start again. She was also horrid to the girls she employed and paid them too little and bullied them.

Madame Olympia had had five husbands. All these husbands had disappeared in very odd ways, mostly after they had made wills leaving her all their money. She *said* that they had died, but it was odd that a werewolf with weak, blue eyes and a bald patch had appeared in Epping Forest, very much frightening the inhabitants, just after she had reported her first husband's death. The second and third husbands had vanished within a year of each other, and each time the girls in the beauty parlor were struck by the way madame's necklace of human teeth suddenly got very much longer. The fourth Mr. Olympia really did run his Jaguar into a lamppost, but the fifth . . . well, no one knew for certain what had happened to him, but the coffin in which he was carried to his funeral was most *suspiciously* light.

And now she was after Arriman the Awful, Wizard of the North!

As soon as she had heard of the competition she had come straight up to Todcaster and "persuaded" Monalot to sell her house. Monalot hadn't wanted to go, of course: she'd sobbed and moaned and pleaded; after all, she wasn't a banshee for nothing. But by the time Madame Olympia had suggested just a few of the things she might do to her, and to Percy, if she didn't, Monalot had been very glad to sell her house and take a nice package tour round the world. Very glad indeed.

Mr. Leadbetter had begun to explain the rules of the competition. The witches were to wear black gowns and masks so that the judges would not go by the way they looked but by the blackness of their magic. They were to draw numbers out of a hat and do their tricks in the order that they drew. They were to hand in a list of anything they might need for the contest: dragons' blood, sieves to go to sea in, and so on, so that they would be ready in good time. . . .

Madame Olympia hardly bothered to listen. One look at the other witches and she had known she would win. The little golden-haired thing was quite fetching, but anyone could see what was wrong with *her*. Oh, yes, she'd be Queen of Darkington all right. And then . . . !

Hardly waiting for Mr. Leadbetter to finish, she rose to her feet and stretched. "See that my aardvark is watered and fed, please," she ordered carelessly. "I'm going to change for dinner."

And she glided out of the room, leaving the other witches boiling and bubbling with indignation.

"Cocky, sneering cow, who does she think she is?" said Nancy Shouter. "Hope she drops dead."

And for once, her twin agreed with her.

It was a long time before Belladonna slept that night. Dinner had been excellent, but even before the bandage fell from Mother Bloodwort's chin into her mushroom soup, Belladonna had not been really hungry. Then there was a fuss about Ethel Feedbag, who had a double bed and wanted to share it with her pig, and when Belladonna got to her room at last there was still Doris in the bath, waving to her and wanting to be noticed.

But it was none of that that worried Belladonna. It was the glimpse she had had, passing an open door, of Madame Olympia, standing in a gold negligee, her black hair falling round her shoulders, the aardvark cowering at her feet. She was looking into the magic mirror that had been left for Monalot and laughing—a low and truly evil sound.

"You wanted power and darkness, you Wizard of the North," Belladonna heard her say. "Well, power and darkness you shall have!"

And it was with the sound of the new witch's horrible laughter still in her ears that Belladonna fell asleep at last.

CHAPTER 5

BELLADONNA WAS still worried when she awoke. It seemed to her certain that Madame Olympia would win the competition and become Mrs. Canker, and she feared most dreadfully for Arriman.

She got up and went to the open window, and at once a family of bluetits flew onto her shoulder and started telling her a long story about a nesting box that wasn't fit for a flea to sleep in and the shocking way that people carried on, taking their milk bottles in too soon and keeping cats.

Belladonna sighed. She could cope with one bluetit in her hair, but a whole family always gave her a headache.

"You can stay, but in my straw basket," she said, managing for once to be firm.

Doris, fortunately, was still asleep, her body bleached

to the whiteness of the bath, her vile eyes peacefully closed. Belladonna cleaned her teeth and went downstairs. The rooms were deserted and silent still. She didn't feel like the other witches this morning; she didn't feel like anybody. And slipping out of a side door into the street, she began to walk away from the hotel.

She walked and she walked and she walked, letting her feet carry her where they would, and presently she found that she had left the pleasant gardens and smart shops which surrounded the Grand Spa Hotel and was in a poor and slummy part of the town where the houses were neglected and dirty, orange peel and broken glass littered the gutters, and mangy dogs foraged in the dustbins.

She crossed a mean little square with a few dusty laurel bushes, a boarded-up lemonade stall, and a public lavatory, and found herself in front of a large, gray building with curtains the color of bile. A flight of mottled stone steps led from the side of the building into a patch of gravel and scuffed earth which might once have been a garden. And there, hunched on the low wall which ran beside the pavement, was a small boy. He was looking down at something that he held cupped in his skinny hands and making that kind of hiccuping noise that people make when they are trying not to cry.

What was cupped in the boy's hands was an earthworm. And the name of the boy—a name he hated—was Terence Mugg.

When he was a very small baby, Terence Mugg had been found wrapped in a newspaper in a telephone kiosk behind the railway station. The newspaper had smelt of vinegar, and the lady who found it had thought at first that it was a packet of fish and chips. However, when the fish and chips packet burst and put out a small, pink hand, she screamed and ran for a policeman.

At the police station, Terence was fed and clothed and photographed in the arms of a pretty policewoman. But when his picture appeared in the paper no one said, "Ooh!" and "Aah!" and "Isn't he sweet?," and no one wrote in offering to adopt him (though an old gentleman wrote in offering to adopt the policewoman). Terence just wasn't that kind of baby. There were even people cruel enough to say they might have left him in a telephone kiosk themselves.

So poor Terence was sent to the Sunnydene Children's Home in the most dismal part of Todcaster, and Matron christened him "Terence" after an actor she fancied at the time and "Mugg" because she said, "With a mug like that, what else can he be called?"

Babies in children's homes usually get adopted quite

quickly, but not Terence. Not only was he an unusually plain baby, but he spent the first five years of his life getting not only chicken pox and whooping cough, but really quite unusual things like brain fever and dermatitis and croup. Naturally nobody wants to adopt a baby whose entire head is swathed in bandages or whose face is covered with spots or who can't digest cheese without turning as yellow as a lentil. By the time he was five and had started at the local school, Terence had quite given up hope of finding a family to love him.

"We'll have *that* one with us for life," Matron would say nastily as Terence crept past her like a battered little snail. "No Mrs. Right's going to come along for *him*."

People who are lonely and unloved often turn to animals for company, and that was what Terence had done. Only, of course, at the Sunnydene Children's Home, Matron did not allow proper pets. So it was little things—small spiders and hurrying wood lice and shiny beetles—that Terence played with when he was out in the waste patch they called a garden, or found under paving stones on the way to school.

It was in this way that he had found Rover.

Rover was an earthworm, a pale pink, slender animal with a mauve bulge in the middle, a pointed end, and a peaceful way of crawling along the ground.

Terence had liked him immediately. There was something a little special about Rover. He did not seem quite like other worms, who often appear to have no notion of doing anything beyond burrowing down into the soil. Rover would curl into knots around Terence's fingers or lie quietly in the palm of his hand, and sometimes he would rear up his pointed end in a most intelligent way. Terence had found him in a tub of earth outside a chemist's shop, and he'd sneaked him into the home and found a place for him in the garden—a jam jar filled with leaf mold which he was careful to keep damp because his teacher had told him that earthworms breathe through their skins and should never get dry. He'd buried the jam jar behind a pile of bricks and told no one—only Billy, who was deaf and hadn't been adopted either. Billy was another person who didn't bother living things.

And there Rover had lived as happily as anything until last night when Matron had found Terence and Billy talking to him when they should have been inside getting ready for bed.

"How *dare* you!" she had shouted, charging down the garden like an ill-tempered camel. "Come inside at once! And throw that disgusting, unsanitary worm away immediately!"

And when Terence did not instantly do what he was told, she snatched Rover's jar and turned it upside down, scuffing at the leaf mold with her sharp and spiky shoes.

She had hurt Rover. Hurt him badly. He was no better this morning: there was a wound in his middle where the skin was broken and his insides were spilling out in a terrible way. Rover wasn't moving, either; he just lay there, perfectly still and stretched in Terence's hand.

He was going to die.

"Hallo!" said a soft and musical voice above his head, and Terence, looking up, saw the most beautiful girl he had ever seen—a girl he would have been frightened of except that her blue eyes looked sad, and sadness was something Terence knew about. "My name is Belladonna," the gentle voice went on. "What's yours?"

The little boy flushed. "Terence Mugg," he said, staring up at her through his big, steel-rimmed spectacles. "And this," he swallowed, "is Rover. Only," he said, keeping his voice steady with an effort, "I think he's going . . . to die."

Belladonna looked carefully at the worm. She did not think Rover was an odd name for an earthworm.

She knew at once that he was called Rover because Terence dreadfully wanted a dog and knew he would never get one. And she knew, too, that Terence was right about Rover. The worm was very, very sick.

"May I hold him for a moment?" she asked.

Terence hesitated. When somebody that belongs to you is going to die you feel you should hold on to him and help him right to the end. But when he saw the look on Belladonna's face he carefully opened his hand and gave her his worm.

Belladonna bent over Rover and her hair fell like a golden curtain, inside which the wounded worm lay snug and warm. Then she began to croon a little song.

Terence had never heard a song like the one that Belladonna sang. It was about dampness and the soft darkness of the rich earth and about the patient worms who had turned it through the years. It was a song about pinkness and wetness and roundness, and while she sang it, Terence felt that he, too, was an earthworm and understood the soul of all earthworms and always would. Then she blew three times on her cupped hands and parted them.

"Let's see now," she said.

"Oh!" said Terence. *"Oh!"*

The little jagged place where Matron's shoe had hit the earthworm's side was quite closed over. Rover's skin was smooth again, there was no scar, and even as

Terence gazed at him, Rover reared up his pointed end in just the jaunty way he used to.

Terence was possibly the ugliest little boy that Belladonna had ever seen, but now his face was shining like an archangel's. "He's better! He's all right again! You *healed* him! Oh, Rover, you're fine again, you're better than before!" He looked up at Belladonna. "Only you didn't give him any medicine or anything. Are you a vet, then?" But his face was puzzled because he had seen vets and they did not look like Belladonna.

"Well, not exactly," said Belladonna. "But sometimes I can—" She broke off and flinched. Quite the most unpleasant voice she had ever heard was coming at her from the top of the steps.

"Where is that dratted boy," it whined. "Skulking in the garden again! Really, I don't know why they bothered to fish him out of the telephone kiosk, he's been nothing but trouble since the day he arrived."

The unpleasant voice belonged to a tall, bony woman with a yellowish skin and a nose you could have cut cheese with.

"It's Matron," whispered Terence as he drew closer to Belladonna.

"Oh, there you are, you wretched boy! Well, come in at *once* or you'll have no lunch. And if you've still got that slimy worm I'm going to flush him down the lavatory, and you after him!"

She began to charge down the steps, and Belladonna could feel Terence shrinking beside her. "No,"
he said. "Please. I'll put him away."

Matron took no notice at all. She had reached the
bottom step and was coming at them along the gravel
path. "As for you," she said, glaring at Belladonna,
"I'd like to know what you're doing, trespassing in a
private garden."

"Will you take him?" Terence whispered.

Belladonna nodded and slipped Rover into her
hand. Then she put her arm round Terence's shoulders. And as she felt the shivers that shook his thin little frame, a great anger shot through her. Belladonna
was almost never angry, but she was angry now. Very
angry.

Belladonna closed her eyes. She took a deep breath.
And then she called on a god that white witches do not
usually call on. "Oh, great Cernunnos, you horned
one, please help me halt this *revolting* woman!"

Matron was coming closer. Closer still . . . Then
suddenly she stumbled and looked back at her left
foot. She tugged at it. She pulled. Nothing happened.
Matron's left foot would not move.

"Oh!" gasped Terence. *"Look!"*

A little bulge had appeared at the tip of Matron's
left shoe. Then the leather burst open and a green
root appeared and began to snake along the ground

and bury itself in the soil. From the side of the shoe came another root, and another. . . . The roots grew thicker and stronger; gnarled they were now, like the roots of an ancient beech and always pushing down, down into the ground.

"Help!" shrieked Matron. "Help! *Eek!*"

It was happening to the other foot now. From her heels, her toes, her ankles, her knobbly knees . . . Roots that began soft and green and became thicker and more twisted as they grew downward; roots like great creepers, like ropes—and all tethering Matron as if with bands of steel to the ground.

"Help!" shrieked Matron again. But no one heard her, and now the roots were coming out of her waist, her arms. . . . And then she could shriek no more because a tendril had sprung out of her upper lip and was snaking down toward the ground, closing her mouth as firmly as a trap.

"*Oh!*" said Terence once again. He was still nestling against her skirt, but when Belladonna looked down she saw that he wasn't frightened, just amazed. "You did it!" said Terence, "I know you did it. You're magic, aren't you? You're a witch!"

Belladonna nodded. She, too, was very much excited, because rooting people to the ground is magic all right, but it is not really very white. Rooting a begonia or a cabbage or a clump of wallflowers is white

because begonias and cabbages and clumps of wallflowers like to have roots and cannot live without
them. But rooting matrons is a different matter. If it
wasn't actually *black* magic, it was certainly fairly gray,
and Belladonna's eyes were shining as she looked at
Terence.

"You've brought me luck," she said. "You and
Rover. That's the blackest thing I've done, *ever.*"

"You mean you usually do white magic, like healing
people and so on?" said Terence. It struck Belladonna
that he seemed to have a natural feeling for magic and
not to show any of the fears one would expect in so
nervous a boy. "But do you *want* to be black?"

"Yes, I do. I do terribly," said Belladonna. And she
explained about the competition and Arriman. She
was too shy to tell Terence that she loved Arriman, but
she thought he had probably guessed. He was that kind
of little boy. Suddenly a thought struck her. "Terence,
you don't think . . ." She looked down at the worm,
now distinctly perky and inclined to tie himself into knots
around her finger. "You don't think that Rover . . .
that he might be a *familiar.* I never had one, you know.
The other witches did, but I didn't. Do you think"—
Belladonna was growing very excited now—"do you
think it was because I was holding Rover that I managed to root Matron?"

"It might be." Terence was as excited as she was.

"Only I thought familiars were usually black cats and hares and goats and things?"

"Oh, no." And Belladonna explained about the octopus called Doris, and Madame Olympia's aardvark, and the cloud of flies.

"He's so little," said Terence. There was a pause, broken only by a furious, suffocated grunt from Matron, up whose legs a large black spider was steadily marching. "But if he has helped you," Terence went on bravely, "then you must have him. Take him with you so's you win the competition."

Belladonna was incredibly touched.

"I couldn't, Terence. I couldn't separate you two. You belong together. Anyway, I haven't a hope of winning the competition even so."

But Terence now was clutching her arm and looking up at her, his eyes pleading.

"If you couldn't separate us, couldn't you . . . Oh, please, *please* couldn't you take me with you? Witches have servants, I know they do. Imps and . . . fiends and things. I'd do anything for you, *anything.*"

"Oh, Terence, I'd love to, but how can I? I'm staying in this posh hotel and they'd never let you come. And anyway, witches don't really mix with ordinary people, you know. It never comes right."

But her voice trailed away as she said it, for what was "right" for Terence about the Sunnydene Children's

Home? And what would happen to him when Matron stopped being rooted? Belladonna had absolutely no idea how long the spell would last, and the glitter in Matron's eye as she tugged uselessly at her roots boded extremely ill for Terence.

Terence did not say anything. He just stood there, dejected and beaten, but still holding out his worm to her.

"Oh, heck," said Belladonna suddenly, making up her mind. "Let's just *do* it. It may come right."

She climbed over the low wall and turned, stretching out a hand to Terence. Then, followed by the strangled grunts of the rooted Matron, they ran together down the road.

CHAPTER 6

WHEN BELLADONNA GOT BACK to the hotel, she took Terence straight to the manager's office to see Mr. Leadbetter and the ogre.

She found them in a bad way. There had been a row about Ethel Feedbag's pig, which was not house-trained, and when the manager complained, Ethel (who had not been well brought up) said: "Oh, go and teach your grandmother to suck eggs!" Unfortunately, she had been clutching her hazel wand at the time and the next moment the manager found himself in a nursing home in Bexhill-on-Sea holding out a raw egg to his mother's mother, a frail old lady who had been looking forward to her morning porridge and was very much annoyed.

The muddle had taken a long time to clear up, and then it was discovered that Mother Bloodwort, who had been riding up and down in the hotel lift all morning, had got jammed between floors. Trying to remember the spell for making things go up in the air, she had got mixed up and become a coffee table once again, and since coffee tables cannot press emergency buttons, she had caused a great deal of trouble to the engineers.

But when they saw Belladonna, the secretary and the ogre both cheered up and greeted Terence most politely.

Belladonna lost no time in explaining about Terence and the horrible home. "And he's brought this absolutely *marvelous* familiar!" she went on. "He made me able to do a really quite black thing. Me!"

The ogre and Mr. Leadbetter looked around the room, wondering if they had missed a stampeding bufflalo or a wolverine with slavering fangs, but all they could see was a small and skinny boy, his gaze fixed wonderingly on the ogre's single eye.

"Show them, Terence," said Belladonna.

So Terence felt in his pocket and lifted out Rover and put him carefully down on Mr. Leadbetter's blotter. The secretary and the ogre bent over him and their hearts sank—a small, pale worm whose bristles, as he crawled across the paper, made a delicate soughing noise like autumn leaves stirred by the softest of winds. And for a moment they'd really hoped!

70

"Shall I try the typewriter?" Belladonna asked eagerly. "Like you wanted me to yesterday? A nest of vipers, wasn't it? Come on, Terence."

So Terence picked up Rover and stood beside her, and Belladonna rested her fingertips lightly on the little worm's mauve and slightly bulgy middle and closed her eyes. And, lo and behold, the typewriter vanished with a puff and there on the desk was a writhing mass of hissing vipers with darting tongues and slitty, yellow eyes.

"Poor little things," said Belladonna, forgetting her blackness for a moment. "They look awfully dry."

"Vipers is born dry," said Lester, "so don't you go fretting yourself."

But the look he exchanged with Mr. Leadbetter was eager and excited. If Belladonna could get black so quickly, there was hope yet!

"Amazing!" said Mr. Leadbetter. He looked at Rover again to see if he had missed anything: a hidden poison sac, a lethal sting—but the worm now crawling peaceably up Terence's sleeve was exactly what he seemed: gentle, modest, and moist.

"So, I was wondering," said Belladonna, putting her arm around Terence's shoulder, "if Terence could *possibly* stay for a bit? Rover belongs to him, and though he offered to give him to me, I just *couldn't* take him away."

Mr. Leadbetter looked worried. What would the manager say to another guest? And what about the other witches? Would it start an absolute avalanche of witch friends and relations coming to stay at the hotel? Fishy little Wracks and quarreling Shouter cousins and small Feedbags in nasty Wellington boots?

Terence said nothing. He just stood there, waiting. He was not a boy who had ever hoped for much.

Mr. Leadbetter cleared his throat. "It so happens," he began, "that I have a sister. Amelia, her name is. Amelia Leadbetter."

The ogre and Belladonna looked at him anxiously. They knew how hard he had been working and that overwork can drive people a little mad.

"She didn't, in fact, marry," Mr. Leadbetter went on. "But she might have done. There was a swimming bath attendant who was very fond of her."

The others waited.

"I'm not saying that the swimming bath attendant was called Mugg," the secretary went on, "because he wasn't. His name, actually, was Arthur Hurtleypool. I remember it because jokes were made about hurtleying into the pool, that kind of thing. Still, if he *had* been called Mugg and if he had married my sister Amelia and if the marriage had been blessed with a son, then this son," finished the secretary, "would undoubtedly have been my nephew."

"Your nephew, Terence!" said Belladonna, seeing the light.

"Precisely. And what more natural than that my sister, Amelia, having to go into the hospital to have her appendix out, should send Terence to stay with me?"

"Oh, Mr. Leadbetter, you're wonderful," cried Belladonna, throwing her arms around the secretary, a thing he very much enjoyed.

Terence looked as though he'd swallowed a lighted candle. But when he spoke it was to say haltingly: "If I was your nephew, shouldn't I have . . ." He was too shy to finish, but his eyes went to the back of Mr. Leadbetter and lingered there. The secretary was a modest man, so much so that he usually wore his stump inside his trousers, but Terence was a boy who noticed things.

"A tail?" said Mr. Leadbetter.

Terence nodded.

"I could make him a little one," said Belladonna. "Even without Rover. Making tails is *growing* magic, and there's nothing whiter than that. But I don't know. . . . I feel Terence is sort of perfect as he is."

Terence looked up quickly. Surely Belladonna was mocking him? But no—her periwinkle eyes were very clear and very loving as she looked at him, and he had to turn away because a lump had come up in his throat.

"Quite honestly, Terence," said Mr. Leadbetter, "if

you *can* manage without one, it would be better. There is, you *see,* the problem of sitting down. And my sister Amelia—your mother, that would be—was perfectly tailless, as far as I recall."

Terence didn't keep on about it after that. To be able to be near Belladonna, to know that *his* worm might help her to gain her heart's desire, was happiness enough. Only someone really greedy and undisciplined would also expect a tail.

"I'll tell you one thing, though," said Lester. "I wouldn't say anything about Rover being such a powerful familiar. I'd let Terence look after Rover and pretend he was just a pet, that's what I'd do. If it gets around that Rover's giving Belladonna even half a chance of winning the competition, I wouldn't give a fig for *his* chances."

"Oh, no, *surely,* no one would hurt an innocent worm like that!" said Belladonna.

"Now, Belladonna, try *thinking* black as well as acting it. There's already been some hanky-panky with Doris. Lurching about the bath she was, drunk as a lord and a nasty pea green color with it—and Ms. Wrack saying Doris never touched a drop and someone must have forced it down her throat."

"Oh, *poor* Doris—is she all right now?" cried Belladonna.

"Well, it seems she'd been on the bath salts. But it

just shows," said Lester darkly. "I wouldn't trust any of those witches as far as I could throw them, let alone that Madame Olympia."

A chill spread round the room as they remembered the enchantress's cruel smile and the necklace of human teeth.

"And what about those Shouter chickens? You know how they follow you about. One peck at Rover and you'll be back to bloomin' begonias," the ogre went on.

Belladonna saw the sense of this. "They wouldn't *mean* to, of course; they'd feel dreadful afterward, but all the same . . ." She turned to Terence. "All right, you shall be Rover's *bodyguard* and keep him, and when I want to do some magic you can come over and stand beside me and I'll touch Rover without anyone seeing."

"That's the ticket," said the ogre.

It was decided that Terence should sleep on a camp bed in Mr. Leadbetter's room and make himself useful generally until it was time to go to Darkington, and when Belladonna had turned the vipers back into a typewriter again, she and Terence went to wash their hands for lunch.

In the afternoon, Mr. Leadbetter took the witches to a big department store called Turnbull and Buttle to buy the long, black gowns and hoods that they were to wear for the competition. He had hoped to have Lester to help him, but Arriman had sent for the ogre, spiriting him away just as he was about to lift a spoonful of banana fritter to his mouth, and it was Mr. Leadbetter alone who had to shepherd the witches up to the third floor and stop Mabel Wrack from leaping onto the fish slab and return the cigarettes that had mysteriously flown through the air into the handbags of the Shouter twins and explain to the young man behind the glove counter that he couldn't immediately marry Belladonna.

Fortunately the gowns were waiting for them: black ones with hoods like schoolteachers used to wear, and long enough to reach right down to the ground and cover Mother Bloodwort's slippers and Ethel Feedbag's Wellies, so that with the black carnival masks that Turnbull and Buttle had ordered specially, there really was no way of telling which witch was which.

But when it came to Madame Olympia's turn to try on her gown, she made a nasty scene. All day, the enchantress had kept snootily to her room, insisting that meals be sent up to her, ordering incredible delicacies for the aardvark, and putting out seventeen pairs of shoes for the poor boot boy to clean.

Now she looked at her plain cotton gown and said:

"Are you out of your *mind*? Do you imagine I can perform magic in that *rag*!"

"I'm afraid all the witches have to be dressed alike," said Mr. Leadbetter. "It's one of the rules of the competition."

"Then the rules must be broken," said the enchantress, fixing Mr. Leadbetter with an evil and glittering eye.

It is impossible to say what would have happened next, but just at that moment Mother Bloodwort, who had been resting on a low gilt chair, gave a shriek of excitement.

"It's me toe! Me big toe! It's happened. I can feel it!"

Belladonna put down her gown and hurried over to her. "What has, Mother Bloodwort?"

"It's my turning-myself-young-again spell! I've been working on it all week, and just now me big toe gave this splutter. More of a *spurt* it was, really. Like a spring chicken it felt, rarin' to go."

She began to scrabble under her musty skirt, removed her stockings, shook off a couple of the small, gray bandages which clung like dead mice around her ankles, and stuck her naked foot into the air.

The stunned shop assistants drew closer; the witches clustered around.

"It is . . . *pinker* than the others, I'm almost sure," said Belladonna at last. "And sort of . . . fuller-looking."

77

"Rubbish," said Nancy Shouter. "It's exactly like the others and nasty with it."

"You've made the whole thing up," said Mabel Wrack, pursing her codlike lips.

"And your toenails need cutting."

The unkind remarks of the other witches came thick and fast. And it had to be admitted that Mother Bloodwort's toe did look exactly like all the others: yellow and bent with little tufty hairs.

But Mother Bloodwort was not to be put down. "You'll see one day, all of you. When I get the rest of the spell, you'll see, I'll be so young you'll have to put me into nappies!"

But she allowed Belladonna to help her on with her stockings and lead her back to the bus. It had been rather an exciting day.

When Lester found himself spirited away to Darkington in the middle of his banana fritter, he had a feeling that his master was up to no good, and he was right. Arriman had sent for him to tell him that the witches couldn't stay at the hall during the competition.

"But sir—" began Lester.

Arriman, who was in his library, waved a hand.

"Don't try to persuade me, Lester. Even if they stay in the east wing as you suggested, even if they're completely covered in their hoods and gowns, I just can't face it."

Lester tried not to show it, but he was annoyed. It seemed to him that Arriman was doing everything he could to make the contest as difficult as possible. After all, if you wanted a black witch, what was the use of fussing about a few warts with whiskers on them or a sea slug over someone's eye? For a moment, he wondered whether to mention Madame Olympia. Arriman hadn't seen her yet and she might be more his type. About Belladonna he decided to say nothing. The disappointment if she didn't win would be bad enough without raising any hopes.

"Well, where are they to stay, then?" he asked.

Arriman brightened. "I had a good idea. I want them to camp in the west meadow, the one opposite the main gate. They'll be out of the way there. Just buy everything you need—those pretty orange tents with little plastic porches and camp stoves and those cunning canvas lavatories. Buy everything," he said grandly, "and send the bill to me."

"But it's October, sir! They'll be freezing!"

"No, no—not at all. Braced is what they'll be. Toned up. Those nylon sleeping bags are very good, I hear. You'll have to excuse me now, Lester—I have the judges arriving tonight."

As he came away from the library, Lester met the Wizard Watcher.

"How do you find him?" asked the Left Head.

"Off his chump," said the ogre. "Wants the witches to camp in the west meadow. Won't have them in the house."

The monster sighed. "He's taken it hard," said the Middle Head. "You can imagine how we feel, letting him down."

"Still, if the wizard didn't cometh, what could we do?" remarked the Left Head.

"And cometh he definitely didn't," the Right Head said.

The monster then told Lester that it had asked for a holiday during the actual contest. It was just going to take a rucksack and go walkabout.

"We'll be back for the wedding, of course," said the Middle Head. "But everyone'll be better for a break."

Lester nodded. He could see that, in spite of itself, the Wizard Watcher felt it had somehow failed in its task and wanted to be alone till it felt better.

"What's with Sir Simon?" he said. "Seems to me the old man's seeing a bit too much of him, eh?"

He had no sooner spoken than there was a moaning sound, followed by the clank of leg armor and the hollow, gloomy specter of the wife-slayer passed through them in the corridor.

"Gone to watch the old man noshing," said the Middle Head disapprovingly.

"Thick as thieves, they are," said the Left Head.

"Gets me down, all that beating his blinking fore-head," complained the Right Head. "I mean, if you've murdered your wives, you've murdered them and that's *it*."

Lester's great craggy brow was so furrowed that the eye patch seemed to be riding a storm-tossed sea.

"I don't like it," he said. "There's something fishy going on between those two, you mark my words."

He sighed and pulled a saber out of the umbrella stand. There was never anything decent to swallow at the hotel.

"Ready, sir," he called upstairs to Arriman.

And with a whoosh, he was gone.

CHAPTER 7

THE NEWS THAT the witches were to camp hit Mr. Leadbetter extremely hard. Once, before he came to work for Arriman, he had taken a camping holiday in the south of France. He could remember a huge ironmonger's daughter from Berlin who had lost her way back to her tent at night and fallen like a felled ox across his guy ropes. He could remember an old Greek lady cutting her toenails into the sinks, and three sunburnt Italian men who had stumped up and down with blaring transistors. He remembered the dead toad caught in the slatted floor of the shower block and the hairy housewife from Luxembourg who had sat on the steps of her caravan shaving her legs. And when he remembered that these were *ordinary* people, the thought of what the witches would make of camping made him groan aloud. "Sometimes I don't know what

I've done to deserve it, Lester, honestly I don't," he said to the ogre.

But of course he went out, good secretary that he was, and ordered everything he could think of: tents and sleeping bags and folding chairs, and had the stuff sent up to Darkington. Then he borrowed the manager's top hat and wrote the numbers one to seven on bits of paper and put them inside the hat and left it on the piano stool in the ballroom ready for the witches to draw lots on the following day for their place in the contest.

"Perhaps Madame Olympia would care to draw first?" he suggested, when he had gathered them together after breakfast.

So the enchantress, dragging her aardvark by his rhinestone collar, came forward and put her hand into the hat.

"Is this some sort of joke?" she said disdainfully, putting the thing she had just pulled out onto the piano stool.

It was an egg.

There was only the shortest of pauses and then it began: "That is an egg laid by *my* chicken," said Nancy Shouter.

"Oh, no it isn't. That is an egg laid by *my* chicken. I could tell that egg anywhere."

The other witches came closer. There is always excitement when a familiar lays an egg. There could so easily be a small dragon inside or a dark stain which could be trained to grow up into a fiend—anything—and for once they could see what the Shouter twins were quarreling about.

Mr. Leadbetter sighed. He did so want to get on with drawing lots.

Ethel Feedbag now stepped forward. Working at the egg packing station, she was reckoned to be an expert.

"That egg," she pronounced, "be, simply—an egg."

This, of course, set the Shouters off again.

"How *dare* you suggest that *my* chicken could lay an ordinary egg."

"Not your chicken! *My* chicken!"

Ethel shrugged. Nancy Shouter picked up the egg. Nora Shouter tried to pull it away from her. The next second they were all peering down at the mess of yellow yolk, transparent white, and bits of shell sploshed across the carpet.

Ethel was perfectly right. Whichever of the chickens had laid it, the thing was simply an egg.

When at last they got round to drawing lots it worked out like this: Mabel Wrack was number one, which meant that she would be the first to do her trick, Ethel Feedbag was number two, and the Shouter twins had drawn three and four. Mother Bloodwort was number five, and Madame Olympia was number six. And the witch who would do her trick last, on the actual night of Halloween, and who had drawn number seven—was Belladonna.

"Fine Halloween that'll be," sneered Nancy Shouter. "Blinking nightingales all over the place and angels singing the Hallelujah Chorus, I shouldn't wonder."

Once, those words would have hurt Belladonna badly, but not now. Only half an hour earlier, with Rover and Terence, she had turned the ashtray in her bedroom into a hideous, grinning skull.

There was only one more thing for the witches to do, and in a way it was the most important of all. They had to decide on which piece of magic they were going to do and make lists of all the things they needed for it so that they could be got ready and waiting for them at the hall. All the other witches seemed to know—you could hear them plotting and whispering and hiding bits of paper from each other all over the hotel—but not Belladonna. Being black needs a lot of practice and a completely different way of thinking to being white, and when she tried to imagine a trick foul and vicious enough to please Arriman, her mind just went completely blank.

"Oh, Terence, I *wish* I knew what to do," she said to the little boy who was sitting beside her on the bed.

Even in the two days since he had left the home, Terence seemed to have changed. His mud-colored eyes had grown bright and eager, his hair was no longer plastered to his head but bounced with life, and he wore his spectacles at quite a jaunty angle on the end of his nose. Happiness is almost as good as magic for altering a person's looks.

"I suppose Mabel Wrack will do some watery, fishy kind of trick," Belladonna went on. "And Ethel Feedbag's sure to do something countryish, and Madame Olympia . . ." But the thought of Madame Olympia's trick was horrible in a special sort of way, and Belladonna left her sentence unfinished.

She picked up the mirror. Arriman was playing solitaire—not cheating exactly but sometimes rearranging the cards a little. The look on his dark, brooding face, the white hair in his curse curl, made her heart turn over. She was just going to put the mirror down again when a gray, wavering shape passed over its surface, and she saw Arriman look up eagerly.

"Is that Sir Simon?" asked Terence. It was his first sight of the wicked specter.

Belladonna nodded. "He's his special friend."

"Why is he banging at his forehead like that?" Terence wanted to know.

"It's guilt. Because he killed all his wives. It makes a

plashing noise, Lester says, but we can't hear it because the mirror's silent."

"Is that all he does?" Terence asked. "Can't he speak or anything?"

Belladonna shook her head. "You've got to remember he's been dead for four hundred years. Whatever it is people speak with must have got very withered up by now." She sighed. "It must be so *lonely* for Arriman, having a friend who can't say anything. I mean, a plashing sound is not the same."

Suddenly Terence gave a little cry and Belladonna saw that behind his spectacles his bright, mud-colored eyes were positively sparkling with excitement.

"Belladonna, I've had a *marvelous* idea! For your trick. Why don't you raise Sir Simon? Bring him back to life?"

Belladonna stared at him. "Terence, I *couldn't*. Not *possibly*. That's the blackest magic in the whole world. Witches didn't just get burnt at the stake for that; they got hung and drawn and quartered and rolled up into little balls of *dung*."

Terence didn't seem to think this mattered. "But you want to be black, don't you? What's the point of being just a little bit black? If you're going to win, surely you have to do the most awful thing there is?"

"Yes, but I'd never *do* it. Arriman hasn't been

able to do it, and Lester says he's tried and tried and tried."

"Arriman hasn't got Rover," said Terence.

Belladonna was silent. The little boy's faith in his worm was somehow catching.

"Oh, Terence, do you really think I could?"

"Of *course* you could. And think how happy you'd be making Arriman. That's what you want when you love someone, isn't it? To make them happy?"

So he *had* guessed her secret.

"Yes," said Belladonna quietly, "that's what you want."

She got up and went over to the wooden box that Terence had fitted out for Rover to live in when he wasn't in the matchbox in his pocket. Just to know that the worm was there, cradled deep in layers of damp, rich earth, made her feel at once more evil, more wicked, and more dark.

"What shall I put on my list, then? There are awful things you need for necromancy. Warm sheep's blood, I think and . . . *pits* . . . and things."

Terence considered. "I wouldn't bother with all that," he said. "I think all that stuff's just for people who haven't got Rover. I reckon you've just got to *think* black."

So Belladonna got a sheet of hotel note paper out of the bureau and wrote, *Witch Number Seven: Nothing*, and went downstairs to give it to the secretary and the ogre.

Mr. Leadbetter had just finished reading the lists handed in by the other six witches, after which he had done something most unusual. He had sat down. Not even the pain as his stump grated against the seat could keep him on his feet. He had expected the witches to want a few things like crucibles and thuribles (whatever they were), a bit of wax for making images, perhaps a spot of moonwort or of mercury—that kind of thing. But no; the witches had really gone to town.

"Seven princesses!" cried Mr. Leadbetter, holding up the list that the chambermaid had written out for witch number five. "What does she think I am?"

Lester pulled skillfully at the handle of the saber sticking from his mouth and drew it from his gullet.

"These'll have to go up to the hall," he said, coming to stand behind the secretary. "We'll get the easy stuff, but the old man'll have to magic up the rest on the day. *I'm* not going into Turnbull and Buttle's to ask for seven princesses of the blood royal, nor are you."

Mr. Leadbetter nodded. Much as he hated failing Arriman, he could see that Lester was right.

It was just then that Belladonna knocked and slipped in quietly with her list.

"The dear girl," said Mr. Leadbetter when he'd read it. "She's never any trouble."

But secretly, the ogre and the secretary were anxious and dismayed. Did it mean that Belladonna had gone white again? That she wasn't even going to try? What kind of magic could one do with *nothing*?

Meanwhile, at Darkington Hall, the visiting judges had arrived.

When the competition had first been suggested, Arriman had thought of having a whole panel of judges as they do for the Miss World contest or the Olympic Games. But people who really knew about magic were getting hard to find, and anyway now that he had *seen* some of the witches, Arriman felt so gloomy that he just wanted to get everything over in the simplest way possible. He had written to a lady called The Hag of the Dribble to ask if she would come and be a judge, but she hadn't answered—probably there wasn't any writing paper in Dribble—and what he was left with was an extremely old, rather frail ghoul called Henry Sniveler and a genie called Mr. Chatterjee.

Mr. Chatterjee, like most genies, lived in a bottle out of which he swooshed if someone said the right words and remembered to unscrew the top. He was an Indian genie and felt the cold so dreadfully that mostly he liked to stay inside the bottle and talk through the glass. As his accent was rather strong, this made it difficult to understand him, but he was a very fine judge of magic, having lived so long in the East, where they do a lot of interesting things like sending people up on flying carpets and then bringing them down suddenly so that their behinds become impaled on spikes.

Mr. Sniveler was a very different sort of person: a dark-faced, silent ghoul who lived behind a slaughter-house in a satanic northern town and spent the night for-aging in dustbins for unspeakable, bloodred things, some of which he ate and some of which he collected. Ghouls are not particularly good at magic, but there is nothing darker, gloomier, or more evil than a ghoul, and Arri-man knew that he had been very lucky to get him.

So now the three of them sat at dinner around the carved oak table in the great hall, where the firelight flickered, the ravens croaked in the rafters, and, on a rug, the weary Wizard Watcher rested its head. Arriman was in low spirits—the witches were due to arrive in a couple of days—and kind Mr. Chatterjee, who was dining inside his bottle because of the drafts, was doing his best to cheer him up.

"Oh, my goodness, it will not be so bad, I think, to have a wife," he said in his soft voice, sucking up a piece of spaghetti which Arriman had dropped in for him. Although tiny, he was most beautifully dressed in a white turban and a scarlet tunic frogged with gold.

The ghoul did not see it like that. "Yak!" he said. And presently, when he had swallowed a fish finger: "Ugh."

Arriman was just beginning to explain about the contest and how it should be judged when there was the usual plashing and moaning and Sir Simon appeared through the tapestry and thrust his pale and ghastly face at Arriman.

"You see," said the wizard gloomily. "He's trying to warn me. Seven times he's been married and each time his wife drove him to murder. Quite simply *drove* him."

"Oh, dearie me!" said Mr. Chatterjee, very much upset. "How has he been murdering so many, please?"

Arriman shrugged. "The usual methods, I suppose. Drowning, stabbing, strangulation—that kind of thing."

"Then it is good he is only a ghost," said the little genie, "or your new wife will perhaps be number eight."

Arriman threw him a sharp look from beneath his devilish eyebrows. "It's only his *own* wives he kills," he said. But for a while he stared abstractedly into the fire as though turning a new and important idea over in his mind.

"Well now, gentlemen," he said at last. "To business. I thought each witch should be given ten points. Two for darkness, two for power, two for presentation. . ."

There was a swoosh and Mr. Chatterjee came out of his bottle, growing almost to normal size as he did. Like most genies, he was very serious about his work.

And for the next hour, while the shadows lengthened and the Wizard Watcher slept, the judges of the Miss Witch of Todcaster contest bent over their task.

CHAPTER 8

$\mathcal{T}$HE WITCHES' CAMPING wasn't as bad as Mr.
Leadbetter had thought it would be. It was worse.

Not that there was anything wrong with the campsite. The campsite was very nice. Mr. Leadbetter had
ordered a caravan for Mother Bloodwort, who had
seemed to him too old to do well under canvas, and
tents and a toilet block with showers and absolutely the
latest kind of chemical loo. But the witches hadn't been
in the west meadow for twenty-four hours before pandemonium set in.

For a start, Mother Bloodwort never got into her
caravan at all. Madame Olympia nabbed it straightaway, no one knew how, and sat inside it with the aardvark, despising the other witches and refusing to take
her turn at any of the chores. Nancy and Nora Shouter
spent the first night quarreling about which of them

had the better camp bed and ended by sticking penknives into each other's air mattresses. Ethel Feedbag's pig escaped from its pen and crashed into Mother Bloodwort's tent, sending the old witch flying just as she was trying to fix a mouse-blood poultice under her nightdress, and Mabel Wrack insisted on using the cooking cauldron to give Doris a bubble bath, which made the breakfast porridge taste very strange indeed.

It was Belladonna, of course, who was left to fetch the water and do the cooking and the washing up, and however hard she tried to please everybody—braising cod's eyes for Mabel Wrack and roasting squashed hedgehogs on hot bricks for Ethel Feedbag—she got nothing but grumbles and sneers for her pains.

And Belladonna had her own troubles. Mr. Leadbetter and the ogre were back in their old rooms up at the hall, and as Terence was supposed to be Mr. Leadbetter's nephew, he had been given a little room beside the secretary's in the servants' wing. This meant that Rover, too, was far away at the end of the long drive, sleeping in his wooden box under Terence's window. And with her familiar out of reach, Belladonna's old trouble was coming back, and coming back badly. The very first morning she had woken to find that her sleeping bag had come out in a rash of passionflowers— great, pollen-loaded things that tickled abominably and made her sneeze, and when she opened the flap of her tent she found six twitch-eared, bright-eyed baby rabbits waiting for her, their paws in the air.

"I'm not a white witch now, you know," she said crossly. But of course she let them in and conjured up a patch of lettuce for them out of her groundsheet, and it was clear to everybody that they were to stay.

But if life was hard on the camping site in the west meadow, it wasn't exactly easy at the hall. Mr. Sniveler, the ghoul, who was sleeping in the tapestry room, found it difficult to break the habit of years and spent the night scooping fungus off the cellar walls and filching raw mince from the refrigerator and taking them to bed. This meant that he was usually very tired during the day and fell asleep all over the place, waking up suddenly to say things like, "Blood!" or "Slime!" which made it difficult to carry on a sensible conversation. Poor Mr. Chatterjee had caught a cold and sat inside his bottle sneezing miserably so that the glass misted up and he couldn't see out. As for Arriman, well, as Lester said: "Anyone would think he was goin' to have his bloomin' head chopped off instead of getting hitched, the way he's carrying on."

In the bustle and fuss that led up to the start of the competition, Terence turned out to be worth his weight in gold. He ran errands, found the wizard's socks, removed the bits of bandage with scabs on them from Mr. Sniveler's bed, and stuffed Mr. Chatterjee's bottle with paper tissue so that the little genie could blow his swollen nose. And everything he did, he did happily and with delight because Darkington, with its devilish maze and stinking laboratory and ghastly zoo, seemed to him the most enchanting place in the whole world.

But what Terence did whenever he could be spared was to study Sir Simon Montpelier, and quite soon he knew as much about the wicked wife-slayer as Arriman himself. He learned that the specter usually appeared first in the broom cupboard, where he limbered up with a couple of groans, half a dozen eerie thumps, and a wail or two, before settling into the serious business of smiting his forehead with a plashing sound. Then, still plashing for all he was worth, the unhappy phantom would set off through the laundry room, up the stairs to the library, pass through a couple of book-cases and a stuffed bison, and end up in the great hall, popping out through a tapestry of a man being stuck full of arrows while being burnt at the stake, and ruining the appetite of whomever was at dinner.

"You'll see," said Terence to Belladonna, who was stirring the witches' supper over the campfire. "He'll be absolutely terrific when he's raised. When you get close to him, his face is all sort of loathsome and ruined-looking. When he bursts through the wall, *alive*, it'll be a sensation."

"Oh, Terence, I do hope so," said Belladonna. The baby rabbits hadn't gone, nor had the passionflowers, and the tree behind her tent was bearing golden pears. "Tell me," she went on, "how is he? Is he still so sad?"

She meant Arriman, of course. The great magician was seldom from her mind.

"Well, he is a bit. But you've got to remember that he's never seen you and that he doesn't know you're going to win."

"No," said Belladonna. "He certainly doesn't know *that.*"

But already she felt blacker and more hopeful. It was always like that when Terence came.

And so, at last, after all the preparations and the fuss, the first day of the contest dawned.

Mabel Wrack—witch number one—had got up early and stood for two hours under the shower so that her legs did not dry out on her big day. She had dressed with care, fastening the sea-slug brooch beneath her gown, but she was not nervous. Owing to Mrs. Wrack having been a mermaid, Mabel was one quarter fish and, as is well known, fishes are cold-blooded and never get excited.

As everyone had expected, Mabel had decided to do

her trick beside the sea. The place she had chosen was called the Devil's Cauldron: a sandy bay flanked by brooding granite cliffs and strewn with jagged rocks to which dark seaweed slimily clung.

Backing the sand was a strip of turf, and it was here, at a trestle table which Lester had dragged out for them, that the judges sat. Arriman the Awful, wearing his robe with the constellations on it, was in the middle; Mr. Chatterjee (inside his bottle on account of the nippy breeze) was on the magician's left, and on the right—pale and exhausted after a night of hideous wandering—dropped Mr. Sniveler. The other witches, gowned and masked so that Arriman couldn't catch even an accidental glimpse of them, were huddled behind a clump of gorse bushes—all except Madame Olympia, who had stayed snootily inside her caravan.

Arriman now got up to make a speech. He declared the Ms. Witch of Todcaster contest open and welcomed all the competitors. He reminded them of the rules—any witch practicing black magic on another witch or her familiars would be disqualified, the competitors must not show their faces, and the judges' decision was final. Then he sat down and Mr. Leadbetter, shouting through a megaphone like a film director, said:

"Witch number one—step forward!"

There was clapping from the other witches, and from some villagers who had come up the cliff path, and Mabel emerged from behind the gorse bushes. Only the lower part of her face showed beneath the mask, but it was enough to make Arriman hope frantically that she was going to go to sea in a sieve and drown.

"Present your list!" ordered Mr. Leadbetter, and Mabel went up to the judges' table with her piece of paper. In the neat hand of a practiced shopkeeper, Mabel had written:

1. *One gong (loud)*
2. *Some golden rings*
3. *A drowned sailor*

"The manager of the hotel was kind enough to lend us his gong," said Mr. Leadbetter. "And we got the golden rings from Woolworth's. But there is this matter of the drowned sailor."

"Hm," said Arriman, looking rather sick. There is a place called Davy Jones's locker under the sea, where the bodies of drowned sailors are supposed to be kept, but he had never fancied it. Messy, it sounded, as though things would have been nibbled at, and, of all things, Arriman hated a *mess*.

Then he had an idea and smiled. "Hand me my wand, Leadbetter," he said, and shut his eyes. The next second a large gray skeleton stuck together with bits of wire swirled through the air and landed at the sea witch's feet.

"I wanted a *fresh* one," complained Ms. Wrack. "One with some meat on him. It's for bait."

"If witch number one is not satisfied," snapped Arriman, fire shooting from his nostrils, "she may withdraw from the contest."

"Oh, all right," said Mabel sulkily. "But he's a very funny shape."

This was certainly true. The skeleton had, in fact, belonged to the biology lab of a large comprehensive school in the Midlands, and the poor gentleman hadn't exactly been a sailor but an undertaker who liked messing about in boats and had fallen, in the year 1892, into the Shropshire Union Canal. Owing to the carelessness of the children, and the fact that the biology master was the kind who couldn't keep order, the skeleton had got badly jumbled. The skull was back to front, three finger bones were missing, and for some reason he seemed to have had three thighs.

"Announce the trick you will perform," Mr. Leadbetter shouted through his megaphone.

Mabel Wrack turned to face the judges. She had taken Doris out of her bucket and thrown the familiar's tentacles carelessly round her shoulders like a mink stole, while she held the animal's round body under her arm, squeezing it for power and darkness like someone playing the bagpipes.

Then she spoke.

"I SHALL CALL FORTH THE KRAKEN FROM THE DEEP," she said.

There was a stunned silence. The Kraken! That dread and dangerous monster that has lain since the dawn of time beneath the surface of the sea, dragging ships to their doom, creating by its lightest movement, tidal waves that could drown cities!

"Oh, Terence," whispered Belladonna, "I'm scared, aren't you? Fancy Mabel Wrack being able to do *that*!"

And indeed all the onlookers were a little bit ashamed. They had never taken the fishy witch too seriously and now . . .

Even Arriman the Awful was impressed. "Instruct witch number one to proceed," he said.

Mabel Wrack stepped forward to the edge of the ocean. The sea witch was no slouch, and she had prepared her act with care. She would begin by peppering the sea with golden rings to fetch up the underwater spirits who were known to be extremely fond of jewelry and would then come and help her when she called them to her aid. As for the drowned sailor, he was meant to lure the Kraken from his lair and so make it easier for the spirits to find him.

She put Doris back in her bucket and threw the rings one by one into the foam. Then she raised her arms, and the skeleton of the undertaker who had liked messing about in boats rose slowly up in the air, turned a somersault, and tumbled into the waves.

"Levitation," said Arriman. "Quite neat. Give her a mark for that, don't you think?" The thought of seeing a Kraken had quite cheered him up.

Next, Mabel picked up the gong and thumped it with a resounding wallop, which sent the seabirds flying up in terror. Then:

> *"Mighty Spirits of the Deep*
> *Pray you waken from your sleep.*
> *Come as fast as you are able*
> *Come and help your sister, Mabel,"*

chanted Ms. Wrack. She had decided to go into poetry for the contest. This may have been a mistake. Some witches have a feeling for poetry, some haven't. Ms. Wrack hadn't.

> *"From thunderous reef and mighty grot*
> *The dreaded Kraken must be got. . . ."*

"What's a grot?" whispered Mother Bloodwort pettishly from behind the gorse bushes.

"It's short for grotto, I think," Belladonna whispered back. "Sort of a cave." Though she knew that she had no chance of winning now—who could do anything more terrible than call up a Kraken—she was looking at Ms. Wrack with shining eyes. There just wasn't a mean streak anywhere in Belladonna.

The pause which followed was an anxious one. Even Arriman wondered if he had been hasty. Would there be flooding? Whirlpools? Cannibalism? There are too many stories of witches summoning up evil forces which they cannot then control.

The pause lengthened. The ghoul, unable to take the strain, dropped off to sleep, and still the wind soughed, and the gray sea foamed and boiled against the rocks.

But now there was a change. The sky seemed to darken. The white crests of the waves died away to leave a creeping, wrinkled skin of water. The wind dropped. The sea birds fell silent.

What came next was a strange heaping up of the water into a mound that grew and grew and became a huge tower topped with foam. And now the tower reared upward, bent, and turned to race—a great tunnel of boiling, churning water—toward the shore.

The witches huddled together. Terence's hand crept into Belladonna's, and at the judges' table, Arriman reached for the genie's bottle and screwed on the top.

Just in time. The towering wave had landed with a thunderous crash upon the sand. And when the foam and turmoil had died down, the onlookers blinked.

Ms. Wrack had called on the spirits of the deep to help her find the Kraken, and it was perhaps natural that these should be mermaids. But the four ladies who now sat on the beach were fleshy and no longer young, and they seemed to be rather pointlessly clutching a large black handbag, each of them holding on to it with a pudgy arm. The rings which Ms. Wrack had sent them glistened on their fingers, and their lower halves were sensibly covered in tail cozies of knitted bladder wrack, but all of them were topless, and Arriman had already flinched and closed his eyes.

Ms. Wrack stepped closer—and her mouth opened in horror.

"Septic suckerfish!" she swore under her breath.

And indeed it was the most appalling luck! Of all the mermaids in the ocean, she had managed to call up her mother's four unmarried sisters: Aunt Edna, Aunt Gwendolyn, Aunt Phoebe, and Aunt Jane!

For a moment, Mabel panicked. There is probably nothing less black or magical in the whole world than a person's aunt. Then she remembered that the top half of her face was covered by a mask. With luck, she would not be recognized. There had been a bit of a split in the family when her mother had opted for legs. So, disguising her voice as well as she could, she began:

"Summoned here, I bid thee hearken,
You have been to fetch the Kraken
Search the corners of the ocean—"

She broke off, trying to find a rhyme for "ocean," and also wondering a bit whether an ocean really *had* corners. But she needn't have bothered because all four of her aunts were talking at once, taking no notice of each other or of her.

"My dear, we're so glad you called! We've been worried *sick*!"

"Not knowing what to do for the best, you see."

"When that oil rig went through his mother's head—"

"Skull shattered; not a hope, poor soul—"

"It's *meant*, I said to Edna, didn't I, dear?"

"You did, Phoebe. It's *meant*, you said."

"*Someone* knows what's right."

The aunt who had just spoken broke off, edged closer, peered at Mabel Wrack. "Funny, I'd swear I'd seen you before. Those nostrils . . . that mouth . . ."

Still clutching their handbag, the mermaids waddled toward her on their tails.

"It can't be, of course. But isn't she the *spit* of poor Agatha!"

"The spit!" echoed Aunt Jane.

Mabel Wrack retreated backward, but it was too late.

"It *must* be Agatha's little girl. The one she had with the fishmonger after the operation. It *is* her, I'm sure. Mabel, wasn't she called?"

"Mabel! Dear little Mabel!"

Terribly exicited, the aunts dropped their handbag at last and surrounded their niece with a great flopping of tails and waving of pink, plump arms.

"Stop it!" hissed Mabel furiously. "This is a competition. Keep *away*! And speak in verse, you're disgracing me."

There was a moment of outraged silence while Mabel continued to glare angrily at her relations. It was a silly thing for her to do. Mermaids are famous for being touchy, and so, of course, are maiden aunts.

"Oh, very well," said Aunt Edna haughtily. "We know when we aren't wanted, don't we?"

"It was you that called *us*, you know."

"Such airs—just because her father had legs and a shop."

As they spoke, the mermaids began to waddle huffily away, speaking over their shoulders as they went.

"We were going to stay and give you a few hints, but we won't bother now."

"Don't blame *us* if you don't know how much sieved sea quirt to give."

"Speak in verse, indeed!"

And with a last, offended sniff, the four mermaids dived back into the water and were gone.

"Stop!" shouted the desperate Ms. Wrack. "Come back! You've left your handbag!"

It was a dreadful moment. The mermaids had gone, the mighty Kraken still slumbered beneath the deep, and on the face of Arriman the Awful there was a look that froze the marrow in one's bones.

And now this handbag . . .

Only, was it a handbag? For even as they watched, the object on the sand seemed to give a kind of judder. Next it puffed itself out into a round, smoothed dome like the top of a tadpole or of a small and very squidgy flying saucer. In the middle of this dome, two slits now appeared and a pair of shining, tear-filled, sky-blue eyes stared upward at Ms. Wrack.

"Oh, my gawd," said Lester, with whom the penny had already dropped.

The thing now went into a kind of private struggle and from its round, dark blancmange of a body there appeared, one by one, eight wavery, wobbly legs, each ending in a blob-shaped foot. Peering closer, the onlookers could see, at the rim of the saucer, a round hole from whose reddened edges the little finger bone of the undertaker sadly hung. Aunt Jane had given it to him to help him with his teething.

Even with the evidence there before their eyes, no one could quite believe it. They watched in silence as the "handbag" raised itself once more, tottered a few pathetic steps, and fell in a despairing, quivering heap before Ms. Wrack.

"Mummy?" it said in a piteous voice. "Mummy?"

The sea witch stepped back in disgust; Terence clung tightly to Belladonna to stop her running forward; the ghoul woke suddenly and said: "Spittle!"; and Arriman the Awful rose from his seat.

"What in the name of devilry and darkness is that THING?" he thundered.

He knew, of course. You could say a lot about Arriman, but not that he was thick.

"That, sir," said the ogre, "is a Kraken. A baby Kraken. A very young baby Kraken indeed."

Hearing voices, feeling himself unwanted by the very witch who had called him from the sea, the Kraken, his eyes, his whole body streaming with tears, now began to totter wetly to the table where the judges sat. Three times he fell, his legs hopelessly knotted, and three times he rose again, leaving each time a glistening pool of water, until he reached the chair of Arriman the Awful, Wizard of the North.

"Daddy?" said the Kraken, rolling his anguished eyes upward. And again: "Daddy?"

Everybody waited.

Arriman looked downward and shuddered. "Take it away, Lester. Remove it. Throw it back into the sea."

The ogre did not move.

"You heard me, Lester. It is dribbling on my feet."

"Sir," said the ogre. "That Kraken is an orphan. Its mother's had an oil rig through her head. It'll be two thousand years before that Kraken is old enough to swallow as much as a canoe. If you throw it back now, it'll die."

"So?" said Arriman nastily.

Over by the gorse bushes, Belladonna closed her eyes and prayed. Mr. Chatterjee tried to swoosh out of his bottle, hit his head on the screwed-on top, and fell back, his turban over his dark, kind face.

"Daddy?" said the Kraken, his voice only a whisper now—and raised from the top of his body, a tiny, trembling, and hopeless-looking tail.

"Oh, a plague on the lot of you," cursed Arriman, and scooping up the Kraken, which immediately began to squeak and giggle because it was extremely ticklish, the furious magician left the judges' table and strode away toward the hall.

CHAPTER 9

*M*ABEL'S MARKS WERE announced that night. She had scored four out of a possible ten—a low mark and one that would have been lower if Arriman had had his way. But as kind Mr. Chatterjee pointed out, she had called up the Kraken from the deep and it wasn't her fault that the thing had turned out the way it had.

The low score pleased all the other witches, and Ethel Feedbag, whose turn came on the following day, was heard lurching and roistering round the campfire until long after midnight, hiccuping over her parsnip wine, and falling asleep with her head on her pig and her Wellies dangerously close to the embers. Belladonna, of course, couldn't help feeling a bit sorry for Mabel, who had retired huffily into her sleeping bag with wet towels around her legs, but Terence didn't pretend to be anything but pleased.

"You'll see, Belladonna, you'll win; you're bound to!"

He had brought Rover down earlier, and just by touching the slender, peaceful body of her familiar, Belladonna had been able to turn the passionflowers into bloodshot eyeballs and the golden pears into thumbscrews. She'd left the baby rabbits because, as she said to Terence, it was knowing that she *could* turn them into decayed appendixes that was important.

"How is . . . you know . . . He?" she asked now.

Terence said that Arriman was a little bit upset. He could have said more, but he knew that Belladonna was in love and that nothing hurts people more than to think that someone they love is not altogether perfect. In fact, Arriman had been yelling like nobody's business on account of the Kraken. Absolutely nothing could persuade the Kraken that Arriman was not his father, and the magician had had to change his shoes three times between tea and supper because the thing insisted on sitting on his feet. Krakens make their own wetness from the inside and can breathe in air as well as in water so there was nothing to stop the dreaded denizen of the deep from trying to climb onto Arriman's lap or shedding tears all over his trousers, and the great man was taking it very badly.

"Oh, why didn't the new wizard cometh!" he raged at dinner. "I'd have been spared all this. Lester, take it away!"

"It's you he wants, sir," said the ogre reproachfully. But he scooped the Kraken up and put him in a soup tureen, for what with Sir Simon wailing in the wainscot, Mr. Chatterjee sneezing in his bottle, and the ghoul dribbling raw liver from his mouth, he did feel that perhaps his master had had enough.

The following morning they were up early to see what witch number two was going to do.

Ethel had chosen to perform her trick in a grassy and very beautiful hollow in which, beside a bubbling brook, there grew an oak, an ash, and a thorn.

These three trees have, since the beginning of time, been special trees. Even separately they are special but when they grow together . . . well, anything can happen in a place like that.

"Witch number two—step forward!" shouted Mr. Leadbetter, and Ethel, still wearing beneath her gown the three moldering jerseys she'd slept in, lurched out from behind a rock, pushing a wheelbarrow and calling to her huge and mucky pig.

"Hand in your list!" Mr. Leadbetter ordered, and Ethel walked over to the judges' table, which Lester had set out on a level patch of grass, and put down a crumpled piece of paper in front of Arriman.

The magician read it and passed a weary hand across his forehead. Witch number two wanted: *A man, a woman, and a child.*

"More fuss," he murmured. And then: "Fetch the telephone directory."

So Terence ran up to the hall and came back with the *Todcaster and District Directory,* and Arriman closed his eyes, flicked the pages, and stubbed his finger down on what turned out to be the Bs.

It is not difficult to work a telephone directory. Any wizard worth his salt can do it. You just press your finger down hard on a telephone number, say the right spells, and immediately you can see in your mind's eye the family that lives at that address. After that, summoning them by levitation is just child's play. So now Arriman ignored a Colonel Bellingbotter sitting pinkly in his bath at Todcaster 5930, passed over the Bender sisters doing keep-fit exercise at 2378, and found in the Bicknell family, at Todcaster 9549, exactly what he was looking for.

Mr. and Mrs. Bicknell and their daughter, Linda, were sitting at breakfast in their small semi at 187 Acacia Avenue. Mrs. Bicknell was still in her hair net and curlers; Linda was dressed for school. Linda was fat and her mother was thin; Linda was eight years old and her mother was thirty-five, but what they both liked best was being nasty to Linda's father, Mr. Bicknell, and they were doing it now.

"Why did you put on that stupid shirt?" said Mrs. Bicknell. "It makes you look like an ostrich with the croup."

"Your hair's getting awfully thin on top, Daddy! You'll be bald soon. Won't you look silly when you're bald," said Linda.

"Mrs. Pearce across the road is getting a new washing machine. I suppose you know I've had *my* washing machine for three years?"

"Davina's daddy's buying her a doll that can clean its own teeth. Why don't *you* buy me a doll like that?"

Mr. Bicknell, a small, rather stooped man with a thin, tired face and a lined forehead, just went on quietly eating his cornflakes. He worked hard all day in his grocer's shop, helping the people he served to make their money go further, and when he came home at night he went on helping. He helped his wife with the washing up and fixed shelves and dug the garden, but whatever he did, it made no difference. His wife and his daughter just nagged and nagged and nagged.

"You didn't clean the budgerigar's cage out properly," said Mrs. Bicknell, piling her toast with marmalade. "There's birdseed stuck to the corner."

"Davina says being a grocer is *silly*. Only *silly* people are grocers, Davina says."

"And I wish that just for once you'd—"

But at this point the windows began to rattle violently. Then they burst open and the room was filled with a whirling, roaring wind which lifted Mr. and Mrs. Bicknell and their daughter, Linda, and sent them up and out of the house . . . up and away . . . to land, in what seemed to be just a moment in time, at Ethel Feedbag's feet.

The country witch peered down at them and nodded. Then she stuck her boot under the shrieking, twitching Mrs. Bicknell and the howling, kicking Linda and turned them over on their backs. There was no need to turn over Mr. Bicknell who already lay quietly, looking upward at the sky.

"Announce your trick!" commanded Mr. Leadbetter through his megaphone.

Ethel took the straw from her mouth, burped, and said: "I BE GOIN' TO SHUT THE WOMAN IN THE ASH TREE AN' THE MAN IN THE OAK TREE AN' THAT BAWLIN' BRAT IN THE THORN TREE."

A whisper passed through the audience and they looked at witch number two with a new respect. Imprisonment of human beings in trees is very old magic and it is as black as night. The druids did it, and the witches of ancient Greece and Rome. Even now there are gaunt willows and shuddering alders from whose insides their own spirits have fled, to be replaced by some boastful traveler or careless shepherd who has lain there trapped in slumber for a thousand years.

Only Belladonna, hiding with the other witches, was unhappy. "Those *poor* trees!" she murmured.

And indeed the trees were worth worrying about. The oak was one of those trees that are a whole world of their own: its great scarred trunk was full of clefts and hollows in which squirrels lived, and mice and little scurrying beetles. It stood rooted in a pool of soft green moss; delicate acorn cups clung to its mazed branches, and its crown was a mass of autumn gold.

The ash was as tall, but slender, the smooth gray bark seemingly like silver against the pale blue sky, the key-shaped seeds hanging in bunches from its upward-sweeping boughs. A younger tree than the oak, but proud and regal as a queen.

And lastly, the hawthorn, a most powerful and knowing tree with its writhing trunk, its bloodred berries clustered around the fierce black barbs.

Ethel Feedbag, meanwhile, had fetched a sack from her wheelbarrow and humped it to where the Bicknells lay. It was labeled MANGEL WURZEL MEAL, but it was better not to ask what was really in the powder she now sprinkled over the bawling, slug-faced Linda, her twitching mother, and the tired body of the grocer. Whatever it was, within seconds all three of them lay unconscious on the grass.

Grinning happily, Ethel now pulled up her gown, fumbled under her skirt, and from the elastic of her brown woolen knickers, drew a long black-hilted witches' knife. And as she did so, Arriman gasped and turned a chalky white. He had seen, clear as daylight, the dreaded Wellies beneath the gown.

For a moment, it looked as though the great magician would cut and run, but the ogre and the secretary had already closed ranks behind him, and with a groan he sank back in his seat.

Ethel, meanwhile, was smearing the bark of the thorn tree with a slimy blood-colored paste. Then she picked up her knife and made a single, long slit in its side.

"Oh, Terence, I can't *bear* it!" whispered Belladonna.

"I don't suppose it feels any pain, Belladonna. I expect that's what the ointment was for. To stop it hurting."

They watched breathlessly as the slit, of its own accord, grew wider . . . wider . . . and became, at last, a gaping hole that led to the tree's very heart.

"Not bad," said Arriman, struggling to be fair. "Though I prefer lightning myself. Neater."

Ethel grunted, whacked her pig, and came back to stand with her knife poised over Linda.

"Is she going to kill her?" asked Terence hopefully.

But Ethel was crouching over Linda, murmuring a

spell in a language so ancient and peculiar that none of them could make out a word. Over and over again she chanted, and then slowly the fat, nasty little schoolgirl rose from the grass, stuck her hands in front of her, and began to sleepwalk, like a bewitched suet pudding, toward the tree.

"In!" ordered Ethel, putting a boot in Linda's bottom.

And, lo and behold, Linda wobbled forward into the thorn tree and the sides of the tree came together closer . . . closer . . . and the slit vanished and she was gone.

Next, Ethel went over to the ash. Again she rubbed the tree with ointment, again she made a slit in its side, and again the slit widened to show the dark center of the tree. And now it was Mrs. Bicknell who rose and walked in a trance into the tree and the tree closed around her, and she was gone.

Ethel was just going to start the oak when there was an extremely angry *rustling* noise which began at the hawthorn tree and moved over to where Ethel stood. A second, even angrier rustle, followed. What these were, were the spirits of the thorn and of the ash, and they were in a very nasty temper indeed.

"It is not at *all* convenient for me to be out this morning," said the spirit of the ash.

"You might have *asked*," said the spirit of the thorn.

One cannot actually see tree spirits—they are simply a rustle—but one knows that if one could, they would be green, female, and easily upset.

"Didn't ask you to shift," said Ethel. "Plenty of room for everybody."

"Stay in with that repulsive child!" said the spirit of the thorn. "You must be joking! I'm going home to Mother." And she rustled off in the direction of an old hawthorn standing on the hill, followed by the spirit of the ash, still yammering with indignation.

Ethel shrugged. It took more than a couple of rustles to upset a Feedbag. She had made a slit in the oak tree now and stood back as it opened, groaning and creaking and sending the squirrels and dormice scampering away in terror.

Then Ethel went to fetch Mr. Bicknell and he, too, got up and walked into the tree, and the tree closed over him, and he was gone.

The judges, going over to have a closer look, were pleased. True, the thorn tree bulged at the bottom because of the fatness of Linda's thighs, and its bark had come out in bumpy knots like boils. The golden leaves of the ash, too, were shriveling fast. Still, no passerby could possibly have guessed that three frantic, tortured human beings were imprisoned in this peaceful dell.

But of course there was no question of giving out marks just yet. A true witch must be able to loosen an enchantment as well as weave it.

"Undo the spell!" ordered Arriman.

Ethel had slumped down beside her pig. Now she got up and waddled over to the thorn. Again she made a slit in the tree, again the slit widened—and out on the grass like a crumpled maggot rolled Linda Bicknell.

Next, Ethel slit open the ash, and the lovely tree seemed to sigh with relief as Mrs. Bicknell, sticky with sap and minus three of her curlers, fell out onto the turf.

Smirking now, Ethel went over to the oak. Again she slit it, again she stood back and waited.

Nothing happened.

"Out!" ordered Ethel, jerking her head.

Still nothing.

Beneath the mask, Ethel's round face flushed with temper.

"Out!" she said, stamping her foot.

Silence. Then, from the depths of the great tree, a quiet voice said: *"No!"*

Ethel's face darkened to beetroot. "It's over," she hissed. "You come on out!"

But inside the oak tree, the tired grocer did not stir. What did come out of the tree was its spirit. Like the spirits of the ash and of the thorn, the spirit of the oak was simply a rustle but an older and a wiser one.

"Leave him be," it said to Ethel Feedbag. "He wants to stay. He likes it in there. Says he'll come out when his wife's ninety and in a wheelchair and can't nag, and his daughter's left home for good."

"Stay in t' tree?" roared Ethel, angry as a bull.

"That's right," rustled the spirit. "Says he's never been so happy in his life. He's no bother to me; he just wants to sleep most of the time. His wife used to snore and kick him around the bed, you know how some women do. I don't mind him, he's company— and you can see *he* doesn't mind."

This was true. Unlike the thorn which had come out in boils, or the ash whose leaves had shriveled, the great oak tree stood calm and undisturbed by the grocer in his depths.

"Just do us up again, dear," ordered the spirit. "It's getting drafty. He'll be all right in there for fifty years or so; I'll see he doesn't go moldy. Then someone can let him out and the poor bloke can lead a decent life."

So Ethel closed the tree up again. What else could she do? But when Linda and her mother had been sent back to Acacia Avenue and Ethel's marks came through, they were low; four out of ten, the same as Mabel's. What else could one expect? There is nothing black about shutting someone into a tree who simply loves it there.

But if Ethel was furious, Arriman was as happy as a lark. Whatever else happened, he wouldn't have to marry the witch with the Wellies. All through supper he laughed and joked—until he went upstairs, heard the steady drip-drip of water, and found that the Kraken had climbed onto his bed.

*N*O ONE EVER FORGOT what happened when witch number three did her trick. It was really very horrible in a way that no one could have imagined, and even Arriman, used as he was to terror and disaster, could never think of it, in years to come, without feeling quite giddy and faint.

Witch number three was Nancy Shouter, and when she announced her trick there was a great deal of interest.

"I AM GOING," she said, "TO MAKE A BOTTOMLESS HOLE."

To make a bottomless hole is not easy. A bottomless hole is not a hole that comes out in Australia; a hole that comes out in Australia is a hole that comes out in Australia—it is not bottomless. No, bottomless is something very different. Bottomlessness is a mysteri-

125

ous nothingness that goes on forever; it is an interminable blackness; it is no echo, no plop when something drops into it, no glimmer of water in its depths. Not only that, a bottomless hole has a demonic and unusual power—anyone coming too close has an almost uncontrollable longing to throw himself into it.

Everyone, therefore, was pleased, and Mr. Chatterjee, becoming muddled in his excitement, said, "Oh, that is good! A bottom with no hole!"

So Nancy got to work. She had chosen the east lawn, quite close to the house, to do her trick, and she went about it in a businesslike manner, stubbing out her cigarette, putting her chicken down on the bonnet of the caterpillar tractor that Mr. Leadbetter had hired for her, and setting the motor in motion so that the heavy rotary blades could dig into the soil.

It was a mild and pleasant day. The other witches were clustered in the little summer house, where they could see without being seen by Arriman. Even Madame Olympia had turned out with her aardvark. At the judges' table, which Lester had raised on wooden blocks so that they could see the digging better, Arriman tried to forget the awful night he'd spent with the Kraken, and his anxiety about the Wizard Watcher (who was sending brave but homesick postcards from places like Brighton and Southend-on-Sea), and prepared to give witch number three a chance.

Nancy certainly seemed to know her job. True, her chicken was against her. All along, the Shouter chickens had been rather a washout as familiars. They never crowed thrice or flapped threateningly or erected their wattles, and altogether they looked more like old-age pensioners evicted from a battery than the kind of bird one finds in fairy stories or in fights.

All the same, Nancy was doing all right. From working with the railway, both the Shouter twins were good with mechanical things, and after about an hour Nancy drove the tractor away to the other side of the lawn and the real task began.

Because, of course, at this stage the thing was simply a hole. Nancy had dug up some old drainpipes, part of a tin bath, an old ham bone of the Wizard Watcher's, and masses and masses of shale and sludge. She had made a deep hole, a good hole, the kind of hole little boys stand and gape at on the way to school, but though its bottom was a long way down, it was still *there*.

But now the magic began. First Nancy circled the hole with her wand, scratching a witches' pentacle deep into the surrounding soil. Five times she walked widdershins round the hole and five times she walked *not* widdershins, keeping always to the far side of the magic symbol. Then she put down her wand, picked up her chicken, and, raising it aloft, turned to the north.

"Spirits of the earth, I bid thee SUCK THE BOTTOM FROM THIS HOLE!" she intoned.

Then, still holding her chicken, she turned to the west: "Spirits of fire, I bid thee BURN THE BOTTOM FROM THIS HOLE!" cried Nancy Shouter.

Then she turned to the east and bade the spirits of the air BLOW THE BOTTOM FROM THE HOLE. But now, the chicken had had enough. It fluttered, squawking, from her arms, and it was chickenless that Nancy turned to the south and commanded the spirits of the water to DROWN THE BOTTOM OF THE HOLE.

After which she said the Lord's Prayer backward— and the spell was complete.

It is always hard, the bit between the end of a piece of magic and the time when it is supposed to work. No one is good at waiting, and witches least of all. Nancy had begun most irritably to tap her toes when the scream began.

It was a scream such as no one could have imagined. A scream as if a million giants were being disemboweled with red-hot pincers—a scream that grew louder and more unendurable each second, till everyone present thought that their skulls must shatter with the pain of it.

And how could it be otherwise? For this was the

scream of a hole losing the only thing it has—its bottom.

When the noise had died away at last and the pain in their ears had gone, the judges walked over to where Nancy stood. Taking care not to go too close because of the fearsome power a bottomless hole has to draw things into it, they examined, discussed, and considered.

And they were pleased. Arriman was nodding, Mr. Chatterjee, in his bright turban, was bobbing up and down, and the white exhausted face of the old ghoul had cracked into something almost like a smile.

For while it is true that there is not much you can actually *do* with a bottomless hole, at least it cannot possibly turn out to be someone's aunt like the mermaids, nor can it make anybody happy as Mr. Bicknell had been made happy by being shut into a tree. As they returned to the table, it was clear that the judges were going to give Nancy a much higher mark than they had awarded to Ethel Feedbag or Mabel Wrack.

But before they could make an announcement there was a scuffle from the summer house; Belladonna cried: "Oh, please, don't!"—and then Nora Shouter, shaking herself loose, catapulted onto the east lawn, brandishing her chicken as she came.

"You're a cheat!" she screamed, charging up to her twin. "You're a liar and a twister and a cheat! That's *my* chicken you've got there! You've done your trick with *my* chicken so it doesn't count."

"I have *not* done my trick with your chicken! I have done my trick with *my* chicken!"

"You haven't!"

"You have!"

Face-to-face on the east lawn, the Shouter sisters' fury and loathing reached new heights.

"And anyway," yelled Nora, "I don't believe your hole is bottomless. It's just a hole!"

"My hole is *so* bottomless!"

"No, it isn't!"

"Yes, it is!"

Arriman had risen from his seat, his devilish eyebrows meeting in an angry frown, and in the summer house, Belladonna covered her face. But nothing could stop the Shouters now. Both had put down their chickens and stood facing each other with murder in their eyes.

"If you say my hole isn't bottomless once more, I'll finish you, you worm-eaten stick," screamed Nancy, forgetting the contest, forgetting everything.

"It isn't bottomless! It isn't bottomless! It isn't bottomless!" screamed Nora, quite eaten up with jealousy and temper.

What happened next, happened with terrifying speed.

Nancy stepped forward and pushed her sister hard, sending her reeling, to fall backward with her legs in the air. Then, as Nora tried to rise, Nancy pushed her again and she fell, this time inside the magic pentacle.

Even then, Nancy might have saved her twin. But she stood there, unmoving, her face suffused with an evil, gloating triumph as Nora half rose, swayed—and tottered, *of her own accord,* toward the round, black maw. . . . Right at the edge, she managed to pause, and tried desperately to take a step backward. Too late! There was a hideous, roaring, sucking noise, Nora's arm went up. . . . And then the hole took her and she was gone.

The campsite, that night, was silent as the grave. Arriman, white with shock, had disqualified witch number three and ordered the east lawn to be cleared. Nancy, though, had hardly seemed to hear what he said, but just stood there, blindly gazing at the spot where her sister had last stood, and in the end it was Belladonna who led her away and put her to bed in the tent she had shared with Nora.

"Doesn't matter which of our chickens is which now, does it?" was all Nancy said as Belladonna settled the sad brown birds into their coops.

And Belladonna, who knew perfectly well which chicken was which, and always had, agreed that it didn't matter now. It didn't matter at all.

The horribleness of what had happened kept everyone in a state of shock throughout the following day, which was the one on which Nora should have done her act. Mr. Chatterjee stayed curled in his bottle like a baby that doesn't want to be born, Arriman didn't even notice when the Kraken dribbled into his best elastic-sided boots, and at the campsite the witches stopped bickering for once, shamed by the tragedy that had overtaken them.

But the strangest thing of all was what had happened to Nancy.

Nancy had turned overnight from a loudmouthed, bossy, chain-smoking witch into a timid, shrunken person who just lay on her camp bed in her vest and knickers refusing to wash or dress or eat, and telling anyone who came near that it didn't matter which chicken was which.

"She's going off her nut, you mark my words," said Mother Bloodwort. "I've seen it before. She's flipped."

Terence couldn't understand it. "She hated Nora so *much*, didn't she, Belladonna? So why is she so upset?"

Belladonna crinkled her forehead, trying to work it out.

"I suppose . . . hating Nora was sort of a *part* of

Nancy. I mean, it was what being Nancy was *about*. And now Nora's gone, she isn't anybody. Just a wraith."

But however worried they were about Nancy, the contest had to go on. So later that afternoon, Terence and Belladonna set off for the woods behind the campsite and practiced with Rover, turning the golden bracken fronds into leprous fingers and conjuring little spitting dragons from a bramble bush. They had discovered that Rover's power was so strong that it could work from *inside* the matchbox even when Terence held it closed, and this was a great help because with the box open, Rover had wandered about rather a lot.

"Funny, I thought I heard someone moving over there, behind those elms," said Belladonna, as they sat resting in a grassy clearing, letting Rover crawl confidingly across their hands.

They peered through the trees, but there was no one there. Yet both of them had had an eerie feeling of being watched, and by someone far more sinister than lumbering Ethel or fishy Mabel Wrack.

"Perhaps we'd better put him away," said Terence, scooping Rover back into his box. They had kept his incredible power secret from the other witches and they meant to go on doing so.

And if they could not see the cunning enchantress

loping away from the clearing, who could blame them?
She had taken on a form much used by witches: that of
a fleet and silent hare. But no real hare ever had in its
eyes the look that was in this one's: evil and calculating
and unutterably cruel.

CHAPTER 11

THE FOLLOWING DAY it was Mother Blood-wort's turn. She had spent the whole of the evening before in a last desperate attempt at the turning-herself-young-again spell, rushing from her tent to the toilet block and back again with little jars of crushed gall bladder from the inside of murderers, powdered mandrake picked under a dying moon, and a whole lot of other noxious things which she rubbed into herself, croaking weird rhymes as she did so.

But it hadn't helped. As she was announced by Mr. Leadbetter and tottered out into the Italian garden, she was unmistakably Mother Bloodwort, warts, whiskers, cloud of flies, and all.

Arriman of course, recognized her at once. But to the surprise of Mr. Leadbetter and the ogre, he did not try to escape. The reason for this was simple. He had decided that if the witch with the whiskers won the contest, he, Arriman the Awful, would kill himself. He would do this in some very dramatic way, perhaps by plunging over the cliff into the boiling waters of the Devil's Cauldron, or by shooting himself with a silver dueling pistol, or by falling onto one of the swords that Lester was always swallowing, but he would do it.

So he was quite calm as witch number five hobbled toward him and handed in her list, and he stayed calm until he'd read it.

It was Mother Bloodwort who wanted the seven princesses. She was going to do an old-fashioned trick, but a very famous one: the one in which seven beautiful maidens of the blood royal turn into seven black swans, doomed to wing their way across the waters of the world through all eternity.

There is probably nothing sadder or more romantic in all magic than this spell. One minute you have these lively, bright-eyed girls with all life before them, and often a prince or two in the offing—and then there comes this ghastly moment when their golden hair turns into black down, their rosebud mouths become beaks, their pretty feet in silver slippers change into webbed toes . . . until at last the great black tragic birds fly away into the sunset never to return.

As a setting for this trick, Mother Bloodwort had chosen the Italian garden, which lay beside the lake.

137

Arriman hadn't got round to much blighting and smiting there, and it was a beautiful spot with urns, statues, and wide gravel paths which swept down to the shimmering water.

But now the great magician had read her list. "Seven princesses!" he roared. "Seven! You must be mad!"

Mother Bloodwort, however, was not to be put off.

"Aye. Seven. Proper ones. Royal."

"I can't just whirl princesses through the air like commoners, you know," said Arriman. "The thing has to be done properly. Decent transport and all that. And they're not in the telephone directory."

But Mother Bloodwort, obstinate old witch that she was, just stood there, waiting.

Arriman sighed. "Tell everyone to go away for an hour, Leadbetter," he said. "I'll have to go to my laboratory for this. And send me that nephew of yours. He's a useful lad, and I could do with an extra pair of hands."

So Mr. Leadbetter took the witches back to the camp, and Terence, beaming with pride, followed Arriman and the ogre into the laboratory with its bubbling crucibles and fiendish flasks.

"Actually there is a *sort* of telephone directory for princesses," said the magician. "It's called the *Almanach de Gotha*. Run and get it from the library, boy. It's a big, gold-bound book on the second shelf as you go in."

Terence was back in no time, his eyes shining with excitement.

"Hm," said Arriman. "Let's see. There's a Spanish family descended from Carlos the Cruel, I believe. Yes . . . good, there seems to be a daughter. And we ought to find something in Austria. What about the Habsburgs—they're certainly royal enough."

"Can't we have a *British* princess?" said Lester.

Arriman shook his head. "Not wise, I think." He continued to flick the pages. "We shall have to scrape the barrel a bit. Still, let's get to work."

For nearly an hour, Arriman magicked: murmuring spells, twirling his wand, going backward and forward between his potions and his vellum-bound books. Once he said: "Strange, I feel an unusual force in this room. Things are coming through much faster than usual." But though Terence exchanged a look with Lester, he said nothing. Rover was in his pocket, but if Belladonna was to win the contest, the worm's special power *had* to be kept a secret.

"Right," said the magician. "You can fetch them all back now. The last one's just come through."

Because, sure enough, there, rather beautifully arranged round the rim of a fountain, were seven princesses. Arriman had kept his word and all of them were of the blood royal, but that was as far as he'd been able to go. It was no use pretending that they were a matching set of lovely girls. The Princess Olga Zerchinsky, for example, a niece of one of the last grand dukes of Russia, was ninety-two and crippled with rheumatism so that Arriman had had to conjure her up in a wheelchair. On the other hand, an African princess, descended from King Solomon himself, was lying asleep in her cradle. The Spanish princess, though beautifully dressed in couture, unfortunately had a wooden leg, and the Indian princess was almost invisible in a cloud of exhaust from her motorcycle. There was another young princess from America wearing Levi's and a T-shirt emblazoned with *I AM BATMAN'S FRIEND* (her ancestors had left France when Louis Philippe lost his throne), and there was a middle-aged Austrian one whose nose came down over her chin because she was a Habsburg and they have been famous through history for being the ugliest rulers in the world. And there was an Eastern princess in silken trousers who had Mr. Chatterjee swooshing out of his bottle with excitement.

Mother Bloodwort, meanwhile, had announced her trick. "I AM GOING TO TURN SEVEN PRINCESSES OF THE BLOOD ROYAL INTO SEVEN BLACK SWANS," she said. Then, feeling perhaps that something was missing, she added: "TEE HEE," which was the nearest she could get to evil, cackling laughter.

She then vanished behind a statue of the god, Pan, and returned with a broomstick. It was the crummiest, most moth-eaten broomstick anyone had ever seen—Mother Bloodwort had made it herself from brushwood she had found at the back of the camping site—but everyone was pleased because it meant she was going to do hobbyhorse magic. This is the kind where you ride round and round your victims going faster and ever faster, dizzying them with your speed and

your spells, until the transformation is complete. It is old-fashioned magic, but it can be very powerful.

So now Mother Bloodwort went over to the fountain, blew a hole in her cloud of flies, and stood peering at the princesses. Then she laid her wrinkled hand on the Spanish one in her turquoise gown.

"You!" she said, pulling her forward on to the gravel path.

Arriman had hypnotized the princesses as they came so that Princess Juanita followed the old crone obediently, her wooden leg clacking a little as she walked.

Mother Bloodwort now mounted her broomstick, groaning as she heaved her stiff old legs over the handle, which she had greased with the melted body fat of maddened skunks, and began to ride around and around the royal Spanish lady.

> *"Hattock away, ye magic broom*
> *Send this princess to her doom!"*

shrieked Mother Bloodwort.

Faster she rode, and faster, sending her hood tumbling back and her white hair streaming, while her cloud of flies clung desperately to her flushed face and heaving chest.

So crazy did she look, so exhausted and old, that no one really expected the magic to work. But they were wrong. Strange and terrible things were happening to the Princess Juanita.

Her hair had wavered . . . vanished. . . . Her head was shimmering . . . and now it was covered in feathers, and her full, pouting mouth was changing . . . yes, changing into a beak!

"She's done it, Terence! Mother Bloodwort's done it!" cried Belladonna joyfully from the pavilion.

Once more, Mother Bloodwort circled the doomed princess. Then she dismounted and stood back.

"Drat!" said Mother Bloodwort.

For while it was true that she had completely transformed the princess into a bird, that bird was not a swan. It was a duck and, the princess having had trouble with her leg, it was a *lame* duck.

Everybody stared gloomily at the enchanted bird as it waddled, quacking, toward the water. Why there is such a difference between a duck and a swan it is hard to say. There just is. This one seemed to be a Khaki Campbell and not to be at all the sort of person that a prince might fall in love with, recognizing it for the imprisoned soul it was.

But Mother Bloodwort was not daunted. Leaving the duck to stare moodily at a clump of reeds, she took her broomstick back to the fountain and led out the Eastern princess, lovely as an orchid in her shimmering trousers and golden blouse.

"Oi!" moaned Mr. Chatterjee. He had never married, not being sure if his wife would settle in a bottle, and the Princess Shari was all that he desired.

Again the princess followed the old witch meekly; again Mother Bloodwort rode around and around her on her broomstick, reciting her rhyme.

"It's going to work this time," whispered Belladonna to Terence. "Look, the feathers are black! It'll be a lovely swan, you'll see."

They watched, breathless, as Mother Bloodwort slowed down and dismounted.

"I see that I am to be spared nothing," muttered Arriman the Awful, while beside him, Mr. Chatterjee howled with pain.

For the bird now tottering like an overfed alderman toward the lake was a fat, sleek, and foolish-looking penguin.

For a moment, Mother Bloodwort was very much put out. But once more she pulled herself together, and, coughing up a number of dead flies, she re-greased her broomstick and went to fetch the American princess with her pigtail and her T-shirt.

But the princess did not seem to be as hypnotized as the others.

"This is ridiculous," she complained. "What a joke. Make me a black swan or I'll call my lawyer."

But it was not to be. And of all the heartrending things they'd had to watch, one of the worst was seeing a great-great-great-granddaughter of Louis Philippe sitting on a branch and saying in that silly way that budgies have, even in America: "Please give Polly a cracker. Polly wants a cracker, please."

It was Belladonna who knew what was going to happen next. Mother Bloodwort had dropped her broom, her shoulders sagged, her cloud of flies grew silent.

"Don't!" cried Belladonna. "Oh, please, Mother Bloodwort, don't!"

Too late. Already the budgie, looking surprised,

had hopped onto the thing that now stood, four square, upon the path beside the lake.

The ghoul woke and said, "Vomit!" Mr. Chatterjee shook his turbaned head sadly from side to side. And Arriman the Awful rose from his seat.

"No one," he said, "can accuse me of not doing my bit for wizardry and darkness. But there is one thing I will not do and that is *marry a coffee table!*"

And pulling his mantle close about him, the outraged wizard strode away.

CHAPTER 12

ON THE NIGHT BEFORE Madame Olympia was due to do her trick, Terence had a dream. Not a dream, really—a nightmare—a truly horrible one in which he was back at the Sunnydene Home with all the miseries and cruelties he knew so well.

In his dream, Terence was looking for something. Something terribly important, but he didn't know what it was, and growing more and more frantic, he ran through the drab cold rooms, opening battered locker doors, tearing the lids off serving dishes with their soggy dumplings and clammy meatballs, snatching the rough gray blankets from the iron beds. And all the time, as he searched, he heard the sound of laughter—jeering, taunting laughter. Unable to bear it, Terence ran down the mottled steps into the garden.

"I'll find it," said Terence. "I'll find it here."

He bent down and pressed his hands against the gravel, but the laughter was growing louder and more malevolent, and then, suddenly, rearing up in his path, was the dreaded figure of Matron with her sneering lips and baleful eyes, Matron, grown ten foot tall and still trailing the roots which had tethered her—roots which he saw were now made of plaited, blood-stained *human* teeth.

"I *must* find it!" sobbed the little boy.

"You'll never find it! You'll never find it!" screamed Matron. And as her pointed shoe, sharpened to a saw blade, came up to cut him in half, Terence woke.

At first, just finding that he was in his little room at the hall, wearing Mr. Leadbetter's pajama top and miles away from Matron, was a tremendous relief. But this dream was one it didn't seem easy to shake off.

What had he been looking for so desperately? What had Matron said he'd never find? And suddenly, awake, Terence knew what he had not known when he was sleeping.

Rover. It was Rover he'd been looking for.

Only that was silly. Rover was safe in his box. Terence had said good night to him only an hour ago and he'd been in splendid shape, rippling along the rim of the washbasin like an anaconda.

Still, he'd just make absolutely sure. Jumping out of bed, Terence turned on the light and went over to Rover's box, which stood where it always stood, under the window.

He lifted the lid.

"Rover?" he called.

The worm was underground; he usually was, and turning the moist, crumbly earth over with his hands, Terence began to search for his friend.

He was a long way down. And gradually, as he searched, Terence's movements became faster and his breath seemed to stick in his throat.

Even then he didn't panic, but went to fetch a newspaper from the pantry and, spreading the sheets out on the floor, upended Rover's box.

In the thinly spread scattering of earth, the truth could no longer be denied.

Rover was gone.

An hour later, the ogre, the secretary, and Terence were in Mr. Leadbetter's room, desperately deciding what to do. The ogre had rubbed his eye patch onto the back of his head. Mr. Leadbetter was pacing the floor, and Terence, still in the secretary's pajama top, was crouched on the bed like a worried fledgling on a nest.

"I suppose it wouldn't be possible to use another

earthworm for the competition?" said Mr. Leadbetter, coming to rest for a moment.

Terence shook his head. "Belladonna said she'd tried being black sometimes with other worms when I was up at the hall and it didn't work at all. It isn't *any* worm that makes her black; it's Rover."

"But if we got another worm and *told* her it was Rover—" began Mr. Leadbetter, and broke off because he knew he was being silly. Belladonna could tell each ladybird from all its fellows, call a dozen grimy sparrows on a rooftop by their names. It was as foolish to think that all dogs looked alike as it was to imagine that she couldn't tell Rover from every earthworm in the world.

"It's only Friday," said Terence in a rather shaky voice. To him, Rover had not been just a powerful familiar; Terence had lost a dear and valued friend. "It's Madame Olympia's turn tomorrow and Sunday's a free day, isn't it. So by the time Belladonna does her trick on Monday night, don't you think Rover might be"—he gulped and pulled himself together—"might be found?"

The ogre and Mr. Leadbetter exchanged glances. Terence believed that Rover was simply lost, and they thought it was better he went on thinking so. They had their own suspicions, but the boy had quite enough to bear.

"I wouldn't bank on it, son," said Lester, laying his enormous hand on Terence's shoulder.

"I suppose we'll just have to give up all hope of Belladonna winning," said the secretary wearily.

"*No!*" Terence had jumped from the bed and his voice was strong again. "No! We mustn't give in. Look—Belladonna's just got to win the actual competition, hasn't she? I mean, once Arriman's seen her he's bound to want to marry her and by that time maybe Rover'll have turned up. So can't we *fake* her trick? *Pretend* to have raised Sir Simon?"

"Get someone to impersonate the ghost, do you mean?"

"That's right," said Terence eagerly. "There could be lots of smoke and spotlights and things, like in a pantomime. And then this horrible specter suddenly appearing—*alive!*"

Mr. Leadbetter looked shocked. "That would be cheating, surely?"

Terence turned to him, surprised. "Well, cheating's black, isn't it? And blackness is what Arriman wants."

Mr. Leadbetter saw the logic of this. "But who could we get to take the part of Sir Simon?"

"Ought to be a professional," said Lester. "An actor. I used to know some when I was in the fair, but not now."

"Wait a minute," said Mr. Leadbetter. Now that he

had got used to the idea of cheating, his brain was beginning to tick over once again. "You know my sister Amelia? The one that's Terence's mother and didn't marry the swimming bath attendant?"

The others nodded.

"Well, she keeps a boardinghouse for theatricals in Todcaster. You know, actors and people connected with the stage generally. I wonder if she could find us someone to impersonate Sir Simon?"

"We'll have to move fast," said Lester. "There's only two days and one of them's a Sunday. And I don't really see how I can leave the old man with that Madame Olympia due to do her trick tomorrow."

"And I can't either," said Mr. Leadbetter. "She's asked for some most complicated stuff. Strobe lights and amplifiers and goodness knows what. Oh, dear!"

"*I* can go," said Terence.

There was a pause. Terence had looked wonderfully better since he'd come to the hall, but he was still the smallest and skinniest boy imaginable. And Todcaster was thirty miles away: it meant a train and then a bus into the town.

"Amelia'd look after you," said Mr. Leadbetter slowly. "But . . ." His voice trailed away. He was too polite to say that he didn't think an actor or anyone else would take much notice of Terence.

"Wait a minute," said the ogre. "I've got an idea.

The old man's been making paper money: fivers, tenners, the lot. Says he's sick of humping bags of gold around. I'll just go and have a look."

He was back in a few minutes with a large wallet crammed to bursting with notes.

"If you take these you'll be all right," said Lester. "No one'll care a stuff what size you are when they see these. And remember, not a word to Belladonna! She's got to believe that she's really raising Sir Simon and that it's Rover she's touching inside his box. However nutty she is on Arriman, she'll never cheat to get him and that's for sure!"

And then, at last, they went to bed to wait for dawn.

But one light still burnt at Darkington. A single lamp in the window of Madame Olympia's caravan where the enchantress sat gloating over something she held in her cruel, rapacious fingers. Something moist and gentle which, greedy as she was, she prized beyond any jewel.

She had always been certain she would win the competition. But now . . . *No one* could beat her now!

BELLADONNA WOKE on the morning of Madame Olympia's trick feeling worried and out of sorts. The bloodshot eyeballs on her sleeping bag had gone very pink and fragrant in the night and she had a nasty feeling that they might be turning into the begonias she was so often troubled with. Then there was Mother Bloodwort, who'd been so upset by the budgerigar that not all Belladonna's coaxing could get her to remember the undoing spell for being a coffee table, and Belladonna had had to drag her into her own tent and just hope she'd come round in time. And being Belladonna, she was worried about the flies. Were they all right inside the coffee table; what did they *think*?

But of course she cooked breakfast for the others

and took a cup of tea to Nancy Shouter (who still lay on her camp bed in her vest and knickers telling everyone that it didn't matter which chicken was which) and then she followed Mabel Wrack and Ethel Feedbag up to the hall.

When she reached the steps leading to the south terrace, she met Mr. Leadbetter and the ogre, who told her that Terence had gone into Todcaster to do some errands for Arriman.

"Oh, dear!" said Belladonna. "He'll miss Madame Olympia's trick, and he's so *fond* of magic."

And feeling ridiculously miserable at the thought of spending the day without the little boy, she went to look for the other witches and find a hiding place from which to watch.

Madame Olympia had chosen to do her trick in the underground vaults and cellars of Darkington Hall itself; a cold, dark, echoing warren of passages which opened into a wide cave, as big as several rooms, where in the olden days prisoners had been tortured to death or left to starve. No daylight ever reached this subterranean maze, and as Arriman strode to his place at the judges' table, holding the genie's bottle under his cloak against the cold, he shivered and pulled his collar round his ears.

But when witch number six strode into the cave, his

mood changed. For here, at last, was a witch to be taken seriously.

One moment they were sitting in a dark and gloomy cellar, the next, the cave was aflame with flashing lights that changed from sulfurous yellow to livid green and searing crimson, casting strange and flickering shadows on the walls. Next, the vault was filled with a pulsing, sobbing, shrieking sound as the music of "The Groaning Gizzards," amplified to screaming pitch, pierced the eardrums of the listeners with a song about greed and wretchedness and hate.

Having thus set the stage, the enchantress walked over to the judges' table and bowed low. She was wearing the hood and gown that Arriman had insisted on, but she did not look at all like Mother Bloodwort or Ethel Feedbag or Mabel Wrack. In the secrecy of her caravan, the enchantress had sewn a thousand jet-black sequins onto her gown, which now trembled and glittered in the light of the strobes, as did the rhinestones on the collar and lead of her sinister familiar. Witch number six was tall and carried herself like a queen, and she had looped her necklace of ninety-three molars, fifty-seven incisors, and eleven wisdom teeth so as to make a column of palest ivory round her throat.

"THE SYMPHONY OF DEATH PERFORMED BY A CAST OF THOUSANDS," announced Madame Olympia.

Arriman nodded. He didn't understand a word but it sounded good, and the witch's low, husky voice sent a most agreeable shiver up his spine.

Madame Olympia stepped into the center of the cave. Then she closed her eyes and raised, not her wand, but a whip. A whip like no other in the world. Stolen from an accursed Egyptian tomb, its thongs were made of the plaited skins of human slaves; its lapis lazuli handle had been wrought by an ancient sorcerer so powerful that it had meant death even to know his name.

Three times Madame Olympia laid the whip across the back of the aardvark, charging it with the evil beast's devilish power. Then she cracked the whip—and everybody gasped.

A minute before, the cellar had been empty. Now, from every nook and cranny, from the walls, the ceiling, the floors, from the very air itself, there came tumbling and squeaking and clawing, a hundred, two hundred, five hundred—a thousand huge gray rats.

Not ordinary rats. Lurching, swollen, putrid-eyed rats with scabrous tails and bloated fleas clinging to their matted fur. Rats with death in their filmed eyes—vicious, maddened, *plague-bearing rats!*

Belladonna, hiding behind a pillar, gasped with terror, turned to take Terence's hand, and remembered that he was not there. The ogre said, "Cor!"

and Arriman the Awful leaned forward intently in his seat.

There were so many rats now that they could not all put their diseased and twisted feet on the ground but walked on each other's faces, climbed on each other's backs. . . . And now Madame Olympia turned off the music of "The Groaning Gizzards" and adjusted the amplifier so that it was the squeaks and squeals and hideous scamperings of the rats, magnified beyond bearing, that filled the cave.

Once more she flicked her whip and now, unbelievably, each one of the deformed and frightful animals swelled and swelled . . . grew to twice its size . . . three times. . . . Rats the size of large dogs, now, so that the beasts' heavy scaly tails thumped like hawsers against the stones. And the fleas, those dreaded carriers of bubonic plague, fell off them, large as saucers.

Smiling her cruel, complacent smile, the enchantress watched as the sickening monsters in their thousands filled the cave, pressing each other against the walls, stamping each other underfoot, their whiskers flicking like thongs into the oozing eyes and twitching limbs of their fellows. And still more rats appeared, layer upon layer of them till the cave was filled almost to the roof with the misshapen, screeching monsters.

Only the ghoul was smiling now. The ogre, though the bravest of men, had pulled Mr. Leadbetter away to stand behind Arriman, and the three witches, their differences forgotten, clung together trembling.

Again the enchantress cracked her whip—and they saw that Madame Olympia had not come to the end of her devilry. For even as they watched, the flesh, the hair, the eyes, and skin of the giant rats began to pucker up, to shrivel—and then to vanish altogether till the whole cellar was packed with skeletons. But skeletons which still ran and climbed and fought and bit. Eyeless, hairless, tailless, these were still rats, and on the walls their shadows reared and capered in a grotesque and frightful dance of death.

"Is good, is very good," said Mr. Chatterjee inside his bottle, but he was shaking like a leaf, and Belladonna, almost fainting with disgust, could be glad at least that Terence was not there.

Another crack of the whip, and, lo, the giant rats were clothed in their own flesh again: their gray fur returned, their rheumy eyes, their scabrous tails. But the most horrible part of the trick was still to come. For as they heard the last crack of the whip, all the rats were seized at the same moment with a passionate and uncontrollable desire for *the taste of each other's flesh.* It was cannibalism run riot, cannibalism in its most ghastly form, as the rats sank their yellow teeth into thighs and shoulders and cheeks, and slowly devoured each other—crunch by horrendous crunch.

"I can't bear it," said Belladonna beneath her breath.

There were fewer rats now, and fewer, as more and more twitching bodies vanished into the maws of their fellows. Soon only fifty rats were left, then twenty, then five. . . .

And then one . . . A single, huge rat sitting on its torn haunches in the middle of the floor, blood dripping from a wound in his side, and the still-twitching tail of his neighbor vanishing down his gullet.

Even then it was not quite done. For now this last rat was seized with the most terrible madness of all, and, gasping, the onlookers saw it begin, slowly and relentlessly, to *eat itself.*

Madame Olympia waited till the dripping jaws hung in the air. Then she flicked her whip, the jaws vanished—and she turned to the judges and bowed.

"The Symphony of Death is completed," said Madame Olympia.

And laughed . . .

CHAPTER 14

ADAME OLYMPIA GOT nine out of ten for her "Symphony of Death," as near full marks as could be. The ghoul loved her trick, and though Mr. Chatterjee's teeth went on chattering for a long time inside his bottle, he too thought she was very, very clever. Not even the nastiest caliph in the *Arabian Nights* had done anything more horrible.

"Why did I only give her nine out of ten?" Arriman asked himself that evening. "Why not full marks?" Because it was he who held back. The other two had been willing to go the whole hog and give her that last mark also.

What had prevented him, he wondered? For certainly no witch could touch her for darkness. And the style, the flair! Those strobe lights and that single rat left in the middle of the floor eating its own flesh!

Standing there in his dressing gown, Arriman remembered her low and evil laughter—very attractive it was, really—and that proud toss of the head. No, no one would beat her, that was for sure. There was only one witch to go, and from what he'd heard she was just a little slip of a thing, not to be taken seriously. No, witch number six would be Mrs. Canker, all right. She'd known it herself.

"That was a very fine show today, don't you think, Lester?" he called to the ogre, who was running his bath.

Lester came out of the bathroom looking steamy and rather tired.

"Very fine, sir," he said, his voice expressionless.

"Those flickering lights and the skeletons and those giant fleas. I really liked them, didn't you?"

"Very much, sir."

"Of course, some people would have thought it wasn't necessary to make the rats actually . . . eat each other up like that. I mean, I myself have never gone in much for that sort of thing."

"No, sir."

"But you couldn't have anything blacker. And she was quite good-looking, I think. I didn't see any warts, did you? Or . . . er, whiskers? And I'm almost sure she wasn't wearing Wellies."

"No, she wasn't wearing Wellies, sir."

"So I'm very glad she's won. Well, she's sure to have. Very glad indeed. I think she'll make me an excellent wife. I shouldn't think she'll get things to eat each other very much once we're married. There'll be just straightforward blighting and smiting, wouldn't you say?"

"Yes, sir. Your bath is ready, sir."

"You're not very forthcoming tonight, Lester. What's the matter with you?"

"I'm a little tired, sir."

"Are you? Well, I'll tell you what. Fetch Leadbetter's nephew, Terence. He can scrub my back for me. A nice boy, I'm fond of him."

"I'm afraid he isn't here, sir," said Lester after a short pause. "He's gone to visit . . . his mother."

"Has he? Dear me. That'll be Leadbetter's sister, I suppose. Pity. He'd have enjoyed today, I think," said the magician, untying his dressing gown cord. "Er . . . those were *human* teeth she was wearing round her neck?"

"Undoubtedly, sir."

"Yes. I thought so. It's a new fashion, I suppose. I mean, one must keep up with the times."

Arriman took off his trousers, his socks, and his shoes, and was just about to start on his underpants when the usual plashing sound was heard behind the wainscot.

"Oh, my gawd," said Lester, who was in no mood for Sir Simon.

But before he could make his getaway, the wicked spook came waveringly through the paneling and thrust his pallid, guilty face at Arriman.

"Hello, hello!" said the magician, cheering up as always at the sight of his friend. "I've great news for you. I've found a truly black witch. Looks like a certain winner."

The specter stood in silence, his eye sockets dark and inscrutable.

"I know you aren't into marriage much, but you'll like her. Great style. She did this amazing trick where all these rats . . . ate each other up. Of course, it's not for people with weak stomachs."

Still silent, the specter stood and plashed.

"Oh, blast you!" said Arriman, suddenly furious. "Why don't you *say* something?"

The wizard was in his bath, and Lester, who'd finished scrubbing his back, was out in the corridor talking to Mr. Leadbetter, when a cry of anguish rent the air.

"Lester! Come back! It's trying to get in with me. Take it away!"

Lester did not move.

"Aren't you going to go to him?" asked Mr. Lead-better.

"Not likely."

"But it's the Kraken. It's trying to get in the bath with him."

"I know it's the Kraken. It always tries to get in the bath with him."

"But—" began Mr. Leadbetter, as another despairing cry came from Arriman.

"Look," said the ogre, rubbing his eye patch. "Last night that bloke sent seven princesses back to seven different countries, and three of them blinking budgies, lame ducks, and penguins before he got to them. A month ago he brought down a ton of toads on the tax inspector's hatchback. What's to stop him sending the Kraken back into the sea or turning him into an umbrella stand or something?"

"You mean he likes being followed about and so on?"

"Likes it?" said the ogre. "He loves it. Laps it up. Can't get enough. You mark my words, if he marries and has a kid he'll be the biggest sucker in the world. Anyone calling that bloke "Daddy" and he's a goner, devilry and wizardry or no."

They both fell silent. The thought of Arriman's marriage lay like a stone on their chests. For Terence hadn't yet returned, and even if he managed to hire an actor, was there really any hope that they'd manage to deceive Arriman?

"Will you stay on if he marries . . . Madame Olympia?" said Mr. Leadbetter, who could hardly bring himself to say the enchantress's name.

Lester shook his craggy head. "Don't think I could," he said. "Goodness knows it goes against the grain to leave the poor bloke, but she really gives me the creeps. I wouldn't put it past her to turn me into a bloomin' baboon *and* get me to nosh meself into the bargain."

"It's the boy I'm worried about," said Mr. Leadbetter. "If anything happens to Terence, Belladonna'll never get over it."

"It won't," said the ogre. "He may be gnat-sized, but he's got a head on his shoulders, that boy. Even now, I wouldn't put it past him to bring home the bacon."-

"I do hope you're right, Lester," said the secretary, rubbing his aching tail. "I do very much hope so."

Lester *was* right. No harm had befallen Terence, and midday had found him ringing the doorbell of Amelia Leadbetter's terrace house on the outskirts of Todcaster.

At first when he'd seen again the dreary houses and mean streets of the town he'd been so unhappy in, Terence had felt uneasy and afraid. Ms. Leadbetter's boardinghouse was not far from the Sunnydene Home, and when Terence thought of Matron and her bullying it was as though the last exciting days at Darkington had never been. But then he remembered that he was there to help Belladonna and not to worry about himself, and it was with renewed courage that he rang the bell.

Ms. Leadbetter might not have a tail but she was a brisk and sensible woman, and when she'd read the note her brother had written, and given Terence a cup of tea and a tuna sandwich, she got down to business.

"Now it says here you want an actor to take part in a show up at the hall? Someone tall and used to costume work, is that right?"

Terence nodded. "If he could be used to talking in that old-fashioned way, you know, with 'haths' and 'quothees' and things in it?"

"Shakespearean." Amelia Leadbetter nodded. "Well, there's plenty of unemployed actors around. It's not a comic you want, then? It's straight lead?"

"Oh, yes. He plays a knight in armor. It's a very good part. Sort of a star part."

"And it's got to be someone who can keep a secret. Now, let's see . . . " She leaned across and filled Terence's mug once more with scalding tea. "There's Bert Danby, but he's a boozer and you can never trust a boozer. Then there's Dave Lullingworth—he's down to doing cat food adverts on the telly—but Dave would tell his life story to a brick wall. Wait a minute! I've got it.

Yes, Monty Moon. He's a bit long in the tooth now, but with the right makeup he'll pass. Monty hasn't worked for years, but he was at Stratford once. In fact I'm not sure he didn't play the ghost in Hamlet."

Terence was very excited. "He sounds just right!" he said. An actor who was actually used to playing ghosts was more than he had hoped for.

So Amelia rang up Mr. Moon, who by good luck was at home and agreed to come around immediately.

Monty Moon turned out to be tall and pale and stooped, with a large balding head and a way of tucking in his chin so that it didn't show any sags or wrinkles. When he saw Terence he looked surprised and a little stuffy, but when he saw the wallet Terence had laid casually open on the table he got a lot less stuffy at once.

Five minutes later, they were deep in conversation.

"Now, I understand I'm to play a wicked, wifeslaying specter who suddenly finds himself brought back to life—is that correct?"

"That's right."

"Now, fill me in, dear boy, fill me in. I must get right *inside* this part. How many wives have I slain? What sort of armor do I wear? Am I bloodstained?"

So Terence told him everything he could think of about Sir Simon, and Mr. Moon wrote it all down in his little notebook.

"And he doesn't wear his helmet or anything," finished Terence. "The top of him is clear and so are his hands so that he can beat his forehead with a plashing sound."

"Like this?" asked Mr. Moon, bringing his arm around in a sweep and striking dramatically at his forehead.

"Well, yes, but it makes a softer noise. Sort of sloshier."

"Don't worry, dear boy. I'll get it right on the night. Now what about the sound effects? Anything special you want when I appear? Howling dogs? Tempests? Crowing cockerels? Just say the word."

They went on discussing things for another hour and deciding what Terence should get ready in the way of skulls, necromancy incense, and so on, for while it had been all right for Belladonna to write "Nothing" on her list when they had Rover to rely on, now that her trick was to be faked, the more props there were, the better. When Mr. Moon heard that he was to get five hundred pounds now and another five hundred if he succeeded in convincing everybody that he was really Sir Simon brought back to life, he promised of his own accord to bring an electrician and a stage manager who had their own van and would help him set the thing up.

"You'll see, dear boy, it'll be a first-rate show. I always did my best work in costume parts. Now just draw a little map for me to show me how we can get into the hall the night before and rig up one or two effects. A trapdoor would have been nice, but one can't have everything."

When they had finished, Terence went to thank Ms. Leadbetter. Returning to say good-bye to Mr. Moon, he found the actor still standing in the middle of the room, bringing his arm in a sweep round to his forehead, practicing and practicing his plashing sound. And knowing that he had found somebody who took his work seriously, Terence went contentedly away.

CHAPTER 15

*A*RRIMAN WOKE ON the Sunday before Halloween with a headache. Like Terence, he had had a dream and a dream with teeth in it. He'd seen this necklace floating in the air with five brand-new molars on it: cusps, fillings, and all. Arriman had known at once that they were *his* teeth, and he'd started making teeth-calling noises like the noises you call cows in to be milked with, or chickens to be fed. But the teeth wouldn't come to him; they sort of sneered and floated away—and then Arriman woke and had been almost glad to hear, from under the lid of the soup tureen, the muffled cries of "Daddy! Daddy!" with which the Kraken greeted the dawn.

Mr. Chatterjee was already breakfasting inside his bottle, looking cheerful and relaxed. The climate of the north of England didn't really suit him, and as

171

soon as witch number seven had done her trick he was going to fly home to Calcutta.

"Well, we've got the day free," said Arriman, who was always jolly at breakfast. "Witch number seven's not going to do her trick till tomorrow night. Myself, I think I'll do a little smiting and blighting today; I'm getting short of exercise. What about you, Sniveler?"

But the ghoul, sitting hunched and exhausted over his kidneys, didn't answer. He almost never did.

So Arriman went off and blighted some fir trees and cleft some boulders in twain and called in a thunderstorm from the west—clean, old-fashioned magic which he enjoyed—and thought how nice it had been when the Wizard Watcher had sat peacefully at the gate and his oak trees had not been filled with sleeping grocers and lost witches had not bubbled about in bottomless holes on his east lawn.

"Well, tomorrow it'll all be over," he thought. "Tomorrow I'll know for certain who my wife is going to be. No, I'm being silly. I know *now*."

After which he went to find Mr. Leadbetter to ask him for some milk of magnesia tablets. Magician or no, Arriman had a stomachache.

Meanwhile, down at the campsite, Belladonna sat wretchedly by the campfire, facing the fact that Arriman the Awful was lost to her forever. Even before the enchantress did her trick, Belladonna had not really hoped to win, though when Terence was with her she'd sometimes felt confident and strong. Now, all hope was gone.

She reached for the magic mirror. Arriman was gulping down small white pills. He looked tired and anxious, but what was that to do with her? It would be Madame Olympia now who'd comfort him and smooth the curse curl from his furrowed brow.

Her sad thoughts were interrupted by a fierce rocking noise behind her, followed by a scrabble and a swoosh, and Mother Bloodwort crawled out of Belladonna's tent, her flies sticking like a doormat around her head. The old witch had been a coffee table far too long, and as she collapsed onto the camp stool that Belladonna pulled out for her, she looked very battered and confused.

"What happened?" she asked, blinking. "Was the last one a swan?"

"I'm afraid not," said Belladonna gently. "It was a budgerigar. A very intelligent one. It asked for a biscuit."

"Not the same, though, is it?" the old witch remarked. "Don't know what went wrong. Didn't get a very high mark, I suppose?"

"Well . . . three out of ten. Not bad, really. More than I'll get, anyway."

Mother Bloodwort kicked off her slippers so that the fire could get at her bunions and stared sadly into the flames.

"It wouldn't have made any difference if you'd managed the swan bit," said Belladonna, trying to comfort the old woman. "Because Madame Olympia would have won, anyway. She did this absolutely terrifying thing with rats. The 'Symphony of Death,' it was called. She got nine out of ten: no one can possibly beat her."

"The 'Symphony of Death,' eh?" said Mother Bloodwort thoughtfully. "I've heard of that. Very black, that is, *very* nasty. There's not too many witches could do that even in my day. I should think she'd gobble up poor Arriman as soon as look at him. Good job he's got nice teeth."

"Oh, no, *no*! Don't say that!" cried Belladonna. "Arriman's the mightiest wizard in the world! She couldn't hurt him, she couldn't!"

"Oh, well, maybe not," said Mother Bloodwort. She sighed. "I suppose marriage wouldn't really have suited me. I've lost the habit, I reckon, and that turning-myself-young-again spell doesn't seem to be up to much."

She got up creakingly, went to fetch her tin with the coronation on the lid, and began to shake her head into it, blowing on the flies as they fell to change them into maggots. "Best be getting ready for lunch, I suppose."

But before Mother Bloodwort could move, Ethel Feedbag and Mabel Wrack came lurching up to them, both heaving with rage.

"Look!" said Mabel, putting down the bucket in which she was taking Doris for her midday stroll and pointing with a shaking arm at the enchantress's caravan.

"Stuck-up, snooty cow!" raged Ethel Feedbag.

Belladonna looked up, frowning.

"How strange," she said.

Madame Olympia's caravan was the kind with a little stove and a chimney. And of course, as she was a witch, the smoke from her chimney was blowing against the wind. But that wasn't what had made Ethel and Mabel so mad. Madame Olympia had magicked the smoke so that it came out in letters: the letter *O* followed by the letter *C* again and again, standing out as clear as could be against the deep blue sky of autumn.

"What does it mean?" asked Belladonna, puzzled.

"What do you think it means?" snarled Mabel Wrack. "Those are her new initials, of course. Olympia Canker. She's letting us all know she's won."

"But she hasn't won! She *hasn't*!"

The voice was a new one, and Belladonna, hearing it, sprang to her feet.

"Terence! Oh, I'm so glad you're back! You've no idea how much I've missed you."

But though he hugged her as lovingly as always, Terence's mud-colored eyes were fixed on the enchantress's chimney and his jaw was set.

"You're going to beat her, Belladonna. You're going to get ten out of ten tomorrow. You'll see!"

CHAPTER 16

*I*N THE GREAT HALL at Darkington, the clock struck eleven. An hour till the true beginning of Halloween, the Feast of the Dead, when the shades of the departed draw closer, for a few dread hours, to those they have left behind.

In a dozen sconces, the tall candles burnt with a sickly flame; logs of gnarled and knotted alderwood, like ancient severed limbs, hissed and spat in the grate, and the wind, howling through the rafters, eerily stirred the tapestry of the gentleman being shot with arrows while burning at the stake.

Belladonna, waiting for her turn, was as white as a sheet under her gown and mask. Terence had taken her through her trick again and again. He'd told her that everything would be ready, laid out on a great refectory table covered with a cloth, and that he himself would be hiding underneath it, ready to hand her Rover at the right moment and prompt her if she forgot anything. And waiting behind a tall embroidered screen with the other witches, she could see that he'd been as good as his word. The table, with its candlesticks, its grinning skull, and portrait of Sir Simon, looked just like one of those dreadful necromancy altars she'd seen in books. But that only made her more horribly afraid of the deed she was about to do.

"Witch number seven—step forward!" commanded Mr. Leadbetter.

The secretary was looking tired and careworn. However much he argued with himself, it seemed to him that cheating was *not* the same as wizardry and darkness. Cheating, whichever way you looked at it, was *mean*. And what if Monty Moon let them down and all they'd done was make Belladonna look a fool?

But Belladonna, trying to stop her knees from trembling, was walking toward the judges' table, and, pulling himself together, Mr. Leadbetter said:

"Announce your trick!"

Belladonna turned and bowed low to the judges. Her voice shook a little on the first words, but she lifted her head bravely and her clear young voice reached even to the farthest corner of the hall.

"I AM GOING TO BRING SIR SIMON MONTPELIER

BACK FROM THE DEAD," said Belladonna, allowing herself a lingering look at Arriman as he sat, brooding and a little bored, between the other judges.

But at her words, the magician leaned forward, furiously frowning, and a spurt of fire burst from his left ear. Going to do necromancy, was she? A deed so difficult that he, Arriman the Awful, had failed at it again and again. A little slip of a witch, not up to his shoulder. How *dared* she?

For a moment, it looked as though Arriman was going to make a scene. But even as he brought his fist down, ready to bang it on the table, his curiosity got the better of him. It was impertinence, of course, the most appalling cheek. Still, it wouldn't hurt to let her try. Perhaps she had guessed how achingly he longed for his plashing, ghostly friend.

So Belladonna stepped forward to the table with its long cloth and candlesticks and skull, and as she did so, Terence slipped Rover's closed box into the pocket of her gown. Then she took a pin from her other pocket and, jabbing it into her finger, let a drop of blood fall, like a red pearl, into the incense pot. And immediately there was a flash, and a sheet of rose and amethyst and orange smoke rose almost to the roof.

"Thank gawd," said Lester, who believed that if you had to cheat it was best to cheat good and proper. He'd heard a van drive into the courtyard at dawn, but that was the only sign of Monty Moon and his crew, and he'd begun to have doubts.

"Let there be darkness!" said Belladonna. And instantly, every candle guttered and went out, and the hall was plunged into inky impenetrable night.

Belladonna let the darkness and silence stay there for a moment, making everyone's flesh crawl a little. Then she took up the hollow skull and walked over to the magic triangle that Terence had chalked out for her below the tapestry.

"Do you hear me, shades of the underworld?" cried Belladonna, raising the skull.

They heard her. First came a low and fearful murmuring which swelled to a cacophony of cackling, screaming, and screeching, and under the table, Terence sighed with relief. Mr. Moon had been as good as his word—and better.

Belladonna's teeth were chattering badly now. It seemed that Terence was right and that with Rover to help her there was no limit to her darkness. But she went on bravely, and putting down the skull, she fetched the portrait of Sir Simon and held it aloft.

"I call upon thee, shades, to release from eternal torment the spirit of this man!" she intoned.

More screams and yells from the spirits, while in the rafters, the ravens hideously croaked.

"Sir Simon Montpelier, Knight of Darkington, I command thee to appear!" cried Belladonna.

The jabbering and screeching died away, and now, in the black silence of the hall, there appeared a series of white, disembodied lights which bobbed and flickered, giving off at the same time an almost unendurable stench of decay.

"Corpse candles," murmured Mother Bloodwort, drawing her skirt away from one which had come too close.

Then, all in the same second, the corpse candles went out, and over the hall there spread a coldness such as they had never before experienced: the coldness of the tomb, the grave, of death itself.

"I wonder how he did that?" murmured Lester, whose respect for Mr. Moon was growing every minute. "Some sort of chemical, I suppose."

But now the coldness was passing and everyone's gaze was drawn upward to the wall on the left of the chimney breast. For the tapestry of the man stuck with arrows while burning at the stake was beginning to glow and shine and shimmer with a most unearthly light.

Belladonna felt in her pocket for a last squeeze of Rover's box. She was incredibly tired and her knees felt like water, but she wouldn't weaken now. And taking up a wand from the table, she struck the ground thrice and, prompted by Terence, who had been whispering the spells with her all along, she said the words that are older than any book of magic in the world:

"Allay fortission! Fortissio Roa!" cried Belladonna.

The glow around the tapestry grew stronger. The clock struck midnight. And as the last chime died away, there crept around the edge of the hanging, slowly and gropingly—a hand. A white hand, limp and long-fingered, with an emerald riding one knuckle.

For a few moments, the hand just hung there. Then it felt for the sides of the tapestry and with a sudden violent gesture, tore it from the wall and threw it on the ground.

And there stepped from the stone recess—wan and weary, but definitely alive—the figure of an Elizabethan knight.

A shriek of joy from Arriman broke the stunned silence.

"Sir Simon! Is it really you?" he cried, pushing

back his chair so hard that it crashed to the ground. And dashing forward he seized the specter's hands in his own.

"Aye, 'tis I," intoned Sir Simon. His voice was high and reedy, like an oboe playing something sad. "Ye see before ye the guilty, tainted flesh of Sir Simon Montmorency Montpelier."

"Oh, I can't believe it! But yes, yes, I can feel you; you're solid! And look at that vein throbbing in your left temple! Oh, happy, happy day! What ecstasy! What bliss!"

Sir Simon removed his left hand from Arriman's grasp and brought it up to his forehead. The plashing sound was much, much better than when he'd been a ghost: more solid, wetter, in every way more *real.*

Arriman was quite overcome. "The talks we'll have! The confidences! The walks! The delights of nature we will share! My dear, dear fellow, this is the best day of my life!"

Then, remembering at last that this was a competition, Arriman turned to the other judges.

"Ten out of ten, gentlemen, are we agreed?"

The ghoul nodded—he'd have liked the whole world to be inhabited by people who were dead—and kind Mr. Chatterjee smiled.

But these words were never heard by Belladonna. Overcome by fatigue, terror, and strain, Belladonna had fainted.

*B*ELLADONNA WOKE IN a four-poster bed in a room at the very top of the north tower at Darkington. Mr. Leadbetter and the ogre had carried her there after the end of the competition, while Terence hopped round her, worrying about her and congratulating her at the same time. Belladonna couldn't remember much about it now; only that she'd been anxious about the baby rabbits and about not having a toothbrush, and that Terence had said he'd go down to the campsite and see to everything.

How long ago had that been, she wondered. It still seemed to be dark, but now she felt refreshed and very happy. She'd done it! She'd won! She was to be the bride of Arriman, to be with him always, to stroke his mustache and massage his ankles if they swelled and share his secrets, his hopes, and his fears.

"Oh, glory!" said Belladonna, and smiling, fell asleep once more.

But a *happy* white witch, a white witch blissfully in love, can be a disaster. While Belladonna slept the room began to fill with exquisite saucer-sized snowflakes, each a perfect, six-pointed star, and the flakes did not melt but alighted softly on the hangings of the bed, the embroidered rug, the washstand. An enameled musical box burst from the chest of drawers and began to play a dreamy Viennese waltz; strings of gold and silver tinsel draped themselves across the ceiling, and the windowsills filled with rows of crystal goblets brimful of Knickerbocker Glories.

But Belladonna, knowing nothing of all this, slept on.

While Belladonna lay dreaming in the tower room, Arriman sat in the library talking to Sir Simon Montpelier. Arriman had suggested that the knight might like to slip into something more comfortable than the breastplate and leg armor he had worn for four hundred years, and though he'd murmured something about his underclothes not being quite the thing, the wife-slayer was now wearing Arriman's second-best dressing gown—a maroon one appliquéd with fiends and pitchforks—and was telling the magician the story of his life.

185

"So the Lady Anne was the first of your wives?" inquired Arriman, pushing the whisky decanter toward his friend.

"Even so," agreed Sir Simon. "She was the one I drowned. Ere the cock crew thrice, I drowned her. I had to. She madeth the sleeping chamber rumble as if cleft in twain."

"Ah! She snored, you mean?" said Arriman. "Very distressing, that. Nothing worse."

The knight nodded and plashed a little.

"Then I wedded the Lady Mary. Her I took by the throat and fastened my foul fingers around."

"Strangulation." Arriman nodded.

"She hath cheateth me of my victuals," said the knight.

"Fiddled the housekeeping, did she? In that case she deserved everything she got. And the next one?"

"Next I espoused the fair Olivia. Her I walled up in the privy for looking with favor upon the knave who emptied of her slops."

Arriman shook his head. "Terrible, terrible. What you've been through!"

Sir Simon went on to tell the magician about the Lady Julia, whom he'd stabbed in the buttery because she had a horrid little dog that yapped, and the Lady Letitia, whom he'd thrown over a cliff because she guzzled, and he was just about to start on the Lady Henrietta, whom he'd knocked off with a poisoned halibut because she drove him nutty walking in her sleep, when there was a knock at the door and the ogre entered.

"The Kraken's in his tureen waiting for you to say good night, sir, and I've laid out your pajamas. Is there anything else you require?"

"No, no, Lester, that's fine. You can go to bed."

"I've put Sir Simon in the green room," said Lester, winking at Mr. Moon, "on account of it being handy for the bathroom, like."

"Good, good," said the magician impatiently. There was still one more wife to go and he wanted to hear about her.

"There was a postcard from the Wizard Watcher by the late post, sir," the ogre continued. "It has reached Skegness and hopes to be back the day after tomorrow."

He had got through to the magician at last. "Now that is good news! I'm really glad about that. I wouldn't have liked it to miss the wedding."

But the word "wedding" had a bad effect on Arriman. His brooding face darkened and he drained his whisky in a single desperate gulp. "You've no idea what women do, Lester. Sir Simon's been telling me. They snore and have little dogs and walk in their sleep. And those are just *ordinary* women! I mean, this witch . . . she must be really very black to do necromancy. I should think a witch as black as that would have some pretty nasty habits."

"Not necessarily, sir," said Lester.

"And if she's blacker than me . . . I mean, I don't want to be *henpecked*. I can't imagine anything sillier than a henpecked wizard."

"Sir," said Lester, losing his patience, "you haven't even *seen* witch number seven. And anyway, what about your duty to wizardry and darkness? What about this blighting black baby you're going to have? What," said Lester, "did we have this blinking contest *for*?"

The magician sighed. "Yes, yes, you're quite right, Lester. I'll go and see her first thing in the morning and fix the date."

As Lester left the room, Arriman was leaning forward eagerly and saying: "And the last one? The Lady Beatrice, wasn't it? What did she do?"

"Smelled," said Sir Simon gloomily. "Most vilely and horribly hath she smelled."

And having come to the end of his wives, the knight poured himself another whisky and began again at the beginning.

Arriman kept his word, and the next morning saw him climbing the curved steps to Belladonna's tower.

The magician wasn't feeling too good. Sir Simon had told him about his murdered wives not once but three times, and though Arriman understood how much the wife-slayer needed to talk after four hundred years of only plashing, he did feel very tired. Nor were the ogre and the secretary, following close behind him, exactly full of beans. They'd spent the night worrying in case the real Sir Simon burst clanking through the paneling and gave the game away, and they didn't really like the way Monty Moon was settling into his part. That was the trouble with actors. You could get them *on*stage, but getting them off was another matter.

"Leadbetter, you wouldn't lie to me," said Arriman, turning round. "Is she covered in warts? I mean, *covered*?"

"No, sir. Not at all."

"What about her fingers and toes? All there, are they? No . . . stumps, for example? Nothing webbed or anything? Nothing *clawed*?"

"No, sir."

The magician climbed a few more steps and turned again.

"And . . . er . . . nothing personal, you understand, because yours is charming. I mean, it's part of you, but it could be awkward in a wife. In short, Leadbetter, has she got . . . a tail? You know, one of those forked jobs, a bit black and bushy?"

"No, sir," said the secretary. "Witch number seven is tailless."

"And her name is Belladonna?"

"That's right."

"Belladonna Canker. Ah, well."

And reaching the top step, Arriman paused, took a deep breath—and threw open the door.

Belladonna was sitting up in bed. The sun, streaming through the east window, had turned her hair into a shower of gold; her eyes were bright with happiness and blue as a summer sky, and she was singing a sweet and foolish little song: the kind with roses in it and springtime and love. Rather a lot of love.

Arriman stood stock-still in the doorway, unable to move.

"Who . . . is this?" he stammered.

"That is Belladonna, sir. Witch number seven. The winner of the contest!"

"You're not pulling my leg?"

"No, sir."

"She's not . . . er . . . in an enchanted state? I mean, she hasn't taken on another shape just to bamboozle me? She looks like that all the time?"

"All the time, sir."

Belladonna, meanwhile, was gazing rapturously at Arriman, her heart in her eyes. This was the closest she had ever been to him, and she was drinking in the flaring nostrils, the tufty ears, the curve of his noble nose.

"Belladonna!" said the magician, stepping forward. His voice throbbed, his eyes burnt, and his chest heaved like a pair of bellows.

"Arry?" murmured Belladonna shyly, from beneath lowered lashes.

"Arry! All my life I've wanted someone to call me Arry."

Lester and Mr. Leadbetter exchanged glances. Things were turning out exactly the way they'd hoped, but they hadn't reckoned on being quite so embarrassed.

"Leadbetter, we must be married at once! Tomorrow at the latest!" said Arriman, who was now sitting on Belladonna's bed and grasping both her hands.

Mr. Leadbetter sighed. It was just like Arriman to spend weeks grumbling about having to get married and then fall in love like a ton of bricks and make trouble for everyone.

"I'm afraid that's impossible, sir. There are the wedding invitations to be sent, the food to be ordered, the bride's clothes to be bought. Three weeks is the shortest I can manage it in."

"Three weeks! I can't wait three weeks! Can you wait three weeks, my pretty?"

"Oh, my gawd," murmured Lester. He had forgotten how absolutely ridiculous people sounded when they were in love.

But now at last the really peculiar look of the tower room had got through to Arriman, and without letting go of Belladonna's hands, he looked with surprise at the exquisite snowflakes, the strings of gold and silver tinsel, the shimmering moonstones now dripping from the mouth of the wash jug.

Catching every movement of her beloved's eyes, Belladonna flushed and said: "I'm sorry about all this. It happened while I was asleep. You see, Arry, I feel I should tell you that I used to be white."

"No, no, my treasure," said the magician dotingly.

"That's quite impossible. Your hair is so golden, your cheeks are so pink, your eyes are such a lovely, lovely blue."

"I don't mean that," said Belladonna. "I mean, my *magic* was white. I was a white witch."

She had got through to Arriman at last. A spasm crossed his face. "My dearest love, you mustn't *say* such things!"

"Oh, it's all right. I'm not white now. I'm very, very black. Well, you saw how black I was. *Rover* made me—" She broke off with a little cry. "Oh, how dreadful of me! How selfish and cruel! I left Rover in his matchbox all night! Oh, poor, poor Rover; he'll be so dry and sad—Terence will never forgive me."

She had freed her hands from Arriman's and, jumping out of bed, ran to the chair where her gown was lying.

"Here it comes!" whispered the ogre.

Belladonna had found the matchbox, had opened it, was staring at it while the color drained from her face.

When she spoke it was in a voice so full of anguish and disbelief that they hardly recognized it.

"Rover's gone," said Belladonna. "He's *gone!*"

There was a long and dreadful pause. "I have to find him, Arry, I have to. He's my familiar, you see. Without him, I'm nothing."

She began to search desperately, lifting up the Knickerbocker Glories, pushing aside the snowflakes. Arriman had started to help her when he saw the ogre beckoning to him from the other side of the room.

"Sir," said Lester, when he'd got his master outside the door. "It's my belief that it ain't no good looking because that worm ain't lost. He's been stolen. I've thought so all along."

"All along? But Belladonna's only just noticed that he's gone," said Arriman, looking puzzled.

Lester saw that he'd made a mistake. If he told Arriman that Rover had been gone before the raising of Sir Simon, he'd get suspicious at once. Belladonna had made it clear that her blackness came from Rover, so if there was no Rover there was no blackness, and that led right back to Sir Simon not being Sir Simon at all but an actor called Monty Moon.

194

"I can't go into that now, sir," he said. "But I can tell you one thing. Rover may be a good performer, but he's not up to shutting a matchbox after he's crawled out of it. No, that worm's been nicked and I'll bet my bottom dollar I know who did it."

"Who?"

"Witch number six. That Madame Olympia. Leadbetter thinks the same."

"Oh, no! Surely not!" Arriman was very shocked. "The one with the interesting, cruel smile and the . . . er . . . rats?"

Lester nodded. "And if I'm right we ought to be getting down to her caravan quick. The witches are due to go back tomorrow."

Arriman was frowning. The more he remembered the "Symphony of Death," the more he thought it would be better not to meet the enchantress head-on.

"I think we'd better take her by surprise," he said. "And that means disguises. How would you like to be a rabbit, Lester?"

"Not at all, sir."

"Oh, come on! Be a sport!"

"No, sir. Absolutely and definitely, *no.*"

While Arriman and the ogre were talking, Madame Olympia was packing her things.

Since Belladonna had won the competition, the enchantress had been in such a towering rage that she had made three holes in the floor of the caravan where she had stamped her feet. She had also come out in a rash from sheer temper, and it was this which made her decide to go back to London immediately, to her beauty parlor, where she could mix some creams and ointments to get rid of it. Then she planned to come back like the queen in *Snow White* with a poisoned apple or some poisoned stays which she would sell to Belladonna at the door and which would kill her. Except that probably Belladonna did not *wear* stays— people did not seem to nowadays—so she would have to think of something else.

So now she came out of the caravan to do one last job, and that was to throw some rubbish she did not want onto the fire. Some nasty, useless, disappointing rubbish that she wanted to get rid of once and for all. And as she did so, a rabbit and a fox ran between her legs and bounded into the caravan.

If she had bothered to look, she might have noticed that the fox was an unusually handsome one with a great bushy autumn-colored tail, and that the rabbit, which looked cross, had only a single eye. But she only turned round furiously and said: "Get out at *once*, you dirty animals. Shoo!"

But of course they weren't dirty animals anymore.

Sitting at the table were Arriman the Awful and the ogre.

"Good morning," said Arriman, polite as always.

"How dare you!" screamed the enchantress. "How *dare* you break in like this?"

Arriman looked at her. An enchantress's power is useless on someone who is truly in love. Arriman could see her now as she really was and he did not like what he saw.

"We believe you may have something that belongs to my fiancée," said the magician. "Her familiar, to be exact."

"Her familiar? What on earth are you talking about? I've a perfectly good familiar of my own, as you can see." Madame Olympia kicked the cowering aardvark with the heel of her shoe.

Then she shut her eyes and began to gabble something under her breath. But before she could get any further, Lester, following a signal from his master, had taken the full milk jug and upended it over the enchantress's head.

"Phloo," spluttered Madame Olympia. *"Guggle!"*

Milk is a well-known antidote to magic, almost as good as eating roses or holding a rowan twig.

"Quick! Search the caravan!" ordered Arriman, while the enchantress, groping for a towel, used some words that even Lester had not heard before.

So they searched the caravan, turning out the built-in cupboards, opening Madame Olympia's half-packed suitcase, feeling under the bed.

Nothing. Not a sign of Rover.

"You see," jeered the enchantress. "Turn the caravan inside out for all I care."

She flung herself out of the caravan and, picking up the little bundle of rubbish, walked with a gleeful smile toward the fire.

It was Arriman who caught on first and ran after her, the ogre following.

"Stop! Stop! Let's see what you're burning."

"Never!" shouted the enchantress, and laughed.

Then she brought her arm over in an arc and threw her bundle onto the flames.

Arriman did not stop for any of the spells that would have made him fireproof, or any magic words that would have doused the flames. Instead, he plunged his hand into the red-hot blaze and drew out the crumpled bundle just as it had begun to catch.

And there—dry and bewildered-looking at the bottom of a cornflake packet—was Rover!

Belladonna, sitting wistfully in a chair in the tower room, greeted the earthworm with a shriek of joy. But then she saw the magician's hand.

"Oh, Arry! You're hurt! How dreadful!"

And she took his hand and bent over it and began to croon one of her wholeness songs about the beauty of new skin and the cleverness of having five fingers, and almost at once, the pain disappeared and the blisters also.

"My angel! My little blossom! You've healed me!" cried Arriman, growing more and more besotted.

"Yes, but that was the *old* me," said Belladonna hastily. "The new me is quite different, Arry. If you give me Rover, I'll show you."

The ogre handed her the worm, which he'd damped down and fettled up with some moist earth as they came.

"What would you like, Arry?" she said. "Shall I turn the tinsel into some moldering thighbones, perhaps? Sort of in a crisscross pattern? And what about making the snowflakes into gaping wounds? You do *like* gaping wounds?"

"I adore them, my angel. They're almost my favorite thing."

So Belladonna closed her eyes while the ogre and Mr. Leadbetter and Arriman stood and watched.

The next half hour was one that none of them ever forgot. Belladonna worked and she worked and she worked, not once letting the strain and puzzlement show on her face. But at the end of the time, she put down Rover and threw herself with a wail of anguish onto the bed.

"It's hopeless!" she cried. "Quite, quite hopeless. You must forget me, Arry. You must wed another. My blackness has absolutely and completely gone!"

The others looked round the room once more. The strings of gold and silver tinsel were still there, but between them there sparkled a chain of most delightful fairy dolls. In the center of each exquisite, still unmelted snowflake shone a diadem of flawless pearls. But it was the pots of pink and rather blobby flowers which had sprung up all over the place that made Lester's voice, when he spoke, sound like a voice from the tomb.

"Begonias," said the ogre, shaking his gigantic head. "Bloomin' *begonias*."

It was in this moment of complete despair that Arriman showed himself a most true and noble lover.

"My angel!" he said, gathering Belladonna into his arms. "What does it matter? You can fill the whole place with Knickerbocker Glories and those . . . er . . . pink blobby things, and it wouldn't matter to me. All I care about is you!"

But though she let her head rest for a moment on his manly shoulders, Belladonna was firm.

"No, Arry; you have a duty. Remember what the competition was about? 'Darkness is All,' you said. Suppose we had—" Her voice broke but she pulled herself together. "Suppose we had a white baby? Or even a gray baby? What could a baby like that do with a devilish maze and a fiendish laboratory and all the other lovely things you've worked so hard to make? How could a white baby keep wizardry and darkness alive in the land? You don't just belong to yourself, Arry. You belong to all the doom and dastardry and devilment in the world, and I'd never forgive myself if I let you forget what was right."

And nothing that the desperate wizard could say would shake her.

"I'll go as soon as I can get my things together," she said, keeping her voice steady with an effort. "If I'm so white that I can ruin a powerful familiar like that, the farther away I am the better. Only I must say good-bye to Terence and give Rover back to him." She turned to Mr. Leadbetter and the ogre who were standing miserably by the door. "By the way, where *is* Terence? I haven't seen him for ages."

The ogre frowned. "He wasn't at the campsite," he said.

"Are you sure?" said Mr. Leadbetter sharply. "He said he was going down to the campsite to get Belladonna's things and help the witches clear up. I was sure he'd spent the night down there. You know what boys are with tents."

And, their great sorrow laid aside for a moment, they all looked at each other with a new anxiety.

Where *was* Terence?

CHAPTER 18

ERENCE, AT THAT MOMENT, was locked in
a small dark room with high barred windows in the
place he feared and hated more than any other in the
world. For the worst thing that could have happened to
Terence had happened. Matron had come unrooted;
she sent out an alarm; he'd been recaptured as he ran
across the road to go to the campsite, and now he was
back in the home.

It had happened so suddenly that he'd had no
chance to defend himself. A police car had been waiting outside the gates (even policemen didn't dare to go
inside the gates at Darkington). Two men had stepped
out of the car and grabbed him, and before he knew
where he was, he was inside the car and driving at sev-
enty miles an hour back to Todcaster.

The policemen had been quite kind, only telling

him what a stupid thing it was to run away: children were always caught in the end, they said. Apparently a tradesman who delivered groceries to the home had seen Terence at the station on the day he went to find Ms. Leadbetter and had noticed him buying a ticket back to Darkington.

But if the policemen had been fatherly enough, Matron had received the woebegone little boy with a gloating triumph. She said nothing about the rooting; most probably she had forgotten it (there is often loss of memory after rooting), but she had not forgotten her grudge against Terence. And now, after a night spent on a lumpy mattress with only a bowl of claggy porridge for his breakfast, he was waiting for her to come and punish him.

The door opened and Matron entered. She was yellower and more like a camel than ever, and she began at once: "Now then, what are we going to do with you? Beat you? Send you to Borstal? Keep you locked up for good?"

On she went, scolding and threatening, while Terence cowered against the wall and wondered why God hadn't given people earlids as well as eyelids so that they could shut out such dreadful sounds. And all the while, his anxious thoughts raced back to Darkington. Had Belladonna noticed yet that Rover had gone? Had Arriman learned that Sir Simon was a fake? Would anyone miss him and try to find him or would they think he'd run away because he didn't like it at the hall? No, they couldn't think that; they *couldn't.*

Matron was still standing over him, shouting and blustering, the stream of ugly words pouring out of her mouth like pitch. She'd have liked to hit Terence, to knock him against the wall, but there were stupid health inspectors who came round these days and made trouble. One had actually had the nerve to tell her that her methods were old-fashioned. Still, there were plenty of things you could do that didn't leave marks. A pinch under the wrist, for example. Matron had a special line in pinches.

"So just you remember, my boy. One squeak out of you, one more bit of trouble and you'll stay in this room for the rest of your life, do you understand?"

Terence nodded. In the few hours since he'd been back at the home, all his sparkle and bounce had gone. Terence could stand the blackest magic and enjoy it, but unkindness and spite just finished him.

And so the grayness and misery of the home closed over Terence once again. By the time he'd eaten his boiled fish and black-eyed potatoes at the scrubbed dining table, had his fingernails inspected, and put on his mackintosh for the boring walk they always took when there was no school—past the Formica factory, left at the gasworks, and back down a long road of seedy terrace houses—he'd almost forgotten that only a few hours ago life had been an exciting and wonderful thing.

But just as the line of children, led by the assistant matron, a watery lady called Ms. Kettle, was crossing the road back to the home, a strange thing happened. Terence heard his name called and, looking up, he saw Ms. Leadbetter carrying a shopping basket and waving her umbrella.

"Wait!" she shouted. "I want to speak to you!"

She marched up to Terence, ignoring Ms. Kettle, who was wittering away at the head of the line, and said: "Just the person I wanted to see. Though what you're doing here, I don't know. I thought you were staying with my brother."

"I was," said Terence. "But they caught me." He looked up at her eagerly. "If you could tell Mr. Leadbetter I'm here, *please*. I don't want him to think—"

"Come along, Terence Mugg. No loitering," called Ms. Kettle sharply.

But Ms. Leadbetter, who had once thrown a drunken actor down three flights of stairs, was not at all cowed by Ms. Kettle.

"What I was going to say," she said, bending down and speaking quickly into Terence's ear, "was that I've just had a message from the hospital. From poor

Monty Moon. He's so sorry he's had to let you down. It was the van—the one belonging to the electrician. Monty says the tires were worn to a shred, but he wouldn't listen. Anyway, they ran into a ditch on the way to Darkington and the whole lot of them were taken to the hospital. Just cuts and bruises, but poor Monty didn't really come round till this morning. It was last night, wasn't it, that he was supposed to do the show?"

Terence was looking at her in amazement.

"Yes," he said. "It was last night. But he didn't let us down. He did do the show. He was there."

"No, he wasn't. Not Monty. He's been in the hospital since Sunday and the stage manager and electrician with him. He never got to Darkington at all. That's what's worrying him, on account of having taken the five hundred pounds."

But now Ms. Kettle had had enough. She left the front of the line, yanked Terence by the arms, and marched him away.

Terence made no move to resist. He had too much to think about.

If Monty Moon had never got to Darkington, who had appeared from behind the tapestry? Who was the Elizabethan knight they had "raised"? Could it be . . . didn't it *have* to be . . . Sir Simon Montpelier himself?

So Belladonna had really done it! But Rover hadn't been there, that was certain. The box Terence had handed Belladonna was empty. And without Rover, Belladonna was absolutely white.

Where had all that darkness come from, then? What did it mean?

"Take your coat off, you lazy boy, and don't stand there dreaming," said Ms. Kettle, who took her tone from Matron.

Terence didn't even hear.

The afternoon darkened. The children had beans on toast. Ms. Kettle read them a story from *Struwelpeter* about a boy who had his thumbs cut off, and then they all trooped up to bed. Lying in his iron cot, looking at the same crack in the ceiling that he'd looked at for years and years, Terence heard Billy, in the next bed, begin to snuffle and cry.

"What is it, Billy?" asked Terence.

"I'm thirsty; I want a drink."

"Well, why don't you go and get one?"

"I'm scared," said Billy. He was partly deaf and wet his bed and was always in trouble too.

"I'll go," said Terence.

He slipped out of bed and tiptoed out into the corridor toward the bathroom. Matron and Ms. Kettle were talking in the hall below—and they were talking about him.

"Of course, he is a troublemaker," Ms. Kettle agreed. "But I've always felt, Matron, that you dislike him particularly."

"Dislike him? Of course I dislike him. And I've every reason to. Look!"

She held up her hand, and Ms. Kettle peered at it.

"The little finger, do you mean?"

"Yes," shouted Matron. "The little finger I do mean. The little finger that Terence Mugg bit to the bone and mutilated when he was brought to me, a babe in arms, and I bent over to say 'Ickle bickle boo' to him as I do to all my babies. Even now I get shooting pains in it when I knit."

"Goodness," said Ms. Kettle. "And he was only three weeks old, wasn't he, when they brought him from the kiosk? Most unusual!"

"Everything about that horrible child is unusual. He gives me the creeps. Do you know, whatever you do to him, he never cries? Never. He'll sit there with his eyes like saucers and he'll wince with pain, but he's never shed a tear in all the time he's been here. It's unnatural, that's what it is, and I'll knock it out of him, see if I don't!"

A sharp noise from the top of the stairs made them both turn round. Terence was standing on the landing in his pajamas. He was standing perfectly still, as though in a state of shock, and the glass of water he'd been fetching for Billy lay in splinters at his feet.

"How *dare* you, Terence Mugg! How *dare* you get out of bed! Just you wait, you've gone too far this time. You've gone too far!"

Terence waited. He felt very queer. There was a sort of roaring in his ears and the landing felt as though it were rocking and swaying beneath his feet.

Matron was on the first step . . . the second. . . . Now she was almost up to him, her arms outstretched to get him by the shoulders and shake him.

Terence took a long deep breath. He closed his eyes. . . .

CHAPTER 19

*T*HE WIZARD WATCHER, returning from a holiday it hadn't enjoyed at all, arrived at Darkington the following morning, and as all three heads agreed, it was like coming back to a blinking funeral.

Arriman and Belladonna sat hopelessly entwined on the big sofa in the black drawing room, gazing into each other's eyes. Belladonna had packed her straw basket and folded her tent and was only waiting for Terence to be found before going away forever to a life of loneliness, begonias, and pain.

Except that it was beginning to look as though Terence never *would* be found. Mr. Leadbetter (who'd quite forgotten that the little boy was not really his nephew) had rung every hospital in the district in case there'd been an accident, but no one had news of him and the anxiety was dreadful.

Meanwhile the Kraken wasn't exactly helping by tottering back and forth saying "Daddy!" to Arriman and "Mummy!" to Belladonna and making both of them extremely wet. Nor did the wife-slayer take any notice of the fact that everyone was so upset, but plashed up and down droning on about how he'd smothered Lady Beatrice, strangled Lady Mary, and knocked off Lady Henrietta with a halibut.

It was to this scene of misery that the Wizard Watcher returned, and it made no bones about saying that it wasn't the sort of homecoming it had expected.

Not that Arriman wasn't terribly pleased to see it; he was, and immediately introduced Belladonna, whom the monster took to at once.

"Very nice," said the Middle Head, looking her up and down.

"Better than all those goose-pimpled girls at Brighton," said the Left Head, who had not felt really happy at the seaside.

"When's the wedding?" asked the Right Head.

But this, of course, started all the unhappiness off again, and the lovers went back to the business of sighing and looking into each other's eyes, leaving the ogre and Mr. Leadbetter to explain the events that had led up to this day.

The Wizard Watcher did what it could to cheer everybody up, but after half an hour during which the

Kraken kept trying to climb up its tail, Sir Simon told it in horrid detail what Lady Olivia had said to the lavatory attendant, and Arriman had declared for the hundredth time that he would die without Belladonna, the monster had had enough.

"Proper carry-on in here," said the Middle Head. "It's worse than Blackpool."

"Let's go out and get some fresh air," said the Right Head.

"Good idea," said the Left Head. "Get that little perisher off our tail, anyway."

And twitching the Kraken carefully onto the floor, the monster waddled out into the park.

An hour passed. Mr. Leadbetter had made a list of police stations and was just about to pick up the phone to try again for news of Terence, when they heard the great oak door in the hall burst open with a resounding crash. Next came the sound of footsteps pounding upstairs; then the drawing room door flew open as if pushed by a hurricane and the Wizard Watcher came skidding into the room. Its heads were trembling, its eyes were blazing, and they could actually *see* its heart pounding in its chest. Never had anyone known the monster in such a state, and for a moment its excitement was such that it simply could not speak. Then the Middle Head began and the other two joined in.

"The new wizard cometh!"

"He *cometh!*"

"Right *now,* he cometh!"

Arriman rose with shaking knees and went to the window, and everybody followed him.

Stumbling with exhaustion, his small face lifted to the windows of the hall, Terence Mugg was coming up the drive.

CHAPTER 20

*A*RE YOU SUGGESTING we don't know our job?" said the Middle Head, looking very hurt.

"Yes, are you? I mean, you *made* us, you know," said the Left Head.

"No, no, my dear fellow," said Arriman, who knew how sensitive the monster was. "It's just . . . well, you see, this is Leadbetter's nephew. We've all been rather anxious about him. Of course you haven't met him, you were away during the contest, but that's who it is. Terence's the name. Terence Mugg."

Terence was sitting on the sofa next to Belladonna, who had rushed up to him, half carrying him into the room, and was now feeding him with cauliflower soup and bananas, pale things she'd been able to magic up quickly till Lester could get to the kitchen and rustle up a steak.

Now he stood up. Already being with the people he loved had made his cheeks glow and chased the weariness from his face.

"Actually, sir," he began. "Actually, I think maybe—" But here he broke off because it was so difficult to explain. He didn't really believe it himself yet and had walked all the way from Todcaster rather than try anything that might not work and prove him wrong. So instead he felt in his pocket and took out a piece of string, an apple core, an India rubber—and at last a blue tin punched with holes.

Terence opened the tin. Inside it was a small spider with hairy legs and a black cross on its back.

"What is it?" asked Arriman as they all craned forward.

Terence swallowed.

"It's . . . Matron, sir," he said.

So then he began to explain, growing more confident as his story unfolded. And as he talked it all became quite clear, and the only surprising thing was that no one had suspected it before.

He began by telling what he'd overheard at the home, and as he spoke they could see the tiny baby carried in and snapping at Matron with his full set of teeth so that she had hated him bitterly from that day. They could see a small boy who never cried because wizards, like witches, cannot shed tears, but a small boy who knew nothing of his powers because unlike Mr. and Mrs. Canker, who had wisely encouraged their little Arriman, Terence had grown up in a place where people were ignorant and blind.

And then, when he'd first met Belladonna, Terence went on, he'd felt—oh, not just that he loved her ("Everyone," said Terence, "loves Belladonna.") but a sort of feeling of *belonging,* and from the first moment, when she'd tried to root Matron, Terence had said her spells along with her and worked with her and *felt* with her. "Whatever she did," he said, "I had to do it, and sometimes I said extra spells of my own. Only I thought it was Rover the blackness came from—we both did. I was *sure* it was Rover. But then I met Ms. Leadbetter and she told me that Mr. Moon had never come to the hall at all, he'd had an accident. But Sir Simon *did* appear, and I knew it couldn't be Rover because Rover had already gone. So—"

But this part was news to Lester and Mr. Leadbetter, and gobbledegook to Arriman and Belladonna, and Terence had to stop while everybody explained everything to everyone else. Arriman was most displeased to think that his servants had tried to play a trick on him, but when they explained that it was only because they were so sure that Belladonna was the wife for him, he couldn't really make a fuss.

"Anyway," Terence went on, "I couldn't understand *what* had happened because I knew Belladonna was quite white without the earthworm. So if it wasn't Rover and it wasn't her, who was it? And then when they said that about me biting so hard when I was a tiny baby, everything sort of clicked into place, and when Matron came charging upstairs at me, I just shut my eyes and—well, there she is."

And he held out the tin inside which the spider was scuttling dementedly to and fro.

The rejoicing after Terence had finished his story may be imagined. Belladonna hugged him and kissed him; Lester seized a saber and gulped it down joyfully in a single swallow; Arriman came and pumped him by the hand.

"My dear, dear boy, what happiness, what joy! What a relief! Don't you see, all our problems are solved. You shall stay here and attend to wizardry and darkness, and Belladonna and I can be married and live happily ever after!"

"Oh, Arry, so we can, so we can!" cried Belladonna, rushing into his arms. "It doesn't matter what color our babies are now, does it, with a mighty wizard like Terence to take charge of things?"

"Am I really going to be a *mighty* wizard?" said Terence, his eyes shining.

Arriman turned to him, his dark face serious for a moment.

"You have a great gift, my boy," he said. "A great gift. Necromancy at your age! I couldn't have touched it. Why, if I called the thunder before the lightning I was as pleased as punch. No, it's my belief you're going to extend the frontiers of wizardry and darkness to unheard-of depths. Of course, there's a lot of work before you, but you understand that, I'm sure."

"Oh, yes, sir; I'll work like *anything*."

In the excitement and happiness which followed, everyone was careful to give the Wizard Watcher his due, and the useful monster sat there, contented smiles on its faces, receiving the congratulations it knew it had deserved.

"Yes, it's a relief," said the Middle Head, nodding graciously. "No use pretending it isn't."

"Those nine hundred and ninety days just sitting

there took it out of us," said the Left Head, "not to mention the chilblains."

"Still, all's well that ends well," said the Right Head.

There was only one slight snag which Mr. Leadbetter, drawing aside his employer, pointed out to Arriman.

"If Sir Simon's real, sir, which it seems he is, what's to become of him? Because it's my belief that if anyone else has to hear about Lady Mary or Lady Julia or Lady Letitia who guzzled, there'll be murder done, and it won't be him doing it."

Arriman nodded. A look of deep wickedness had come into his fiery eyes.

"Actually, Leadbetter, I have just had a very neat idea about Sir Simon. A very neat idea indeed. But first we must have our wedding party. I want you to invite everybody. All the witches that took part in the contest, for a start."

"Even the enchantress, sir?" said Mr. Leadbetter, frowning.

Arriman smiled.

"*Particularly* the enchantress," he said.

CHAPTER 21

THE DAY OF the wedding dawned, and from all over the land there came kobbolds and kelpies, goblins and noggles, furies and fiends, to share the magician's happiness and to meet the new wizard whose coming had been foretold by the gypsy Esmeralda and whose power was said to be greater even than Arriman's own.

No handsomer couple than the bridal pair could be imagined. Arriman was in antlers and a gold-patterned cloak; Belladonna's ink black dress was loose and flowing and in her glorious hair she wore only a single, simple bat. It was the little short-eared bat that had invented an Aunt Screwtooth for her at the coven, and it had flown up specially to be with her on her great day.

In the center of the table, on a blue velvet cushion that the ogre had fitted with a special sprinkler, lay

Rover, looking rosy and peaceful now that it was understood that he was not a powerful familiar but just an ordinary worm. Opposite him in a high chair sat the Kraken, squeaking with excitement. Belladonna had managed to put him into nappies in spite of his eight legs, and with his underneath wrapped in snow-white muslin, he looked, as Terence said, almost like a bridesmaid or perhaps a page.

None of their friends had failed them. Mr. Chatterjee had flown back from Calcutta; the ghoul had left his slaughterhouse. Even Ms. Leadbetter, though she didn't hold with magic, was there, bringing news of the Sunnydene Home's new Matron, a fat and friendly lady whom the children loved. (The old Matron had been let loose in the rose garden, where she was making herself useful eating aphids and other insect pests, as spiders will.)

And the witches were there. However much they had sneered at Belladonna, now that she was Mrs. Canker and Wizardess of the North, they were only too ready to be friendly.

Belladonna, of course, forgave them everything. Not only that, but when the feasting and roistering had died down a little, she laid a hand on Arriman's arm and said: "Arry, shouldn't we grant everyone a wish? Isn't that the thing to do at weddings?"

"Well, my treasure, if that's what you want. Of

course, granting wishes isn't exactly *black*. Still, on such a happy day . . . We'll get Terence to do it; it'll be good practice."

It would take too long to tell what all the brownies and kelpies and noggles wanted, and anyway it was mostly money. Mr. Chatterjee didn't need a wish because he'd tracked down the Princess Shari (the one who'd been a penguin) and was engaged to be married. The ghoul and Ms. Leadbetter didn't hold with wishes, and Ethel Feedbag had fallen asleep with her head on her plate and couldn't be roused.

But Mother Bloodwort knew exactly what *she* wanted.

"It's that turning-myself-young-again spell," she said to Terence. "I can't get it right myself, but you can. About twenty, I'd like to be, or maybe eighteen. Gladys Trotter, the name was, and I'd like to be dressed nice."

But when the wish had been granted and Mother Bloodwort stood staring into the mirror at the young girl she had been, a very odd look spread across her face.

"I don't like it," she said at last. "I'm sorry, but you'll have to turn me back again. All that swollen flesh and those bulgy pink cheeks . . . And what did I want all that hair *for*?"

So Terence turned her back again, and the old woman went back contentedly to her shack, where she lived for many more years being sometimes a coffee table and sometimes a witch, and not doing any harm to anyone because she had forgotten how.

After that it was Mabel Wrack's turn and what *she* wanted was to have her legs turned back into a mermaid's tail. She said she was sick of them itching and sick of humping Doris about in polyethylene buckets and she felt bad, she said, about the way she had treated her aunts. "For when all's said and done, water's thicker than blood and you can't beat a wet family," said Mabel, "so if you'll drop me off at that bit of cliff where I did my trick, I'll find them soon enough."

So the wedding guests, glad of some fresh air after all that eating, trooped off to the Devil's Cauldron, and Terence gave Mabel a splendid tail and two gill slits for breathing underwater, and Belladonna kissed Doris lovingly above her vile red eyes. And sure enough, as Mabel hit the waves, they could all see, distinctly, a set of plump and motherly arms pulling the witch and her octopus down into the foam.

But when Nancy Shouter told the little boy what *she* wanted, Terence turned pale. For what Nancy wanted was no less than the impossible. She wanted Terence to

225

reverse the bottomless hole, to turn it inside out and see if somewhere in its bottomlessness, her sister Nora might be found.

"I don't know if I can do that," said Terence anxiously.

But with Arriman's hand reassuringly on his shoulder, he walked bravely to the east lawn, and the wedding guests followed.

If anyone had doubted up to then that Terence was a great and mighty wizard, they did not doubt again. For Terence just walked up to the hole with its notices saying DANGER and KEEP OUT and took them down. Next, with his shoes, he scuffed out the pentacle of protection. And then he stepped forward and spoke to the hole.

No one heard the words he used. What passed between him and it remains secret till the end of time. But the hole obeyed him; it knew its master—and with a frightful scream, a roaring judder, and a fearful lurch, it gave up its bottomlessness, turned inside out, and from its newfound bottom, dredged up the crumpled, bewildered body of Nancy Shouter's twin.

"Nora!" cried Nancy, rushing forward and sending her chickens flying.

"Nancy!" cried Nora, rushing into her sister's arms.

Taking no notice of anyone, the two sisters stood there, hugging each other and laughing for joy.

Then: "You look a proper mess," said Nancy Shouter. "You're all crumpled."

"Of course I'm crumpled, you stupid stick," said Nora. "What do you expect? You shouldn't have pushed me into the hole in the first place."

"I didn't push you; you fell."

"I didn't."

"You did."

And quarreling happily, the two sisters picked up their chickens and walked away.

But when Terence, carried shoulder-high by the wedding guests, got back to the banqueting hall to grant the enchantress *her* wish, he found her chair empty except for a pair of moth-eaten stays which she had bought in the Portobello Road and poisoned in her parlor. Madame Olympia, it seemed, had returned to London—and with her had gone no less a person than Sir Simon Montpelier!

"So my plan worked!" said Arriman gleefully, rubbing his hands.

"I'll say it worked," said the ogre. "I put the love philter in each of their drinks like you told me, and you should have seen them! The plasher down on his knees asking her to marry him and measuring her neck for a noose at the same time. And her accepting him and trying to get a squint at his molars to see how they'd look on her necklace. I nearly died!"

"A well-matched pair," said Arriman. "I wonder which of them will knock the other off first." He turned to Belladonna. "Am I not clever, my little kitten?"

And Belladonna, gazing at him adoringly, said: "The cleverest person in the world!"

But the best part of any party is the bit where the guests have gone and the family is left alone, tired and content.

Terence lay on the hearth rug, chatting to Rover; Lester was sharpening his bedtime sword. Arriman had

taken off his antlers, and he and Belladonna were curled up on the sofa making plans. They were going to build a little house on the other side of the park—quite close to the hall but not too close, so that Terence would learn to manage on his own. Arriman was going to write a book and Mr. Leadbetter was already wondering how to stop the magician jumbling up the pages and getting the typewriter ribbon jammed and putting the carbon paper in the wrong way around.

So happy and peaceful did everybody feel that it was quite a while before they noticed that the Wizard Watcher wasn't quite itself. Its round and beautiful eyes were suspiciously moist and it was allowing the Kraken to slide down its tail as though it didn't really care what happened.

"Is anything the matter?" asked Arriman. Now he came to think of it, the Watcher hadn't really been itself at the party. It'd eaten hardly anything, and talking had seemed an effort.

The monster shook its head.

"It's nothing," said the Middle Head in a low voice.

"Not anything, really," said the Left Head.

"We're only making a fuss," the Right Head agreed.

By this time, of course, everyone was desperate, and Terence, who had loved the monster from the moment he saw it, put down Rover and came over, quite pop-eyed with concern.

"Please!" said Arriman. "You must tell us! That's what friends are for. To share things with."

The monster sighed heavily.

"Well," said the Middle Head. "It's obvious really, isn't it?"

"I mean, what are Wizard Watchers *for*?" said the Left Head.

"They're for watching for wizards, aren't they?" put in the Right Head.

"So when a wizard's been *found*," said the Middle Head, "there isn't much use for a Wizard Watcher, is there?"

"Sort of *spare*, a Wizard Watcher is then, isn't he?" said the Left Head.

"You could say useless. Redundant. Finished," said the Right Head, dashing away a tear.

There was an absolutely ghastly silence while everyone took in the monster's grief and pain.

Then Belladonna stepped forward, her eyes alight.

"How *could* you be so foolish?" she said to the three heads. "Surely you know that Wizard Watchers aren't just for watching FOR wizards? They're for watching OVER wizards. I thought everyone knew that!"

The monster lifted its heads.

"Terence may be a mighty and terrible wizard, but he's a very young one," Belladonna went on, while the little boy nodded eagerly.

"And skinny with it," said the Middle Head.

"Undernourished, you could say," said the Right Head.

"Short of sleep, I shouldn't wonder," said the Left Head.

"It's my belief a cup of warm milk in the middle of the day wouldn't hurt," said the Middle Head.

"Nor some hot soup at night. You can't beat hot soup, I always say."

"And plenty of fresh air . . ."

Everyone sighed with relief. The monster had withdrawn into a corner, busy and interested, and they could hear it working out a routine in which a young wizard could blight and smite and blast and wither, but *sensibly*.

"You'll be all right now," said Belladonna, drawing the little boy close.

And the wizard who in years to come would be known as Mugg the Magnificent, Flayer of the Foolish and Master of the Shades, looked up at her with shining mud-colored eyes and said:

"Oh, yes! There'll be no one in the world as all right as me!"

THE SECRET OF
PLATFORM 13

The Secret of
PLATFORM 13

· · · · · · · · · · ·

Eva Ibbotson

Illustrated by Sue Porter

Dutton Children's Books

· NEW YORK ·

Library of Congress Cataloging-in-Publication Data

Ibbotson, Eva.
The secret of platform 13 / Eva Ibbotson; illustrated by Sue Porter.
—1st American ed.
p. cm.
Summary: Odge Gribble, a young hag, accompanies an old wizard,
a gentle fey, and a giant ogre on their mission through a magical
tunnel from their Island to London to rescue their King and Queen's
son, who had been stolen as an infant.
ISBN 0-525-45929-4
[1. Fairy tales.] I. Porter, Sue, ill. II. Title.
PZ8.I25Se 1998
[Fic]—dc21 97-44601 CIP AC

First published in the United States 1998 by Dutton Children's Books,
a member of Penguin Putnam Inc.
375 Hudson Street, New York, New York 10014
Originally published in Great Britain 1994 by Pan Macmillan
Children's Books, London.
Typography by Semadar Megged and Richard Amari
Printed in U.S.A.
First American Edition

9 10

For Laurie and for David

THE SECRET OF

PLATFORM 13

IF YOU WENT into a school nowadays and said to the children: "What is a *gump?*" you would probably get some very silly answers.

"It's a person without a brain, like a chump," a child might say. Or:

"It's a camel whose hump has got stuck." Or even:

"It's a kind of chewing gum."

But once this wasn't so. Once every child in the land could have told you that a gump was a special mound, a grassy bump on the earth, and that in this bump was a hidden door which opened every so often to reveal a tunnel which led to a completely different world.

They would have known that every country has its own gump and that in Great Britain the gump was in a place called the Hill of the Cross of Kings not far from the river Thames. And the wise children, the ones that read the old stories and listened to the old tales, would have known more than that. They would have known that this particular gump opened for exactly nine days every nine years, and not one second longer, and that it was no good changing your mind about coming or going because nothing would open the door once the time was up.

But the children forgot—everyone forgot—and perhaps you can't blame them, yet the gump is still there. It is under Platform Thirteen of King's Cross Railway Station, and the secret door is behind the wall of the old gentlemen's cloakroom with its flappy posters saying "Trains Get You There" and its chipped wooden benches and the dirty ashtrays in which the old gentlemen used to stub out their smelly cigarettes.

No one uses the platform now. They have built newer, smarter platforms with rows of shiny luggage trolleys and slot machines that actually work and television screens which show you how late your train is going to be. But Platform Thirteen is different. The clock has stopped; spiders have spun their webs across the cloakroom door. There's a Left-Luggage Office with a notice saying NOT IN USE, and inside it is an umbrella covered in mold which a lady left on the 5:25 from Doncaster the year of the Queen's Silver Jubilee. The chocolate machines are rusty and lopsided, and if you were foolish enough to put your money in one, it would make a noise like "Harrumph" and swallow it, and you could wait the rest of your life for the chocolate to come out.

Yet when people tried to pull down that part of the station and redevelop it, something always went wrong. An architect who wanted to build shops there suddenly came out in awful boils and went to live in Spain, and when they tried to relay the tracks for electricity, the surveyor said the ground wasn't suitable and muttered something about subsidence and cracks. It was as though people knew *something* about Platform Thirteen, but they didn't know what.

But in every city there are those who have not forgotten the old days or the old stories. The ghosts, for example . . . Ernie Hobbs, the railway porter who'd spent all his life working at King's Cross and still liked to haunt round the trains, he knew—and so did his friend, the ghost of a cleaning lady called Mrs. Partridge who used to scrub out the parcels' office on her hands and knees. The people who plodged about in the sewers under the city and came up occasionally through the manholes beside the station, they knew . . . and so in their own way did the pigeons.

They knew that the gump was still there and they knew where it led: by a long, misty, and mysterious tunnel to a secret cove where a ship waited to take those who wished it to an island so beautiful that it took the breath away.

The people who lived on it just called it the Island, but it has had all sorts of names: Avalon, St. Martin's Land, the Place of the Sudden Mists. Years and years ago it was joined to the mainland, but then it broke off and floated away slowly westward, just as Madagascar floated away from the continent of Africa. Islands do that every few million years; it is nothing to make a fuss about.

With the floating island, of course, came the people who were living on it: sensible people mostly who understood that everyone did not have to have exactly two arms and legs, but might be different in shape and different in the way they thought. So they lived peacefully with ogres who had one eye or dragons (of whom there were a lot about in those days). They didn't leap into the sea every time they saw a mermaid comb her hair on a rock. They simply said, "Good morning." They understood that Ellerwomen had hollow backs and hated to be looked at on a Saturday and that if trolls wanted to wear their beards so long that they stepped on them every time they walked, then that was entirely their own affair.

They lived in peace with the animals too. There were

a lot of interesting animals on the Island as well as ordinary sheep and cows and goats. Giant birds who had forgotten how to fly and laid eggs the size of kettle drums, and brollachans like blobs of jelly with dark red eyes, and sea horses with manes of silk that galloped and snorted in the waves.

But it was the mistmakers that the people of the Island loved the most. These endearing animals are found nowhere else in the world. They are white and small with soft fur all over their bodies, rather like baby seals, but they don't have flippers. They have short legs and big feet like the feet of puppies. Their black eyes are huge and moist, their noses are whiskery and cool, and they pant a little as they move because they look rather like small pillows and they don't like going very fast.

The mistmakers weren't just *nice*, they were exceedingly important.

Because as the years passed and newspapers were washed up on the shore or refugees came through the gump with stories of the World Above, the Islanders became more and more determined to be left alone. Of course they knew that some modern inventions were good, like electric blankets to keep people's feet warm in bed or fluoride to stop their teeth from rotting, but there were other things they didn't like at all, like nuclear weapons or tower blocks at the tops of which old ladies shivered and shook because the lifts were bust, or battery hens stuffed two in a cage. And they dreaded being discovered by passing ships or airplanes flying too low.

Which is where the mistmakers came in. These sensitive creatures, you see, absolutely adore music. When you play music to a mistmaker, its eyes grow wide and it lets out its breath and gives a great sigh.

"Aaah," it will sigh. "Aaah . . . aaah . . ."

And each time it sighs, mist comes from its mouth: clean, thick, white mist which smells of early morning and damp grass. There are hundreds and hundreds of mistmakers lolloping over the turf or along the shore of the Island, and that means a lot of mist.

So when a ship was sighted or a speck in the sky which might be an airplane, all the children ran out of school with their flutes and their trumpets and their recorders and started to play to the mistmakers . . . And the people who might have landed and poked and pried saw only clouds of whiteness and went on their way.

Though there were so many unusual creatures on the Island, the royal family was entirely human and always had been. They were royal in the proper sense—not greedy, not covered in jewels, but brave and fair. They saw themselves as servants of the people, which is how all good rulers should think of themselves, but often don't.

The King and Queen didn't live in a golden palace full of uncomfortable gilded thrones which stuck into people's behinds when they sat down, nor did they fill the place with servants who fell over footstools from walking backward from Their Majesties. They lived in a low white house on a curving beach of golden sand studded with cowrie shells—and always, day or night, they could hear the murmur and slap of the waves and the gentle soughing of the wind.

The rooms of the palace were simple and cool; the windows were kept open so that birds could fly in and out. Intelligent dogs lay sleeping by the hearth; bowls of fresh fruit and fragrant flowers stood on the tables—and anyone who had nowhere to go—orphaned little hags or seals with sore flippers or wizards who had become depressed and old—found sanctuary there.

And in the year 1983—the year the Americans put a woman into space—the Queen, who was young and kind and beautiful—had a baby. Which is where this story really begins.

The baby was a boy, and it was everything a baby should be, with bright eyes, a funny tuft of hair, a button nose, and interesting ears. Not only that, but the little Prince could whistle before he was a month old—not proper tunes, but a nice peeping noise like a young bird.

The Queen was absolutely besotted about her son, and the King was so happy that he thought he would burst, and all over the Island the people rejoiced because you can tell very early how a baby is going to turn out, and they could see that the Prince was going to be just the kind of ruler that they wanted.

Of course as soon as the child was born, there were queues of people round the palace wanting to look after him and be his nurse: Wise Women who wanted to teach him things and sirens who wanted to sing to him and hags who wanted to show him weird tricks. There was even a mermaid who seemed to think she could look after a baby, even if it meant she had to be trundled round the palace in a bath on wheels.

But although the Queen thanked everyone most politely, the nurse she chose for her baby was an ordinary human. Or rather it was three ordinary humans: triplets whose names were Violet and Lily and Rose. They had come to the Island as young girls and were proper trained nursery nurses who knew how to change nappies and bring up wind and sieve vegetables, and the fact that they couldn't do any magic was a relief to the Queen who sometimes felt she had enough magic in her life. Having triplets seemed to her a good idea because looking after babies goes on night and day, and this way there would always be someone with spiky red hair and a long nose and freckles to soothe the Prince and rock him and sing to him, and he wouldn't be startled by the change because however remarkable the baby was, he wouldn't be able to tell Violet from Lily or Lily from Rose.

So the three nurses came and they did indeed look after the Prince most devotedly and everything went beautifully—for a while. But when the baby was three months old, there came the time of the Opening of the Gump—and after that, nothing was ever the same again.

There was always excitement before the Opening. In the harbor, the sailors made the three-masted ship ready to sail to the Secret Cove; those people who wanted to leave the Island started their packing and said their good-byes, and rest houses were prepared for those who would come the other way.

It was now that homesickness began to attack Lily and Violet and Rose.

Homesickness is a terrible thing. Children at boarding schools sometimes feel as though they're going to die of it. It doesn't matter what your home is like—it's that it's yours that matters. Lily and Violet and Rose loved the Island and they adored the Prince, but now they began to remember the life they had led as little girls in the shabby streets of north London.

"Do you remember the Bingo Halls?" asked Lily. "All the shouting from inside when someone won?"

"And Saturday night at the Odeon with a bag of crisps?" said Violet.

"The clang of the fruit machines in Paddy's Parlour," said Rose.

They went on like this for days, quite forgetting how unhappy they had been as children: teased at school, never seeing a clean blade of grass, and beaten by their father. So unhappy that they'd taken to playing in King's Cross Station and had been there when the door opened in the gump and couldn't go through it fast enough.

"I know we can't go Up There," said Lily. "Not with the Prince to look after. But maybe Their Majesties would let us sail with the ship and just look at the dear old country?"

So they asked the Queen if they could take the baby Prince on the ship and wait with him in the Secret Cove—and the Queen said no. The thought of being parted from her baby made her stomach crunch up so badly that she felt quite sick.

It was because she minded so much that she began to change her mind. Was she being one of those awful drooling mothers who smother children instead of letting them grow up free and unafraid? She spoke to the King, hoping he would forbid his son to go, but he said: "Well, dear, it's true that adventures are good for people even when they are very young. Adventures can get into a person's blood even if he doesn't remember having them. And surely you trust the nurses?"

Well, she did, of course. And she trusted the sailors who manned the ship—and sea air, as everybody knows, is terribly good for the lungs.

So she agreed and had a little weep in her room, and the nurses took the baby aboard in his handwoven rush basket with its lace-edged hood and settled him down for the voyage.

Just before the ship was due to sail, the Queen rushed out of the palace, her face as white as chalk, and said: "No, no! Bring him back! I don't want him to go!"

But when she reached the harbor, she was too late. The ship was just a speck in the distance, and only the gulls echoed her tragic voice.

CHAPTER 2

MRS. TROTTLE was rich. She was so rich that she had eleven winter coats and five diamond necklaces, and her bath had golden taps. Mr. Trottle, her husband, was a banker and spent his days lending money to people who already had too much of it and refusing to lend it to people who needed it. The house the Trottles lived in was in the best part of London beside a beautiful park and not far from Buckingham Palace. It had an ordinary address, but the tradesmen called it Trottle Towers because of the spiky railings that surrounded it and the statues in the garden and the flagpole.

Although Larina Trottle was perfectly strong and well and Landon Trottle kept fit by hiring a man to pummel him in his private gym, the Trottles had no less than five servants to wait on them: a butler, a cook, a chauffeur, a housemaid, and a gardener. They had three cars and seven portable telephones, which Mr. Trottle sat on sometimes by mistake, and a hunting lodge in Scotland where he went to shoot deer, and a beach house in the South of France with a flat roof on which Mrs. Trottle lay with nothing on, so as to get a suntan, which was *not* a pleasant sight.

But there was one thing they didn't have. They didn't have a baby.

As the years passed and no baby came along, Mrs. Trottle got angrier and angrier. She glared at people pushing prams, she snorted when babies appeared on television gurgling and advertising disposable nappies. Even puppies and kittens annoyed her.

Then after nearly ten years of marriage, she decided to go and adopt a baby.

First, though, she went to see the woman who had looked after her when she was small. Nanny Brown was getting on in years. She was a tiny, grumpy person who soaked her false teeth in brandy and never got into bed without looking to see if there was a burglar hiding underneath, but she knew everything there was to know about babies.

"You'd better come with me," Mrs. Trottle said. "And I want that old doll of mine."

So Nanny Brown went to fetch the doll, which was one of the large, old-fashioned ones with eyes that click open and shut, and lace dresses, and cold, china arms and legs.

And on a fine day toward the end of June, the chauffeur drove Mrs. Trottle to an orphanage in the north of England, and beside her in the Rolls-Royce sat Nanny Brown, looking like a cross old bird and holding the china doll in her lap.

They reached the orphanage. Mrs. Trottle swept in.

"I have come to choose a baby," she said. "I'm prepared to take either a boy or a girl, but it must be healthy, of course, and not more than three months old, and I'd prefer it to have fair hair."

Matron looked at her. "I'm afraid we don't have any babies for adoption," she said. "There's a waiting list."

"A *waiting list!*" Mrs. Trottle's bosom swelled so much that it looked as if it were going to take off into space. "My good woman, do you know who I am? I am Larina Trottle! My husband is the head of Trottle and Blatherspoon, the biggest merchant bank in the City, and his salary is five hundred thousand pounds a year."

Matron said she was glad to hear it.

"Anyone lucky enough to become a Trottle would be brought up like a prince," Mrs. Trottle went on. "And this doll which I have brought for the baby is a real antique. I have been offered a very large sum of money for it. This doll is priceless!"

Matron nodded and said she was sure Mrs. Trottle was right, but she had no babies for adoption, and that was her last word.

The journey back to London was not a pleasant one. Mrs. Trottle ranted and raved; Nanny Brown sat huddled up with the doll in her lap; the chauffeur drove steadily southward.

Then just as they were coming into London, the engine began to make a nasty clunking noise.

"Oh no, this is too much!" raged Mrs. Trottle. "I will *not* allow you to break down in these disgusting, squalid streets." They were close to King's Cross Station, and it was eleven o'clock at night.

But the clunking noise grew worse.

"I'm afraid I'll have to stop at this garage, Madam," said the chauffeur.

They drew up by one of the petrol pumps. The chauffeur got out to look for a mechanic.

Mrs. Trottle, in the backseat, went on ranting and raving.

Then she grew quiet. On a bench between the

garage and a fish-and-chip shop sat a woman whose frizzy red hair and long nose caught the lamplight. She was wearing the uniform of a nursery nurse and beside her was a baby's basket . . . a basket most finely woven out of rushes whose deep hood sheltered whoever lay within.

The chauffeur returned with a mechanic and began to rev the engine. Exhaust fumes from the huge car drifted toward the bench where the red-haired woman sat holding on to the handle of the basket. Her head nodded, but she jerked herself awake.

The chauffeur revved even harder, and another cloud of poisonous gas rolled toward the bench.

The nurse's head nodded once more.

"Give me the doll!" ordered Larina Trottle—and got out of the car.

For eight days the nurses had waited on the ship as it anchored off the Secret Cove. They had sung to the Prince and rocked him and held him up to see the sea birds and the cliffs of their homeland. They had taken him ashore while they paddled and gathered shells, and they had welcomed the people who came through the gump, as they arrived in the mouth of the cave.

Traveling through the gump takes only a moment. The suction currents and strange breezes that are stored up there during nine long years have their own laws and can form themselves into wind baskets into which people can step and be swooshed up or down in an instant. It is a delightful way to travel but can be muddling for those not used to it, and the nurses made themselves useful helping the newcomers onto the ship.

Then on the ninth day something different came through the tunnel . . . and that something was—a smell.

The nurses were right by the entrance in the cliff when it came to them and as they sniffed it up, their eyes filled with tears.

"Oh Lily!" said poor Violet, and her nose quivered.

"Oh Rose!" said poor Lily and clutched her sister.

It was the smell of their childhood: the smell of fish and chips. Every Saturday night their parents had sent them out for five packets, and they'd carried them back, warm as puppies, through the lamplit streets.

"Do you remember the batter, all sizzled and gold?" asked Lily.

"And the soft whiteness when you got through to the fish?" said Violet.

"The way the chips went soggy when you doused them with vinegar?" said Rose.

And as they stood there, they thought they would die if they didn't just once more taste the glory that was fish and chips.

"We can't go," said Lily, who was the careful one. "You know we can't."

"Why can't we?" asked Rose. "We'd be up there in a minute. It's a good two hours still before the Closing."

"What about the Prince? There's no way we can leave him," said Lily.

"No, of course we can't," said Violet. "We'll take him. He'll love going in a swoosherette, won't you, my poppet?"

And indeed the Prince crowed and smiled and looked as though he would like nothing better.

Well, to cut a long story short, the three sisters made their way to the mouth of the cave, climbed into a wind basket—and in no time at all found themselves in King's Cross Station.

Smells are odd things. They follow you about when you're not thinking about them, but when you put your nose to where they ought to be, they aren't there. The nurses wandered round the shabby streets, and to be honest they were wishing they hadn't come. The pavements were dirty, passing cars splattered them with mud, and the Odeon Cinema where they'd seen such lovely films had been turned into a bowling alley.

Then suddenly there it was again—the smell—stronger than ever, and now, beside an All Night garage, they saw a shop blazing with light and in the window a sign saying FRYING NOW.

The nurses hurried forward. Then they stopped.

"We can't take the Prince into a common fish-and-chip shop," said Lily. "It wouldn't be proper."

The others agreed. Some of the people queuing inside looked distinctly rough.

"Look, you wait over there on the bench with the baby," said Rose. She was half an hour older than the others and often took the lead. "Violet and I'll go in and get three packets. We're only a couple of streets away from the station—there's plenty of time."

So Lily went to sit on the bench, and Rose and Violet went in to join the queue. Of course when they reached the counter, the cod had run out—something always runs out when it's your turn. But the man went to fetch some more and there was nothing to worry about: they had three-quarters of an hour before the Closing of the Gump, and they were only ten minutes' walk from the station.

Lily, waiting on the bench, saw the big Rolls Royce draw up at the garage . . . saw the chauffeur get out and a woman with wobbly piled-up hair open the window and let out a stream of complaints.

Then the chauffeur came back and started to rev up . . .

Oh dear, I do feel funny, thought Lily, and held on tight to the handle of the basket. Her head fell forward and she jerked herself awake. Another cloud of fumes rolled toward her . . . and once more she blacked out.

But only for a moment. Almost at once she came round and all was well. The big car had gone, the basket was beside her, and now her sisters came out with three packets wrapped in newspaper. The smell was marvelous, and a greasy ooze had come up on the face of the Prime Minister, just the way she remembered it.

Thoroughly pleased with themselves, the nurses hurried through the dark streets, reached Platform Thirteen, and entered the cloakroom.

Only when they were safe in the tunnel did they unpack the steaming fish and chips.

"Let's just give him one chip to suck?" suggested Violet.

But Lily, who was the fussy one, said no, the Prince only had healthy food and never anything salty or fried.

"He's sleeping so soundly," she said fondly.

She bent over the cot, peered under the hood . . . unwound the embroidered blanket, the lacy shawl . . .

Then she began to scream.

Instead of the warm, living, breathing baby—there lay a cold and lifeless doll.

And the wall of the gentlemen's cloakroom was moving . . . moving . . . it was almost back in position.

Weeping, clawing, howling, the nurses tried to hold it back.

Too late. The gump was closed, and no power on earth could open it again before the time was up.

But in Nanny Brown's little flat, Mrs. Trottle stood looking down at the stolen baby with triumph in her eyes.

"Do you know what I'm going to do?" she said.

Nanny Brown shook her head.

"I'm going to go right away from here with the baby. To Switzerland. For a whole year. And when I come back I'm going to pretend that I had him over there. That it's my very own baby—not adopted but *mine*. No one will guess; it's such a little baby. My husband won't guess either if I stay away—he's so busy with the bank, he won't notice."

Nanny Brown looked at her, thunderstruck. "You'll never get away with it, Miss Larina. Never."

"Oh yes, I will! I'm going to bring him back as my own little darling babykins, aren't I, my poppet? I'm going to call him Raymond. Raymond Trottle, that sounds good, doesn't it? He's going to grow up like a little prince, and no one will be sorry for me or sneer at me because they'll think he's properly mine. I'll sack all the servants and get some new ones so they can't tell tales, and when I come back, it'll be with my teeny weeny Raymond in my arms."

"You can't do it," said Nanny Brown obstinately. "It's wicked."

"Oh yes, I can. And you're going to give up your flat and come with me because I'm not going to change his nappies. And if you don't, I'll go to the police and tell them it was you that stole the baby."

"You wouldn't!" gasped Nanny Brown.

But she knew perfectly well that Mrs. Trottle would. When she was a little girl, Larina Trottle had tipped five live goldfish onto the carpet and watched them flap themselves to death because her mother had told her to clean out their bowl, and she was capable of anything.

But it wasn't just fear that made Nanny Brown go with Mrs. Trottle to Switzerland. It was the baby with his milky breath and the big eyes which he now opened to look about him and the funny little whistling noise he made. She wasn't a particularly nice woman, but she loved babies, and she knew that Larina Trottle was as fit to look after a young baby as a baboon. Actually, a lot *less* fit because baboons, as it happens, make excellent mothers.

So Mrs. Trottle went away to Switzerland—and over the Island a kind of darkness fell. The Queen all but died of grief, the King went about his work like a man twice his age. The people mourned, the mermaids wept on their rocks, and the schoolchildren made a gigantic calendar showing the number of days which had to pass before the gump opened once more and the Prince could be brought back.

But of all this, the boy called Raymond Huntingdon Trottle knew nothing at all.

CHAPTER 3

ODGE GRIBBLE was a hag.

She was a very young one, and a disappointment to her parents. The Gribbles lived in the north of the Island and came from a long line of frightful and monstrous women who flapped and shrieked about, giving nightmares to people who had been wicked or making newts come out of the mouths of anyone who told a lie. Odge's oldest sister had a fingernail so long that you could dig the garden with it, the next girl had black hairs like piano wires coming out of her ears, the third had stripey feet and so on—down to the sixth who had blue teeth and a wart the size of a saucer on her chin.

Then came Odge.

There was great excitement before she was born because Mrs. Gribble had herself been a seventh daughter, and now the new baby would be the seventh also, and the seventh daughter of a seventh daughter is supposed to be very special indeed.

But when the baby came, everyone fell silent and a cousin of Mrs. Gribble's said: "Oh dear!"

The baby's fingernails were short; not one whisker grew out of her ears; her feet were absolutely ordinary.

"She looks just like a small pink splodge," the cousin went on.

So Mrs. Gribble decided not to call her new daughter Nocticula or Valpurgina and settled for Odge (which rhymed with splodge) and hoped that she would improve as she grew older.

And up to a point, Odge did get a little more hag-like. She had unequal eyes: the left one was green and the right one was brown, and she had one blue tooth—but it was a molar and right at the back; the kind you only see when you're at the dentist. There was also a bump on one of her feet which just could have been the beginning of an extra toe, though not a very big one.

Nothing is worse than knowing you have failed your

parents, but Odge did not whinge or whine. She was a strong-willed little girl with a chin like a prizefighter's and long black hair which she drew like a curtain when she didn't want to speak to anyone, and she was very independent. What she liked best was to wander along the seashore making friends with the mistmakers and picking up the treasures that she found there.

It was on one of these lonely walks that she came across the Nurse's Cave.

It was a big, dark cave with water dripping from the

walls, and the noise that came from it made Odge's blood run cold. Dreadful moans, frightful wails, shuddering sobs . . . She stopped to listen, and after a while she heard that the wails had words to them, and that there seemed to be not one wailing voice but three.

"Ooh," she heard. "Oooh, *ooh* . . . I shall never forgive myself. Never!"

"Never, never!" wailed the second voice.

"I deserve to die," moaned a third.

Odge crossed the sandy bay and entered the cave. Three women were sitting there, dressed in the uniform of nursery nurses. Their hair was plastered with ashes, their faces were smeared with mud—and as they wailed and rocked, they speared pieces of completely burnt toast from a smoldering fire and put them into their mouths.

"What's the matter?" asked Odge.

"What's the *matter*?" said the first woman. Odge could see that she had red hair beneath the ashes and a long, freckled nose.

"What's the MATTER?" repeated the second one, who looked so like the first that Odge realized she had to be her sister.

"How is that you don't know about our sorrow and our guilt?" said the third—and she too was so alike that Odge knew they must be triplets.

Then Odge remembered who they were. The tragedy

had happened before she was born, but even now the Island was still in mourning.

"Are you the nurses who took the Prince Up There and allowed him to be stolen?"

"We are," said one of the women. She turned furiously to her sister. "The toast is not burnt enough, Lily. Go and burn it some more."

Then Odge heard how they had lived in the cave ever since that dreadful day so as to punish themselves. How they ate only food that was burnt or moldy or so stale that it hurt their teeth and never anything they were fond of, like bananas. How they never cleaned their teeth or washed, so that fleas could jump into their clothes and bite them, and always chose the sharpest stones to sleep on so that they woke up sore and bruised.

"What happened to the Prince after he was stolen?" asked Odge. She was much more interested in the stolen baby than in how bruised the nurses were or how disgusting their food was.

"He was snatched by an evil woman named Mrs. Trottle and taken to her house."

"How do you know that," asked Odge, "if the door in the gump was closed?" (Hags do not start school till they are eight years old, so she still had a lot to learn.)

"There are those who can pass through the gump even when it is shut, and they told us."

"Ghosts, do you mean?"

Violet nodded. "My foot feels comfortable," she grumbled. "I must go and dip it in the icy water and turn my toes blue."

"What did she do with him? With the baby?"

"She pretended he was her own son. He lives with her now. She has called him Raymond Trottle."

"Raymond Trottle," repeated Odge. It seemed an unlikely name for a prince. "And he's still living there and going to school and everything? He doesn't know who he is?"

"That's right," said Rose, poking a stick into her ear so as to try and draw blood. "But in two years from now, the gump will open and the rescuers will go and bring him back and then we will stop wailing and eating burnt toast and our feet will grow warm and the sun will shine on our faces."

"And the Queen will smile again," said Lily.

"Yes, that will be best of all, when the Queen smiles properly once more."

Odge was very thoughtful as she made her way back along the shore, taking care not to step on the toes of the mistmakers who lay basking on the sand. The Prince was only four months older than she was. How did he feel, being Raymond Trottle and living in the middle of London? What would he think when he found out that he wasn't who he thought he was?

And who would be chosen to bring him back? The

rescuers would be famous; they would go down in history.

"I wish I could go," thought Odge, nudging her blue tooth with her tongue. "I wish *I* could be a rescuer."

Already she felt that she knew the Prince; that she would like him for a friend.

Suddenly she stopped. She set her jaw. "I *will* go," she said aloud. "I'll make them let me go."

From that day on, Odge was a girl with a mission. She started school the following year and worked so hard that she was soon top of her class. She jogged, she threw boulders around to strengthen her biceps, she studied maps of London, and tried to cough up frogs. And a month before the gump was due to open, she wrote a letter to the palace.

When you have worked and worked for something, it is almost impossible to believe that you can fail. Yet when the names of the rescuers were announced, Odge Gribble's name was not among them.

It was the most bitter disappointment. She would have taken it better if the people who *had* been chosen were mighty and splendid warriors who would ride through the gump on horseback, but they were not. A wheezing old wizard, a slightly batty fey, and a one-eyed giant who lived in the mountains moving goats about and making cheese . . .

The head teacher, when she announced who was going in Assembly, had given the reason.

"Cornelius the Wizard has been chosen because he is *wise*. Gurkintrude the fey has been chosen because she is *good*. And the giant Hans has been chosen because he is *strong*."

Of course, being the head teacher, she had then gone on to tell the children that if they wanted to do great deeds when they were older, they must themselves remember to be wise and good and strong, and they could begin by getting their homework done on time and keeping their classroom tidy.

When you are a hag it is important not to cry, but Odge, as she sat on a rock that evening wrapped in her hair, was deeply and seriously hurt.

"I am wise," she said to herself. "I was top again in algebra. And I'm strong: I threw a boulder right across Anchorage Bay. As for being good, I can't see any point in that—not for a mission which might be dangerous."

And yet the letter she had written to the King and Queen had been answered by a secretary who said he felt Miss Gribble was too young.

Sitting alone by the edge of the sea, Odge Gribble ground her teeth.

But there was another reason why those three people had been chosen. The King and Queen wanted their son to be brought back quietly. They didn't want to unloose a lot of strange and magical creatures on the city of London—creatures who would do sensational tricks and be noticed. They dreaded television crews getting excited and newspapermen writing articles about a Lost Continent or a Stolen Prince. As far as the Island was a Lost Continent, they wanted it to stay that way, and they were determined to protect their son from the kind of fuss that went on Up There when anything unusual was going on.

So they had chosen rescuers who could do magic if it was absolutely necessary but could pass for human beings—well, more or less. Of course, if anything went wrong, they had hordes of powerful creatures in reserve: winged harpies with ghastly claws; black dogs that could bay and howl over the rooftops; monsters with pale, flat eyes who could disguise themselves as rocks. . . . All these could be sent through the tunnel if the Trottles turned nasty, but no one expected this. The Trottles had done a dreadful thing; they would certainly be sorry and give up the child with good grace.

Yet now, as the rescuers stood in the drawing room of the palace ready to be briefed, the King and Queen did feel a pang. Cornelius was the mightiest wizard on the Island; a man so learned that he could divide twenty-three-thousand-seven-hundred-and-forty-one by six-and-three-quarters in the time it took a cat to sneeze. He could change the weather and strike fire from a rock, and what was most important, he had once been a university professor and lived Up There so that he could be made to look human without any trouble. Well, he *was* human.

But they hadn't realized he was quite so old. Up in his hut in the hills one didn't notice it so much, but in the strong light that came in from the sea, the liver spots on his bald pate did show up rather, and the yellowish streaks in his long white beard. Cor's neck wobbled as if holding up that domed, brain-filled head was too much for it. You could hear his bones creaking like old timbers every time he moved, and he was very deaf.

But when they suggested that he might find the journey too much, he had been deeply offended.

"To bring back the Prince will be the crowning glory of my life," he'd said.

"And I'll be there to help him," Gurkintrude had promised, looking at the old man out of her soft blue eyes.

"I know you will, dear," said the Queen, smiling at her favorite fey. And indeed, Gurkintrude had already brought up a little patch of hair on the wizard's bald head so as to keep him warm for the journey. True, it looked more like grass because she was a sort of growth goddess, a kind of agricultural fairy, but the wizard had been very pleased.

If the Queen couldn't go herself to fetch back her son (and the Royal Advisors had forbidden it), there was no one she would rather have sent than this fruitful and loving person. Flowers sprang from the ground for Gurkie, trees put out their leaves—and she never forgot the vegetables either. It was because of what she did for those rich, swollen things like marrows and pumpkins—and in particular for those delicious, tiny cucumbers called gherkins which taste so wonderful when pickled —that her name (which had been Gertrude) had gradually changed the way it had.

And Gurkintrude, too, would be at home in London because her mother had been a gym mistress in a girls' school and had run about in gray shorts shouting, "Well Played!" and "Spiffing!" before she came to the Island. Gurkie had adored her mother, and she sometimes talked to her plants as though they were the girls of St. Agnes School, crying, "Well grown!" to the raspberries or telling a lopsided tree to "Pull Your Socks Up and Play the Game."

The third rescuer was lying behind a screen being tested by the doctor. Hans was an ogre—a one-eyed giant—a most simple and kindly person who lived in the mountains putting things right for the goats, collecting feathers for his alpine hat, and yodeling.

As giants go he was not very big, but anyone bigger would not have been able to get through the door of the gentlemen's cloakroom. Even so, at a meter taller than an ordinary person, he would have been noticed, so it had been decided to make him invisible for the journey.

This was no problem. Fernseed, as everyone knows, makes people invisible in a moment, but just a few people can't take it on their skin. They come out in lumps and bumps or develop a rash, and it was to test the ogre's skin that the doctor had taken him behind the screen. Now he came out, carrying his black bag and beaming.

"All is well, Your Majesties," he said. "There will be no ill effects at all."

Hans followed shyly. The ogre always wore leather shorts with embroidered braces, and they could see on his huge pink thigh a patch of pure, clear nothingness.

But he was looking a little worried.

"My eye?" he said. "I wish not seed in my eye?" (He spoke in short sentences and with a foreign accent because his people, long ago, had come through a gump in the Austrian Alps.)

Everyone understood this. If you have only one eye, it really matters.

"I don't think anyone will notice a single eye floating so high in the air," said the Chief Advisor. "And if they do, he could always shut it."

So this was settled and the Palace Secretary handed Cornelius a map of the London Underground and a

briefcase full of money. There was always plenty of that because the people who came through the gump brought it to the treasury, not having any use for it on the Island, and the King now gave his orders.

"You know already that no magic must be used directly on the Prince," he said—and the rescuers nodded. The King and Queen liked ruling over a place where unusual things happened, but they themselves were completely human and could only manage if they kept magic strictly out of their private lives. "As for the rest, I think you understand what you have to do. Make your way quietly to the Trottles' house and find the so-called Raymond. If he is ready to come at once, return immediately and make your way down the tunnel, but if he needs time—"

"How could he?" cried the Queen. "How could he need time?" The thought that her son might not want to come to her at once hurt her so much that she had to catch her breath.

"Nevertheless, my dear, it may be a shock to him, and if so," he turned back to the rescuers, "you have a day or two to get him used to the idea, but whatever you do, don't delay more than—"

He was interrupted by a knock on the door, and a palace servant entered.

"Excuse me, Your Majesties, but there is someone waiting at the gates. She has been here for hours, and though I have explained that you are busy, she simply will not go away."

"Who is it?" asked the Queen.

"A little girl, Your Majesty. She has a suitcase full of sandwiches and a book and says she will wait all night if necessary."

The King frowned. "You had better show her in," he said.

Odge entered and bobbed a curtsey. She looked grim and determined and carried a suitcase with the words ODGE GRIBBLE—HAG painted on the side.

The Queen smiled—almost a proper smile now that she was soon to see her son. "Aren't you Mrs. Gribble's youngest?" she said in her soft voice.

"Yes, I am."

"And what can we do for you, my dear? Your sisters are well, I trust?"

Odge scowled. Her sisters were very well, showing off, shrieking, flapping, digging the garden with their long fingernails, and generally making her feel bad. But this was no time for her own problems.

"I want you to let me go with the rescuers and fetch the Prince," said Odge. "I wrote a letter about it."

The King's secretary now stepped forward and said that Miss Gribble had indeed offered her services, but he had felt that her youth made her unsuitable.

The King nodded and the Queen said gently: "You *are* too young, my dear—you must see that yourself."

"I'm the same age as the Prince," said Odge. "Almost. And I think it would be nice for him to have someone young."

"The rescuers have already been chosen, " said the King.

"Yes, I know. But I don't take up much room. And I think I know how he might feel. Raymond Trottle, I mean."

"How?" asked the Queen eagerly.

"Well, a bit muddled. I mean, he thinks he's a Trottle and he thinks Mrs. Trottle is his mother and—"

"But she isn't! She isn't! She's a wicked woman and a thief."

"Yes, that's true," said Odge. "But if he's a royal prince, it will be difficult for him to hate his mother and—" She broke off, not wanting to say more.

"It could be a dangerous journey," said the Queen.

Odge drew herself up to her full height, which was not very great. Her green eye glinted and her brown eye glared. "I am a hag," she said huffily. "I am Odge-with-the-Tooth." She stepped forward and opened her mouth very wide, and the Queen could indeed see a glimmer of blue right at the back. "Darkness and Danger is meat and drink to hags."

The King and Queen knew this to be true—but it

was absurd to send such a little girl. It was out of the question.

"Sometimes I cough frogs," said Odge—and blushed because it wasn't true. Once she had coughed something that she thought might be a tadpole, but it hadn't been.

"Why do you want to go?" asked the King.

"I just want to," said Odge. "I want to so much that I feel it must be *meant*."

There was a long pause. Then the Queen said: "Odge, if you were allowed to go, what would you say to the Prince when you first saw him?"

"I wouldn't *say* anything," said Odge. "I'd bring him a present."

"What kind of a present?" asked the King.

Odge told him.

CHAPTER 4

"WELL, THIS IS IT!" said Ernie Hobbs, floating past the boarded-up Left-Luggage Office and coming to rest on an old mailbag. "This is the day!"

He was a thin ghost with a drooping moustache, still dressed in the railway porter's uniform he'd worn when he worked in the station. Ernie hated the newfangled luggage trolleys, taking the bread out of the mouths of honest men who used to carry people's suitcases. He also had a sorrow because, after he died, his wife had married again, and when he went to haunt his old house, Ernie could see a man called Albert Fisher sitting in Ernie's old chair with a napkin tied round his nasty neck, eating the bangers and mash that Ernie's wife had cooked for him.

All the same, Ernie was a hero. It was he who had seen Mrs. Trottle snatch the baby Prince outside the fish shop and tried to glide after the Rolls-Royce and stop her—and when that hadn't worked, he'd bravely floated through the gump (although wind tunnels do awful things to the stuff that ghosts are made of) and brought the dreadful news to the sailors waiting in the Cove.

Since then, for nine long years, Ernie and the other station ghosts had kept watch on the Trottles' house, and now they waited to welcome the rescuers and show them the way.

"Are you going to say anything?" asked Mrs. Partridge. "About . . . you know . . . Raymond?"

She was an older ghost than Ernie and remembered the war and how friendly everyone had been, with the soldiers crowding the station and always ready for a chat. Being a specter suited her: her legs had been dreadful when she was alive—all swollen and sore from scrubbing floors all day, and she never got over feeling as free and light as air.

Ernie shook his head. "Don't think so," he said. "No point in upsetting them. They'll find out soon enough."

Mrs. Partridge nodded. She never believed in making

trouble—and a very pale, frail ghost called Miriam Hughes-Hughes agreed. She'd been an apologizing lady—one of those people whose voices come over the loudspeaker all day saying "sorry" to travelers because their trains are late. No one can do that for long and stay healthy, and she had died quite young of sadness and pneumonia.

They were a close band, the specters who haunted Platform Thirteen. The Ghosts of the Gump, they called themselves, and they didn't have much truck with outsiders. There was the ghost of a train spotter called Brian who'd got between the buffers and the 9:15

from Peterborough, and the ghost of the old woman who'd lost her umbrella and still hovered over the Left-Luggage Office keeping an eye on it. . . . And there were others haunting shyly in various parts of the station, not wanting to put themselves forward, but ready to lend a hand if they were needed.

The hands of the great clock moved slowly forward.

Not the clock on Platform Thirteen, which was covered in cobwebs, but that of the main one. Eleven-thirty . . . eleven forty-five . . . midnight . . .

And then it happened! The wall of the gentlemen's cloakroom moved slowly, slowly to one side. A hole appeared . . . a deep, dark hole . . . and from it came swirls of mist and, very faintly, the smell of the sea. . . .

Mrs. Partridge clutched Ernie's arm. "Oooh, I am excited!" she whispered.

And indeed it was exciting; it was awesome. The dark hole, the swirling mist . . . and now in the hole there appeared . . . figures. Three of them . . . and hovering high above them, a clear blue eye.

"Welcome!" said Ernie Hobbs. He bowed, the women curtsied.

And the rescuers stepped forward into the light.

It has to be said that the ghosts were surprised. They knew that the Prince was to be brought back without a fuss, but they had expected . . . well . . . something a bit fiercer.

Of course they could see that the ancient gentleman now tottering toward them was a wizard. His face was very wise, and there seemed to be astrological signs on his long, dark cloak, though when they looked more carefully they saw they were pieces of very old spaghetti in tomato sauce. The wizard's ear trumpet, which he wore on a string around his neck, had tangled with the cord holding his spectacles so that it looked as if he might choke to death before he ever set out on his mission, and though they could see a place on his shoulder where a mighty eagle must have once perched, it was definitely not there anymore. Yet when he came forward to shake hands with them, the ghosts were impressed. How you shake hands with a ghost matters, because of course you feel nothing, and someone who isn't a true gentleman can just wave his hands about in midair and make a ghost feel really small.

"I am Cornelius the Mighty," said Cor, "and I bring thanks from Their Majesties for your Guardianship of the Gump."

He then introduced Gurkintrude.

The fey was wearing a large hat decorated with flowers, but also with a single beetroot. It was a living beetroot—Gurkie would never have worn anything that was dead—and she carried a basket full of important things for gardening: a watering can, some brown paper bags, a roll of twine. . . . The ghosts knew all about these healing ladies who go about making things better for everyone, and they had seen fairy godmothers in the pantomime, but Mrs. Partridge was a bit worried about the hat. The beetroot suited Gurkie—it went with her kind pink face—but of course vegetables are not worn very much in London.

But it was the third person who puzzled the Ghosts of the Gump particularly. Why had the rulers of the Island sent a little girl?

Odge's thick black hair had been yanked into two pigtails, and she wore a pleated gym slip and a blazer with "Play Up and Play the Game" embroidered on the pocket. The uniform was an exact copy of the one that the girls of St. Agnes wore in the photograph that Gurkie's mother had had on her mantelpiece, but the ghosts did not know that—nor did they understand why the suitcase she was clutching, holding it out in front of her like a tea tray, was punched full of holes.

Fortunately the Eye at least belonged to the kind of rescuer they had expected. Because they themselves were often invisible, the ghosts could make out the shape of the ogre even though he was covered in fern-seed. They could see his enormous muscles, each the size of a young sheep, and his sledgehammer fists, and while the embroidered braces were a pity, they thought that he would do very well as a bodyguard.

Cornelius now explained that they were disguised as an ordinary human family. "I am a retired university professor, Gurkintrude is my niece who works for the Ministry of Agriculture, and Odge is her goddaughter on the way to boarding school." As for the ogre, he told them, he would stay invisible, closing his eye when necessary but not, it was hoped, bumping into things.

"And the dear boy?" Gurkintrude now asked eagerly. "Dear little Raymond? He is well?"

There was a pause while Ernie and Mrs. Partridge looked at each other, and the ghost of the apologizing lady stared at the ground.

"He's very well," said Ernie.

"In the pink," put in Mrs. Partridge.

"And knows nothing?"

"Nothing," agreed Ernie.

It now struck the rescuers that there was very little bustle round the gentlemen's cloakroom and that this was unusual. Last time the gump had opened there'd been a stream of people going down: tree spirits whose trees had got Dutch elm disease, water nymphs whose ponds had dried up, and just ordinary people who were fed up with the pollution and the noise. But when they pointed this out to Ernie, he said: "Maybe they'll come later. There's nine days to go."

Actually, he didn't think they'd come later. He didn't think they'd come at all, and he knew why.

"Let us plunge into the bowels of the earth," said Cornelius who wanted to be on his way.

But the Underground had stopped running and so had the buses. "And I wouldn't advise waking Raymond Trottle in the middle of the night," said Ernie. "I wouldn't advise that at all!"

So it was decided they would walk to Trottle Towers

and rest in the park till morning. There was a little sum-mer house hidden in the bushes, close to Raymond's back door where nobody would find them. The only problem was the wizard, who was too tottery to go far, and the giant solved that by saying: "I pig him on back."

This seemed a good idea. Of course they'd have to watch out for people who'd be surprised to see an old gentleman having a piggyback in midair, but as the ghosts were coming along to show them the way, that wouldn't be difficult.

Odge had gone back into the cloakroom to do some-thing to her suitcase. They could hear a tap running and her voice talking to someone. Now, as she stomped after the others down the platform, Ernie took a closer look at her—at the unequal eyes, the fierce black eyebrows which met in the middle . . . and a glimmer of blue as she yawned.

Not just a little girl, then. A hag. Well, they could do with one of those with what was coming to them, thought Ernie Hobbs.

"Goodness, isn't it grand!" said Gurkintrude, looking at the house, which was as famous on the Island as Buckingham Palace or the castle where King Arthur had lived with his knights.

Gurkie was right. Trottle Towers was *very* grand. It had three stories and bristled with curly bits of plasterwork and bow windows and turrets in the roof. The front of the house was separated from the street by a stony garden with gravel paths and a high spiked gate. On the railings were notices saying TRADESMEN NOT ADMITTED and IT IS STRICTLY FORBIDDEN TO PARK— and on the brickwork of the house were three burglar alarms like yellow boils.

The back of the house faced the park, and it was from here that the rescuers had come. The ghosts had returned to the gump. Dawn was just breaking, but inside the house everything was silent and dark.

Then as they stood and looked, a light came on downstairs, deep in the basement. The room had barred windows and almost no furniture so that they could see who was inside as clearly as on a stage.

A boy.

A boy with light hair and a friendly, intelligent face. He was dressed in jeans and a sweater—and he was working. On a low table stood a row of shoes—shoes of all shapes and sizes: boots and ladies' high-heeled sandals and gentlemen's laceups—and the boy was cleaning them. Not just rubbing a cloth over them, but working in the polish with a will—and as he worked, he whistled; they could just hear him through the open slit at the top of the window.

And the rescuers turned to each other and smiled, for they could see that the Prince had been taught to work; that he wasn't being brought up spoilt and selfish as they had feared. Something about the way the ghosts had spoken about Raymond Trottle had worried them, but the boy's alert face, the willing way in which he polished other people's shoes, was a sign of the best possible breeding. This was a prince who would know how to serve others, as did his parents.

The boy finished the shoes and carried them out. A second light went on, and they saw him enter a scullery, fill a kettle, and lay out some cups and saucers on a tray. This job too he did neatly and nimbly, and Odge sighed, for it was amazing how right she had been about the

Prince; he was just the kind of person she wanted for a friend, and she held on even tighter to the suitcase, glad that she had brought him the best present that any boy could have.

The scullery light went off, and a light appeared between the crack in a pair of curtains which the boy now drew back. As he did this, they could see his face turned toward them: the straight, light hair lapping the level brows, the wide-set eyes and the pointed chin. Then he made his way to the bed and set the tray down beside a fierce-looking lady who didn't seem to be thanking him at all, but just grabbed her cup.

"That must be Mrs. Trottle," whispered Gurkintrude. "She doesn't look very loving."

The boy's tasks were still not done. Back in the scullery, he took out a mop and a bucket and began to wipe the floor. Was he perhaps working a little *too* hard for a child who had not yet had breakfast? Or was he on a training scheme? Knights often lived like this before a joust or a tournament—and boy scouts, too.

But nothing mattered except that the Prince was everything a boy should be and that the day they brought him back to his rightful home would be the most joyful one the Island had ever known.

"Can't we go and tell him we're here?" asked Odge.

There was no need. The boy had come out of the back door carrying a polythene bag full of rubbish which he put in the dustbin. Then he lifted his head and saw them. For a moment he stood perfectly still with a look of wonder on his face, and it was almost as though he was listening to some distant, remembered music. Then he ran lightly up the basement steps and threw open the gate.

"Can I help you?" he asked. "Is there anyone you want to see?"

Cor the Wise stepped forward. He wanted to greet the Prince by his true name, to bow his head before him, but he knew he must not startle him, and trying to speak in an ordinary voice (though he was very much moved) he said: "Yes, there is someone we want to see. You."

The boy drew in his breath. He looked at Gurkie's round, kind face, at the grassy patch on the wizard's head, at Odge who had turned shy and was scuffing her shoes. Then he sighed, as though a weight had fallen from him, and said: "You mean it? It's really me you've come to see?"

"Indeed it is, my dear," said Gurkintrude and put her arm round him. He was too thin and why hadn't Mrs. Trottle cut his hair? It was bothering him, flopping over his eyes.

The boy's next words surprised them. "I wish I could ask you in, but I'm not allowed to have visitors," he said—and they could see how much he minded not being able to invite them to his house. "But there's a bench there under the oak tree where you could rest, and I could get you a drink. No one's up yet, they wouldn't notice."

"We need nothing," said Cor. "But let us be seated. We have much to tell you."

They made their way back into the park, and the boy took out his handkerchief and wiped the wooden slats of the seat clear of leaves. It was as though he was inviting them to his bench even if he couldn't invite them to his house. Nor would he himself sit down, but stood before them and answered their questions in a steady voice.

"You have lived all your life in Trottle Towers?" asked Cor.

"Yes." A shadow spread for a moment over his face as though he was looking back on a childhood that had been far from happy.

"And you have learnt to work, we can see that. But your schooling?"

"Oh, yes; I go to school. It's across the park in a different part of London."

Very different, he thought. Swalebottle Junior was in a rowdy, shabby street; the building was full of cracks and the teachers were often tired, but it was a good place to be. It was the holidays he minded, not the term.

The ogre had managed to follow them to the bench

with his eye shut, but the Prince's voice pleased him so much that he now opened it. Cor frowned at him, Gurkie shook her head—they had been so careful not to startle the Prince, and invisible ogres *are* unusual; there is nothing to be done about that. But the boy didn't seem at all put out by a single blue eye floating halfway up the trunk of the tree.

"Is he . . . or she . . . I don't want to pry, but is he a friend of yours?"

Hans was introduced, and the visitors made up their minds. The Prince was entirely untroubled by magic; it was as though the traditions of the Island were in his blood even if he hadn't been there since he was three months old. It was time to reveal themselves and take him back.

"Was that Mrs. Trottle to whom you brought a cup of tea?" asked Cor. "Because we have something to say to her."

The boy smiled. "Oh, goodness, no!" he said. "Mrs. Trottle lives upstairs. That was the cook."

Cor frowned. He was an old-fashioned man and a bit of a snob, and he did not think it absolutely right that a prince should have to take morning tea to the cook.

But Odge had had enough of talking.

"I've brought you something," she said in her abrupt, throaty little voice. "A present. Something nice."

She put the suitcase down on the grass. The words

ODGE GRIBBLE—HAG had been painted out. Instead she'd written THIS WAY UP. HANDLE WITH CARE.

The boy crouched down beside her. He could hear the present breathing through the holes. Something alive, he thought, his eyes alight.

It was at this moment that, on the first floor of Trottle Towers, someone began to scream.

All of them were used to the sound of screaming. Odge's sisters practically never stopped, banshees wailed through the trees of the Island, harpies yowled, and the sound of bull seals calling to their mates sometimes seemed to shake the rafters. But this was not that sort of a scream. It was not the healthy scream of someone going about their business; it was a whining, self-pitying, blackmailing sort of scream. Odge refastened the catch of her suitcase in a hurry; Gurkintrude put her arm round the Prince, and the Eye soared upward as Hans got to his feet.

"What is it, dear boy?" asked Gurkie, and put her free hand up to her head as though to protect the beet-root from the dreadful noise.

"Is it someone having an operation?" said Cornelius. "I thought you had anesthetics?"

The boy shook his head. "No," he said. "It's nothing like that. It's Raymond."

A terrible silence fell.

"What do you mean, it's Raymond?" asked Cor when he could speak again. "Surely you are Raymond Trottle, the supposed son of Mr. and Mrs. Trottle?"

The boy shook his head once more. "No. Oh, goodness, no! I'm only the kitchen boy. I'm not anybody. My name is Ben."

As he spoke, Ben moved away and stood with his back to the visitors. It was over, then. It wasn't him they'd come to see; he'd been an idiot. When he'd seen them standing there he'd had such a feeling of . . . homecoming, as though at last the years of drudgery were over. It was like that dream he had sometimes—the dream with the sea in it, and soft green turf, and someone whose face he couldn't see clearly, but who he knew wanted him.

Only dreams were things you woke from, and he should have known that it was not him but Raymond the visitors had come to find. Everything had always belonged to Raymond. All his life he'd been used to Raymond living upstairs with everything he wished for and parents to dote on him. Raymond had cupboards full of toys he never even looked at and more clothes than he knew what to do with; he was driven to his posh school in a Rolls-Royce, and just to tear the wrapping paper from his Christmas presents took Raymond hours.

And so far Ben hadn't minded. He was used to living with the servants, used to sleeping in a windowless cupboard and working for his keep. You couldn't envy Raymond, who was always whining and saying: "I'm bored!"

But this was different. That these strange, mysterious, interesting people belonged to Raymond and not to him was almost more than he could bear.

"You're sure he isn't being tortured?" asked Cor as the screams went on.

"Quite sure. He often does it."

"*Often?*" said the wizard and shook out his ear trumpet in case he had misheard.

Ben nodded. "Whenever he doesn't want to go to school. Probably he hasn't done his homework. I usually do it for him, but I couldn't yesterday because I was visiting my grandmother in hospital."

"Who is your grandmother?" Odge wanted to know.

"She's called Nanny Brown. She used to be Mrs. Trottle's Nanny, and she still lives here in the basement. She adopted me when I was a baby because I didn't have any parents."

"What happened to them?"

Ben shrugged. "I don't know. They died. Mr. Fulton thinks they must have been in prison because Nanny never mentions them."

Talking about Nanny Brown was difficult because

she was very ill. It was she who protected him from the bullying of the servants—even the snooty butler, Mr. Fulton, respected her—and if she died . . .

The rescuers were silent, huddled together on the bench. Hans had closed his eye and was covering his face with his invisible hand. He was used to the silence of the mountains and felt a headache coming on. Odge was crouched over the suitcase as though to comfort what was inside.

It was a *child* who was making that noise; the child they had come so far to find. And the boy they liked so much had nothing to do with them at all!

CHAPTER 5

WHAT IS IT, my angel, my babykins, my treasure?" said Mrs. Trottle, coming into the room.

She had been making up her face when Raymond's
screams began. Now her right cheek was covered in
purple rouge, and her left cheek was still a rather nasty
gray color. Mrs. Trottle's hair was in curlers, and she
gave off a strong smell of Maneater because she always
went to bed covered in scent.

Raymond continued to scream.

"Tell Mama; tell your Mummy, my pinkyboo," begged Mrs. Trottle.

"I've got a pain in my tummy," yelled Raymond. "I'm ill."

Mrs. Trottle pulled back the covers on Raymond's huge bed with its padded headboard and the built-in switches for his television set, his two computers, and his electric trains. She put a finger on Raymond's stomach, and the finger vanished because Raymond was extremely fat.

"Where does it hurt, my pettikins? Which bit?"

"Everywhere," screeched Raymond. "All over!"

Since Raymond had eaten an entire box of chocolates the night before, this was not surprising, but Mrs. Trottle looked worried.

"I can't go to school!" yelled Raymond, getting to the point. "I can't!"

Raymond's school was the most expensive in London; the uniform alone cost hundreds of pounds, but he hated it.

"Of course you can't, my lambkin," said Mrs. Trottle, drawing her finger out of Raymond's middle. "I'll send a message to the headmaster. And then I'll call a doctor."

"No, no—not the doctor! I don't want the doctor; he makes me worse," yelled Raymond—and indeed the doctor was not always as kind to darling Raymond as he might have been.

Mr. Trottle now came in looking cross because he had sat on his portable telephone again and asked what was the matter.

"Our little one is ill," said Mrs. Trottle. "You must tell Willard to drive to the school after he has dropped you at the bank and let them know."

"He doesn't look ill to me," said Mr. Trottle—but he

never argued with his wife, and anyway he was in a hurry to go and lend a million pounds to a property developer who wanted to cover a beautiful Scottish island with holiday homes for the rich.

Raymond's screams grew less. They became wails, then snivels . . .

"I feel a bit better now," he said. "I might manage some breakfast." He had heard the car drive away and knew that the danger of school was safely past.

"Perhaps a glass of orange juice?" suggested Mrs. Trottle.

"No. Some bacon and some sausages and some fried bread," said Raymond.

"But, darling—"

Raymond puckered up his face, ready to scream again.

"All right, my little sugar lump. I'll tell Fulton. And then a quiet day in bed."

"No. I don't want a quiet day. I feel better now. I want to go to lunch at Fortlands. And then shopping. I want a laser gun like Paul has at school, and a knife, and—"

"But, darling, you've already got seven different guns," said Mrs. Trottle, looking at Raymond's room, which was completely strewn with toys he had pushed aside or broken or refused to put away.

"Not like the one Paul's got—not a sonic-trigger activated laser, and I want one. I *want* it."

"Very well, dear," said Mrs. Trottle. "We'll go to lunch at Fortlands. You do look a little rosier."

This was true. Raymond looked very rosy indeed. People usually do when they have yelled for half an hour.

"And shopping?" asked Raymond. "Not just lunch but shopping afterward?"

"And shopping," agreed Mrs. Trottle. "So now give your mumsy a great big sloppy kiss."

That was how things always ended on days when Raymond didn't feel well enough to go to school—with Raymond and Mrs. Trottle, dressed to kill, going to have lunch in London's grandest department store.

The name of the store was Fortlands and Marlow. It was in Piccadilly and sold everything you could imagine: marble bathtubs and ivory elephants and sofas that you sank into and disappeared. It had a food hall with a fountain where butlers in hard hats bought cheeses that cost a week's wages, and a bridal department where the daughters of duchesses were fitted for their wedding gowns—and none of the dresses had price tickets on them in case people fainted clean away when they saw how much they cost.

And there was a restaurant with pink chairs and pink tablecloths in which Raymond and his mother were having lunch.

"I'll have shrimps in mayonnaise," said Raymond, "and then I'll have roast pork with crackling and Yorkshire pudding and—"

"I'm afraid the Yorkshire pudding comes with the roast beef, sir," said the waitress. "With the pork you get applesauce and red-currant jelly."

"I don't like applesauce," whined Raymond. "It's all squishy and gooey. I want Yorkshire pudding. I *want* it."

It was at this moment that the rescuers entered the store. They too were having lunch in the restaurant. When Ben had told them how Raymond was going to spend the day, they decided to follow the Prince and study him from a distance so that they could decide how best to make themselves known to him.

"Only I want Ben to come," Odge said.

Everyone wanted Ben to come, but he said he couldn't. "I don't have school today because they need the building for a council election, and I promised my grandmother I'd come to the hospital at dinnertime."

But he said he would go with them as far as Fortlands and point Raymond out because the Trottles had gone off in the Rolls and no one had seen him yet. Hans, though, decided to stay behind. He didn't like crowded places, and he lay down under an oak tree and went to sleep, which made a great muddle for the dogs, who didn't understand why they couldn't walk through a perfectly empty patch of grass.

Gurkie absolutely loved Fortlands. The vegetable display was quite beautiful—the passion fruit and the pineapples and the cauliflowers so artistically arranged —and she had time to say nice things to a tray of broccoli which looked a little lonely. In a different sort of shop, the rescuers might have stood out, but Fortlands was full of old-fashioned people coming up from the country, and they fit in quite well. The only thing people did stare at a bit was the beetroot in Gurkie's hat, so she decided to leave it in the fountain to soak quietly while she went up to the restaurant. It was as she was bending over the water to look for a place where the beloved vegetable would not be noticed that she saw, beneath the water weed, a small, sad face.

Bending down to see more clearly, she found that she had not been mistaken.

"Yes, it's me," said a slight, silvery voice. "Melisande. I heard you were coming." And then: "I'm not a mermaid, you know, I'm a water nymph. I've got feet."

"Yes, I know, dear; I can see you've got feet. But you don't look well. What are those marks on your arms?"

"It's the coins. People chuck coins into the fountain all day long, heaven knows why. I'm all over bruises— and the water isn't changed nearly often enough."

And her lovely, tiny face really did look very melancholy.

"Why don't you come down with us, dear?" whispered Gurkintrude. "The gump's open. We could take you wrapped in wet towels; it wouldn't be difficult."

"I was going to," said the nymph sadly. "But not now. You've seen him."

"The Prince, do you mean? We haven't yet."

"Well, you will in a minute; he's just gone up in the lift. There was a lot of us going, but who wants to be ruled by *that?*"

She then agreed to hide the beetroot under a water lily leaf, and Gurkie hurried to catch up with the others. The nymph's words had upset her, but feys always think the best of people, and she was determined to look on the bright side. Even if Mrs. Trottle had spoilt Raymond a little, there would be time to put that right when he came to the Island. When children behave badly, it is nearly always the fault of those who bring them up.

"There he is," whispered Ben. "Over there, by the window."

There was a long pause.

"You're sure?" asked Cor. "There can be no mistake?"

"I'm sure," said Ben.

He then slipped away, and the rescuers were left to study the boy they had come so far to find.

"He looks . . . healthy," said Gurkintrude, trying to make the best of things.

"And well-washed," agreed the wizard. "I imagine there would be no mold behind his ears?"

Odge didn't say anything. She still carried the suitcase, holding it out flat like a tray, and had been in a very nasty temper since she discovered that Ben was not the Prince.

What surprised them most was how like his supposed mother Raymond Trottle looked. They both had the same fat faces, the same podgy noses, the same round, pale eyes. They knew, of course, that dogs often grew to be like their owners, so perhaps it was understandable that Raymond, who had lived with the Trottles since he was three months old, should look like the woman who had stolen him, but it was odd all the same.

The visitors had looked forward very much to having lunch in a posh restaurant, but the hour that followed was one of the saddest of their lives. They found a table behind a potted palm from which they could watch the Trottles without being noticed, and what they saw got worse and worse and worse. Raymond's shrimps had arrived, and he was pushing them away with a scowl.

"I don't want them," said Raymond. "They're the wrong ones. I want the bigger ones."

As far as Gurkie was concerned, there was no such thing as a wrong shrimp or a right shrimp. All shrimps were her friends, and she would have died rather than eat one, but she felt dreadfully sorry for the waitress.

"The bigger ones are prawns, sir; and I'm afraid we don't have any today."

"Don't have any *prawns*," said Mrs. Trottle in a loud voice. "Don't have any prawns in the most expensive restaurant in London!"

The waitress had been on her feet all day, her little girl was ill at home, but she kept her temper.

"If you'd just try them, sir," she begged Raymond.

But he wouldn't. The dish was taken away and Raymond decided to start with soup. "Only not with any bits in it," he shouted after the waitress. "I don't eat bits."

Poor Gurkie's kind round face was growing paler and paler. The Islanders had ordered salad and nut cutlets, but she was so sensitive that she could hear the lamb chops screaming on the neighboring tables, and the poor stiff legs of dead pheasants sticking up from people's plates made her want to cry.

Raymond's soup came and it did have bits in it—a few leaves of fresh parsley.

"I thought I asked for *clear* soup," said Mrs. Trottle. "Really, I find it quite extraordinary that you cannot bring us what we want."

The rescuers had been up all night; they were not only sad, they were tired, and because of this they forgot themselves a little. When their nut cutlets came, they were too hard for the wizard's teeth. He should have mashed them up with his fork—of course he should. Instead, he mumbled something and in a second the cutlets had turned to liquid. Fortunately no one saw, and the liquidizing spell is nothing to write home about—it was used by wizards in the olden days to turn their enemies' bones to jelly—but it was embarrassing when they were trying so hard to be ordinary. And then the sweet peas in Gurkintrude's hat started to put out tendrils without even being told so as to shield her from the sight of the Prince fishing with his fingers in the soup.

The Trottles' roast pork came next—and the kind waitress had managed to persuade the chef to put a helping of Yorkshire pudding on Raymond's plate, though anyone who knows anything about food knows that Yorkshire pudding belongs to beef and not to pork.

Raymond stared at the plate out of his round pale eyes. "I don't want roast potatoes," he said. "I want chips. Roast potatoes are boring."

"Now Raymond, dear," began his mother.

"I want *chips*. This is supposed to be my treat, and it isn't a treat if I can't have chips."

Odge had behaved quite well so far. She had glared, she had ground her teeth, but she had gone on eating her lunch. Now though, she began to have *thoughts* and the thoughts were about her sisters—and in particular about her oldest sister, Fredegonda, who was better than anyone on the Island at ill-wishing pigs.

Ill-wishing things is not all that difficult. Witch doctors do it when they send bad thoughts to people and make them sick; sometimes you can do it when you will someone not to score a goal at football and they don't. Odge had never wanted to ill-wish pigs because she liked animals, but she had sometimes wanted to ill-wish people, and now, more than anything in the world, she wanted to ill-wish Raymond Trottle.

But she didn't. For one thing she wasn't sure if she could, and anyway she had promised to behave like the girls of St. Agnes whose uniform she wore.

"I want a Knickerbocker Glory next," said Raymond. "The kind with pink ice cream and green ice cream and jelly and peaches and raspberry juice and nuts."

The waitress went away and returned with Mrs. Trottle's caramel pudding and the Knickerbocker Glory in a tall glass. It was an absolutely marvelous one—just to look at it made Odge's mouth water.

Raymond picked up his spoon—and put it down again.

"It hasn't got an umbrella on top," he wailed. "I always have a plastic umbrella on top. I won't eat it unless I have a—Ugh! Eek! Yow! What's happened? I didn't touch it, I didn't, I *didn't!*"

He was telling the truth for once, but nobody believed him. For the Knickerbocker Glory had done a somersault and landed facedown on the table, so that the three kinds of ice cream, the jelly, the tinned peaches, and the raspberry juice were running down Raymond's trousers, into his socks, across his flashy shoes . . .

Odge had not ill-wished Raymond Trottle. She had been very good and held herself in, but not completely. She had ill-wished the Knickerbocker Glory.

CHAPTER 6

"I WANT SOME BRANDY for my teeth," said Nanny Brown.

She lay in the second bed from the end in Ward Three of the West Park Hospital, in a flannel nightdress with a drawstring round the neck because she didn't believe in showing bits of herself to the doctors. She had been old when Mrs. Trottle persuaded her to come to Switzerland with the stolen baby, and now she was very old indeed; shriveled and tired and ready to go because she'd said her prayers every day of her life, and if God wasn't waiting to take her up to heaven she'd want to know the reason why. But she was cross about her teeth.

"Now, Mrs. Brown," said the nurse briskly, "you know we can't let you soak your teeth in that nasty stuff. Just pop them in that nice glass of disinfectant."

"It isn't nice, it's smelly," grumbled Mrs. Brown. "I've always soaked my teeth in brandy, and then I drink the brandy. That's how I get my strength."

And she had needed her strength, living in the Trottles' basement helping to look after Raymond, but keeping an eye on Ben. She didn't hold with the way Larina was bringing up Raymond; she could see how spoilt he was going to be, and when he was three she'd handed him over to another nanny, but she wouldn't let Larina turn her out—not with Ben to look after. Mrs. Trottle might threaten her with the police if she said anything about the stolen baby, but the threat worked both ways. "If you turn me out, and the boy, I'll tell them everything, and who knows which of us they'll believe," Nanny Brown had said.

So she'd stayed in Trottle Towers and helped with a bit of sewing and ironing, and turned her back on what was going on in the nursery upstairs. And she'd been able to see that Ben at least was brought up properly. She couldn't stop the servants ordering him about, but she saw to his table manners and that he spoke nicely and got his schooling, and he was a credit to her.

That was the only thing that worried her—what would happen to Ben if she died. Mrs. Trottle hated Ben; she'd stop at nothing to get him sent away. But I'm going to foil her, thought Nanny Brown. Oh yes, I'm going to stop her tricks.

"There's a burglar under my bed," she said now. "I feel it. Have a look."

"Now, Mrs. Brown," said the nurse, "we don't want to get silly ideas into our head, do we?"

"It isn't silly," said Nanny peevishly. "London's full of burglars, so why not under my bed?"

The nurse wouldn't look though; she was one of the bossy ones. "What will your grandson say if you carry on like that?" she said, and walked away with her behind swinging.

But when Ben came slowly down the ward, the old woman felt better at once. She'd been strict with him: no rude words, eating up every scrap you were given, yet she didn't mind admitting that if she loved anyone in the world, it was this boy. And the other patients smiled too as he passed their beds because he was always so polite and friendly, greeting them and remembering their names.

"Hello, Nanny."

He always called her Nanny, not Grandma. She'd

told him to, it sounded better. Now he laid a small bunch of lilies of the valley down beside her, and she shook her head at him. "I told you not to waste your money." She'd left him a few pounds out of her pension when she went into hospital and told him it had to last. Waste was wicked, but her gnarled fingers closed round the bunch and she smiled.

"How are you feeling?" Ben asked.

"Oh fine, fine," lied Nanny Brown. "And you? What's been going on at home?"

Ben hesitated. He wanted to tell Nanny about his mysterious visitors, about how much he liked them . . . the strange feeling he'd had that they belonged to him. But he'd promised to say nothing and anyway he'd been wrong because they didn't belong to him. So he just said: "Nothing much. I've got onto the football team and Raymond's had another screaming fit."

"That's hardly news," said Nanny Brown grimly. And then: "No one's been bothering you? That Mr. Fulton?"

"No, not really. But . . . do you think you're coming home soon, Nanny? It's better when you're there."

Nanny patted his hand. "Bless you, of course I am. You just get on with your schooling and remember, once you're grown up, no one can tell you what to do."

"Yes."

It would be a long time though till he was a man,

and Nanny looked very ill. Fear was bad; being afraid was about yourself and you had to fight it, but just for a moment he was very much afraid whether it was selfish or not.

It was very quiet in the ward when the visitors had gone. All the other patients lay back drowsily, glad to rest, but Nanny Brown sat up in bed as fierce as a sparrow hawk. There wasn't much time to waste. And she was lucky: it was the nice nurse from the Philippines who came round to take temperatures. Celeste, she was called, and she had a lovely smile and a tiny red rose tucked into her hair behind her ear. You could only see it when she bent down, but it always made you feel better, knowing it was there.

"Listen, dear, there's something I want you to do for me. Will you get me a piece of paper and an envelope? It's really important or I wouldn't ask you."

Celeste reached for Nanny's wrist and began to take her pulse.

"I'll try, Mrs. Brown," she said. "But you'll have to wait till I've finished my rounds."

And she didn't forget. An hour later she came with the paper and a strong white envelope. "Have you got a pen?"

Nanny Brown nodded. "Thank you, dear; that's a weight off my mind. You're a good kind girl."

Celeste smiled. "That's all right." She looked closely

at the old woman's face. It wouldn't be long now. "I'll just make sure about the burglars," she said.

She bent down to look, and as she did so Nanny Brown could see the little red rose tucked in the jet black hair.

"Bless you," she said—and then, feeling much better, she began to write.

CHAPTER 7

"IS SIMPLE," said Hans. "I bop 'im. I sack 'im. We go through the gump."

The others had returned from Fortlands in such a gloomy mood that the poor ogre could hardly bear it. He'd had a good sleep and when he heard what had happened in the restaurant, he decided that he should come forward and put things right.

Cor shook his head. It was tempting to let the giant bop Raymond on the head, tie him up in a sack, and carry him back to the Island, but it couldn't be done. He imagined the King and Queen unwrapping their stunned son like a trussed piglet . . . realizing that Raymond had had to be carried off by force.

"He must come willingly, Hans," he said, "or the Queen will break her heart."

Ernie Hobbs now glided toward the little summer house where they were sitting. He usually allowed himself a breather in the early evening and had left the other ghosts in charge of the gump.

"Well, how's it going?"

The Islanders told him.

Ernie nodded. "I'm afraid it's a bad business. We've been keeping an eye on him, and he's been going downhill steadily. Mrs. Trottle's a fool and Mr. Trottle's never there—there's no one to check him."

"I suppose there can be no doubt who Raymond is?" asked Cor.

Ernie shook his head. "I saw her steal the baby. I saw her come back a year later with the baby in her arms. What's more, he had the same comforter in his mouth. I noticed it particularly with it being on a gold ring. He'll be the Prince all right."

"And what about Ben?" asked Gurkintrude.

"Ah, he's a different kettle of fish, Ben is. Been here as long as Raymond, and you couldn't find a better lad. He can see ghosts too and never a squawk out of him. The servants treat him like dirt—take their tone from

Mrs. Trottle. It'll be a bad day for the boy when his grandma dies."

He then glided off to watch Albert Fisher eat bangers and mash in his old house and make himself miserable, but first he promised the help of all the ghosts in the city if it was needed. "And not just ghosts—there's all sorts would like to see things come right on the Island," he said.

He had no sooner gone than Ben came hurrying out of the house toward them, and Odge—who had been exercising her present in the shrubbery—crawled out with her suitcase and said "Hello."

"How was your grandmother?" Gurkie asked.

A shadow crossed Ben's face. "She says she's all right but she doesn't look very well to me." And then: "How did it go at lunch?"

"Raymond was awful," said Odge. "I think he's disgusting. I think we should have a republic on the Island and not bother with a prince once the King and Queen are dead."

"*Odge!*" said Gurkie in a warning voice.

Odge hung her head. She had not meant to betray the reason for their journey any more than she had meant to ill-wish the Knickerbocker Glory, but she was a girl with strong feelings.

But Cor had come to a decision.

"I think, Ben," he said, "that you are a boy who can keep a secret?"

"Yes, sir, I am," said Ben without hesitation.

"You see, we shall need your help. You know Raymond's movements and where he sleeps and so on. So we had better explain why we are here."

He then told him about the Island, about the sorrow of the King and Queen, about their quest.

Ben listened in silence, and when they had finished, his eyes were bright with wonder. "I always knew there had to be a place like that. I knew it!" But he was amazed that Raymond had been stolen. "Mrs. Trottle's got his birth certificate framed in her room."

"Well, that just shows she's a cheat, doesn't it?" said Odge. "Who'd want to frame a crummy birth certificate unless they had something to hide?"

"Now, listen, Ben," the wizard went on, "we want you to take us to see Raymond when he's alone. Do you know when that might be?"

"Tonight would be good. The Trottles are going out and Mrs. Flint's meant to listen for him—that's the cook—but all she does is switch the telly on full blast and stay in her sitting room."

"That will do then. And now we must think how to win Raymond's trust and make him come with us. What sort of things does he like?"

This was difficult. Ben could think of a lot of things Raymond *didn't* like. After a pause he said: "Presents. He likes getting things."

"Ah, in that case—"

"*No!*" Odge broke in most rudely. She was clutching the suitcase, and her green eye gave off beams of fury. "I won't give this present to that pig of a boy."

Cornelius rose. "How *dare* you speak like that to your superiors?"

But Odge stood her ground. "This present is special. I brought it up from when it was tiny, and it's still a baby, and I'm not going to give it to Raymond because he's horrible. I'm going to give it to Ben."

Gurkintrude now knelt down beside the hag. "Look, Odge, I know how you feel. But it's our duty to bring back the Prince. The Queen trusted you as much as she trusted us, and it was because you thought of such a lovely present for her son that she said you could come. You can't let her down now."

But it was Ben who changed her mind. "If you promise to do something, Odge, then you have to do it, you know that. And if giving Raymond . . . whatever it is . . . will help, then that's part of the deal."

"Oh, all right," said Odge sulkily. "But if he doesn't treat it properly, I'll let my sisters loose on him, and that's a promise."

It was nine o'clock before the servants were settled in front of the telly and Ben could creep upstairs with his new friends.

Raymond was sitting up in bed with his boom box going full tilt, wriggling in time to the music.

"What do you want?" he said to Ben. "I don't need you. I haven't got any homework to do today because tomorrow's Saturday, and anyway you're supposed to stay in the kitchen."

"I've brought some people to see you," said Ben. "Visitors."

The rescuers entered, and Ben introduced them—all except Hans, who had to crawl through the door on his hands and knees and settled himself down with his eye shut.

Raymond stared at them. "They look funny," he said. "Are they in fancy dress?"

"No, Your Roy—" began Cor and broke off. He had been about to call Raymond "Your Royal Highness," but it was too early to reveal the full truth. "We come from another place."

"What place?" asked Raymond suspiciously.

"It's called the Island," said Gurkintrude. Feys are used to kissing children and being godmother to almost everyone, but Raymond, bulging out of his yellow silk pajamas, looked so uninviting that she had to pretend he was a vegetable marrow before she could settle down beside him on the bed. "It's a most beautiful place, Raymond. There are green fields with wildflowers growing in the grass and groves of ancient trees and rivers where the water is so clear that you can see all the stones on the bottom as if they were jewels."

Raymond didn't say anything, but at least he'd switched off his radio.

"And all round the Island are beaches of white sand and rock pools and cliffs where the seabirds come to nest each spring."

"And there are seals and buzzards and rabbits and crabs," said Odge.

"I don't like crabs," said Raymond. "They pinch you. Is there a pier with slot machines and an amusement arcade?"

"No. But you don't need an amusement arcade—the dolphins will come and talk to you, and the kelpies will take you on their backs and gallop through the waves."

"I don't believe it," said Raymond. "You're telling fibs."

"No, Raymond, it's all true," said Gurkie, "and if you come with us, we'll show you."

Cor opened his briefcase and took out a cardboard folder. "Perhaps you would like to see a picture of our King and Queen?"

He handed the photograph to Raymond. It wasn't one of the official palace portraits with the royal family in their robes. The Queen was sitting on a rock by the sea with one hand trailing in the water. Her long hair was loose, and she was smiling up at the King, who looked down at her, his face full of pride. The picture had been taken before the Prince was stolen and what came out of it most was—happiness.

"They look all right," said Raymond. "But they don't look royal. They're dressed like ordinary people. If I was royal, I'd wear a gold uniform and medals."

"Then you'd look pretty silly by the sea," said Odge, "because the salt spray would make the gold braid go all green and nasty, and your medals would clank and frighten away—"

"Now, Odge!" said Gurkie warningly.

"Could I look?" asked Ben—and Cor took the picture from Raymond and handed it to him.

Ben said nothing. He just stood looking at the photograph—looking and looking as if he could make himself part of it . . . as if he could vanish into the picture and stay there.

But now Raymond sat up very straight and pointed to the door. "Eeek!" he shouted. "There's a horrible thing there! An eye! It's disgusting; it's creepy. I want my mummy!"

The others turned their heads in dismay. They knew how sensitive the ogre was, and to call such a clean-living person "creepy" is about as hurtful as it is possible to be. And sure enough, a tear welled up in Hans' clear blue eye, trembled there . . . and fell. Then the eye vanished, and from the space where the giant sat, there came a deep, unhappy sigh.

But Odge now came to the rescue. She had promised to behave like the girls of St. Agnes who said: "Play Up and Play the Game" and she said: "Raymond, I've brought you a present, a really special one. I brought it all the way from the Island. Look!"

The word "present" cheered Raymond up at once, and he watched as she lifted her suitcase onto the bed and opened it.

"What is it?" Raymond asked.

But he didn't shudder this time; he looked quite pleased. And the person who wasn't pleased with what lay inside, cradled in layers of moss, would have been made of stone. A very small animal covered in soft, snow-white fur, with big paws lightly tipped with black. His eyes, as he woke from sleep, were huge and very dark, his blob of a nose was moist and whiskery and cool, and as he looked up at Raymond and yawned, you could see his strawberry-pink tongue and smell his clean milky breath.

"I've never seen one of them," said Raymond. "It's a funny-looking thing. What is it?"

Odge told him. "It's a mistmaker. We have hundreds of them on the Island; they get very tame. I got this one because his mother got muddled and rolled on him. She didn't mean to, she just got mixed up."

She lifted the little animal out and laid him on the satin quilt. The mistmaker's forehead was wrinkled like a bloodhound's; he had a small, soft moustache, and his pink, almost human-looking ears had big lobes like you find on the ears of poets or musicians.

"Why is it called a mistmaker?" asked Raymond.

"I'll show you," said Odge. "Can you sing?"

"Of course I can sing," said Raymond. "Everyone can sing."

"Well, then, do it. Sing something to it. Put your head quite close."

Raymond cleared his throat. "I can't remember any

words," he said. "I'll play it something on my radio." He turned the knob and the room was filled with the sound of cackling studio laughter.

"You try, Ben," ordered Odge. "You sing to it."

But Ben didn't sing. He whistled. None of them had heard whistling quite like that; it was like birdsong, but it wasn't just chirruping—it had a proper tune: a soaring tune that made them think of spring and young trees and life beginning everywhere. And as Ben whistled, the little animal drew closer . . . and closer still . . . he pressed his moist nose against Ben's hands; the wrinkles on his worried-looking forehead grew smoother . . .

"Aaah," sighed the mistmaker. "Aaah . . ."

Then it began. At first there was only a little mist; he was after all very young . . . and then there came more . . . and more . . . Even from this animal only a few weeks old there came enough cool, swirling mist to wreathe Raymond's bed in whiteness. The room became beautiful and mysterious; the piles of neglected toys disappeared, and the fussy furniture . . . and the Islanders drank in the well-remembered freshness of early morning and of grass still moist with dew.

Raymond's mouth dropped open. "It's weird. I've never seen that. It isn't natural."

"Why isn't it natural?" asked Odge crossly. "Skunks make stinks and slugs make slime and people make sweat, so why shouldn't a mistmaker make mist?"

Raymond was still staring at the little creature. No

one at school had anything like that. He'd be able to show it off to everyone. Paul had a tree frog and Derek had a grass snake, but this would beat them all.

"You'd be able to play with mistmakers all day long if you came to the Island," said Gurkie. "You will come, won't you?"

"Nope," said Raymond. "I'd miss my telly and my computer games and my Scalextric set. But I'll keep him."

He made a grab for the mistmaker, but the animal had given off so much mist that he was less pillow-shaped now, and nimbler. Jumping off the bed, he landed with a thud on his nose and began to explore the room.

They watched him as he ran his whiskery moustache along Raymond's toy boxes, rolled over on the rug, rubbed himself against a chest of drawers. Sometimes he disappeared into patches of mist, then reappeared with one ear turned inside out which is what happens to mistmakers who are busy.

The wizard cleared his throat. Now was the time to come out with the truth. Such a snobby boy would surely come to the Island if he knew he would live there as a prince.

"Perhaps we should tell you, Raymond, that you are really of noble—"

He was interrupted by another and even louder shriek from Raymond.

"Look! It's lifted its leg! It's made a puddle on the carpet! It's dirty!"

Odge looked at him with loathing. "This mistmaker is *six weeks old!* They can be house-trained perfectly well but not when they are infants. You made enough puddles when you were that age, and it's a *clean* puddle. It isn't the puddle of someone who guzzles shrimps and roast pork and greasy potatoes."

Ben had already been to the bathroom for a cloth and was mopping up. Mopping up after Raymond was something he had been doing ever since he could remember. Then he gathered up the mistmaker, who was trembling all over and trying to cover his ears with his paws. You cannot be as musical as these animals are without suffering terribly from the kind of stuck-pig noises that Raymond made.

"You keep him downstairs, Ben," ordered Raymond. "You can feed him and see he doesn't mess up my room. But remember, he's *mine!*"

CHAPTER 8

ODGE AND GURKIE spent the night curled up on the floor of the little summer house. It was a pretty place with a fretwork verandah and wooden steps, but no one used it now. Years ago the roof had begun to leak, and instead of mending it, the head keeper had put up a notice saying: PRIVATE. NO ADMITTANCE. Dark privet bushes and clumps of laurel hid it from passersby. Only the animals came to it now: sparrows to preen in the lopsided birdbath; squirrels to chatter on the roof.

Nearby, a patch of snoring grass showed where the ogre rested. Ben had smuggled the mistmaker into his cupboard of a room.

But Cornelius could not sleep. He longed to conjure up a fire to keep his old bones warm, but he thought it might be noticed, and after a while he took his stick and wandered off toward the lake. The Serpentine it was called because it was wiggly and shaped like a serpent, and he remembered it from when he had lived Up Here. Londoners were fond of it; people went boating there and caught tiddlers, and brave old gentlemen broke the ice with their toes in winter and swam in it, getting goose pimples but being healthy.

But it wasn't just old men with goose pimples or lovers canoodling or children sailing their boats that came here. There were . . . others. There had been mermaids in the lake when Cor was a little boy, each tree had had its spirit, banshees had wailed in the bushes. And on Midsummer's Eve they had gathered together and had a great party.

Midsummer's Eve was in two days' time. Did they still come, the boggarts and the brownies, the nymphs and the nixies, the sproggans and the witches and the trolls? And if so, was there an idea there? If Raymond saw real magic—saw the exciting things that happened on the Island, would that persuade him to come?

Cor's ancient forehead wrinkled up in thought. Then

he raised his stick in the air and said some poetry—and seconds later Ernie Hobbs, who had been sleeping on a mail bag on Platform Thirteen of King's Cross Station, woke up and said: "Ouch!" Looking about him, he saw that Mrs. Partridge, who'd been flat out on a luggage trolley, was sitting up and looking puzzled.

"I've got a tingle in my elbow," she said. "Real fierce it is."

At the same time, Miriam Hughes-Hughes, the ghost of the apologizing lady, rolled off the bench outside the Left-Luggage Office and lay blinking on the ground.

It was Ernie who realized what had happened.

"We're being summoned! We're being sent for!"

"It'll be the wizard," said Mrs. Partridge excitedly. "There isn't no one else can do tricks like that!"

Wasting no more time, they glided down the platform and made their way to the park. They found Cornelius sitting on a tree stump and staring into the water.

"Did you call us, Your Honor?" asked Ernie.

"I did," said Cor. He then told them what had happened earlier in Raymond's room: "We went to tell him who he was, but the noise he made was more than anyone could bear. We had to leave."

The ghosts looked troubled. "We should have warned you, maybe," said Ernie, "but we thought he might be better with you."

"Well, he wasn't." Cor rubbed his aching knees. "Hans wants to bop the Prince on the head and carry him through the gump in a sack, but I think we must have another go at persuading him to come willingly. So I want you to call up all the . . . unusual people who are left Up Here and ask them to put on a special show for Raymond. Wizards, will o' the wisps . . . everyone you can find. Ask them to do the best tricks they can, and we'll build a throne for Raymond and hail him as a prince."

"A sort of Raymond Trottle Magic Show?" said Mrs. Partridge eagerly.

Ernie, though, was looking worried. "There's always a bit of a do on Midsummer's Eve, that's true enough. But . . . well, Your Honor, I don't want to throw a damper, but magic isn't what it was up here. It's what you might call the Tinkerbell Factor."

"I don't follow you," said the wizard.

"Well, there's this fairy . . . she's in a book called *Peter Pan*. Tinkerbell, she's called. When people say they don't believe in her, she goes all woozy and feeble. It's like that up here with the wizards and the witches and all. People haven't believed in them so long they've lost heart a bit."

"We can only do our best," said Cornelius. "Now, tell me, what's the situation about . . . you know . . ." He spoke quietly, not knowing who might be listening in the depths of the lake. "*Him*, the monster? Is he still there?"

"Old Nuckel? They say so," said Ernie. "But no one's

seen him for donkey's years. Have you thought of calling him up?"

"I was wondering," said Cor. "I happen to have my book of spells with me. It would make a splendid ending to the show."

The ghosts looked respectful. Raising monsters from the deep is very difficult magic indeed.

"Well, if that doesn't fetch the little perisher, nothing will," said Mrs. Partridge—and blushed, because nasty or not, Raymond Trottle was, after all, a prince.

It was incredible how helpful everyone was. Witches who worked in school kitchens trying to make two pounds of mince go round a hundred children said they would come, and so did wizards who taught chemistry and stayed behind to make interesting explosions after the children had gone home. An animal trainer who trained birds for films and television, and was really an enchanter, promised to bring his flock of white doves so that the evening could begin with a flypast.

Melisande, the water-nymph-who-was-not-a-mermaid, swam through the outlet pipe at Fortlands and spoke to her uncle who was a merrow and worked the sewers, dredging up stuff which people had flushed down the loo by mistake or lost in the plughole of the bath, and he too said he would come and do a trick for Raymond.

"Really, people are so *kind*," said Gurkie as she ran

about jollying along the tree spirits who had agreed to do a special dance for Raymond on the night.

And she was right. After all, it wasn't as though they didn't know what Raymond was like—that kind of thing gets around—but everyone wanted the King and Queen to be happy. The Island mattered to them; it was their homeland even if they themselves hadn't been there, and there seemed to be no end to the trouble they were prepared to take.

The ghosts, during these two days, were everywhere; helping, persuading, taking messages. Even Miriam Hughes-Hughes stopped apologizing and found a Ladies' Group of Banshees—those pale, ghastly women who wail and screech when something awful is going to happen, and they agreed to come and sing sad songs for the Prince. A troll called Henry Prendergast who lived in the basement of the Bank of England said he thought he could manage some shape-shifting, and Hans tried to forget the hurt that Raymond had done him by calling him creepy, and practiced weight lifting till his muscles threatened to crack. As for Odge Gribble, she went off by herself in the Underground to visit an aunt of her mother's. The aunt was an Old Woman of Gloominess and absolutely marvelous at turning people bald, and she promised to bring some friends along from her sewing circle and amuse Raymond by making donkey's tails come out of people's foreheads and that kind of thing.

But it was Cor who worked himself hardest. Hour after hour, he sat by the lake with his black book practicing his monster-raising spell. He didn't eat, he scarcely slept, but he wouldn't stop. There was something special about the Monster of the Serpentine, only he couldn't remember what it was. There was a lot he couldn't remember these days, but he wasn't going to give up. There was nothing Cor wouldn't have done to bring back the Prince—unbopped and unsacked—to the parents who wanted him so much.

The only thing that still worried the rescuers was how to make Raymond Trottle come to the park. Of course it would be easy to call him by magic as Cor had called the ghosts, but they had promised faithfully not to use any magic directly on the Prince.

It was Ben who thought of what to do. "There's a boy at Raymond's school called Paul who's the son of a duke. Raymond would do anything to keep up with him. If we pretend that Paul's giving a secret party by the lake, I'm sure Raymond will come." Then his face became troubled. "Of course, it's cheating, I suppose. It's a lie."

But Cor was firm about this. "Bringing Raymond back to the Island is like a military campaign. Like a war. In a war, a soldier might have to tell a lie, but he'd still be serving his country."

Ben's plan worked. Melisande knew a siren who worked in Fortlands showing off the dresses, and she "borrowed" a posh invitation card, and Ben pretended that Paul had bribed him to deliver it.

And just before twelve o'clock on Midsummer's Eve, Raymond Trottle, in his jazziest clothes, arrived at the edge of the lake—and found a great throne which the trolls had built for him and a host of people who raised their arms and hailed him as a prince.

"A prince?" said Raymond. "Me?"

"Yes, Your Highness," said the Wizard, and told Raymond the story of his birth.

Raymond listened and, as he did so, a smug, self-satisfied smile spread across his face.

"I always knew I was special," he said. "I knew it"— and he climbed onto his throne.

CHAPTER 9

THERE HAD BEEN NOTHING like it for a hundred years.

The witches had made a circle of protection round the lake which no one could cross; everything inside it was invisible to any stray wanderers. Light came from the flaring torches of the wizards and from the glow-worms which Gurkie had coaxed into the trees—hundreds of them, glimmering and winking like stars. And there were real stars too: the night was clear, the moon shone down calmly on the revels.

"Doesn't it look *beautiful!*" whispered Ben. He hadn't expected to be allowed to watch, but Odge had told him not to be silly.

"Of course you're watching. We'll hide in the shrubbery with the mistmaker; no one will mind you being there."

And they didn't. It was strange how well Ben fit in. He spoke to the ghosts as easily as the Islanders, and even Odge's aunt, the Old Woman of Gloominess, had patted him on the head without turning him the least bit bald.

The Raymond Trottle Magic Show began with a fly-past of Important Birds.

First a skein of geese flew in perfect formation across the moon, dipping their wings in salute as they passed over the Prince. Next the enchanter who had brought them called up a cloud of coal-black ravens who swooped and circled over Raymond's head—and then he stretched out an arm, and from a tree full of nightingales came music so glorious that Ben and Odge vanished for a moment as the mistmaker folded his paws over his chest and sighed.

Last came three dozen snow-white doves, which did the most amazing aerial acrobatics and turned to green, to orange, to pink, as the wizards changed the light on their flares. Then one bird left the flock, pulled a sprig of greenery from a laurel bush, flew with it in his beak to Raymond's throne—and laid it in his lap. It was just like this that the dove in the ark had come to Noah and shown him that his troubles were over, and all the watchers were very much moved.

And what did Raymond Trottle say? He said: "I've seen that on the telly."

But now the waters of the lake began to shimmer and shine. Then slowly, very slowly—three spouts of water rose from the center, and on the top of each spout sat a beautiful girl who began to sing and comb her hair.

"Of course, there are far more mermaids than this on the Island, Your Royal Highness," said Cor who was standing beside the Prince.

Not only more but of better quality, thought the wizard, who was beginning to realize what Ernie had meant when he said magic wasn't what it was. One of the mermaids came from the Pimlico Swimming Baths, and the chlorine in the water hadn't done much for her voice; the second had cut her hair into spikes after a pop group came to give an open-air concert by the lake where she lived, so though she could sing, she couldn't really comb. As for the third lady, she was Melisande from the fountain at Fortlands, and as she sang and combed, she kept pointing to her feet. No one knew why she minded so much about being taken for a mermaid, but she did.

Everyone clapped when it was over, though Raymond didn't seem very excited, and then Melisande's uncle, whom they called the Plodger, came forward. He was wearing his wellies and the woolly hat he wore to work in the sewers, but he bowed very respectfully to the Prince and said: "I shall search for the treasure of the lake."

He then walked to the water's edge . . . plodged into the shallows, kept on till the water came to his waist, his chin, his woolly hat . . . and disappeared!

No one was worried about this because merrows can breathe under water, but they were very interested.

The Plodger was gone a long time, and when he came back he was holding a large fish by the tail. The fish was flopping and wriggling, and the Plodger, though covered in slime and waterweed, looked pleased.

The wizards and witches whispered among themselves because they knew what was coming, and in the bushes Odge said: "This is going to be good; he's found a Special Carp!"

The Plodger came right up to Raymond; he still held the fish upside down, and the fish went on wriggling and thrashing its tail. Then suddenly it gave a big hiccup and out of its mouth there came—a beautiful ring! Swallowing rings is something certain fish do—one can read about it in the fairy tales—but finding a fish who has done it when you're wandering about on the bottom of a gray and murky lake is really difficult, and from the watchers there came another burst of clapping.

The Plodger then thanked the fish and threw him back into the lake, and Raymond looked at the ring.

"It isn't gold," he said. "It isn't a proper one. You couldn't get money for it in a shop."

Cor shook his head, and the merrow went off looking hurt. It was true that the ring had come out of a Christmas cracker, but what had that to do with anything? The special fish had trusted him; he had given up the ring that had been in his stomach for ten years—the ring that was part of his life as a fish—and all the Prince wanted to know was if he could sell it in a shop.

After that came the chorus of banshees. They'd had a busy week wailing in a football stadium because they knew that England was going to lose the European Championship, but they'd taken a lot of trouble, putting on their white shrouds and looking properly sinister and sad. And the songs were sinister and sad too—songs about darkness and dread and doom and decay.

When the banshees had finished, Raymond wanted to know if they were going to be sawn in half.

"There's always people sawn in half when there's magic on the telly," he said.

Needless to say, the banshees didn't stay around after that, and Hans came on to do some weight lifting.

The ogre had washed off his fernseed and looked truly splendid in his leather shorts and his embroidered braces and the kneesocks with the tassel on the side.

First he picked up a park bench, twirled it over his head, and put it down. Then he plucked out a concrete drinking fountain, balanced it on his nose—and put it back. And then he turned to the statue of Alderman Sir Harold Henfitter, which had been put up a month before. The alderman was cast in bronze and rested on a slab of marble, and even Hans had to pull and tug several times before he could free him from the ground.

But he did it. Then he counted to one . . . to two . . . to three . . . and threw the ten-ton alderman into the air!

Everyone waited. They waited and waited, but nothing happened. Nothing ever *would* happen—and that was the point, of course. The alderman had been thrown with such force that he would never come down again. Even now, Sir Harold Henfitter is going round and round somewhere in space and will go on doing so until the end of time.

It is not easy to believe what Raymond did after this amazing trick. He pointed with his fat finger at the giant's midriff. He giggled. And then he said: "A button's come off his braces!"

No one could believe their ears. Making personal remarks is rude at any time, but at a moment like this! It was true there had been a slight twang as the button went missing—but it was only on one side, and the ogre's leather shorts had hardly slipped at all.

Still, the show had to go on. The wizards did some tricks with the weather, making it rain on one side of the lake and snow on the other, and calling up a rumble of thunder with lightning following *afterward*—and then it was time for refreshments.

Gurkie was in charge of these, and instead of arranging for an ice-cream lady to come with her tray, she had laid on something very special. She ran to the big elm growing by the water and called to the glowworms to come so that the tree was lit as brightly as on a stage. Then she tapped the bark and spoke softly to the tree—and lo, every one of its branches began to bear fruit. There were peaches like golden moons; apples whose red skins glistened; pears as big as two fists put together.

"We beg Your Highness to refresh himself," said Gurkie.

Raymond got out of his throne and waddled over to the tree. Then he said: "I don't like fruit; it's got pips in it. I want a gobstopper."

Everyone lost heart a little after that. Cor didn't know what a gobstopper was; they hadn't had them when he lived Up Here, and even when the troll called Henry Prendergast drew one for him, he didn't feel like conjuring one up. There is very little magic done with gobstoppers anywhere in the world—and in the end a kind witch who worked as a school cook got on her bicycle and found an all-night garage that sold sweets and brought one for Raymond, who sucked it, moving it from cheek to bulging cheek all through the second part of the show.

This began with Odge's aunt and her sewing circle. There were seven of these Old Women of Gloominess, and though all of them were fierce and hairy, Odge's aunt was definitely the fiercest and the hairiest. The ladies struck each other with baldness; they made newts come out of each other's nostrils; they gave each other chicken pox . . . And in the bushes, Odge sighed.

"Do you think I'll ever be like that?" she asked.

"Of course you will," said Ben stoutly. "You've just got to get a little older."

Gurkie's tree spirits came next. To get a spirit to leave his tree is not easy, but Gurkie had such a way with her that one by one they all stepped out: the old, gnarled spirit of the oak; the tall, gray slightly snooty spirit of the ash; the wavery spirit of the willow . . . The dance they did was as ancient as Stonehenge—only three humans had been allowed to watch it in a thousand years—and Raymond Trottle sat there, moving his gobstopper from side to side—and yawned.

And now came Cor's big moment. He walked to the edge of the lake, and the wizards and the witches, the banshees and the trolls all held their breath.

The wizard closed his eyes. He waved his wand and spoke the monster-raising spell . . . and nothing happened. Once more he raised his wand, once more he said the spell . . .

Still nothing . . . Cor's shoulders sagged. He was too old. His power was gone. For the third and last time, the wizard drew on his strength and spoke the magic words. He had turned away, the watchers were shaking their heads—and then there appeared on the waters of the lake a kind of . . . shudder. The shudder was followed by a ripple . . . then a whole ring of ripples, and from the center of the ring there came . . . slowly, very slowly . . . a head.

It was a large head, and human—but unusual. The head was followed by a neck, and the neck was followed by shoulders and a chest, but what came after that was not a man's body, it was the body of a horse.

And everybody remembered what it was that was different about a nuckelavee.

It wasn't that it had a man's head and a horse's body. Animals that are partly people, and people that are partly animals, are two a penny where there is magic. No, what was unusual about the nuckelavee was that he didn't have any skin.

As the monster looked about him, wondering who had called him from the deep, they could see the blood rushing about inside his arteries and his windpipe taking in air. They could see the curving shape of his stomach as it churned the nuckel's food; even the creature's

heart, patiently pumping and pumping, was as clear as if they were seeing it through glass.

No one could take their eyes off him; they were entranced! To be able to see a living body in this way—to be allowed to study the marvelous working of the muscles and nerves and glands—was an honor they could hardly believe, and a young cousin of the troll called Henry Prendergast decided then and there to become a doctor.

Of course, they should have known what was to come. They should have known that Raymond Trottle would spoil this amazing and wonderful moment—a moment so special that none of them forgot it as long as they lived. They should have known that this boy with his bulging cheeks and piggy eyes would hurt and insult this awe-inspiring creature, and he did.

"Eeek!" said Raymond. "Ugh! It's disgusting; it's creepy. I don't like it!"

Well, that was that, of course. The nuckel sank—and from the onlookers there came a great groan, for they knew it would be a hundred years before the monster showed himself again and they could once more study this miracle of nature.

After that, there was nothing to do except get to the end. The troll called Henry Prendergast shape-shifted himself into a bank manager and a policeman, and the witches did a few interesting things with toads; and then everybody raised their torches and hailed Raymond as Prince of the Island—and it was done.

"Well, Your Highness," said Cor, but he spoke without any hope. "Now do you see what powerful forces you would rule over if you came to the Island? Will you come with us?"

Raymond shrugged. "Well, I dunno. I don't think I fancy it." And then, "You didn't make gold, did you? I thought all wizards could make gold. Can you make it?"

"Certainly we can make it, Your Highness. Any wizard worth his salt can make gold, but it isn't very interesting to watch."

"I don't believe you. I don't believe you can do it."

Cor turned and clapped his hands, and three wizards came to him at once.

"His Highness wishes us to make gold," he said wearily. "Find me some base metal—a bit of guttering from a drainpipe . . . an old bicycle wheel . . . anything."

The wizards vanished and came back with a load of junk metal which they laid on the ground close to Raymond. "Shall we do it, sir?" they asked because Cor was looking desperately tired. But the old wizard shook his head. "Just light the fire," he said.

When it was lit, he bent over it. He didn't even bother to get out his wand or to consult his book of spells. Making gold is something wizards learn to do in the nursery.

Raymond, who had hardly seemed interested when the mermaids sang from a water spout, or the nuckel rose from the deep, couldn't take his eyes from what Cornelius was doing.

The old bicycle wheel, the tin cans glowed . . . flared . . . the flames turned green, turned purple, turned red . . . Cor muttered. Then there was a small thud, and the center of the fire was filled with a mass of molten metal which glinted and glittered in the light of the flares.

"Is that it? Is that really gold?" asked Raymond.

"Yes, Your Highness," said Cor. He blew on the metal, cooled it, and handed it to Raymond.

"And if I come to the Island, can you make more of it? As much as I want?"

The wizard nodded. "Yes, Your Highness." He could have said that no one used gold on the Island—that they either swapped things or gave them away, but he didn't.

"Then I'll come," said Raymond Trottle.

CHAPTER 10

"HURRY UP, BOY," said Mr. Fulton, giving Ben a push. "You've got the potatoes to bring in from the cellar still, and there's the brass strip to polish and the milk bottles to swill."

The butler was a tall, grim man who ruled with a rod of iron and never smiled.

"He's in a dream this morning," said Mrs. Flint. "I've had to tell him three times to wipe down the stove." Cooks are often fat and cheerful, but she was thin and cross and seemed to hate the food she prepared.

Only the housemaid, Rosita, gave Ben a kind glance. The boy looked thoroughly washed out, as though he hadn't slept.

Rosita was right. Ben had scarcely closed his eyes after he crept in from the park the night before. He was glad, of course, that Raymond had agreed to go with the rescuers; he *had* to be glad. Cor and Gurkie had been so relieved that their job was done, but as he dragged the heavy sack of potatoes up the cellar steps he felt as wretched as he had ever felt in his life.

In half an hour, Raymond would leave the house and never come back. On Monday morning, he went to the house of a Mrs. Frankenheimer, who gave him exercises to cure his flat feet and knock-knees. Mrs. Frankenheimer was very easy-going and wouldn't notice if he didn't turn up, and he was going to meet the rescuers at the corner of her street instead of going to school. Just about the time that Ben would be sitting in his classroom and opening his arithmetic book, Raymond would be stepping out onto the sands of the Secret Cove.

As he went to fetch his schoolbag, Ben's foot bumped against the cat tray under his bed. He had already almost house-trained the mistmaker even in the three days he had hidden him in his room. The animal was incredibly intelligent, and the realization that he would never see him again suddenly seemed more than he could bear.

Ben had accepted his life—the early-morning chores, the drudgery again when he came home at night, but that was before he had found people who really understood him and were his friends.

And he had quarreled with Odge.

"You're coming with us, of course," Odge had said. "You're coming to the Island."

And he'd said: "I can't, Odge."

The hag had been furious. "Of course you can. If you're worried about Raymond being such a pain, you needn't be, because if he isn't any better by the time he's grown up, I'll start a revolution and have his head chopped off; you can rely on that!"

"It isn't Raymond, Odge. I don't care about him. It's my grandmother. She took me in because I had nobody, and I can't leave her now she's ill. You must see that."

But Odge hadn't seen it. She'd stamped her feet and called him names, and even when Cor had agreed with Ben and said you had to stand by people who had helped you, she went off in a huff.

Well, it didn't matter now. He'd never see any of them again.

Ben usually liked school, but this morning the shabby old building with the high windows made him feel as though he was in a trap. And to make things worse, his usual teacher was ill and the student who took over was obviously terrified of kids. It would be uproar all morning, thought Ben—and he was right.

At break he didn't join his friends but went off on his own to a corner of the play-yard. You had to take one day at a time when things were bad, Nanny had said. "You can always take just one more step, Ben," she told him, but today it seemed as though the steps would lead down the grayest, dreariest road he could imagine.

There was a grating in the asphalt, covering a drain, and he crouched down beside it, wondering if the Plodger was somewhere nearby in his wellies . . . and that made him think of Melisande and the nuckel with his interesting face . . . Well, that was over, and forever. He'd never see magic again, not an ordinary boy like him.

For a moment, he wondered whether to change his mind. The gump was still open. The rescuers had trusted him; they had told him where it was. They hadn't told Raymond, but they'd told him. He closed his eyes and saw the three-masted sailing ship parting the waves . . . saw the green hump of the Island with its golden sands, and the sun shining on the roofs of the palace . . .

Then the picture vanished and there was another picture in its stead. An old woman lying in a high hospital bed, shrunken, ill, watching for him as he came down the ward.

The teacher blew her whistle. The children began to stream back into the building, but Ben still lingered.

Then he looked up. A small girl was coming across the road toward him. She wore an old-fashioned blazer;

her thick black hair was yanked into two pigtails, and she was scowling.

Ben scrambled to his feet. He tried to be sensible—he really tried—but a lump had come into his throat, and he stretched his hand through the bars like a prisoner.

"Oh, Odge," he said. "I am so *terribly* pleased to see you!"

Raymond had not kept his promise. He had not turned up at the corner of Mrs. Frankenheimer's street as he said he would. They had waited and waited, but he had not come.

"We should have known that the pig boy would double-cross us," said Odge. "The others are in an awful state. Gurkie keeps saying if she'd been a fuath, it wouldn't have happened, which is perfectly ridiculous."

"What's a fuath?"

"Oh, some really vile swamp fairy with all sorts of nasty habits. And the giant keeps talking about bopping and sacking and how it was all his fault because he didn't—and the wizard looks about two hundred years old. He really loves the King and Queen."

"But where is Raymond, then?"

"Well, that's it; nobody knows. He's not in the house—the ghosts have haunted all over. Mrs. Trottle's gone as well—Ernie thinks that Raymond must have blabbed, and she's done a bunk with him. And it's serious, Ben. There are only five more days till the Closing. He's got to be found."

Ben drew himself up to his full height, and the hag thought how fearless he looked suddenly, how strong. "Don't worry, Odge. We'll find him; I absolutely know we will."

Ernie was right. Raymond had blabbed. When his mother came to wake him and told him to hurry or he'd be late for Mrs. Frankenheimer, Raymond yawned and said: "I don't have to go to Mrs. Frankenheimer again. Not ever."

Mrs. Trottle sat down on the edge of his bed, sending waves of Maneater over the coverlet, and put her pudgy hand on Raymond's forehead.

"Now, don't be difficult, sweetikins. You know Mrs. Frankenheimer is going to make your feet all beautiful—and you really can't miss school again. The headmaster was quite cross last week. Just think, if you were expelled and had to go to a common school with ordinary children."

Raymond stretched his arms behind his head and smirked. "I don't have to go to school again either. I'm never going to school anymore. I'm a prince."

"Well, of course, you're a prince to your Mummy, dear," said Mrs. Trottle, giving him a lipsticky kiss. "But—"

"Not that kind of prince; I'm really one. I'm going to go away and rule over hundreds of people on a secret island."

"Yes, dear," said Mrs. Trottle. "That's a very nice dream you've had, but now please get dressed."

"It's not a dream," said Raymond crossly. "They told me. The old man in the park. And the lady with the beetroot in her hat. I'm going to be a famous ruler and I don't have to do anything I don't want to ever again."

Mrs. Trottle went on tutting and taking no notice. Then as she picked up Raymond's jacket, which he had thrown on the floor, she noticed grass stains on it, and in his buttonhole, a spray of ivy. Her eyes narrowed.

"Raymond! What is the meaning of this? You've been out after I put you to bed!"

Raymond shrugged. "You can't tell me what to do

now," he said. "And Dad can't either because I'm a prince, and they're coming to show me the secret way back this morning."

Mrs. Trottle now became very alarmed. She hurried into Mr. Trottle's dressing room and said: "Landon, I think Raymond's in danger. People have been giving him drugs—dreadful drugs—to make him believe all sorts of things. It's a plot to kidnap him and hold us up to ransom, I'm sure of it."

"Nonsense," said Mr. Trottle, stepping into his trousers. "Who would want to kidnap Raymond?"

This was not a fatherly thing to say, but Mr. Trottle's mind was on the bank.

"Anyone who knows we're rich. I'm serious. They've persuaded him that he's a prince so as to lure him away."

"Well, he isn't, is he?" said Mr. Trottle.

"Landon, will you please listen to me. I'm very worried."

"Then why don't you contact the police?"

"Certainly not!" There were all sorts of reasons why Mrs. Trottle didn't want the police snooping around in Trottle Towers. Then suddenly: "I'm going to take Raymond away. I'm going into hiding. Now. This instant. You can stay here and change the locks and look out for anything sinister."

She wouldn't wait a minute longer. Mrs. Trottle was a stupid woman, but when it came to protecting her son, she could move like greased lightning. Taking no notice as Raymond sniveled and whined and said he was a prince, he really was, she packed a suitcase. Half an hour later, she and Raymond drove away in a taxi, and no one who worked in Trottle Towers knew where they had gone.

The search for Raymond went on all that day and well into the next.

Everyone helped. The Ghosts of the Gump got in touch with the ghosts in all the other railway stations and soon there wasn't a train which drew out of London without a spectre gliding down the carriages looking for a fat boy with a wobble in his walk and his even wobblier mother.

The mermaids and the water nymphs checked out the riverboats in case the Trottles meant to escape by sea. The enchanter's special pigeons flew the length and breadth of the land delivering notes to road workers and garage men who might have seen the Trottles' car —and the train spotter called Brian (the one who got between the buffers and the 9:15 from Peterborough) sat all day by the computer at Heathrow, checking the passenger lists, though electricity is about the worst thing that can happen to a spectre's ectoplasm.

Ben had not returned to school after Odge came for him. He'd asked the headmaster for the afternoon off, and because he'd looked so peaky when he first came, the head had agreed.

"Don't come back till you're properly well," he had said—and that was something he didn't say to a lot of children.

But though Ben searched Trottle Towers for clues and tried to get what he could out of the servants, he too drew a blank. Mr. Trottle had returned at lunchtime with a locksmith and told everyone that his wife and son would be away for a long time. And that was all that anybody could discover.

Ben's first thought was that Mrs. Trottle had taken Raymond to her home in Scotland, but one of the banshees, who came from Glasgow, telephoned the station master at Achnasheen, and he swore there was no sign of the Trottles.

"You'd notice them soon enough," he'd said, "with their posh kilts they've got no right to wear, and their bossy ways."

The rescuers had returned to the summer house which now became the headquarters of the search. They had bought some blankets, and a primus and kettle, and some folding chairs—and Hans had painted up the notice saying PRIVATE: NO ADMITTANCE which blocked the path. Fortunately the head keeper was on holiday so nobody disturbed them, but just to make sure, Gurkie had spoken to the bushes that grew so thick and tangled that anybody passing by could see nothing. She had planted out the beetroot from her hat because people did seem to stare rather, and to stop it being lonely she had made a vegetable patch from which huge leeks and lettuces erupted. And a pink begonia on the other side of the lake had made such a fuss because it wanted to be near her that she'd moved it so as to grow beside the wooden steps.

But even though she could feed everyone and make them comfortable, Gurkie still worried dreadfully and thought she should have been a fuath.

"No, you shouldn't, Gurkie," said Ben firmly. "You being a fuath, whatever that is, is a perfectly horrible idea and it wouldn't have helped at all."

Nor would he let the giant moan on because he hadn't bopped and sacked the Prince.

"Raymond'll be found, I'm absolutely sure of it," said Ben.

Ben was changing, thought Odge; he was becoming someone to rely on. She watched as he put down a bowl of milk for the mistmaker. The animal had taken to lurching after Ben wherever he went and making offended noises when he wasn't immediately scratched on the stomach or picked up and spoken to. There was going to be a fuss from the mistmaker when they had to go back and part from Ben, thought Odge, and she wondered whether she should kill Ben's grandmother.

Killing people was the sort of thing hags were meant to do, but it had not been allowed on the Island, and without any practice it was probably a bad idea.

But what mattered now was finding Raymond. All that afternoon, all the evening and well into the night, they searched and searched—the wizards and the witches, the ghosts and the banshees and the trolls . . . and as soon as day broke they began again—but it was beginning to look as though Raymond and his mother had vanished from the face of the earth.

CHAPTER 11

THE QUEEN LEANT OUT of her bedroom window. She leant out so far that she would have fallen but for a dwarf whom the King had put in charge of holding her feet. He had been holding her feet for days now because she did nothing except look out to sea and watch for the three-masted ship.

"Oh, where is it?" she said for the hundredth time. "Why doesn't it come?"

There were men all over the Island peering through

telescopes, the dolphins searched the seas, and the talking birds—the mynahs and the parrots—were never out of the air. The instant the ship was sighted, rockets would flare up, but the Queen went on watching, her long hair streaming over the sill, as though by doing so she could will her son to come to her.

But the dwarf now sighed—he was growing tired—and the Queen dragged herself away and went into the next room which she had prepared for the Prince. His old, white-curtained cradle still stood in the corner, but the palace carpenters had made him a beautiful bed of cedar wood and a carved desk and a bookcase because she knew without being told that the Prince would love to read. She hadn't made the room fussy, but the carpet, with its pattern of mythical beasts and flowers, had taken seven years to make—and there was a wide window seat so that he could sit and look out over the waters of the bay.

But would he ever sit there? Would she ever come in and see his bright head turn toward her?

The King, coming into the room, found her in tears again.

"Come, my dear," he said, putting his arms round her, "there are five days still for the rescuers to bring him back."

But the Queen wouldn't be comforted. "Let me go to the Secret Cove, at least," she begged. "Let me wait there for him."

The King shook his head. "What can you do there, my love? You would only fret and worry, and your people need you."

"I would be closer to him. I would be near."

The King said nothing. He was afraid of letting his wife go near the mouth of the gump. If she lost her head and went through it, he could lose her as he had lost his son.

"Try to have patience," he begged her. "Try to be brave."

The King and Queen were not the only people on the Island to worry and grow afraid. The schoolchildren had been given a holiday during the nine days of the opening, but they had decorated the school with flowers and hung up banners saying WELCOME TO THE PRINCE. Now the flowers were wilting, the banners hung limp after a shower of rain. The bakers who had baked huge, three-tiered cakes for the welcoming banquet began to prod them with skewers, wondering if they were going stale and they should start again. The housewives who had ironed their best dresses shook them out and ironed them all over again because they'd grown crumpled.

As for the nurses in the cave, they had ordered a crate of green bananas before the Opening so that the second the ship was sighted they could rip it open and help themselves to the firm, just-ripened fruit—but when no news came, they nailed it up again, and now they were back to wailing and eating burnt toast.

Then that night the square began to fill up with some very strange people.

There had been rumors, quite early on, of discontent in the north of the island. Not just the kind of grumbling you always get from people who have not been chosen for a job they are sure they could do. Not just Odge's sisters complaining because their baby sister had been chosen and not them. Not just grumpy giants saying, what do you expect, sending a milksop who yodels to bring back the Prince? No . . . this was more serious discontent, and from creatures that were to be reckoned with.

And that evening, the evening of the fourth day of the Opening, they came, these discontented people of the north. They came in droves, filling the grassy square in front of the palace, and turned their faces up to the windows, and waited . . .

Strange faces they were too: the blue-black faces of the neckies with their lopsided feet . . . the slavering-tongued sky yelpers, those airborne hellhounds with their saucer eyes and fiery tongues, and the squint-eyed faces of the harridans.

There were hags in the square who made Odge's sisters look like tinsel fairies; there was a bagworm as long as a railway carriage; there was even a brollachan—one of those shapeless blobs who crawl over the ground like cold jellies and can envelop anyone who gets in the way.

And there were the harpies! They had elbowed their way to the front, these monstrous women with the wings and claws of birds—and even the fiercest creatures who waited with them gave them a wide berth.

"Tell them to choose a spokesperson, and we will hear what they have to say," said the King.

But he knew why they had come and what they had to say, for these creatures of the North were as much his subjects as any ordinary schoolchild or tender-hearted fey. Not only that, they were useful. They were the police people. There was no prison on the Island—there was no need for one. No burglar would burgle twice if it meant a hellhound flying in through his window and taking pieces out of his behind. Any drunken youth going on the rampage soon sobered up after a squint-eyed harridan landed on his chest and squeezed his stomach so as to give him awful dreams—and you only had to say the word "harpy" to the most evil-minded crook and he went straight then and there.

And it was a harpy—the chief harpy—who pushed the others aside and came in to stand before the King.

She called herself Mrs. Smith, but she wasn't married and it would have been hard to think of anyone who would have wanted to sit up in bed beside her drinking tea. The harpy's face was that of a bossy lady politician, the kind that comes on the telly to tell you not to eat the things you like and to do something different with your money. Her brassy permed hair was strained back from her forehead and combed into tight curls, her beady eyes were set on either side of a nose you could have cut cheese with, and her mouth was puckered like a badly sewn buttonhole. A string of pearls was wound round her neck; a handbag dangled from her arm, and she wore a crimplene stretch top tucked into dark green bloomers with a frill round the bottom.

But from under the bloomers there came the long, scaly legs and frightful talons of a bird of prey, and growing out of her back, piercing the crimplene, was a pair of black wings which gave out a strange, rank smell.

"I have come about the Prince," said Mrs. Smith in a high, piercing voice. "I am disgusted by the way this rescue has been handled. Appalled. Shocked. All of us are."

Harpies have been around for hundreds of years. In the old days they were called the Snatchers because they snatched people's food away so that they starved to death, or fouled it to make it uneatable. And it wasn't just food they snatched in their dreadful claws; harpies were used as punishers, carrying people away to dreadful tortures in the underworld.

Mrs. Smith patted her hair and opened her handbag.

"No!" said the King and put up his hand. The handbags of harpies are too horrible to describe. Inside is their makeup—face powder, lipstick, scent . . . But what makeup! Their powder smells of the insides of slaugh-

tered animals, and one drop of their perfume can send a whole army reeling backward. "Not in the palace," he went on sternly.

Even Mrs. Smith obeyed the King. She shut her bag but once again began to complain.

"Obviously that feeble fey and wonky wizard have failed; one could hardly expect anything else. And frankly my patience is exhausted. Everyone's patience is exhausted. I insist that I am sent with my helpers to bring back the Prince."

"What makes you so sure that you can find him?" asked the King.

The harpy twiddled her pearls. "I have my methods," she said. "And I promise he won't escape us." She lifted one leg, opened her talons, covered in their sick-making black nail varnish, and closed them again—and the Queen buried her face in her hands. "As you see, my assistants are ready and waiting." She waved her arm in the direction of the window, and sure enough there were four more loathsome harpies, like vultures with handbags, standing in the light of the lamp. "I'll take a few of the dogs as well, and you'll see, the boy will be back in no time."

By "dogs" she meant the dreaded sky yelpers with their fiery breath and slavering jaws.

The Queen had turned white and fallen back in her chair. She thought of Gurkie with her gentle, loving ways . . . of Odge showing them the baby mistmaker she meant to give to the Prince . . . and old Cor, so proud to do this last service for the court. Why had they failed her? And how could she bear it if her son was snatched by bossy and evil-smelling women?

Yet how long could they still delay?

The King now spoke.

"We will wait for one more day," he said. "If the Prince has not been returned by midnight tomorrow, I will send for you all and choose new rescuers to find him. Till then everyone must return to their homes so that the Queen can sleep."

But when the Northerners had flown and slithered and hopped away, the King and Queen did anything but sleep. All night long, they stared at the darkness and thought with grief and longing and despair of their lost son.

CHAPTER 12

MRS. TROTTLE WAS IN the bath. It was an enormous bath shaped like a seashell. All round the edge of the tub were little cut-glass dishes to hold different kinds of soap and a gold-plated rack stretched across the water so that she could rest her box of chocolates on it, and her body lotions, and the sloppy love story she was reading. On the shelf above her head was a jar of pink bath crystals which smelled of roses, and a jar of green crystals which smelled of fern, and a jar of yellow crystals which smelled of lemon verbena, but the crystals she had put into the water were purple and smelled of violets. Mrs. Trottle's face was covered in a gunge of squashed strawberries which was supposed to make her look young again; three heated bath towels waited on the rail.

"Ta-ra-ra *boom*-de-ray!" sang Mrs. Trottle, lathering her round, pink stomach.

She felt very pleased with herself for she had foiled the kidnappers who were after her darling Raymond. She had outwitted the gang; they would never find her babykins now. They would expect her to go to Scotland or to France, but she had been too clever for them. The hiding place she had found was as safe as houses—and so comfortable!

Mrs. Trottle chose another chocolate and added more hot water with her magenta-painted toe. Next door she could hear the rattle of dice as Raymond played ludo with one of his bodyguards. She'd told Bruce that he had to let Raymond win, and he seemed to be doing what he was told. The poor little fellow always cried when he lost at ludo, and she was paying the guards enough.

Reaching for the long-handled brush, she began to scrub her back. Landon was staying at home to find out what he could about the kidnappers. They would probably go on watching the house, and once she knew who they were, she could hire some thugs to get rid of them.

That was the nice thing about being rich; there was nothing you couldn't do.

And that reminded her of Ben. She'd rung the hospital, and though they never told you what you wanted to know, it didn't look as though Nanny Brown was ever coming out again. The second the old woman was out of the way, she'd move against Ben. Thinking of Ramsden Hall up in the Midlands made her smile. They took only difficult children; children that needed breaking in. There'd be no nonsense there about Ben going on too long with his schooling. The second he was old enough, he'd be sent to work in a factory or a mine.

How she hated the boy! Why could he read years before Raymond? Why was he good at sport when her babykin found it so hard? And the way Ben had looked at her, when he was little, out of those big eyes. Well, she'd found a place where they'd put a stop to all that!

As for Raymond, she'd frightened him so thoroughly that there was no question of him wandering off again. He knew now that all the things he thought he'd seen in the park, and earlier in his bedroom, were due to the drugs he had been given.

"There's nothing people like that won't do to you if they get you in their clutches," she'd said to him. "Cut off your ear . . . chain you to the floor . . ."

She'd hated alarming her pussykin, but Raymond would obey her now.

What a splendid place this was, thought Mrs. Trottle,

dribbling soapy water over her thighs. Everything was provided. And yet . . . perhaps the violet bath crystals weren't quite strong enough? Perhaps she should add something of her own; something she had brought from home? Sitting up, she reached for the bottle of Man-eater on the bathroom stool. The man who mixed it for her had promised no one else had a scent like that.

"You're the only lady in the world, dear Mrs. Trottle, who smells like this," he'd said to her.

Upending the bottle, she poured the perfume generously into the water. Yes, that was it! Now she felt like her true and proper self.

She leant back and reached for her book. The hero was just raining kisses on the heroine's crimson lips. Mr. Trottle never rained kisses on her lips; he never rained anything.

For another quarter of an hour, Mrs. Trottle lay happily soaking and reading.

Then she pulled out the plug.

The Plodger liked his job. He didn't mind the smell of the sewage; it was a natural smell, nothing fancy about it, but it belonged. He liked the long dark tunnels, and the quiet, and the clever way the watercourses joined each other and branched out. He could tell exactly where he was—under which street or square or park— just from the way the pipes ran. It was a good feeling knowing he could walk along twenty feet under

Piccadilly Circus and not be bothered by the traffic and the hooting and the silly people trying to cross the road.

It wasn't a bad living either. It was amazing what people lost down the loo or the plughole of a bath, especially on a Saturday night. Not alligators—the stories about alligators in the sewers were mostly rubbish—but earrings or cigarette lighters or spectacles. His father had been in the same line of business, and his grandfather before him: flushers they were called, the people who made a living from the drains. Of course, having some fish blood helped—that's what merrows were, people who'd married things that lived in water. Not that there had been any tails in the family; merrows and mermen are *not* the same. Melisande was quite right to be proud of her feet; tails were a darned nuisance. No one could work the sewers with a tail.

Thinking about Melisande brought a frown to the Plodger's whiskery face. Melisande was all churned up. She'd got very fond of the fey—of all the rescuers—and now she worried because they couldn't find that dratted boy. All yesterday they'd searched, and they were at it again today, scuttling about Up There, but there wasn't any news.

Over his woolly hat the Plodger wore a helmet with a little light in it, and now, bending down, he saw a pink necklace bobbing in the muck. Not real—he could see that at once; plastic, but a pretty thing. It would fetch a few pence when it was cleaned up, and that was good enough for him; he wasn't greedy. Scooping it up in his long-handled net, he tramped on along the ledge beside the stream of sludge. He was near the Thames now, but he wouldn't go under it, not today. There were good pickings sometimes from the busy street that ran beside the river.

He turned right, plodded through a storm relief chamber, and made his way along one of the oldest tunnels close to Waterloo Bridge. You could tell how old it was with the brickwork being so neat and careful. No one made bricks like that nowadays.

Then suddenly he stopped and sniffed. His snout-like nose was wrinkled, his mouth was pursed up in disgust. Something different had just come down. Something horrid and yucky and *wrong*. Something that didn't belong among the natural, wholesome smell of the drains.

"Ugh!" said the Plodger, and shook his head as though he could escape the sickly odor. A rat scuttled past him, and he fancied that it was running away from the gooey smell just as he wanted to do himself. Rats were sensible. You could trust them.

It wasn't just nasty—it was familiar. He'd smelled it before, that sweet, overpowering, clinging smell.

But where? He thought for a moment, standing on the ledge beside the slowly moving sludge. Yes, he remembered now. Not here—in quite a different part of the town.

He was excited now. Moving forward, he examined the inlet a few paces ahead. Yes; that was where it was coming from, running down in a slurp of bathwater. He tilted his head so as to shine the torch down the pipe, making sure he knew exactly where he was.

Then he turned back and hurried away, turning left, right . . . left again. A lipstick case bobbed up quite near him—brand new it looked too—but he wouldn't stop.

Half an hour later, he was lifting the manhole cover on the path between the Serpentine and the summer house inside the park.

No one, at first, could believe the wonderful news. They stood round the Plodger and stared at him with shining eyes.

"You really mean it? You've found the Prince?" asked Gurkie, holding a leek which had sprung out of the ground before she could stop it.

The Plodger nodded. "Leastways, I've found his mother."

"But how?" Cornelius was completely bewildered. Surely the Trottles weren't hiding in the sewer?

The Plodger answered with a single word.

"Maneater," he said.

"Maneater?" The wizard shook out his ear trumpet, sure he had misheard.

"That rubbishy scent Mrs. Trottle uses. It's got a kick like a mule. I used to smell it when I worked the drains under Trottle Towers. And just now I smelled it again."

The ring of faces stared at him, breathless with suspense.

"Where—oh, please tell us? Where?" begged Gurkie.

"I can tell you for certain," said the Plodger with quiet pride, "because I followed the outlet right back. It came from the Astor. That's where Mrs. Trottle's taken Raymond. She's holed up here in London, and in as clever a place as you can find. Getting the perisher out of there'll be like getting him out of Fort Knox."

The Astor was a hotel, but it was not an ordinary one. It was a super, luxury, five-star, incredibly grand hotel. The front of the hotel faced a wide street with elegant shops and nightclubs, and the back of the hotel looked out over the river Thames with its bridges and passing boats. Gentlemen were only allowed to have tea in the Astor lounge if they were wearing a tie, and the women who danced in the ballroom wore dresses which cost as much as a bus driver earned in a year. The Astor had its own swimming pool and gym and, in the entrance hall, were showcases with one crocodile-skin shoe in them, or a diamond bracelet, and there was a flower shop and a hairdresser and a beauty salon so that you never had to go outside at all.

Best of all was the famous Astor cake. This was not a real cake; not the kind you eat. It was a huge cake made out of plywood, painted pink and decorated with curly bits that looked like icing—and every night while the guests were at dinner, it was wheeled into the restaurant, and a beautiful girl jumped out of it and danced!

Needless to say, ordinary people didn't stay in a hotel like that. It was pop stars and business tycoons and politicians and oil sheiks who came to the Astor, and people of that kind are usually afraid. Pop stars are afraid of fans who will rush up to them and tear their clothes, and politicians are afraid of being shot at by people they have bullied, and oil sheiks and business tycoons like to do their work in secret.

So the Astor had the best security service in the world. Guards with armbands and walkie-talkies

patrolled the corridors, there were burglar alarms everywhere and bomb-proof safes in the basement where the
visitors could keep their jewels. Best of all, there was a
special penthouse on the roof built of reinforced concrete, and the rooms in it had extra-thick walls and
secret numbers and lifts which came up inside them so
that they weren't used by the other guests at all. What's
more, the penthouse was built round a helicopter pad so
that these incredibly important people could fly in and
out of the hotel without being seen by anyone down in
the street.

And it was one of these secret rooms—Number 202
—which Mrs. Trottle had rented for herself and Raymond. Actually, it wasn't one room: it was a whole
apartment with a luxurious sitting room and a bedroom
with twin beds so that Mrs. Trottle could watch over
her babykin even when he slept. Even so, she had
checked into the hotel under a different name. She'd
called herself Lavinia Tarbuck, and Raymond was Ro-
land Tarbuck, and both of them wore dark glasses so
that they stumbled a lot but felt important.

Although the Astor bristled with security men,
Mrs. Trottle had hired two bodyguards specially for
Raymond. Bruce Trout was a fat man with a ponytail,
but the fatness wasn't wobbly like Raymond's; it was
solid like lard. His teeth had rotted years ago because he
never cleaned them and his false ones didn't fit, so they

weren't often in his mouth. They were usually behind the teapot or under the sofa. Not that it mattered. If there was trouble, Bruce could kill someone even without his teeth and had done so many times.

But it was the other bodyguard that was the most feared and famous one in London. Doreen Trout was Bruce's sister, but she couldn't have been more different. She was small and mousy with a bun of gray hair and weak blue eyes behind round spectacles. Doreen wore lumpy tweed skirts and thick stockings—and more than anything, she loved to knit. She knitted all day long: purple cardigans and pink booties and heather-mixture ankle socks . . . Clackety-click, clickety-clack went Doreen's needles from morning to night—and they were sharp, those needles. Incredibly sharp.

There are certain places in the human body which are not covered by bones, and someone who knows exactly where these soft places are does not need to bother with a gun. A really sharp needle is much less messy and scarcely leaves a mark.

Bruce was costing Mrs. Trottle a hundred pounds a day, but for Soft Parts Doreen, as they called her, she had to pay double that.

Mrs. Trottle had made a good job of scaring Raymond. He believed her when she said that everything he'd seen in the park and in his bedroom had been due to dangerous drugs that the kidnappers had put into his food, and when she told him not to move a step without his bodyguards, he did what he was told.

Life in the Astor suited Raymond. He liked the silver trolley that came in with his breakfast, and the waiters calling him "sir," and he liked not having his father there. Mr. Trottle sometimes seemed to think that Raymond wasn't absolutely perfect, and this hurt his son. Best of all, Raymond Trottle liked not having to go to school.

Because the bodyguards were so careful, Mrs. Trottle soon allowed her son to leave his room. So he sat and giggled in the Jacuzzi beside the swimming pool, and went to the massage parlor with his mother, and bought endless boxes of chocolate from the shop in the entrance hall. In the afternoon, the Trottles ate cream cakes in the Palm Court Lounge, which had palm trees in tubs and a fountain, and at night (still followed by the bodyguards) they went to the restaurant for dinner and watched the girl come out of the Astor cake.

She was a truly beautiful girl, and the dance she did was called the Dance of the Seven Veils. When she first jumped out, she was completely covered in shimmering gold, but as she danced she dropped off her first veil . . . and then the next . . . and the next one and the next. When she was down to the last layer of cloth, all the lights went out—and when they came on again, both the girl and the cake had gone.

Raymond couldn't take his eyes off her. He thought he would marry a girl like that when he grew up, but when he said so to his mother, she told him not to be silly.

"Girls who come out of cakes are common," said Mrs. Trottle.

What she liked was the man who played the double bass. He had a soaring moustache and black soulful eyes, and he called himself Roderigo de Roque, but his real name was Neville Potts. Mr. Potts had a wife and five children whom he loved very much, but the hotel manager had told him that he must smile at the ladies sitting close by, so as to make them feel good, and so he did.

Mrs. Trottle liked him so much that on the second night she decided to go downstairs again after Raymond was in bed and listen to him play.

First though, she put a call through to her husband.

"Have you done what I told you? About Ben?"

"Yes." Mr. Trottle sounded tired. "Are you sure . . . ?"

"Yes, I'm perfectly sure," snapped Mrs. Trottle. "Tell the servants he may leave very suddenly, and I don't want any talk about it." She paused for a moment, tapping her fingers on the table and smiling as she thought of the neat plan she had made to get rid of the boy. "Remember, Ben is to be told *nothing*. What about the kidnappers? Any sign of them?"

"No."

"Well, go on watching," said Mrs. Trottle. Then she sprayed herself with Maneater and went downstairs to make eyes at Mr. Potts as he sawed away on his double bass and wished it was time to go home.

CHAPTER 13

ABSOLUTELY EVERYONE wanted to help in rescuing Raymond from the Astor. The ghosts wanted to, and so did the banshees and the troll called Henry Prendergast—and Melisande sent a message to say that she was moving into the fountain in the Astor so as to keep an eye on things.

But before they could make a plan to snatch the Prince, there was something they felt had to be done straightaway, and that was to send a message to the Island.

"They'll be getting so worried, the poor King and Queen," said Gurkie. "And even if everything goes smoothly, it could take another two days to get Raymond out. If they thought he was lost or hurt, it would break their hearts."

But how to do this? Ernie offered to go through the gump again and speak to the sailors in the Secret Cove, but Cor shook his head.

"Your poor ectoplasm has suffered enough," he said.

This was true. There is nothing worse for ectoplasm than traveling in a wind basket, and using ghosts as messengers is simply cruel.

Luck, however, was on their side. The nice witch who worked as a school cook and had fetched Raymond's gobstopper during the Magic Show, had decided to go through the gump immediately and make her home on the Island. She'd gone to work on Monday morning and been told she was being made redundant because the school had to save money, and she didn't think there was any point in hanging about Up Here without any work.

"I don't say as I like Raymond because I don't, but I dare say by the time he's on the throne I'll be under the sod," she said, coming to say good-bye.

Needless to say she was very happy to take a message to the sailors in the Secret Cove, so that problem was solved.

"Tell them there is nothing to worry about. The Prince is found and we hope to bring him very soon," said Cor, who actually thought there was quite a lot to worry about, such as how to get into the Astor, how to bop and sack the detestable boy, how to carry the wriggling creature to the gump. But he was determined not to upset the King and Queen.

So the witch, whose name was Mrs. Frampton, said she would certainly tell them that and made her way to King's Cross Station, and in no time at all she was stepping out onto the sands of the Secret Cove.

No one can be a school cook and work with children and be gloomy, and Mrs. Frampton was perhaps more cheerful than she needed to be. At all events, the message that a sailor (traveling like the wind in a pinnace) carried back to the Island, was so encouraging, that the Queen started to laugh once more and the schoolchildren put fresh flowers in the classroom and everyone rejoiced. Any day now, any hour, the Prince would come! The nurses opened the crate of bananas again—and most importantly, the harpies and the sky yelpers and all the other dark people of the North were told that they would not be needed; that the Prince was found and coming, and all was wonderfully well!

By the second day of watching Raymond, Bruce was thoroughly fed up. When you are a thug and used to being with gangsters, you aren't choosy, but he'd never met a boy who opened a whole box of chocolates and guzzled it in front of someone else without offering a single one. Bruce didn't like the way Raymond whined when he was being beaten at ludo, and he thought a boy sending up for someone to give him a massage when he hadn't taken any exercise was thoroughly weird.

All the same, Bruce did his job. He never let Raymond out of his sight, he kept his gun in its holster, he tasted the food that was sent up in case it was poisoned—and each morning he went into the bathroom as soon as Raymond woke so as to make sure there were no crazed drug fiends lurking behind the tub or in the toilet.

Now, though, he came out looking rather pale.

"There's something funny in there. It felt sort of cold, and the curtain moved, I'm sure of it."

Doreen Trout went on knitting. She knitted as soon as she woke. This morning it was a pair of baby's booties—very pretty, they were, in pink moss stitch, and the steel of the needles glinted in the sun.

"Rubbish," she said. "You're imagining things."

She got up and went into the bathroom. Her empty needle flashed. She waited. No screams followed, no blood oozed from behind the pierced curtains.

"You see," she said. "There's nobody there."

But she was wrong. Mrs. Partridge was there, and a nasty time she was having of it. She was a shy ghost and hated nakedness, but she had set herself to haunt the Trottles' sleeping quarters and get the layout, and though the sight of Mrs. Trottle in her underwear spraying Maneater into her armpits had made her feel really sick, she was determined to stick to her job.

Mrs. Partridge was not the only person watching the Trottles. Cor had decided that a day spent studying their movements was necessary before a proper plan to rescue Raymond could be made. So Ernie was floating through the kitchen quarters looking for the exits, peering at the switchboards which controlled the lights . . . The troll called Henry Prendergast, disguised as a waiter, loaded Raymond's breakfast trolley . . .

And there were others. Down in the laundry room, an immensely sad lady had gotten herself taken on as a temporary laundry maid and wept a little as she counted the sheets and studied the chute which sent the dirty washing down into the basement. She didn't cry because she was particularly troubled, but because she was a banshee, and weeping is what banshees do.

By ten-thirty, Raymond said he was bored.

"I want to go and buy something," he said.

So the Trottles went down in the lift with their bodyguards, and Raymond went into the gift shop in the hotel and grumbled.

"They haven't got the comic I want. And the toys are rubbish."

Mrs. Trottle went shopping too. She decided to buy a beautiful red rose to tuck into her bosom at dinner so that the double bass player would notice it and smile at her.

The flower shop though looked different today, and the lady who served in it seemed to be puzzled.

"Everything's taken off," she said. "Look at that rubber plant—I'll swear it's grown a foot in the night. And that wreath . . . it's twice the size it was."

The wreath was made of greenery and lilies. The hotel always kept wreaths because a lot of the people who stayed at the Astor were old and had friends who died.

Mrs. Trottle bent her head to smell a lily, wondering if the double bass player would prefer her with one of those—and jerked her head back. If it wasn't impossible, she'd have said that someone had pinched her nose.

Someone had. Flower fairies look much like they do in the pictures: very, very small with gauzy wings—but they are incredibly bad tempered because of people sticking their faces into the places where they live and *sniffing*. Seeing the hairy insides of someone's nostrils is not amusing, and though this particular fairy had offered to go to the Astor and help Gurkie, she certainly wasn't going to be *smelled*.

By lunchtime, the secret watchers were feeling thoroughly gloomy. It wasn't just that the bodyguards never let Raymond out of their sight, it was that Raymond himself was such a horrible boy. But it was Melisande who found out just what they were up against in rescuing him.

She had got her uncle to move her into the fountain in the Palm Court, and she was not having a nice time. This was because of the goldfish. In the Fortlands fountain she had been alone. Here she had to share with a dozen, droopy, goggle-eyed, fan-tailed goldfish who flapped their tails in her face and dirtied the water with their droppings and their food.

But Melisande was a trooper. She peeped out from under the leaves; she watched Raymond and Mrs. Trottle guzzle a slab of fudge cake not an hour after they had finished breakfast; she watched the daft way Mrs. Trottle leered at the double bass player when the orchestra played for the guests at tea.

And she watched as Doreen Trout came over to the fountain, sat down on the rim, and—with her eyes still fixed on Raymond—took out her knitting bag.

"Knit two, slip one," murmured Doreen.

Then she turned slightly—so slightly that Melisande hardly noticed it—and one of her needles plunged down into the water.

It was all over in a second, and then she got up and

went back to stand beside Raymond—but the fan-tailed goldfish she had speared lay floating, belly up, between the leaves while his life's blood, draining away, came down on Melisande's shocked and bewildered head.

There was only one thing that cheered up the hidden watchers—and that was the cake!

The cake was beautiful! The way it came in, all pink and glowing, from a door beside the orchestra, the balloons and streamers that came down on top of it . . . and the lovely girl who burst out of it and danced, tossing away her golden veils, while the band played music so dreamy and romantic that it made you weep.

And it was the cake which gave Cor his idea.

All day the watchers had reported to him where he sat in the summer house with his briefcase beside him, taking notes, making maps of the hotel and the street out-side—and thinking. Now he was ready to speak.

It was close on midnight and everyone had come to listen. The Plodger had brought Melisande, carrying her wrapped in a wet towel, and now she sat in the bird-bath looking worried because she felt no one knew quite how dreadful Doreen Trout could be. The ghosts hov-ered on the steps, the troll called Henry Prendergast lay back in a deck chair eating a leek which Gurkie had put into his hand. He did not care for leeks, but he cared for Gurkie and was doing his best with it. Ben had crept out of Trottle Towers, and he and Odge were crouched on the wooden floor watching the mistmaker. Among the banshees and the flower fairies were Odge's great aunt and a couple of ducks.

Cor's plan, like all good plans, was simple. They would use the moment when the girl in the cake finished her dance and the lights went out to capture the Prince.

"Hans will bop him—very, very carefully, of course, using only his little finger—and drop him into the cake as it is wheeled away. No one will think of looking for him there."

"But won't the girl in the cake get a shock when the Prince is thrown in on top of her? Won't she squeak?" asked Gurkie.

Cor shook his head. "No," he said. "Because the girl

in the cake won't be there. The girl in the cake will be somebody else." He looked at Gurkie from under his bushy brows. "The girl in the cake," said the wizard in a weighty voice, "will be—you!"

"Me!" Gurkie blushed a deep and rosy pink. She had always longed to come out of a cake—always—but when her mother was alive, it was no good even thinking about it. Gym mistresses who run about blowing whistles and shouting "Play Up and Play the Game" are not likely to let their daughters within miles of a cake. "You mean I'm to do that dance? The one with the Seven Veils? Oh, but suppose I was left standing in only my—" She didn't say the word "knickers"—she never *had* said it. Saying "knickers" was another thing her mother had not allowed.

"You won't be," said Cor. "The lights will go off before that, when you still have one veil on."

"You'll do it beautifully, Gurkie," said Ben. "They'll go mad for you." And everyone agreed.

"But after that?" said the troll. "How will you get the Prince out of the cake and away? Hans may be invisible, but Raymond won't be, if we're not allowed to use magic on him, and the cake only gets wheeled as far as the artists' dressing room."

Cor nodded. "But there are other things in the dressing room. Such as the instruments that the players in the orchestra use. Among them a large double-bass case."

He paused, and everyone looked at him expectantly, beginning to get the drift.

"As soon as the cake arrives in there, Hans will transfer the Prince into the case—and the double bass player will carry him out of the hotel by the service stairs where a van will be waiting."

"But surely he'll notice," said Ernie. "Raymond must weigh about five times as much as a double bass."

"Yes. But you see it won't be the real double bass player. It'll be Mr. Prendergast." He turned to the troll. "You shape-shifted yourself into a bank manager and a policeman. Surely you can manage a double bass player with a black moustache and a cowlick in the middle of his forehead?"

The troll nodded. "No problem," he said. "I got a good look at him tonight."

The other details were quickly settled. Since they still had over a thousand pounds in banknotes, they were sure they could pay the real girl in the cake to let Gurkie take her place. "And I shall call Mrs. Trottle away with a phone message just before the cake comes in," said Cor. "Odge will pretend to be the double bass player's little daughter and tell the doorman that her father has to come home early. As for you, Ben, you must wait on the fire escape and signal to the van driver as soon as Raymond is packed and ready, so that he can back up against the entrance. And then off we go, all of us, through the gump with a whole day to spare!"

Ben, when the jobs were given out, sighed with relief. He'd been afraid that they wouldn't let him help, and he wanted more than anything to be part of the team.

But he felt guilty too because he knew that Odge thought he was going with them to the island.

"This time you're coming!" said Odge. "You *have* to!"

And Ben had said nothing. It was no good arguing, but you had to do what was right, and leaving Nanny Brown alone, ill as she was, couldn't ever be right. Only he wouldn't let himself think what it would be like after the rescuers had gone. He wouldn't let himself think of anything except how to get Raymond Trottle out of the Astor and bring the King and Queen their long-lost son.

CHAPTER 14

NANNY BROWN moved her head restlessly on the pillow. She was worried stiff. Why had Larina Trottle phoned to ask how she was? Larina didn't care tuppence how she was, Nanny knew that. Surely she couldn't be planning to send Ben away already? In which case Ben ought to have the letter now . . . But what if the police came to the hospital to ask questions? Perhaps they'd pull her out of bed and take her to prison? Ben wouldn't like that; he felt things far too much.

And here he was now! As he sat down beside her and took her hand, she thought what a handsome boy he was turning out to be.

"You've had your hair cut."

Ben nodded. Gurkie had pruned his hair with her pruning shears. She'd offered to curl it too, like she curled the petals of a rose, but Ben didn't think Nanny would like him with curly hair. Thinking of the rescuers made him smile—they were all so excited about tonight and getting Raymond out. Then he looked more closely at Nanny and his heart gave a lurch. She was nothing but skin and bone.

"Does it hurt you, Nanny? Are you in pain?"

"No, of course not," she lied. They'd offered her

some stuff to take away the pain, but she'd never let them dope her when Ben came. "What about Mrs. Trottle? How's she been?"

"She's still away—and Raymond, too."

Nanny nodded. That was all right, then. If Larina was away, she couldn't harm Ben, so the letter could wait. The nurses had promised faithfully to give it to Ben when the time came.

"And the servants?"

"They've been all right. They seem to let me do what I like, almost." But he was puzzled. The servants were almost *too* nice, and Mr. Fulton gave him an odd look now and again, as though he knew something. It made Ben uncomfortable, but he wasn't going to worry Nanny Brown.

And Nanny wasn't going to worry Ben about the nonsense the young doctor had come up with that morning. She knew her time was up, and she certainly didn't mean to go up to heaven stuck full of tubes.

But as Ben left the ward, he found the nice nurse, Celeste, waiting for him.

"Sister'd like a word with you, Ben," she said. "Would you come along to her room?"

The Sister had dark hair and kind eyes. "Ben, you're very young but you're a sensible boy, and there doesn't seem to be anyone else."

Ben waited.

"You're the next of kin, dear, aren't you? I mean, you're the only relation Mrs. Brown has?"

"Yes. I'm her grandson."

The nurse sighed and stabbed her pencil onto a notepad.

"You see, Ben, the doctors are thinking of operating on your grandmother. It would be a shock to her system and cause her some pain, but it might give her a bit longer."

Ben bit his lip. "When would that be?"

"The day after tomorrow. We thought you should know."

The day after tomorrow. The last day of the Opening. It would be all over then and the rescuers gone. Well, if he'd had any doubts, that settled it. To let her go through an operation by herself was not to be thought of.

"I'd like to be there when she comes round," he said. "I'd like to be with her."

"I'll ask the doctor," said the Sister—and smiled at him.

CHAPTER 15

MRS. TROTTLE had got the table she wanted—on the left of the band, which was where the cake came in and really close to the double bass player. She was sure he fancied her; every so often when he wasn't sawing away with his bow, his eyes seemed to meet hers. What a lovely player he was, and what a lovely man!

Raymond was sitting opposite, dressed to kill in a new silk shirt and spotty bow tie, and as she leant forward to wipe the dribble of cream from his chin, Mrs.

Trottle thought there wasn't a better-looking boy in the world. Her husband said she spoiled him, but Mr. Trottle didn't understand Raymond. The boy was sensitive. He *felt* things.

Bruce was standing by the far wall, his eye on Raymond. He was hungry, but no one thought of sending anything over for him to eat. His sister Doreen sat on a chair by the big double doors. Ordinary guests would have been surprised to see a woman knitting all through dinner, but there were enough people there who had used bodyguards in their time, and it gave them a good feeling to know that Soft Parts Doreen was in the room. No terrorists or assassins would get far with her around!

In the phone box across the street from the hotel, Cor was reading the instructions. Or trying to, but his spectacles kept falling off the end of his nose, and he didn't like the look of all those buttons.

"Insert money," mumbled the wizard. "Dial number . . ." But when he dialed it, something gloomy flashed onto the little gray screen and everything went dead. He tried again and the same thing happened. Then suddenly he lost patience. They weren't supposed to use magic on the Prince, but a telephone was different. He spoke the number of the Astor; he turned to the East, he uttered the Calling Spell—and on the reception desk of the hotel, the phone began to ring.

"Oh no! I can't come now." Mrs. Trottle glared at the page who had come to say that she was wanted on the telephone. The double bass player was playing something so dreamy that he must surely be playing it for her alone, and she almost decided to pluck the rose from her chest and throw it at him.

"The gentleman said it was very urgent, Madam," said the page—and Mrs. Trottle got up sulkily and followed him, while Bruce moved closer to Raymond and Doreen shifted slightly in her chair.

Hans now entered the room. He had been incredibly brave and offered to have fernseed even in his eye so that he could be completely invisible and still see where he was going. His little finger was stretched out ready to bop Raymond, and it trembled because the ogre was very much afraid. Suppose he bopped too hard and brought the Prince to the Island with a broken skull? On the other hand, suppose he didn't hit him hard enough so that he squealed when he was thrown into the cake?

If Hans was nervous, poor Gurkie was terrified.

"Oh Mother, forgive me," she muttered. She had been to Fortlands and bought some of the stuff they used for blackout curtains to make the last veil—the one she wore over her underclothes—and the underwear itself was bottle-green Chilprufe because her mother had always told her that it was what you wore next to the skin that mattered, so even if the lights didn't go out at exactly the right time, she would still be decent. All the same, as she stepped into the cake, Gurkie's teeth were chattering. At least the girl who usually did the Dance of the Seven Veils was happy! She'd grabbed the money Cor had given her and even now was going up in a jumbo on the way to sunny Spain.

"Ready?" asked the porter, coming to wheel her in.

"Ready!" squeaked Gurkie, from inside the layers of tissue.

The orchestra burst into a fanfare; balloons and streamers came down from the ceiling—and Gurkie burst out of the cake and began to dance.

Raymond didn't recognize her because even her face was veiled, and the light was rosy and dim, but everyone felt that something beautiful was going to happen, and they were right. Feys have always loved dancing—they dance round the meadows in the early morning, they twirl and whirl on the edge of the sea, and of all the twirlers and whirlers on the Island, Gurkie was the best. She forgot that her mother would have turned in her grave to see her in the dining room of the Astor Hotel like any chorus girl, she forgot that any minute Raymond Trottle would land with a thump on top of her. And as she danced, the orchestra followed the way she moved . . . got slower when she went slowly and quicker when she went fast, and there wasn't a single person in the dining room who could bear to take his eyes off her.

Gurkie dropped the first of her seven veils on the floor. She was thinking of all the lovely things that grew on the Island and of her cucumbers and how she would soon be home, but the people watching her did not know that. They thought she was thinking of them.

And Hans had reached Raymond's table. He was standing in the space left by Mrs. Trottle. He was ready.

The sixth veil dropped. The music got even soupier. Now as she danced, Gurkie was strewing herbs into the room, the sweet-smelling herbs she had brought in her basket to make people sleepy, to make them forget their troubles.

By the back entrance, Odge Gribble was explaining to the porter that her father had to leave early.

"My Mummy isn't well," she said with a lisp—and he nodded and pinched her cheek.

In the lavatory which led out of the dressing room, the troll waited. He looked so like the double bass player that his own mother wouldn't have known him. Ben, crouching on top of the fire escape, kept his eyes on the waiting van.

Back in the dining room, Gurkie dropped her fifth veil . . . her fourth . . . She still spun and whirled, but more slowly now—and the lights were turning mauve . . . then blue.

"Coo!" said Raymond Trottle as she danced past his table.

The third veil now . . . the second. And now Gurkie did begin to worry. What if the lights didn't go out? Was her last veil *really* thick enough?

But it was all right. Hans's little finger was stretched out over Raymond's head.

The orchestra went into its special swirly bit. The lights went out.

And at that moment, Hans bopped!

The getaway van was parked in the narrow road which ran between the back of the Astor and the river. It had been dark for some time; the passing boats had lit their lamps, and light streamed from the windows of the hotel.

The inside of the van was piled with blankets so that the Prince could be made comfortable on the way to the gump. All the rescuers' belongings were there because they were driving straight to the station.

And Odge's suitcase was there, carefully laid flat. The door of the van was open, and plenty of fresh air reached the mistmaker through the holes that Odge had drilled in it, so he should have been content, but he was not. He was too old for suitcases; he was a free spirit; he was used now to being part of things!

Rustling about in the hay, complaining in little whimpers, he put his sharp front teeth against the fiber of the case and found a weak place where the rim round one of the holes had frayed. Getting interested, beginning to see hope, he began to gnaw.

The driver noticed nothing. He had his eyes fixed on the boy who crouched on top of the fire escape. As soon as Ben signaled with his torch, he'd back up against the entrance.

In the dining room of the Astor, the guests waited for the cake; the orchestra played a tango.

"It's awfully hot in here," complained a girl at one of the tables, and called a waiter.

The mistmaker went on gnawing. He was pleased. Something was happening. The hole was getting bigger . . . and bigger . . . and bigger still. His whiskers were already through, and his nose . . .

Then quite suddenly he was free!

Trembling with excitement, he sat up on his haunches and looked about him. And at that moment, one of the waiters opened a window in the dining room, sending the sound of the orchestra out into the night.

Music! And what music! The mistmaker had never heard a full orchestra in his life. His eyes grew huge, his moustache quivered. Then with a bound he leapt out of the van and set off.

The driver's eyes were still on Ben.

Lolloping along like a lovesick pillow, the mistmaker crossed the road, leapt onto the bottom rung of the fire escape, missed . . . tried again. Now he was on and climbing steadily.

"Oom-pa-pa, oom-pa-pa," went the band. The violins soared, the saxophones throbbed . . .

Ben peered down the iron stairs, wondering if he had seen something white crossing the road. No, he must have been mistaken . . .

The Astor was beside the river, and the riverbank

was full of rats. Large, intelligent rats who had dug paths for themselves into the hotel. Panting up the first rung of the fire escape, the mistmaker found a hole in the brick and plunged into it. It came out near the kitchens, behind a store cupboard, and from there another rat-run led into the pantry where the waiters set out the trays to carry into the dining room. He only had to cross a passage, run through an open door . . .

And now he was where he wanted to be—where he absolutely had to be, facing that wonderful sound! He had arrived just as the cake was wheeled away and the room was in darkness, but that didn't matter because the band was still playing and it was a Viennese waltz!

The mistmaker made his way into the middle of the room and sat down. Never, never had he heard anything so beautiful! The fur on the back of his neck lifted; he shivered with happiness; his earlobes throbbed.

"Aaah!" sighed the mistmaker. "Aaah . . . aaah!"

The waves of mist were slight to begin with; he was puffed from the climb and he was overwhelmed. But as the beauty of the music sank deeper and deeper into his soul, so did the clouds of whiteness that came from him.

At one of the tables, an old gentleman began to cough. An angry lady leant across her husband and told the man at the next table to stop smoking.

"I'm not smoking," the man said crossly.

But as the lights came on again, the guests could see

that something odd was happening. The room was covered in a thick white mist—so thick that the Trottles' table could hardly be seen.

"It's smoke!" The room's full of smoke," shouted a girl in a glittery dress.

"No it isn't. It's tear gas!" yelled a bald man and put his napkin to his face.

"It's a terrorist bomb!" cried a fat lady.

Bruce was blundering round Raymond's chair, feeling for the boy. Perhaps he was hiding under the table, trying to get away from the creeping gas? Clutching his gun, he dived under the cloth.

The mistmaker was upset by the ugly shrieking. He moved closer to the band which was still playing. A good orchestra will play through thick and thin.

Once more he gave himself up to the beauty of the music; once more he sighed. But he was getting thinner now; he was no longer pillow-shaped. The whiteness that came from him was not so thick, and in a break in the mist, a woman in a trouser suit stood up and pointed: "Look! It's coming from that horrible thing!" she screeched.

"It's a poisonous rat! It's a rodent from outer space!"

"It's got the plague! They do that; they give off fumes and then they go mad and bite you!"

The cries came from all over the room. A waiter rushed in with a fire extinguisher and squirted foam all over a group of Arabs in their splendid robes. One of the Astor's own guards had seized a walking stick and was banging it on the floor.

And now something happened which put the mist-maker's life in mortal danger. The band gave up. The music stopped . . . and with it, the supply of mist which had helped to hide and shelter him. Suddenly cut off from the glorious sound, the little animal blinked and tried to come back to the real world. Then he began to run hither and thither, looking for the way back.

And Doreen Trout reached for her knitting bag.

In the artists' dressing room, Gurkie had climbed out of the cake. She had a bruise on her shoulder where Raymond's chin had hit her, but she was being brave. The Prince looked crumpled, but his breathing was steady. Only a few minutes now and he'd be stretched out in the van where she could make him comfortable.

"I bopped well?" asked Hans who had followed her into the dressing room.

"You bopped beautifully," said Gurkie.

The troll came out of the toilet and opened the double bass case.

"I'll take the feet," he said, and Hans nodded and went to Raymond's shoulders.

Everything was going according to plan.

It was at that moment that the door to the fire

escape burst open and Ben, ashen-faced and frantic, rushed into the room.

"The mistmaker's escaped," he said. "He's in the dining room. And they're going mad in there. They'll kill him."

"No!" Hans let go of Raymond, who fell back into the cake. "Our duty is to the Prince. You must not go!"

Ben did not even hear him. Before the ogre could move to stop him, he had reached the other door and was gone.

In the dining room, everyone was shrieking and joining in the hunt for the dangerous rodent from outer space. The Arabs whose robes had been squirted with foam were yelling at the waiter; a lady had fainted and fallen into her apple pie.

"There he is!" screamed a woman. "Behind the trolley!" And Bruce aimed, fired—and hit a bottle of champagne, which exploded into smithereens.

The mistmaker was terrified now. The shrieks and thumps beat on his ears like hammer blows; his head was spinning and he ran in circles, trying to find the way out.

"He's got rabies!" yelled a fat woman. "That's how you tell, when they go round and round like that."

"If he bites you, you're finished," shouted a red-faced man. "Get on a table; he'll go for your ankles."

The fat lady did just that, and the table broke, sending her crashing to the ground. "Don't let him get me!" she screamed. "Squash him! Finish him!"

Bruce had seized a chair and was holding it above his head as he stalked the desperate little beast. Now he brought it down with a thump, and one leg came off and rolled away.

"He's missed," moaned the woman on the floor.

Once again Bruce raised the chair, once again he brought it down, and once again he missed.

Doreen Trout had not screamed. She had not thumped. She had not picked up heavy chairs or reached for her gun. All she had done was take out her favorite knitting needle. It was a sock needle of the finest steel and sharper than any rapier. She had judged its length, and it would skewer the animal neatly without any waste.

"Get out of the way, oaf," she hissed at her brother. "I'm dealing with this. Just corner him."

This was easier said than done. The mistmaker, caught in the nightmare, scuttled between the tables, vanished into patches of whiteness, skittered on the foam. But his enemies were gathering. The saxophone player had jumped down from the bandstand and shooed him against the wall; a waiter with a broom handle blocked him as he tried to dive behind the curtains.

And now he was cornered. His eyes huge with fear, he sat trembling and waited for what was to come.

"Stand back!" said Doreen to the crowd—and began to move slowly toward the terrified animal. "Come on, my pretty," she cooed. "Come to your Mummy. Come and see what I've got for you."

The room fell silent. Everyone was watching Doreen Trout, holding her needle as she moved closer, and all the time talking in a coaxing, wheedling voice.

The mistmaker's whiskers twitched. He blinked; the delicate ears became flushed. Here was a low voice; a kind voice. He turned his head this way and that, listening.

"I've got lovely things for you in my bag. Carrots . . . lettuce . . ."

More than anything, the desperate creature wanted kindness. Should he risk it? He took a few steps toward her . . . paused . . . sat up on his haunches. Then suddenly he made up his mind, and in a movement of trust he turned over on his back with his paws in the air as he had done so often when he was playing with Ben and Odge. He knew what came next—that moment when they scratched him so soothingly and deliciously all down his front.

Soft Parts Doreen looked down at the rounded, unprotected stomach of the little beast; at the pink skin still showing where his grown-up fur had not yet come.

Then she smiled and raised her arm.

The next second she lay sprawled on the floor. A boy had come from nowhere and leapt at her, fastening his arms round her throat.

"You murderess! I'll kill you; I'll kill you if you harm him!" shouted Ben.

The attack was so sudden that Doreen dropped her needle, which quivered, point down, in the carpet. Scratching and spitting, she tried to shake Ben off while her free hand crawled like a spider toward the embedded needle.

"Get the boy, idiot!" she spluttered at Bruce.

But that was easier said than done.

Every time it looked as though he could get a shot at Ben, some bit of Doreen got in the way. Anyway, his sister was sure to win—the boy fought like a maniac, but he was half her size, and her hand was almost on the needle. Now she was clawing at his face, and as he pushed her away and tried to free himself, his arm was clear of Doreen's body. Blowing a hole in the boy's arm was better than nothing, and carefully Bruce lifted his gun and aimed.

The next second he staggered back, reeling, while pieces of splintered wood rained down on his shoulders. The double bass player had gone mad and hit him on the head with his instrument.

Except that the real double bass player was up on the bandstand with his hand to his mouth staring down at the man who seemed to be him.

But Doreen's crawling fingers had reached the needle, pulled it out. Holding the glittering steel above Ben's throat, she brought it down in a single, violent thrust—just as Ben, with a superhuman effort, rolled out of her grasp.

"Ow! Help! Gawd!"

Bruce clutched his foot, hopped, tried to pull the needle out of his shoe. Maddened by pain, half stunned by the blow the troll had given him, he seized a brass table lamp.

Ben had turned, trying to catch the mistmaker. He had no time to dodge, no time to save himself. The base of the heavy lamp came down on his skull in a single crushing blow—and as the blood gushed from the wound, he fell unconscious to the ground.

"He's dead!" screamed a woman.

"I hope so," said Doreen softly. "But if not . . ."

She pulled the needle out of her brother's shoe and knelt down beside Ben, searching for the soft hollow beneath his ear.

But then something terrifying happened. As she bent over the boy, she was suddenly pushed back as if by an invisible hand—pushed back so hard that she fell against the plate-glass window, which broke with a crash.

It was incredible but they could all see it—slowly, gently, the wounded boy rose into the air. . . . Higher he rose, and higher . . . Blood still trickled from his scalp, he lay with one arm dangling and his head thrown back . . . lay *in the air*, unsupported and clearly visible above the mist.

"He's going to heaven!" cried someone.

"He's been called up to Paradise!"

And that was how it looked to everyone there. They had seen pictures of saints and martyrs who could do that . . . levitate or lift themselves up and lie there in the clouds.

But that wasn't the end of it. Now the boy who *had* to be dead began to float slowly, gently, away, high over everyone's head . . . until he vanished through the door.

CHAPTER 16

O
N THE MORNING of the eighth day of the Opening, the Royal Yacht set off from the Island, bound for
the Secret Cove.

Not only was the Queen aboard, but the King and
several of his courtiers, for he understood now that the
Queen had to get as close as she could to the place
where the Prince would appear—if he appeared at all.
Two days had passed since the cheerful message from
the witch, and still there was no sign of their son. All

along the King had tried to comfort his wife, but now even he was finding it hard to be brave.

Down below, a special cabin had been prepared for the Wailing Nurses. They had begged to be allowed to come along, but since they hadn't washed for nine years they had to be kept well away from the other passengers. With them had come a new crate of bananas because the first batch had become overripe, and the Queen had managed a smile as she saw it carried aboard because it meant the triplets, at least, still hoped.

As the Royal Yacht drew out of the harbor, a second and much larger boat pulled up its anchors, ready to follow. This was a ship chartered by people on the Island who could not fit onto the King's yacht but who also wanted to be there for the last day of the Opening. Most of these were people who cared very much about the little Prince and longed and longed for him to be brought back safely, even now at the eleventh hour. But some—just a few—were peevish grumblers: people who wanted to gloat over the old wizard and the loopy fey and the conceited little hag when they came back in disgrace. And there were some—there are always such people even in the most beautiful and best-ruled places —who just wanted an outing and a chance to gawp at whatever was going to happen, whether it was good or bad.

The Royal Yacht skimmed over the waves. The charter boat followed more slowly. In their cabin the nurses wailed and tried to think of ways of punishing themselves, but not for long because they became seasick and no one can think of a worse punishment than that.

The Queen would not go below. She stood leaning over the rails, her long hair whipped by the wind, and over and over again she said: "Dear God, please let him come. Please let him come. I will never do anything bad again if only you let him come."

Poor Queen. She never *had* done anything bad; she was not that sort of person.

They had been at sea for only a short time when something happened. The sky darkened; a black thundercloud moved in from the west, and a few drops of rain fell on the deck.

Or was it rain?

The sailors who had been below hurried up the ladders, preparing for a storm. The gulls flew off with cries of alarm; the dolphins dived.

It was not a storm, though, and the swirling blackness was not a cloud. The sky yelpers came first: a pack of baying, saucer-eyed dogs racing overhead, dropping their spittle on the deck where it hissed and sizzled and broke into little tongues of flame which the sailors stamped out.

But it was the harpies which made the Queen sway and the King run to her side.

They flew in formation like geese, with Mrs. Smith at their head and the others in a V shape behind her: Miss Green, Miss Brown, Miss Jones, and Miss Witherspoon. Their handbags dangled from their arms; their varnished talons hung down from their crimplene bloomers . . . and their unspeakable stench beat against the clean, salty air of the sea.

From the charter ship, a cheer went up. These were the real rescuers, the proper ones. And about time too! The King and Queen had waited till the last possible moment before sending in these frightful women, and there were those who thought they had delayed too long.

The harpies flew on, the dogs racing before them. In an hour they would be through the gump. The Queen's knuckles whitened on the rail, but she would not faint; she would bear it.

"There was nothing to do, my dear; you know that," said the King.

The Queen nodded. She did know it. There were twenty-four hours left; only one day. These ghastly creatures were her only hope.

CHAPTER 17

B EN LAY ON THE FLOOR of the summer house, his head pillowed on the wizard's rolled-up cloak. His eyes were closed; his face, in the light of the candles, was deathly pale. Since Hans had carried him out of the Astor, he had not stirred.

Gurkie sat beside him, holding his hand. She had rubbed healing ointment into his scalp; the bleeding had stopped, the wound was closing—but the deeper hurt, the damage to his brain, was beyond her power to heal. And if he never came round again . . . if he lived forever in a coma . . . or if he died . . .

But no one could bear to think of that. Cor sat still as stone in the folding chair. He was shivering, but they hadn't been able to stop him giving his cloak to Ben.

"I am too old," he thought. "I have failed in my mission and brought harm to as brave a child as I shall ever see."

Hans was crouched on the steps. His fernseed had gone blotchy, and every so often a moan escaped him. "Oi," murmured the giant. "Oi." If he had followed Ben at once into the dining room instead of waiting by the Prince, he could have prevented this dreadful accident, and he knew that he would never forgive himself.

The manhole cover on the path now lifted slowly, and the Plodger climbed out, still in his working clothes.

"Any news?" he asked. "Has he come round?"

The wizard shook his head, and the Plodger sighed and made his way back into the sewer. Melisande was going to be dreadfully upset.

It was well past midnight. In Trottle Towers the servants slept, believing that Ben had already been taken to his new "home." The ghosts had come to stand round Ben as he lay unstirring and then had gone back to the guarding of the gump.

It was amazing how many people had come to ask

after Ben, people who should scarcely have known the boy. Wizards and witches, the banshee who had worked in the laundry room of the Astor . . . the flower fairy who had pinched Mrs. Trottle on the nose. It was extraordinary how many people cared.

It was the last day of the Opening. They had expected to be back on the Island by now, but no one even thought of leaving. Ben had helped them from the first moment they had seen him cleaning shoes in the basement of Trottle Towers; he had seemed at once to belong to them. Not one of the rescuers dreamt of abandoning him.

Odge was not with the others as they clustered round Ben. She had gone off by herself and was sitting by the edge of the lake, wrapped in her long black hair.

Ben was going to die; Odge was sure of it.

"And it's my fault," she said aloud. "I brought the mistmaker, and it was because he went to save him that Ben was hurt."

The mistmaker lay beside Ben now; Odge had been able to snatch him up when the ogre brought Ben out of the dining room. If Ben woke, he would see the little animal at once and know that he was all right, but he wouldn't wake. No one could lie there so white and still and not be at death's door.

And if Ben died, nothing would go right ever again. She could grow an extra toe—she could grow a whole crop of extra toes—she could learn to cough frogs, and none of it would be any use. Only yesterday her great-aunt had taught her the Striking People with Baldness Spell, but what did that matter now? Hags don't cry—Odge knew that—but nothing now could stop her tears.

Then suddenly she lifted her head. Something had happened—something horrible! An evil stench spread slowly over the grass and crept through the branches of the trees. . . . The roosting birds flew upward with cries of alarm. A cloud passed over the moon. Running back to warn the others, she saw that they had risen to their feet and were staring at the sky.

The smell grew worse. A mouse in the bushes squealed in terror; a needle of ice pierced the warmth of the summer night.

And then she came! Her rancid wings fluttered once . . . twice . . . and were folded as she came in to land. Her handbag dangled from her arm; the frill round the bottom of her bloomers, hugging her scaly legs, was like the ruff on a poisonous lizard.

"Well, well," sneered Mrs. Smith. "Quite a cozy little family party, I see." She opened her handbag to take out her powder puff—and the rescuers fell back. The smell of a harpy's face powder is one of the most dreaded smells in the world. "One might think that people who have fallen down on their job so completely would at least show some signs of being sorry."

No one spoke. The nail polish on the harpy's ghastly talons, the loathsome hairspray on her permed hair, were making them feel dizzy and sick.

"Candles! Flowers! Giants in embroidered braces! Pshaw!" said Mrs. Smith. She put her claws on Gurkie's begonia and tore it out of the ground. "Well, you know why I'm here. To tell you you're finished. Demoted. *Kaput.* Off the job. I don't know if the King and Queen will forgive you, but if they've got any sense, they won't. You're failures. You're feeble. Pathetic. A disaster. Rescuing a kitchen boy and leaving the Prince!"

Still the rescuers said nothing. They were guilty of everything the harpy accused them of. For they *had* put Ben before the Prince. Hans had struggled with himself for a few minutes, but in the end he and the troll had run back to help Ben and left the true Prince of the Island in a squelchy heap inside the cake. They had forgotten him, it was as simple as that. And Raymond had come to himself and climbed out and even now was probably guzzling Knickerbocker Glories in his room in the hotel. What's more, they hadn't even thought of going back and having another go at getting him out; all they'd thought of was carrying Ben away to safety. They weren't fit to be rescuers; the harpy was right.

"The ghosts told me what happened," said Mrs. Smith. "And if I were the King and Queen, I'd know what to do with you. All that fuss about a common servant boy!"

"He's not a common servant boy, he's *Ben*," raged Odge—and took a step backward as the harpy lifted her dreadful claw and sharpened it once, twice, three times against the step.

"Well, the most useful thing you can do now is keep out of our way," Mrs. Smith went on. "Get yourself through the gump and let us finish the job."

Gurkie put her hand to her heart. She didn't care for Raymond, but the idea of him being carried away in the talons of Mrs. Smith was too horrible to bear.

"How will you operate?" asked the wizard.

"That's none of your business. But some of my girls are sussing out the Astor now. There seems to be a helicopter pad."

She said no more, but in the distance they could hear the baying of a hellhound and a high, screeching voice ordering him to: "*Sit!*"

The harpy flew off then, but the evil she had left in the air still lingered. Then from behind them came a strong young voice.

"Goodness!" said Ben, sitting up and rubbing his head. "What an absolutely *horrible* smell!"

CHAPTER 18

"AND, PLEASE, let us get this clear," said Mrs. Smith. "It is I who will actually snatch the boy. You will help me, of course; you will take care of his mother and the guards, but the Prince is *mine!*"

"Yes, Mrs. Smith," said the other harpies gloomily. "We understand."

They sat in a circle round their chief in a disused underpass not far from the Astor. No one went there after dark; it was the sort of place which muggers loved and ordinary people avoided. All of them would have liked to be the one to snatch the Prince, but they hadn't really expected to be chosen—their leader always kept the best jobs for herself.

Miss Brown, Miss Green, Miss Jones, and Miss Witherspoon were a little smaller than Mrs. Smith, but they had the same rank black wings, the same evil talons, the same stretch tops and bloomers ending in the same frills. They too had handbags full of makeup, but Miss Witherspoon kept a whistle and some dog biscuits in hers. She was the sporting one, the one who trained the dogs.

"You have the sack, Lydia?" asked Mrs. Smith—and Miss Brown nodded.

"And you have the string, Beryl?" she went on—and Miss Green held up the ball of twine.

"Good. We'll parcel him up in the cloakroom—I don't fancy any wriggling as we go through the tunnel." She turned to Miss Witherspoon: "As for the dogs, they'd best stay on the lead till the last moment. I'll give the signal when you should let them go."

One of the black yelpers stirred and got to his feet.

"Sit!" screeched Miss Witherspoon—and the dog sat.

"Now *grovel!*" she yelled—and the great saucer-eyed beast flopped onto his stomach and crawled toward her like a worm.

"Well, that settles everything, I think," said Mrs. Smith. "Just time for a little sleep." She opened her handbag and took out a packet of curlers which she wound into her brassy hair. Then she tucked her head into her wings, as birds do, and in a moment the others heard her snores.

There were only a few more hours before the closing of the gump for nine long years, but it was clear that Mrs. Smith didn't even think of failure. Much as they had wanted to snatch the Prince themselves, the other harpies had to admit that she was the best person for the job.

On the roof of the Astor, Mrs. Trottle waited with her husband and her son. Her suitcase, ready packed, was beside her, and a traveling rug. In ten minutes the helicopter would be there to take them to safety. Mr. Trottle's uncle, Sir Ian Trottle, who lived in a big house on the Scottish border, had offered to shelter them from the madmen who were chasing Raymond.

Her darling babykin hadn't realized that the gang of dope fiends were after him again. When he came round inside the cake, he couldn't remember anything, and she hadn't told him what had happened. And actually she herself wasn't too clear about what had gone on in the Astor dining room. Bruce had told her that he'd thrown the boy for safety into the cake to save him from the clutches of the kidnappers, and she'd rewarded him, but he wasn't much good anymore, limping about and with a bruise on his head the size of a house. And Doreen, who'd been thrown through a window, had cut her wrist so badly that it would be a long time before she could knit. She'd sent them both home, and it was two of the Astor's own guards who were protecting them until the helicopter came.

As for the rest of the babble—something about some boy being lifted up and taken to heaven—Mrs. Trottle put that down to the effect of the poisonous gas that had been let off in the room. By the time she'd got back after some idiot kept her talking on the phone, the dining room was in a shambles and what everyone said was double-dutch.

"I'm hungry!" said Raymond.

"We'll have some sandwiches in the helicopter, dear," said Mrs. Trottle.

"I don't want them in the helicopter, I want them *now*," whined Raymond. He began to grope in Mrs. Trottle's hold-all, found a bar of toffee, and put it in his mouth.

Mrs. Trottle looked up, but there was no sign yet of the helicopter. It was a beautiful clear night. They'd have an easy flight. And as soon as Raymond was safe at Dunloon, she was going to call the police. Once Ben was out of her way and there was no snooping to be done, she'd get proper protection for her little one. And Ben *would* be out of the way—she'd left clear instructions at the hospital. Even now he might be on the way to Ramsden Hall. She'd had a scare with Ramsden— some meddling do-gooders had tried to get the place shut down, but the man who ran it had been too clever for them. Whatever it was called, Ramsden was a good old-fashioned reform school. They didn't actually send children up chimneys because most people now had central heating, but they saw to it that the boys knew their place, and that was what Ben needed. And oh, the relief she'd feel at having him out of the house!

"Here it comes!" said Mr. Trottle, and the guards moved aside the cones and turned up the landing lights, ready for the helicopter to land.

The pilot who'd been sent to fetch the Trottles was one of the best. He had flown in the Gulf War; he was steady and experienced, and of course he would never have taken even the smallest sip to drink before a flight.

And yet now he was seeing things. He was seeing dogs. Which meant that he was going mad because you did not see dogs in the sky; you didn't see stars blotted out by thrashing tails; you didn't see grinning jowls and fangs staring in at the cockpit.

The pilot shook his head. He closed his eyes for an instant, but it didn't help. Another slobbering face with bared teeth and saucer eyes had appeared beside him. There were more of them now . . . three . . . four . . . five.

There couldn't be five dogs racing through the sky. But there were—and they were coming closer. He dipped suddenly, expecting them to be sliced by his propellers, but they weren't. Of course they weren't, because they didn't exist.

High above him, Miss Witherspoon, her handbag dangling, encouraged the pack.

"Go on! See him off!" she shouted. "Faster! Faster!"

Excited by the chase, the dogs moved in. Sparks came from their eyes, spittle dropped from their jaws. The pack leader threw himself at the cockpit window.

The pilot could see the roofs of the Astor below, but every time he tried to lose height, the phantom dogs chivied him harder—and what if those sparks were real? What if they burnt the plane?

"Tally ho!" cried Miss Witherspoon, high in the sky. She blew her whistle, and the dogs went mad.

The pilot made one more attempt to land. Then suddenly he'd had enough. The Astor could wait, and so could the people who had hired him. The Trottles, staring at the helicopter's light as it came down, saw it rise again and vanish over the rooftops.

"Now what?" said Mrs. Trottle, peevishly.

She was soon to find out.

The people of London had forgotten the old ways. They had heard the baying of the phantom yelpers in the sky, and now they could smell the evil stench that came in with the night air, but they spoke of drains, of blocked pipes, and shut their windows.

And the harpies flew on.

"Yuk!" said Raymond, chewing his toffee bar. "It stinks. I feel sick!"

"Well, my little noodle-pie, I did tell you not to eat sweets before—"

Then she broke off, and all the Trottles stared upward.

"My God!" Mr. Trottle staggered backward. "What are they? Ostriches . . . vultures?"

The gigantic birds were losing height. They could see the talons of the biggest one now, caught in the landing lights.

And they could see other things.

"B . . . Bloomers," babbled Mrs. Trottle. "F . . . frills."

"Shoot, can't you!" yelled Mr. Trottle at the guard. "What are we paying you for?"

The guard lifted his gun. There was a loud report, and Mrs. Smith shook out her feathers and smiled. The wings of harpies have been arrow-proof and bullet-proof since the beginning of time.

"Ready, girls!" she called.

The second guard lifted his gun . . . then dropped it and ran screaming back into the building. He had seen a handbag and could take no more.

And the harpies descended.

Each of them knew what to do. Miss Brown landed

on Mrs. Trottle, who had fainted clean away, and sat on her chest. Miss Green picked up the remaining guard and threw him onto the fire escape. Miss Jones pinned the gibbering Mr. Trottle against a wall.

Only Raymond still stood there, his jaws clamped so hard on his treacle toffee that he couldn't even scream.

And then he stood there no longer.

CHAPTER 19

BY THE EVENING of the ninth day, the rescuers could put off their return no longer, but as they made their way to King's Cross Station they felt sadder than they had ever felt in their lives. To come back in disgrace like this . . . to know that they had failed!

Odge, trudging along with the mistmaker's suitcase, was silent and pale, and this worried the others. They had expected her to rant and rave and stamp her feet when Ben once more refused to come with them, but she had behaved well and that wasn't like her. If Odge was going to be ill, that would really be the end.

They had waited till the last minute to make sure Ben had completely recovered from the blow to his head. He'd kept telling them he was fine; he'd helped them to clear up the summer house, sweeping and tidying with a will, and that had made the parting worse because they'd remembered the moment when they first saw him in the basement of Trottle Towers. How happy they'd been when they thought he was the Prince! How certain that they could bring him back!

But there'd been no changing Ben's mind; he wouldn't leave his grandmother. "She's having an operation," he'd said. "I can't leave her to face that alone. Maybe I can come down next time, when the gump opens again."

He'd turned away then, and they knew how much he minded—but Odge hadn't lost her temper the way she'd done before; she'd just shrugged and said nothing at all.

The ghosts were waiting on Platform Thirteen. They looked thoroughly shaken though it was hours since the harpies had come through on their way to rescuing Raymond.

"I tell you, it was like the armies of the dead," said Ernie. "I wouldn't be Raymond Trottle for all the rice in China. They've had engineers here all afternoon looking for blocked drains."

And indeed the harpies' vile stench still lingered. Even the spiders on the stopped clock looked stunned.

Now it was time to say good-bye, and that was hard. The ghosts and the rescuers had become very fond of each other in the nine days they had worked together, but when Cor asked them if they wouldn't come through the gump, they shook their heads.

"Ghosts is ghosts and Islanders is Islanders," said Ernie. "And what would happen to the gump if we weren't here to guard it?"

But the ogre was looking anxiously at the station roof.

"I think we go now?" he said. "I wish not to be under the smelling ladies when they return."

No one wanted that. No one, for that matter, wanted to see the Prince brought back in the harpies' claws like a dead mouse.

They went through into the cloakroom and shook hands. Even the ghost of the train spotter was upset to see them go.

"Please could you take the mistmaker's suitcase for me," said Odge suddenly. "My arm's getting tired."

Gurkie nodded and Odge went forward to the Opening. "I'll go ahead," she said. "I'm missing my sisters and I want to get there quickly."

It says a lot about how weary and sad the rescuers were that they believed her.

· · ·

When he came into the ward, Ben saw that the curtains were drawn round Nanny's bed.

"Has she had the operation?" he asked the nurse. It was Celeste, the one with the red rose in her cap whom everyone loved.

"No, dear. She's not going to have the operation. She's—very ill, Ben. You can sit with her quietly—she'd like to have you there, but she may not say much."

Ben drew aside the curtain. He could see at once that something had happened to Nanny. Her face was tiny; she looked as though she didn't really belong here anymore. But when he pulled a chair up beside the bed and reached for her hand, the skinny, brown-flecked fingers closed tightly round his own.

"Foiled 'em!" said Nanny in a surprisingly clear voice.

"About the operation, do you mean?"

"That's right. Going up there full of tubes! Told them my time was up!"

Her eyes shut . . . then fluttered open once again.

"The letter . . . take it . . ." she whispered. "Go on. Now."

Ben turned his head and saw a white envelope with his name on it lying on her locker.

"All right, Nanny." She watched him, never taking her eyes away, as he took it and put it carefully in his pocket. And now she could let go.

"You're a good boy . . . We shouldn't have . . ."

Her voice drifted away; her breathing became shallow and uneven; only her hand still held tightly onto Ben's.

"Just sleep, Nanny," he said. "I'll stay."

And he did, as the clock ticked away the hours. That was what he had to do now, sit beside her, not thinking of anything else. Not letting his mind follow Odge and the others as they made their way home . . . Not feeling sorry for himself because the people he loved so much had gone away. Just being there while Nanny needed him, that was his job.

The night nurse, coming in twice, found him still as stone beside the bed. The third time she came in, he had fallen asleep in his chair—but he still held his grandmother's cold hand inside his own.

Gently, she uncurled his fingers and told him what had happened.

It was hard to understand that he was now absolutely alone. People dying, however much you expect it, is not like you think it will be.

The Sister had taken him to her room; she'd given him tea and biscuits. Now, to his surprise, she said: "I've been in touch with the people who are going to fetch you, and they're on their way. Soon you'll be in your new home."

Ben lifted his head. "What?" he said stupidly.

"Mrs. Trottle has made the arrangements for you, Ben. She's found a really nice place for you, she says. A school where you'll learn all sorts of things. She didn't think you'd want to go on living with the other servants now your grandmother is dead."

Ben was incredibly tired; it was difficult to take anything in. "I don't know anything about this," he said.

The Sister patted his shoulder. Mrs. Trottle had sounded so kind and concerned on the telephone that it never occurred to her to be suspicious.

"Ah, here they are now," she said.

Two men came into the room. They wore natty suits —one pin-striped, one pale gray—and kipper ties. One of them had long dark hair parted in the middle and trained over his ears; the other was fair, with thick curls. Both of them smelled strongly of aftershave, but their fingernails were dirty.

Ben disliked them at once. They looked oily and untrustworthy, and he took a step backward.

"I don't want to go with you," he said. "I want to find out what all this is about."

"Now come on, we don't want a fuss," said the dark-haired man. "My name's Stanford, by the way, and this here is Ralph—and we've got a long drive ahead of us, so let's be off sharpish."

"Where to? Where are we going?"

"The name wouldn't mean anything to you," said

Ralph, putting a comb through his curls. "But you'll be all right there, you'll see. Now say good-bye to the Sister, and we'll be on our way."

The Sister looked troubled. The men were not what she had expected, but her orders were clear. Ben must not leave the hospital alone and in a state of shock.

"I'm sure everything will be all right, dear," she said. "And of course you'll come back for your Granny's funeral."

The men caught each other's eye, and Ralph gave a snigger. One thing the children at Ramsden Hall did *not* get was time off to go to funerals!

Ben was so tired now that nothing seemed real to him. If the Sister thought it was all right, then perhaps it was. And after all, what was there for him now in Trottle Towers?

He picked up his jacket. The letter was still in his pocket, but he didn't want to read it in front of these unpleasant men.

"All right," he said wearily. "I'm ready."

And then, sandwiched between the two thugs Mrs. Trottle had hired to deliver him to as horrible a place as could be found in England, he walked down the long hospital corridor toward the entrance hall.

It was very late. As she trudged through the streets, Odge was dazzled by the headlights of cars and the silly advertisements flashing on and off. Advertisements for stomach pills, for hairspray, for every sort of rubbish. For a moment she wondered if she was going to be able to stand it. On the Island now it would be cool and quiet; the mistmakers would be lying close together on the beaches, and the stars would be bright and clear. It wasn't a very nice thought that she would never see the Island under the stars again. Well, not for nine years. But in nine years she might be as silly as her sisters, talking about men and marriage and all that stuff.

She stopped for a moment under a lamp to look at the map. First right, first left, over a main road and she'd be there.

London wasn't very beautiful, but there were good things here, and good people. The Plodger was kind, and Henry Prendergast, and even quite ordinary people: shop assistants and park keepers. It wouldn't be too bad living here. And she wouldn't miss her bossy sisters—well, perhaps Fredegonda a little. Fredegonda could be quite funny when she was practicing squeezing people's stomachs to give them nightmares.

The mistmaker she'd miss horribly, that was true, but she couldn't have kept him. The way those idiots had carried on in the Astor had shown her that, and he was old enough now to fend for himself. When the others realized that she hadn't gone ahead—that she'd doubled back and hidden in the cloakroom—they'd see to him, and explain to her parents. And even if she wanted to change her mind, it was too late. In an hour from now, the gump would be closed.

"I am a hag," she reminded herself, because rather a bad attack of homesickness was coming on. "I am Odge-with-the-Tooth."

She turned left . . . crossed the road. She could see the hospital now, towering over the other buildings. Ben would be in there still, and when she imagined him watching by the old woman's bed, Odge knew she'd done the right thing. Ben was clever, but he was much too trusting; he needed someone who saw things as they really were. No one was going to get the better of Ben while she was around, and if it meant living in dirty London instead of the Island, well, that was part of the job.

Up the steps of the hospital now. Even so late at night there were lights burning in the big entrance hall. Hospitals never slept.

"I am Miss Gribble," she said, and the reception clerk looked down in surprise at the small figure, dressed in an old-fashioned blazer, which had come in out of the dark. "And I have to see—"

She broke off because someone had called her name —and spinning round, she saw Ben coming toward her, hemmed in by two men. His face was white, he looked completely exhausted, and the men seemed to be helping him.

"Odge!" he called again. "What are you doing here? Why aren't you—"

The man on Ben's right jerked his arm. "Now then— we've no time to chat."

He began to pull Ben toward the door, but Ben twisted round, trying to free himself.

"She's dead, Odge!" he cried. "My grandmother. She's dead!" His voice broke; it was the first time he'd said that word.

Odge drew in her breath. Then she looked at the big clock on the wall. A quarter past eleven. They could do it if they hurried. Just.

"Then you can come with me!" she said joyfully. "You can come back to the Island."

Ben blinked, shook himself properly awake. He had lost all sense of time, sitting by his grandmother's bed; he'd thought it was long past midnight and the gump was closed. Hope sprang into his eyes.

"Let me *go*!" he said, and with sudden strength he

pulled away from his guard. "I'm going with her!"

"Oh no, you aren't!" Stanford grabbed his shoulders; Ralph bent Ben's arm behind his back and held it there. "You're coming with us and pronto. Now walk."

Ben fought as hard as he knew how, but the men were strong and there were two of them. And the receptionist had gone into her office. There was no one to see what was happening and help. They were close to the door now, and the waiting car.

But Odge had dodged round in front of them.

"No, Ben, no! You mustn't hurt the poor men," she said. "Can't you see how ill they are?"

"Get out of the way, you ugly little brat, or we'll take you, too," said Stanford, and kicked out at her.

But Odge still stood there, looking very upset.

"Oh, how dreadful! Your poor hair! I'm so *sorry* for you!"

Without thinking, Stanford put his hand to his head. Then he gave a shriek. A lump of black hair the size of a fist had come out of his scalp.

"That's how it starts," said Odge. "With sudden baldness. The frothing and the fits come later."

"My God!" Stanford grabbed at his temples, and another long, greasy wedge of hair fell onto the lapel of his suit.

"And your friend—he's even worse," said Odge. "All those lovely curls!"

It was true. Ralph's curls were dropping onto the

tiled floor like hunks of knitting wool while round patches of pink skin appeared on his scalp.

"Usually there's no cure," Odge went on, "but maybe they could give you an injection in here. Some hospitals do have a vaccine—it gets injected into your behind with a big needle—but you'd have to hurry!"

The thugs waited no longer. Holding onto their heads, trying uselessly to keep in the rest of their hair, they ran down the corridor shrieking for help.

"Oh Odge!" said Ben. "*You* did it! You struck them with baldness!"

"Don't waste time," said the hag.

She put her hand into Ben's, and together they bounded down the steps and out into the night.

CHAPTER 20

THE THREE-MASTED SCHOONER was at anchor off the Secret Cove. Beside it lay the Royal Yacht with its flying standard, and the charter boat. A number of smaller craft—dinghies and rowing boats—were drawn up on the beach. The tide was out; the clean firm sand curved and rippled round the bay. In the light of the setting sun, the sea was calm and quiet.

But the King and Queen stood with their backs to the sea, facing the round dark hole at the bottom of the cliff. The cave which led to the gump was surrounded by thorn bushes and overhung by a ledge of rock. It was from there that the Prince would come.

If he came at all . . .

Flanking the King and Queen were the courtiers and the important people on the Island. The head teacher of the school had come on the charter boat and the Prime Minister and a little girl who had been top in Latin and won the trip as a prize.

And standing behind the King and Queen, but a little way off because they still hadn't allowed themselves to wash, were Lily and Violet and Rose. Each of them held a firm, unopened banana in her hand, and their eyes too were fixed on the cave.

There were just two hours still to go before the Closing.

"Your Majesty should rest," said the royal doctor, coming forward with a folding stool. "At least sit down; you're using up all your strength."

But the Queen couldn't sit; she couldn't eat or drink; she could only stare at the dark hole in the cliff as if to take her eyes from it would be to abandon the last shred of hope.

At ten-thirty the flares were lit. Flares round the opening, flares along the curving bay now crowded with people. . . . A ring of flares where the King and Queen waited. It was beautiful, the flickering firelight, but frightening too, for it marked the ending of the last day.

But not surely the end of hope?

Five minutes passed . . . ten . . . Then from the crowd lining the shore there came a rustle of excitement . . . a murmuring—and from the Queen a sudden cry.

A lone figure had appeared in the opening. The King and Queen had already moved toward it, when they checked. It was not their son who stood in the mouth of the cave—it was not anyone they knew. It was in fact a very tired witch called Mrs. Harbottle, holding a carrier bag and looking bewildered. She'd heard about the gump from a sorcerer who worked in the Job Center and decided she fancied it.

The disappointment was bitter. The Queen did not weep, but those who stood close to her could see, suddenly, how she would look when she was old.

Another silence—more ticking away of the minutes. A cold breeze blew in from the sea. Rose and Lily and Violet still held their closed bananas, but Lily had begun to snivel.

Then once more the mouth of the cave filled with figures. Well-known ones this time—and once more hope leapt up, only to die again. There was no need to ask if the rescuers had, after all, brought back the Prince. Cor was bent and huddled into his cloak; Gurkie carried her straw basket as if the weight was too much to bear—and where the fernseed had worn off, they could see the ogre's red, unhappy face.

From just a few people on the shore there came

hisses and boos, but the others quickly shushed them. They knew how terrible the rescuers must feel, coming back empty-handed, and that failure was punishment enough.

Cor was too ashamed to go and greet the King and Queen. He moved out of the light of the flares and sat down wearily on a rock. Gurkie was looking for Odge in the crowd gathered on the beach. She could make out two of Odge's sisters, but there was no sign of the little hag—and trying not to think what a homecoming this might have been, she went to join Cor and the ogre in the shadows.

"We must go and speak to them," said the King. "They will have done their best."

"Yes." But before the Queen could gather up her strength, the child who had won the Latin prize put up her hand.

"Listen!" she said.

Then the others heard it too. Baying. Barking. Howling. The sky yelpers were back!

They burst out of the opening—the whole pack—tumbling over each other, slobbering, slavering, their saucer eyes glinting. Freed suddenly from the tunnel, they hurled themselves about, sending up sprays of loose sand.

But not for long! The smell came first—and then Miss Witherspoon, holding her whistle.

"Sit!" screamed the harpy—and the dogs sat.

"Grovel!" she screeched, and the dogs flopped onto their stomachs, slobbering with humbleness.

"Stay!" she yelled—and they stayed.

Then she stepped aside. The smell grew worse, and out of the tunnel, feet first, came Miss Green, Miss Brown, and Miss Jones. The monstrous bird-women's wings were furled, and one look at their smug faces showed the watchers what they wanted to know.

Turning, the harpies took their place on either side of the tunnel and stretched out their arms with their dangling handbags. "Lo!" they seemed to be saying as they pointed to the opening. "Behold! The Great One comes!"

A cheer went up then and to the sound of hurrahs and the sight of waving hands, Mrs. Smith appeared in the mouth of the cave.

And in her arms—a sack! A large sack, tied at the top but heaving and bulging so that they knew what was inside it was very much alive.

The Prince! The Prince had come!

All eyes went to the King and Queen. The Queen stood with her hand to her heart. He had come in a sack, as a prisoner—but he had come! Nothing mattered except that.

But before she could move forward, the chief harpy put up her arm. She had decided to drop Raymond at the feet of the King and Queen—to sail through the air with him, like the giant birds in the stories. Now she picked up the sack in her talons; unfurled her wings—and circling the heads of the crowd, holding the squirming bundle in her iron claws, she came down and, with perfect timing, dropped it on a hummock of sand.

"I bring you His Royal Highness, the Prince of the Island," said Mrs. Smith—and patted her perm.

The cheering had stopped. No one stirred now, no one spoke. This was the moment they had waited for for nine long years.

The harpy bent down to the sack—and the King banished her with a frown. Later she would be rewarded, but no stranger was going to unwrap this precious burden.

"Your scissors," he said to the doctor.

The doctor opened his black bag and handed them over. The Queen was deathly pale; her breath came in gasps as she stood beside her husband.

With a single snip, the King cut the string, unwound it, loosened the top of the sack. The Queen helped him ease it over the boy's shoulders. Then with a sudden slurp like a grub coming out of an egg, the wriggling figure of Raymond Trottle fell out on the sand.

He wasn't just wriggling; he was yelling, he was howling, he was kicking. Snot ran from his nose as he tried to fight off the Queen's gentle hands.

"I want my Mummy! I want my Mummy! I want to go home!" sobbed Raymond Trottle.

The nurses stepped forward, their unzipped bananas in their hands—and stepped back, zipping them up again. And a great worry fell over the watchers on the shore because even from a distance they could see the Prince kicking out at his parents and hear his screams, and now as the King set him firmly on his feet, they saw his piggy, swollen face and the hiccuping sobs that came from him. Would the Queen not be terribly hurt at the way her son was carrying on?

They needn't have worried. The Queen had straightened herself; and as she lifted her face, they saw that she was looking most wonderfully and radiantly happy. The years fell away from her, and she might have been a girl of seventeen. Then the King followed her gaze, and the watching crowd saw this brave man become transfigured too and change into the carefree ruler they had known.

On the ground, the boy the harpies had brought continued to kick and scream, and the Queen very politely moved her skirt away from him, but she did not run. She moved the way people do in dreams, half gliding, half dancing, as though there was all the time and happiness in the wide world—and the King moved with her, his hand under her arm.

Only then did the onlookers turn their heads to the mouth of the cave and see two figures standing there. One was the little hag, Odge Gribble. The other was a boy.

A boy who for an instant stood quite still with a look of wonder on his face. Then he let go of Odge's hand, and he *did* run. He ran like the wind, scarcely touching the ground—nor did he stop when he reached the King and Queen, but threw himself into their arms as though all his life had led to this moment.

And now the three figures became one, and as the King and Queen held him and encircled him, the watchers heard the same words repeated again and again.

"My son! My son! My *son!*"

CHAPTER 21

ODGE GRIBBLE had moved into the nurses' cave. A week had passed since Ben had gone to the palace to live, and she hadn't heard a single word from him. Now she was going to retire from the world and become a hermit. She had left a note for her mother and her sisters, and she was settling in.

The nurses had eaten burnt toast and slept on stones and poked sticks into their ears, but the things Odge was going to do were much more interesting than that.

She was going to sleep on rusty spikes and eat slime and raw jellyfish. She wasn't going to talk to a living soul ever again, and every day and in every way she was going to get more awful and fearful and hag-like. By the time she was grown up, she would be known as Odge of the Cave, or Odge of the Ocean, or just Odge the Unutterable. The cave would be full of frogs she had coughed; *all* her teeth would be blue, and the bump on her left foot would have turned not into one extra toe, but into seven of them at least.

Now she unpacked her suitcase. It was the one the mistmaker had traveled in, but of course Ben had taken the mistmaker with him to the palace. It was her pet really, but Ben hadn't cared; he'd just gone off with his parents to be a prince and never given her another thought. They said that when people became grand and famous, they forgot their friends, and Ben certainly proved it.

She found a flat boulder which would do as a table and decided to have moldy bladder wrack for lunch. She wouldn't eat with a knife and fork either; she'd eat with her fingers so as to become disgusting as quickly as possible. Now that the nurses did nothing but guzzle beautiful bananas and parade around in frilled dresses which they washed three times a day, it was time someone remembered sorrow and awfulness.

She found the bladder wrack all right; it even had

some little worms crawling on it, but she decided to have lunch a bit later. Not that she was going to be beaten; she'd eat it in the end, all of it. She wasn't going to be beaten by *anything*. No one was going to hurt her again, and she wasn't going back to school either. She had enjoyed school, but she wasn't going to enjoy anything anymore *ever*, and that would show them!

But as she sat with her toes in an icy pool, waiting for them to turn blue and perhaps even drop off with frostbite, she couldn't help thinking how cruel and unfair life was. For it was she who had brought Ben through the gump, and if she hadn't made him open his grandmother's letter as the taxi took them to King's Cross, he might still have argued about coming and perhaps not being welcome on the Island.

Odge could remember every word that Nanny Brown had written.

"Dear Ben," the letter began. "I have to tell you that something very bad was done to you when you were little. You see, you were kidnapped by Mrs. Trottle. She snatched you from your basket near King's Cross Station and carried you off to Switzerland, meaning to pass you off as her own child. But when she got there, she found she was expecting a baby of her own, and after Raymond was born to her, she turned against you and would have sent you away, only I wouldn't let her. No one knows who your real parents are, but they must have loved you very much because you were wearing the most beautiful clothes and the comforter in your mouth was on a golden ring.

"So you must go the police at *once*, Ben, and tell them the truth and ask them to help you find your family—and please forgive me for the lies I told you all those years."

The whole thing had made sense to Odge at once. Ben must have been so much nicer to look at than Raymond, and cleverer, and better able to do things. No wonder Mrs. Trottle had got annoyed and tried to send him away.

And Ben *was* nice—he was as nice as Raymond was nasty—so that it hurt all the more that he had forgotten her. True, the King and Queen had hugged her and the other rescuers and said how grateful they were—and it was true too that the short time between Ben coming through and the Closing had been incredibly busy. Raymond had had to be packed up and thrown into one of the last of the wind baskets that went up to King's Cross, and what the ghosts of the gump thought when they saw him was anybody's guess. And just as Raymond went up, there was a great surge of last-minute people coming down: the Plodger with a bundle of wet cloths which turned out to be his niece Melisande, and the troll called Henry Prendergast, and two of the banshees who'd got wind of the fact that Raymond wasn't the Prince and decided to come to the Island after all.

Even so, Odge had at first not believed that she was forgotten. Every day she had waited at least to be asked to tea at the palace, or thought Ben might ride by her home and ask how she was. Everyone told stories about him—about his white pony, his intelligence, the great wolfhound his father had given him, and the happiness of the Queen who looked so beautiful that the King had had to post a special guard at the palace gates to take in the bunches of flowers which besotted young men left for her.

Well, that's nothing to do with me, thought Odge. I shall stay here in the darkness and the cold and get shriveled and old, and one day they'll find a heap of bones in the corner—and then they'll be sorry.

She was sitting in the mouth of the cave, her hands round her knees, and coughing, when she saw a boy picking his way between the mistmakers on the sands. As he came closer she saw who it was, but she didn't take any notice, she just went on coughing.

"Hello!" said Ben. He looked incredibly well and incredibly happy. She'd have liked to see him wearing silly clothes to show he was royal, but he wasn't—he wore a blue shirt and cotton trousers, and he'd come alone.

"What are you doing?" asked Ben, surprised.

"I'm trying to cough frogs, if you really want to

know," said Odge. "Not that it's any business of yours."

Ben looked round to see if there were any frogs there, but there weren't.

"Odge, I don't know why you're so keen on coughing them. What would you do with them if you did cough them? Ten to one, they'd start thinking they were enchanted princes and wanting you to kiss them and what then?"

Odge sniffed. "I haven't the slightest idea why you've come," she said. "As you see, I've moved in here and I'm going to live here for the rest of my life."

"Why?" asked Ben, sitting down beside her.

Odge drew her hair round her face and disappeared. "Because I want to be alone. I don't want to live in the world, which is full of ingratitude and pain. And I can't help wondering what you're doing sitting on the ground? Why didn't you bring your throne, an important prince like you?"

Ben looked at her amazed. "What on earth's got into you?" he asked.

"Nothing. I told you, I'm going to live here for the rest of my life."

But Ben had seen, in a chink between her hair, the glint of tears. "I see. Well, that's rather a waste because we've spent a whole week decorating your room and furnishing it so as to be a surprise. I suppose I shall just have to tell my parents that you don't want to come, but they'll be terribly disappointed."

"What room?" asked Odge faintly.

"Your room; I've told you. The one next to mine in the palace. It was painted pink, and we didn't think that was right for a hag, so my mother chose a midnight-blue wallpaper with a frieze of bats, and she put a cat door in for the mistmaker, and you've got a huge bed stuffed with raven's feathers—the ravens *gave* their feathers because you're a heroine. It's pretty nice. And my mother drove over to your mother this morning to ask if you could come and live, and your mother said it was all right as long as you visit once a week. So it's kind of a pity about the cave."

He waited. Odge turned her head. Her green eye appeared; then her brown one as she shook back her hair.

"Really? You want me to live with you?"

"Of course. We decided it on the first day, my parents and I," said Ben, and when he said "my parents" his whole face seemed to light up. "Perhaps we should have told you, only I love surprises and I thought maybe you do too."

"Well, yes, I do actually." She scuffed her shoes on the sand. "Only . . . what if I don't turn out to be . . . you know . . . mighty and fearful? Would they want to have a hag that's just . . . ordinary . . . living in a palace? I mean, I may *never* get an extra toe."

Ben got to his feet. "Don't be silly, Odge," he said. You're *you* and it's you we want."

Odge blew her nose and put her pajamas back in the suitcase. Then she gave Ben her hand, and together they walked along the shore toward the welcoming roofs of the palace.

Also by Eva Ibbotson

Which Witch?
The Secret of Platform 13

Island OF THE AUNTS

The

Island

Ethelgonda's
burial
ground

north shore

to the
crystal cave

the
boobrie's
nest

the
stoorworm's
loch

the
Sybil's
cave

mermaid
shed

seal rocks

the
Peggoty

jetty

boathouse

the Hurricane

the
aunts'
house

Island
OF THE
AUNTS

Eva Ibbotson
illustrated by Kevin Hawkes

Dutton Children's Books ✳ *New York*

*To my husband, who really cared about
unusual creatures*

Text copyright © 1999 by Eva Ibbotson
Illustrations copyright © 2000 by Kevin Hawkes
All rights reserved.

CIP Data is available.

Published in the United States 2000 by Dutton Children's Books,
a division of Penguin Putnam Books for Young Readers
345 Hudson Street, New York, New York 10014
www.penguinputnam.com

Originally published in Great Britain 1999
by Macmillan Children's Books, London
Typography by Richard Amari
Printed in USA
First American Edition
ISBN 0-525-46484-0
4 6 8 10 9 7 5 3

Island
OF
THE AUNTS

Chapter 1

KIDNAPPING CHILDREN is not a good idea. All the same, sometimes it has to be done.

Aunt Etta and Aunt Coral and Aunt Myrtle were not natural kidnappers. For one thing, they were getting old, and kidnapping is hard work; for another, though they looked a little odd, they were very caring people. They cared for their ancient father and for their shriveled cousin Sybil, who lived in a cave and tried to foretell the future—and most particularly they cared for the animals on the island on which they lived, many of which were quite unusual.

Some of the creatures that made their way to the Island had come far across the ocean to be looked after, and lately the aunts had felt that they could not go on much longer without help. And "help" didn't mean grown-ups who were set in their ways. "Help" meant children who were young and strong and willing to learn.

So, on a cool, blustery day in April, the three aunts gathered round the kitchen table and decided to go ahead. Some children had to be found, and they had to be brought to the Island, and kidnapping seemed the only sensible way to do it.

"That way we can choose the ones who are suitable," said Aunt Etta. She was the eldest—a tall, bony woman who did fifty press-ups before breakfast and had a small but not at all unpleasant mustache on her upper lip.

The others looked out of the window at the soft green turf, the sparkling sea, and sighed, thinking of what had to be done. The sleeping powders, the drugged hamburgers, the bags and sacks and cello cases they would need to carry the children away in . . .

"Will they scream and wriggle, do you suppose?" asked Aunt Myrtle, who was the youngest. She suffered from headaches and hated noise.

"No, of course not. They'll be unconscious," said Aunt Etta. "Flat out. I don't like it any more than you do," she went on, "but you saw the program on TV last week."

The others nodded. When they first came to the Island, they hadn't had any electricity, but after his hundredth birthday their father's toes had started to turn blue because not enough blood got to his feet, and they

4

had ordered a generator so he could have an electric blanket. After that they thought they might as well have an electric kettle and then a TV.

But the TV had been a mistake because of the nature programs. Nature programs always end badly. First you see the hairy-nosed wombats frisking about with their babies, and then five minutes before the end you hear that there are only twelve breeding pairs left in the whole of Australia. Or there are pictures of the harlequin frogs of Costa Rica croaking away on their lily leaves, and the next minute you are told that they're doomed because their swamps are being drained. Worst of all are the rainforests. The aunts could never see a program about the rainforests without crying, and last week there had been a particularly bad one with wicked people burning and slashing the trees, and pictures of the monkeys and the jaguars rushing away in terror.

"What if *we* became extinct?" Aunt Coral had wondered, blowing her nose. "Not just the wombats and the harlequin frogs and the jaguars, but *us.*"

The others had seen the point at once. If a whole rainforest can become extinct, why not three elderly ladies? And if they became extinct, what would happen to their work and who would care for the creatures that came to the Island in search of comfort and care?

There was another thing that bothered the aunts. Lately the animals that came to the Island simply wouldn't go away again. Long after they were healed, they stayed on—it was almost as if they knew some-thing—and that made more and more work for the aunts. There was no doubt about it, help had to be brought in, and quickly.

So now they were deciding what to do.

"How do you find the *right* children?" asked Myrtle. She looked longingly out at the point where the seals were resting. One of the seals, Herbert, was her special friend, and she would very much rather have been out there playing her cello and singing her songs to him.

"We shall become *Aunts*," said Etta firmly, settling her spectacles on her long nose.

The others looked at her in amazement. "But we *are* aunts," they said. "How can we *become* them?"

This was true. There had been five sisters who had come to the Island with their father many years ago. They had found a ruined house and deserted beaches with only the footprints of sandpipers and herring gulls on the sand, and barnacle geese resting on the way from Greenland, and the seals, quite unafraid, coming out of the water to have their pups.

They had started to repair the house and planted a garden, and then one day they had found an oiled seabird washed up on a rock. . . . Only it turned out not to be an oiled seabird. It was oiled all right, but it was something quite different—and after that, they realized

6

that they had been called to the Island by a Higher Power, and that they had found their life's work.

But one of the sisters, Betty, had not cared for the Island. She hated the wind and the rain and the fish scales in her tea and the eider ducklings nesting in her bedroom slippers. She had gone away and got married to a tax inspector in Newcastle upon Tyne, and now she lived in a house with three kinds of toilet freshener in the loo and sprays to make her armpits smell nice and not a fish scale in sight.

But the point was that she had two children. She called the boy Boo-Boo and the girl Little One (though they had proper names, of course). And horrible though they were, they were children, and because of this, her sisters had become aunts, since all you have to do to become an aunt is have nephews and nieces.

Which is why now the sisters looked so surprised and said: "But we *are* aunts."

"Not that kind," said Etta impatiently. "I mean the kind that live in an office or an agency and call themselves things like *Useful Aunts* or *Universal Aunts* or *Aunts Inc.*—the kind that parents pay to take their children to school and to the dentist or to sit with them when they are ill."

"Why don't the parents do it themselves?" asked Myrtle.

"Because they're too busy. People used to have real

7

aunts and grandmothers and cousins to do it all, but now families are too small, and real aunts go to dances and have boyfriends," said Etta, snorting.

Coral nodded her head. She was the arty one, a large plump person who fed the chickens in a feather boa and interesting jewelry, and at night by the light of the moon, she danced the tango.

"It's a good idea," she said. "You would be able to pick and choose the children—you don't want to end up with a Boo-Boo or a Little One."

"Yes, but if the parents are truly fond of the children, we shouldn't do it," said Myrtle, pushing back her long gray hair.

"Well, of course not," said Etta. "We don't want a hue and cry."

"But if the children are nice, the parents *would* be fond of them," said Myrtle. "And if they aren't, we don't want them either."

Etta sniffed. "You'd be surprised. There are children all over the place whose parents don't know how lucky they are."

They went on talking for a long time, but no one could think of anything better than Etta's plan—not if the position of the Island was to be kept secret, and there was nothing more important than that.

There was one more aunt who would have been useful—not the one with the three kinds of toilet freshener, who was of no use for anything—but Aunt Dorothy, who was next in age to Etta and would have been just the sort of person to have on a kidnapping expedition. But Dorothy was in prison in Hong Kong. She had gone out there to stop a restaurant owner from serving pangolin steaks—pangolins are beautiful, scaly mammals that are getting rare and should never be eaten—and Dorothy had got annoyed and hit the restaurant owner on the head with his own wok, and they had put her in prison. She was due out in a month, but in the meantime only the three of them could go on the mission, and they weren't at all sure about Myrtle because she was not very good out in the world, and when she was away she always pined for Herbert.

"Are you sure you wouldn't rather stay behind, Myrtle?" said Coral now. But Myrtle had decided to be brave and said she thought that she should come along and do her bit.

"Only we won't say anything to Daddy," said Etta. "After all, kidnapping is a crime, and he might worry."

Captain Harper lived upstairs in a big bed with a telescope, looking out to sea. They had mostly given up telling him things. For one thing, he was stone deaf, so that explaining anything took a very long time; and for another, as soon as he saw anybody he started telling them stories about what life had been like when he was a boy. They were good stories, but every single aunt had heard them about three hundred times, so they didn't hang around if they could help it.

But they did go and tell the Sybil. She was the old cousin who had come to the Island soon after them. Sybil was bookish, and one day she had read a book about Greek mythology and about a person called *the* Sybil (not just Sybil) who was a prophetess and could foretell the future. So she had started prophesying about the weather, mumbling on about depressions over Iceland and the windchill factor, and really she didn't get it wrong much more often than the weathermen on the telly. Then she had moved on to other things and had gone to live in a cave with bats because that was where prophetesses were supposed to live. She had stopped washing because she said washing would weaken her powers, so that she was another person one did not visit for too long.

When the aunts told her that they were going to the mainland to kidnap some children, the Sybil got quite excited. Her face turned blue, and her hair began to stand on end, and for a moment they hoped she was going to tell them something important about the journey.

But it turned out that what she was foreseeing was squally showers and what she said was "take seasick pills," which they had decided to do anyway for the boat.

They still had to make sure that their cook, who was called Art, knew exactly what to do while they were away on their mission. Art was an escaped convict who had been washed up in a rowing boat on their shore. He had killed a man when he was young, and now he wouldn't kill anything with arms or legs or eyes—not even a shrimp—but he made excellent porridge. Then they gathered together all the things they would need: chloroform and sleeping powders and anesthetizing darts, which they used for stunning animals that were injured so that they could set their limbs. All of them had things to carry the children away in: Aunt Etta had a canvas holdall, Aunt Coral had a tin trunk with holes bored into it, and Aunt Myrtle had her cello case. They waited for the wind to change so they could sail the *Peggoty* to the next island and catch the steamer; they were terribly excited.

It was a long and difficult journey—many years ago the army had tried to use the Island for experiments in radio signals, and so to keep its position secret, they had changed the maps and forbidden boats to come near it. In the end the army hadn't used it after all, but it was still a forgotten place, and the aunts meant to see that it stayed that way.

"Of course, it won't be a real kidnap because we shan't ask the parents for a ransom," said Etta.

"It'll be more of a child snatch," Coral agreed.

But whether it was a kidnap or a child snatch, it was still dangerous and wicked, and as they waved good-bye to the Island their hearts were beating very fast.

Chapter 2

BY THE TIME she was ten years old, Minette had made the journey between London and Edinburgh forty-seven times. Forty-seven station buffet sandwiches; forty-seven visits to the loo on the train; and forty-seven stomachaches because changing families always churned up her inside.

Minette's father lived in Edinburgh in a tall gray house and was a professor of grammar. Minette's mother lived in a flat in London and was an actress—at least she would have been if anyone had given her any work. They had been separated since Minette was three years old, and they hated each other with a bitter and deadly hatred.

"Tell that louse of a father of yours that he's late with his money again," was the sort of message that Minette's mother usually sent as she took her daughter to King's Cross to put her on the train to Edinburgh.

Or: "No doubt your mother is still running a rooming house for drunken actors," her father would say as he fetched her from the train.

Minette never gave her parents these messages. She made up polite, friendly messages for them to send to each other, but neither her mother nor her father believed her when she delivered them. And on the journey, which took five hours, Minette would look out the window searching for houses where she and her mother and her father would live together one day like an ordinary family with a cat and a canary and a dog. For it went on hurting her, hurting and hurting—not that her parents were separated; lots of children she knew had separated parents—but that they hated each other so much.

On these journeys Minette was usually put in the charge of an aunt. The aunt came from an office called *Useful Aunts,* and what she was like was important because if she talked all the time or wanted to play silly games, Minette couldn't give her mind to finding houses for her parents to live in or imagining beautiful scenes where she was run over and taken to the hospital and her mother and father rushed to her bedside and looked at each other over their daughter's bleeding body and found that they loved each other after all.

Then, as she got up to go on her forty-eighth journey, Minette suddenly realized that it didn't matter *what* kind of aunt they sent to take her because she had given up hope. Her parents would always hate each other, and she would spend the rest of her life traveling from London to Edinburgh and back again, never quite knowing which was her home or where she properly belonged.

And as though someone Up There had heard her, that day they sent her a quite extraordinary aunt.

She was so unlike the other aunts she had traveled with that both Minette and her mother stopped dead as they came up to where she waited, by the bookstall on Platform One of King's Cross Station.

"Are you . . . ?" began Mrs. Danby.

The woman nodded. She was very tall with a small mustache and carried a large holdall that smelled slightly of fish.

"I am your aunt," she said in a deep voice and pointed to her lapel, on which there was a label saying *Unusual Aunts* and, above that, the words *My name is Etta*.

If Minette's mother hadn't been in a hurry to go to the cinema with her latest boyfriend, she might have asked more questions. After all, an *Unusual Aunt* is not quite the same as a *Useful* one, but as it was she handed over the money for the tickets and Minette's lunch, took the cigarette out of her mouth long enough to kiss her daughter, and went away.

And presently Minette and the aunt sat opposite each other in one of those old-fashioned compartments that have no corridor and watched the train make its way through the London suburbs.

Aunt Etta and her sisters had had a hard week in London. They found a boardinghouse full of people like themselves—auntlike persons who had come to town to show their pug dogs at dog shows or go to meetings about setting up retirement homes for ancient donkeys. But they hated the noise and the traffic and the dirty air, and they did not find it easy to get taken on by an agency.

Even when Etta made up an agency and advertised for clients, the children she was given to care for were unspeakable. She took a little boy on a trip down the river who spent the whole time stuffing himself with ice cream and popcorn and crisps and dropping the wrappers in the water. She was sent to take a small girl to have her teeth cleaned and saw her bite the dentist's hand, and she sat with a whining brat called Tarquin Sterndale-Fish who had the measles.

So by the time she met Minette at King's Cross Station, Etta had begun to think that this kidnapping idea was pretty stupid. The world seemed to be full of Boo-Boos and Little Ones, and it was better to become extinct, like the rainforests, than to bring such children to the Island.

Her first sight of Minette did not make her feel hopeful. The child had a crumpled, pinched sort of look; she was small for her age and very thin and looked as though she had been born tired. A meek and feeble child would be quite useless for the work that had to be done. She was also very stupidly dressed, with a load of fluffy pom-poms in her long brown hair and a T-shirt that said *Pinch me and I'll squeal* and a pink plastic handbag shaped like a heart that dangled from her shoulder.

And if Aunt Etta did not like the look of Minette, Minette was not in the least keen on Aunt Etta.

For a while the two of them sat in silence. From time to time, a drop of water fell from the canvas holdall that the aunt had put on the luggage rack onto her topknot of gray hair, but she did not seem to notice it.

"Is something leaking?" asked Minette.

The aunt looked up and shook her head. "The canvas never seems to dry out properly. I use it to move seals about. Only pups of course; a full-grown seal would never fit inside."

Minette began to be interested; her face lost its pinched and troubled look. "Are you a vet then?"

"Not exactly. But that does sort of come into it."

There was another silence. Minette did not like to pry, so she looked out of the window again. They were coming to the first of the dream houses that Minette had chosen to live in with her parents. It was an old stationmaster's house with hanging baskets of flowers and a little gable. And as though she read her thoughts, the aunt said: "What a pleasant place to live in. There might be ghost trains going through at night with interesting specters. That could liven things up."

Minette stared at her. "Do you believe in —"

"Of course," said the aunt briskly. "Certainly. I believe in almost everything, don't you?"

"My father says we mustn't believe anything we can't see or prove," she said.

"Really?"

When they had been traveling for an hour, Minette opened her suitcase and became very busy. She had been wearing pink and orange socks with a border of Mickey Mice. Now she took them off and put on plain white ones. Then she removed the T-shirt that said *Pinch me and I'll squeal* and put on a navy blue one with long sleeves and no writing at all. And lastly she put the dangling handbag back in the suitcase and took out a practical leather purse.

The aunt said nothing, watching as Minette changed from a trendy little dresser to a sensible old-fashioned schoolgirl.

But Minette had not finished. She took out her brush and comb, propped a mirror on her knees, and began to fix her hair into two long, tight braids.

"I always change here," she explained, "because there's nothing interesting to look at out of the window. My father doesn't like clothes with writing. Or funny socks. He thinks they're vulgar. And he hates untidy hair."

"And when you come back, you change back again — put on the pom-poms and unbraid your hair?"

"Yes. My mother likes it loose."

"And you? Which do you like?"

Minette sighed. "I'd like it cut short."

"Well, I have some scissors here. Why don't we cut it?" She opened a very large handbag and took out a pair of scissors.

"Oh no! I couldn't. Then *both* of them would be angry."

Aunt Etta shrugged and dropped the scissors back into her bag. "Actually, long hair can be useful."

"How can it?"

"Oh, for polishing things . . . oyster shells and such- like. And if you fell into the water, it would be some- thing to get hold of."

They had come to the second of Minette's dream houses — a low white house on the bed of a river with a willow tree and a garden sloping down to the water. But this time Minette did not see her mother and father tak- ing tea together on the lawn. She heard her father say- ing, "That willow must come down, it cuts off all the light" — and her mother saying, "If you cut that tree down, I'll have you put in a mental home."

And suddenly, for no reason, she told this strange

woman about her endless journeys from her mother's tiny flat with its smell of face powder and curry from the take-away downstairs, and the tights dripping in the bathroom, to her father's cold, tidy, solemn house with its ticking grandfather clock. And about the silly dreams she'd had of bringing them together and the hopelessness of it all.

"Do you think there might be a third place? Not my father's house or my mother's apartment but somewhere else—by the sea, perhaps? And that one day I might find it?"

She drew back, suddenly frightened, because the fierce aunt was looking at her far too intently.

But Aunt Etta was nodding. "Of course," she said. "Of course there is a third place. There is one for everybody. But it's no good filling it up with people from your old life. If you want to find the third place, you must find it alone."

"But I'm a child. I can't go and live alone."

"Perhaps not. Not exactly. But you might be able to make a new start just the same if you had the courage."

"I don't have courage," said Minette firmly. "I'm a coward." It was one of the few things on which her parents agreed. "I'm frightened of the dark and of diving off the high board and of being bullied."

The train stopped at York, and the aunt bought sandwiches off a trolley. "Now I suggest you go and wash

your hands and freshen up," she said, "because it's time we had our lunch. Which of these sandwiches would you like—egg and cress or cheese and tomato?"

"Cheese and tomato, please."

If Minette had known what was going to happen as soon as she had gone, she would have been very scared indeed. For out of the pocket of her long, navy blue knickers, the aunt took a little box with a brownish powder, which she sprinkled carefully into the center of the cheese-and-tomato sandwich. Then she unzipped the holdall and sat back in her seat with a very contented smile.

"My first one," she murmured to herself. "My very first kidnapping. Oh really, this is most exciting!" And then: "I wonder how Coral is getting on?"

It had been much harder to get Coral to look like an agency aunt. She was the plump one who had been to art school when she was young, and she liked to stand out from the crowd, but she had done her best to look sensible. She wore only two necklaces and one pair of dangly earrings, and the hand-painted squiggles on her robe and matching turban were *peaceful* squiggles, so when she rang the bell of the big house in Mayfair, she felt that she looked as auntlike as she ever would.

The idea of fetching Hubert-Henry Mountjoy from his grandparents' London house and taking him back to

21

his boarding school in Berkshire made Aunt Coral feel extremely glum.

Her first batch of children had been as bad as Etta's: a poisonous, pudgy child who had tried to kick her shins, and a little boy who jumped on a beetle in the park. She was sure that Hubert-Henry Mountjoy would not be her cup of tea—a cold-eyed, snotty little aristo too big for his boots—and she had decided that if she caught him jumping on beetles, she would wallop him hard and give up being an aunt and go home.

As she was shown into the Mountjoys' hall by a snooty maid, she felt worse than ever. The house was huge and dark and cold; there was a big brass gong in one corner; paintings of dead Mountjoys with handlebar mustaches hung on the walls. She waited with the deepest gloom for her first sight of Hubert-Henry in his school uniform.

The door of the drawing room opened. A small boy came out, pushed forward by a tall, white-haired man who looked exactly like the men in the portraits except that he wasn't dead—and her mouth dropped very slightly open.

Hubert-Henry was small and lightly built with jet black hair, olive skin, and huge, very dark eyes. Something about the graceful way he moved and the wary look on his face reminded her of pictures she had seen of the children of South America who made their home among the vines and orchids and broad-leaved trees of the tropical forest.

The old man with the handlebar mustache now spoke. "This is Hubert-Henry," he said in a braying voice. "As you see, he was not born an English gentleman—but we mean to see that he becomes one, eh, Hubert?"

And as he dug the silent little boy in the ribs, Aunt Coral saw a look of such hatred pass over the child's face that she took a step backward and hit her backside on the big brass gong, at which point Hubert-Henry threw back his head and laughed.

A half hour later, they sat side by side in a large black car on the way to Hubert's school. The car was a limo, the kind you hire for weddings and funerals, with a glass partition sealing off the chauffeur. It was a three-hour journey to Berkshire, but the driver had refused to take Hubert-Henry by himself, so Aunt Coral was to deliver him to Greymarsh Towers and hand him over to the matron. The little boy, it seemed, had tried to jump from the train and run away the last time they took him back to his boarding school.

"Are you really called Hubert-Henry?" asked Aunt Coral as they began to leave London behind.

"No."

"What are you called?"

"Fabio."

He had a slight accent. Spanish, perhaps? Or Portuguese?

She hoped he would say more, but he sat silent and sulky. Then: "I said I'd bash the next aunt they fobbed me off with. Bash her really hard."

"Oh, I wouldn't do that," said Coral. "I've got a kick like a mule. It's the hair, you see."

"What hair?"

"The hair on my legs. We've all got hairy legs, me and my sisters. Hair gives you strength; it says so in the Bible. Samson and all that."

But she wasn't really thinking about what she was saying. Aunt Coral was a little bit psychic, as artistic people so often are, which means that she sometimes knew things without knowing how she knew them, and now she dug into her basket, took out a pad and a piece of charcoal, and began to draw.

Fabio, still sulky, turned his head away. When she had finished, she put the picture down on the seat between them. Presently she heard a little gasp. The boy had seized the paper and was devouring it with his eyes, and she saw a single tear run down his cheek.

"Is that what your home was like?" she asked gently.

Fabio nodded. "The tree's right; it was a papaya, and the monkey . . . he was a capuchin, and I tamed him. But there were three huts joined together, not just one—we lived in the end one, closest to the river. The chickens

24

were ours, but the goat belonged to my uncle in the middle house. You've got the pig right, but his stomach was even bigger—it touched the ground."

"So why did you leave, Fabio?" she asked. The homesick child was still staring at the picture she had drawn—the river, the great tree with fruit hanging from its branches, and the fishing boat drawn up on the shore.

"I don't know *exactly*," he said. But he told her what he knew, and she pieced the rest together.

His father, Henry Mountjoy, had been an Englishman, rich, and the owner of a big house in the country; but he was a gambler. He got into debt, and in the end he had gone off to South America to find gold.

Only, of course, he didn't find gold. He fell ill, and Fabio's mother, who was a dancer in a nightclub, had found him half starving in Rio and had nursed him, and after a while he married her.

But he'd ruined his health, and he couldn't get work, and soon after Fabio was born he went back to England. Since then Fabio had lived first with his mother in Rio and then, when she moved in with another man, upriver in the forest with his grandparents and his uncle and his cousins. There were a lot of people in the three huts and very little money, but Fabio had been perfectly happy. His grandfather was an Amorian Indian and knew everything, and his grandmother had worked as a cook for a Portuguese planter and had told the most marvelous stories.

26

Then, just over a year ago, his mother had come with an Englishman in a silly suit who kept mopping his face all the time and wrinkled up his nose when he passed the pig. It turned out that Fabio's father had died and on his deathbed had begged his parents, the old Mountjoys, to bring Fabio to England and bring him up as an English gentleman.

That was the beginning of the nightmare. His mother had insisted that he go. Henry Mountjoy had talked so much about his grand house in England that she wanted her son to have his share. But the grand house had been sold to pay Henry's debts, and Henry's parents took one look at the wild little boy and shuddered.

Since the grandparents were too old to turn Fabio into an English gentleman, this odd thing was to be done in a boarding school. But boarding schools, according to the old Mountjoys, had gone soft. They had tried two from which Fabio had returned much as before, only speaking better English.

Greymarsh Towers, though, was different. The headmaster believed not just in cold baths and stiff upper lips, but in all sorts of things that one would have thought didn't happen anymore, and the boys were vile.

"They call me 'monkey' or 'chopsticks' and try to tie me up. But I'm going to kill them this time. I'm going to kill them, and I'm going to kill the headmaster, and they can take me to prison, and I don't care!"

But before he could get round to killing the headmaster, Fabio started being sick.

They had to pull over the limo outside Slough and on the far side of Maidenhead and at the entrance of a house called The Laurels in Reading; the closer they got to Greymarsh Towers, the sicker Fabio became.

And when she saw Greymarsh Towers, Coral thought that she too would be sick if she had to return there. It was a huge bleak house with iron bars across the windows, and the stone walls looked slimy and cold.

It was now time to act. The chauffeur was supposed to drop them at the school, and she was to make her own way back by train.

"Will you please wait here, Fabio," she said to the boy. "Keep an eye on him, Mr. Fowler. Don't let him run away."

The boy, who had begun to trust her, cowered back in his seat, and Coral marched up to the front door. The smell of Greymarsh would have been enough to put her off for life. Hospital disinfectant, tortured cabbage, lavatories. . . .

As for Matron, she would have made a very good camel: the nose was right, the sneering upper lip, and the distrustful muddy eyes. Except that camels can't help their expressions, and people can.

"I am afraid I have bad news about Hubert-Henry

Mountjoy," said Aunt Coral. "He has been laid low with a bad attack of Burry-Burry fever and can't come back to school at present."

Matron pursed her mouth.

"Well, of course, that is what you expect from foreign children—he probably picked it up in his hut in the jungle."

Since Aunt Coral had just invented Burry-Burry fever, she only nodded and said she would let Matron know as soon as the boy was better. She then returned to the car and said, "I am sorry to tell you that there has been an outbreak of meningitis in the school. Everyone is in quarantine, and Hubert can't go back at present."

The little boy, who had been hunched against the cushions, now sat up and smiled. He had a very nice smile, and Aunt Coral made up her mind.

"Well, I can't take him back," said the surly driver. "I'm going on to another job down in the West Country, and I haven't a minute to waste."

"That's all right," said Coral. "Just take us to the station. We'll make our own way back to London."

Sitting on the station platform, Coral noticed the exact moment when Fabio's happiness at the thought of escaping school changed to misery at the thought of going back to his grandparents' dungeon of a house.

She hadn't had any real doubts, but now she was certain. Should she use chloroform? Or the sleeping powder that Etta used?

Either way, thought Coral, Fabio was the one.

Etta and Coral had been right. Aunt Myrtle should never have been allowed to come on the kidnapping job. Almost as soon as she arrived in London, she was so homesick that she thought she would die. She missed the sound of the waves on the rocks and the scent of the clover and the way the clouds raced across the high clean sky. But most of all, she missed Herbert. She was used to sitting on the point every day and playing the cello to him, and now she began to worry in case he was missing her too.

Or *not* missing her, which would have been even worse.

So by the time she was sent to take Lambert Sprott to the zoo because his father was doing business in New York and his mother was buying clothes in Paris, Aunt Myrtle was in a bad way. Her hair kept falling down, she had a headache, and the map of the zoo looked complicated.

As for Lambert, he was a boy it was not easy to take to. He had pale, distrustful eyes, a tight mouth, and he carried a wallet full of money, a pocket calculator, and his own mobile telephone so that he looked like a shrunken bank manager, except that bank managers have learned to be friendly and Lambert had not.

All the same, she was determined to do her best and to share with the boy the beauty of the animals they saw: the knock-kneed giraffes with their long black tongues, the dignified orangutans with the tufts of red hair under their armpits, the Mississippi alligator, smiling as he steamed in his pool.

"Oh, how fascinating animals are, are they not, Lambert!" she cried, getting carried away. "Look at those bonteboks—the way they carry their heads. And over there, the dear dik-diks—so small but so fast when they run."

Lambert yawned. "They smell," he said.

Myrtle was shocked. "Well, they have their own scent, yes, but so do you. To a bontebok, you would smell of human."

"No, I wouldn't."

Aunt Myrtle sighed, but she was determined not to give up. There must be a flicker of life somewhere in the boy. And there was—when something cost a lot of money, Lambert became quite alert. He told Myrtle that you could get twenty thousand pounds for the horn of the white rhino, and that the Siberian tiger could fetch double that because it was so rare.

"And so beautiful," cried Myrtle. "Look at the markings on its throat."

Lambert yawned again—he was not at all interested in things being beautiful, and he stopped to dial a friend on his mobile telephone, but the friend was out. "I wouldn't mind going shopping," he said. "I've got my own account at Harrods."

But Myrtle had not been told to take him shopping, and, ignoring his whining, she led the way across a little stone bridge and stopped dead.

They had come to the seals. The females lay about like old armchairs, coughing and grunting, but there was one, a young bull seal, who seemed to be staring directly at her.

Tears of homesickness came into Myrtle's eyes; it could have been Herbert's brother lying there! "Oh, Lambert," she said, making a last attempt, "look at the way his whiskers curve and the shine on his skin. Did you ever see anything so lovely?"

"They aren't worth anything," said Lambert in a bored voice. "You can't get any money for seals. They're common."

And then he opened his mouth and yawned once more. He yawned so that Myrtle saw his unhealthy tongue, his tonsils, even the little flap of skin at the back of the throat that stops the food going down the wrong way—and something snapped inside her.

She wouldn't kidnap this loathsome child in a hundred years. The thought of waking up on the Island and knowing he was there made her blood run cold, and she could no more soil her cello case by stuffing the repulsive brat into it than she could fly. She would take Lambert back to his house and tell her sisters that she was a failure as a kidnapper, and she would go home.

Once she had decided this, she felt better, but there was a long afternoon to get through still; one of the longest of her life, it seemed to Myrtle. Lambert lived in a large house bristling with burglar alarms and fitted with ankle-deep carpets, a private bar, a swimming pool, and a kitchen full of gadgets that hummed and pulsed and throbbed, and which she had no idea how to use.

What Lambert's house didn't have in it was any people. His father was busy getting rich, and his mother was busy spending the money he made, so neither of them spent much time at home. Myrtle had been told to wait until the woman who gave Lambert his supper came and then hand him over.

Lambert sat down in front of an enormous telly and started zapping channels in a bored way, and Myrtle made her way to the bathroom to freshen up. She had decided to flush the chloroform down the loo; it bothered her having it when she had given up as a kidnapper.

"What have you got there?" Lambert's suspicious voice made her turn round. He had put his telephone in his pocket and was glaring at her, narrowing his eyes. "You're stealing something. What's in that bottle?"

He leaned forward to try and snatch the bottle. Aunt

Myrtle put it behind her back, but Lambert kicked her hard in the shins, twisted her free arm, and grabbed the bottle. Then he undid the top and put his nose to it.

"Don't!" cried Myrtle. "Put it down, Lambert."

But it was too late. The loathsome boy lay felled and quite unconscious on the floor.

Chapter 3

MINETTE WOKE UP in a strange bed with a lumpy mattress and brass knobs. She was in a big room; shabby, with a threadbare carpet and faded wallpaper in a pattern of parrots and swirling leaves. The curtains breathed slightly in the open windows. A high, mewing noise came from outside.

Then she remembered what had happened, and at once she was very frightened indeed.

She had been eating a sandwich, sitting opposite a strange, fierce aunt who was supposed to be taking her to her father; and suddenly the compartment started going round and round, and the face of the aunt came closer and then farther away . . . and then nothing more. Blackness.

She had been drugged and kidnapped, she was sure of that. She could remember the way the dreadful aunt had peered at her as if she was looking into her soul. Minette knew all about fear, but now she was more afraid than she had ever been. What dreadful fate lay in wait for her? Would they cut off her ear and send it to her parents—or starve her until she did what they wanted?

And what *did* they want? Kidnapping was about getting money out of people, and neither her mother nor her father was rich.

Moving in the bed, she found she was not tied up, but the windows would be barred and the door locked.

Pushing aside the bedclothes, she walked over to the window. She was wearing her own nightdress; the aunt must have kidnapped her suitcase as well. The window was open, and as Minette looked out, she gasped with surprise.

For she was looking at a most incredible view. Down below her was green, sheep-cropped turf studded with daisies and eyebright. A large goose with black legs walked across it, followed by six goslings with their necks stretched out. Beyond the turf the ground sloped to a bay of perfect white sand—and then came the sea.

Minette looked and looked and looked. The sea in the morning light was like a crystal mirror; she could hear the waves turning over quietly on the beach. There were three black rocks guarding the bay, and on them she could make out the dark round heads of seals. White birds circled and mewed, and the air smelled of seaweed and shellfish and wind. It smelled of the sea!

"Oh, it's beautiful," she whispered.

But of course she would not be allowed to go outside. Kidnapped children were kept in dark cupboards and blindfolded. Any minute now someone would come and deal with her. She looked round the room. Old furniture, patchwork rugs, and by the bed—and this was odd—a night-light. She had begged and begged for one at home, but neither her father nor her mother had ever let her have one.

A small snuffling sound made her turn quickly. It had come from behind a screen, covered in cutouts of animals, in the corner of the room.

A fierce dog to guard her? But the noise had not been at all a fierce one.

Her heart pounding, she tiptoed to the screen and looked round it. On a camp bed lay a boy of about her own age. He had very dark hair and sticking-out ears, and he was just waking up.

"Who are you?" he asked, staring at her with big round eyes.

"I'm Minette. And I think I've been kidnapped by an aunt."

The boy sat up. "Me too." He blinked. "Yes, I'm sure. I was supposed to be going back to my grandparents. She gave me a hamburger."

38

"Mine gave me a cheese-and-tomato sandwich."

The boy got out of bed and stretched. He too was wearing his own pajamas. "We'll have to try and escape," he said. "We'll have to."

"Yes. Only I think we're on an island. Come and look."

She didn't know why, but she had had the feeling at once that the sea wasn't just in front of them but all around.

"Wow!" Fabio too was struck by the view. "What a place."

Minette had gone over to the door. "Look, it isn't locked!"

"I'm going out," said the boy. "They don't seem to have taken our clothes away. They're crummy kidnappers."

"Unless it's all a trap." She thought of the films she had seen—holes suddenly opening in the floor with pools of man-eating piranhas or sharks below. "Do you think they've kidnapped us to feed us to something?"

He shrugged. "You'd think they'd choose fatter children than us. Come on, get dressed. I'm going out."

There was no one in the corridor; there was no one on the stairs.

Then, from behind a door across the hallway, they heard a scream, followed by a thump, and then a second scream. Someone in there was being tortured—and it sounded like a child.

Minette leaned back against the wall, white-faced and trembling.

"Come on — quick!" Fabio clutched her arm.

The children ran out across the turf, over the dunes, along the perfect crescent of sand. The tide was out; it was a shell beach; there were Venus shells and cowries and green stones polished like emeralds. No one stopped them; there was no one to be seen. It would have been like Paradise except for that ghastly scream.

"Look," said Fabio.

A group of seals had swum toward the shore and was looking at them, swimming in a semicircle, snorting and blowing. . . . With their round heads they looked like a group of Russian dolls.

The children were silent, looking at the seals, and the seals stared back at them. Then suddenly they turned and swam back into the deep water.

All except one, a bull seal with white markings on the throat, who came close to the shore, and closer, until he was in the shallows with his flippers resting in the sand.

"It's as if he's trying to tell us something."

"He's got incredible eyes," said Minette dreamily. "He doesn't look like a seal at all. He looks as though inside he's a person."

"Well, seals are persons. Everything that's alive is a person really."

But that wasn't what she'd meant.

They took off their shoes and walked on the firm wet sand between the tidemarks toward a cliff covered with nesting kittiwakes and puffins and terns. The tide was still going out, leaving behind its treasures: pieces of driftwood as smooth as velvet, crimson crab shells, bleached cuttlefish bones, whiter than snow. There was no sign of any ship. They might have been alone in the universe.

"What's that noise?" asked Fabio, stopping suddenly.

A deep and mournful sound, a kind of honking, had come from somewhere inland.

"It must be a foghorn," said Minette.

But there wasn't any fog, or any lighthouse to give warning if there had been.

They listened for a few moments, but the sound did not come again, and they ran on along the shore. It was a marvelous island; it seemed to have everything. To their left was a green hill—two hills, actually, with a dip between, the slopes covered with bracken and gorse. The far shore would be wilder, exposed to the wind.

"If we climbed up there, we could see exactly where we are. There might be other islands or a causeway. If we're going to escape, we're going to have to know," said Minette.

They had to get away—that terrible scream still rang in their ears—but Minette couldn't help thinking of where she would be if she hadn't been kidnapped: in her father's dark sitting room trying to get interested in a book until he came back from the university.

Fabio seemed to be having the same sort of thoughts. "I can't help wondering if my grandparents will pay the ransom for me. They're horribly cheap and they don't like me."

Minette tried to think if her parents liked her enough to pay a lot of money to get her back, but when she thought about her parents, her stomach always started to lurch about, so she said, "There's a little path there to the top of the hill."

They began to run toward the gap in the dunes, forgetting the lives they had left behind, forgetting even that awful tortured scream. The wind was at their backs; it was like flying. No one could imagine anything dangerous or dark.

And then it happened! From behind the hummock of sand that had hidden them, there arose suddenly the cruel figures of two enormous women.

It was the evil aunts!

The sinister kidnappers glared at the children, and the children, terrified, stared back. Here was the tall bony aunt with her fierce eyes who had drugged Minette's sandwich, and here was the plump mad person with her scarves flying in the wind who had given sleeping powders to a defenseless boy.

The children reached for each other's hands. Minette

was shaking so much she could hardly stand. What punishment would they be given for escaping from their room?

It was the tall bony aunt, Etta, who spoke. "You're late for breakfast," she said in her fierce and booming voice.

The children continued to stare.

"Breakfast," the other one went on. "You've heard of that? We have it at seven, and the cook gets ratty if he's kept waiting. Go and wash your hands first—the bathroom's at the top of the stairs."

The children ran off, completely puzzled by this way of kidnapping people, and Etta and Coral followed. They were talking about Myrtle, who hadn't stopped crying since she came back.

"She's got to stop blaming herself," said Coral. "Mistakes can happen to anyone."

"Yes. Mind you, Lambert is quite a mistake!"

Breakfast was in the dining room, a big room with shabby leather chairs, which faced the patch of green turf and the bay. All the windows in the L-shaped farmhouse had at least a glimpse of the sea. Even the bathroom, with its huge claw-footed bath and ancient geyser, looked out on the ledge of rock where the seals hauled out of the water to rest.

"Porridge or cereal?" asked Aunt Etta as the children came in.

Minette blinked at her. "Cereal," she managed to say.

"Porridge," said Fabio.

"Please," said Etta briskly, picking up the ladle. "Porridge, *please*."

Fabio was the first to shake himself awake. "This is a very odd kidnap," he said crossly. "And I won't eat anything drugged."

Aunt Etta leaned forward, scooped a spoonful of porridge from his plate, and gulped it down.

"Satisfied?" she said.

Fabio waited to see if she yawned or became dopey. Then he began to eat. The porridge was delicious.

They were both on second helpings when the screams began again. This time they were even worse than before and were followed by sobs and wails and a low shuddering moan. Then the door opened and a woman they had never seen before ran into the room. She had long, reddish gray hair down her back; a bloody scratch ran along one cheek, and she seemed to be quite beside herself.

The children shrank back in their chairs, their fear returning. The woman looked every inch a torturer.

"Really, Myrtle," said Aunt Etta, "I've told the children they mustn't be late for breakfast, and now look at you."

But no one could be cross with Myrtle for long, not even her bossy sister. The scratch on Myrtle's cheek had begun to bleed again, there were tooth marks on her wrist, and though she took a helping of porridge, she was quite unable to swallow it.

And when she was introduced to Minette and Fabio, her tears began to flow again.

"Yours are so nice," she sobbed. "They look so intelligent and friendly."

"That may be," said Etta. "We haven't tried them out yet." She frowned as more bangs and thumps came from across the corridor. "He can't stay in the broom cupboard, Myrtle. What would happen if he were to go for the vacuum cleaner? We'd never get the place cleaned up again."

"It's just for now," said Myrtle. "I gave him my bedroom when he first came round, but I was afraid for the ducklings."

Myrtle often had motherless ducklings keeping warm in her bed and her underclothes drawer.

"I suppose we shall have to *un*kidnap him," said Coral. "But how? No one's going to pay a ransom for Lambert Sprott."

"We could offer to *give* his father some money if he'll take Lambert away," suggested Myrtle, blowing her nose.

"Don't be silly, Myrtle," said Etta. "For one thing, we haven't got any money—and for another, he'd tell everyone about the Island and photographers would come, and journalists." She shuddered. Keeping the position of the Island secret was the most important thing of all.

"We could turn him round and round until he was completely giddy and leave him in a telephone kiosk somewhere on the mainland," said Coral. But she did not sound very convinced by her idea.

Myrtle began to sob again. "I should have left him on the floor," she gulped. "I should never have brought him. But it seemed so cruel just to leave him there unconscious."

"Hush. What's done is done."

But Myrtle couldn't be consoled. "And my cello case smells of the awful child," she wailed. "He puts terrible, perfumed stuff on his hair."

"Perhaps he'll settle down when we've got some breakfast into him."

Judging by the screams and thumps coming from across the corridor, though, this did not seem likely.

But Fabio was getting impatient. "What about *us*? Are you going to unkidnap us?"

The aunts stared at him. "Are you mad?" said Etta. "After all the trouble we took. In any case, you haven't been kidnapped exactly. You've been *chosen*."

Minette and Fabio stared. "How?" asked Minette.

"What do you mean?" inquired Fabio.

Aunt Coral put down her coffee cup. "It's time we explained. But first you'd better come and meet Daddy. He gets upset when things are kept from him."

Captain Harper was a hundred and three years old

and spent most of the day in bed looking at the Island through his telescope.

He was very deaf and very grumpy, and what he saw through the window didn't please him. When he was young, there had been far more geese coming from Greenland—hundreds and thousands of geese—and their feet had been yellower and their bottoms more feathery than the geese that came nowadays. The sheep had been fleecier when he was a boy, and the flowers in the grass had been brighter, and the seals on the rocks ten times larger and fatter.

"Huge, they were," Captain Harper would say, throwing out his arms. "Great big cow seals with big bosoms and eyes like cartwheels, and look at them now!"

No one liked to say that it was partly because he couldn't see or hear too well that things had changed, and when he told the same stories for the hundredth time, his daughters just smiled and tiptoed out of the room, because they were fond of him and knew that being old is difficult.

"Here are the children, Father," yelled Coral. "The ones who have come to stay with us."

The old man put down his telescope and stared at them.

"They're too small," he said. "They won't be a mite of use. You need ones with muscles. When I was their age, I had muscles like footballs."

He put out a skinny arm and flexed his biceps, and

they could see a bump like a very small pea come up on his arm. "We were all strong in those days. There was a boy in my class who could lift the teacher's desk with one hand. Freddie Boyle, he was called. He was the one who put the grass snake down the teacher's trouser leg."

The aunts let him tell the story about the grass snake and the teacher's trouser leg because it was a short one, but when he began on the one about Freddie Boyle's uncle, who'd run over his own false teeth with a milk truck, they shepherded the children out quietly.

"He won't notice," they said.

When they went downstairs again they found Art, the cook, wiping porridge off his trouser leg. He had tried to give Lambert some breakfast and had it thrown in his face.

"Nasty little perisher you've got in there," he said. "Best drown him, I'd say. Shouldn't think his parents would want him back."

Before he escaped and was washed up on the Island, Art had worked in the prison kitchens, which was why he made such good porridge. Because he'd killed a man once, Art didn't like the sight of blood, and it was always the aunts who had to chop the heads off the fish before they went into the frying pan or get the chickens ready for the pot. Another thing Art didn't like to do was anything energetic.

"I don't know my own strength," he would say when

there was anything messy or difficult to be done. "I might forget myself and do someone an injury."

This didn't seem likely—Art was a skinny person who hardly came up to Aunt Etta's shoulder—but he'd quickly locked the door on Lambert and, leaving him to scream for his mobile telephone, retreated to his kitchen.

But Aunt Etta and Aunt Coral now led the children into the garden behind the house. It was time to explain.

The garden was surrounded by gray walls to give shelter from the wind; but no walls on the Island were built so high that they shut out the view of the sea. Aunt Myrtle had gone down to play her cello to the seals. A bumblebee droned on a clump of thrift. It was very peaceful.

"Perhaps I'd better tell you a story," said Etta. "It's a true story, and it begins with five girls coming to an island with their widowed father to look for a new life.

"They found a lovely and deserted place, but ruined, abandoned. All the people who had lived there had left long, long ago. Even the ghost in the old graveyard seemed to have gone away."

Minette sat with her arms hugging her knees and her eyes closed. She loved stories.

"So the girls and their father repaired the house and planted a garden and learned to fish and cut peat and do all the things the Islanders had done before they left. But of course the world outside was changing. Oil was spilled into the sea, and sewage, and trawlers started to use nets that caught even the smallest fish. The water became overheated by nuclear power stations. You'll have learned all that at school."

Minette nodded, but Fabio only scowled. Absolutely *nothing* useful had been taught at Greymarsh Towers.

"Soon the sisters and their father found themselves looking after things that came ashore. Oiled seabirds . . . stunned seals . . . poisoned squids . . . and other things . . ."

Etta paused and looked up at Coral, who raised her eyebrows in a warning way. *Not yet,* said Coral's eyebrows. *Remember what we decided.*

Etta nodded and turned back to the children.

"The sisters worked from dawn to dusk. One of them was an idiot; she started shaving her legs and marrying tax inspectors, so she was no good. And one went off to foreign parts to stop people eating rare animals. And the others got older and became aunts. . . .

"And then one day they realized they might die before long—they might become extinct—and then what would happen to all the creatures? So they decided to find people to carry on after them. Sensible people. Young ones. People who knew how to work."

There was a long pause. Then:

"Us?" said Fabio shyly.

Both aunts nodded.

"Yes," said Aunt Etta. "You."

Chapter 4

SO FABIO AND MINETTE were set to work.

It was the hardest work they had ever done, and it didn't stop from morning to night.

The day began with fifty press-ups on the grass behind the house. Etta was in charge of these, rising up and down on her elbows with her skirt tucked into her navy blue knickers. She had thirty pairs of these, one for each day of the month. The children had seen seven of them on the washing line, and she explained that it made it easier having things the same color and the same shape so one didn't have to think about things that didn't matter—like which of one's knickers were which.

Then they began the chores. The aunts ran a small farm; there were six goats and a cow, and two dozen chickens whose eggs needed to be collected, and fresh straw that needed to be put down.

There were buckets of mash to be taken to the eider ducklings whose mother had been killed in a fishing net, and two seal pups that had to be hand-fed from a bottle. The children had thought feeding the seals might be fun, but it wasn't. The pups prodded and squealed when the milk didn't come fast enough; it was like being bashed into by two blubbery tanks.

A puffin with a splint on his leg lived behind the house, and in a tin bath with a wooden lid was an octopus with eye trouble.

And as they worked, the children were watched — *tested*, you could say — because anyone who was disgusted by a living thing, however odd, was no use on the Island.

Minette was marched down to the strand by Aunt Etta and shown a pile of pink and purple slime.

"These are stranded jellyfish," said Etta. "Put them back into the water. You'd better wear these."

She handed Minette a pair of rubber gloves and stood over her while she carried the wobbling blobs back into the sea.

Fabio was taken to a big tank in the paddock and told to pick up an eel with a skin disease.

"Hold him behind the head while I scrub," Coral ordered him. "He's got scabies."

When they were in bed at night, the children tried to think how to run away. Fabio now slept in a box room next to Minette, and with the door open they could talk.

"We can't stay here and turn into slaves," said Fabio.

"No. Except the aunts are slaves too. They work harder than us."

This was true, but Fabio said it made no difference. "We'll have to steal a boat."

But their beds were warm; they had night-lights; the sea sighed softly beneath their open windows—and before Minette could see even the smallest tiger in the cracks on the ceiling, they were both asleep.

And while they slept, the aunts discussed them.

"Well, so far so good," said Etta. "They haven't squealed or squirmed or wriggled. Yet. Or said 'Ugh!' I can't bear people who say 'Ugh!'"

"And they seem to be keeping to the rules," said Coral.

The rules had been set out on the first day.

"You're not to go near the de-oiling shed in the cove," Etta had said. "Or up to the top of the hill."

"Or to the loch between the hills."

The children had grumbled about this.

"It's exactly like that fairy story about Bluebeard's Castle," said Minette. "You know . . . if you open the seventh door, you'll have your head chopped off."

But they had obeyed—even Fabio, who had been so difficult to control in his grandparents' house. Nothing, though, could stop Fabio from asking questions.

"What's that honking one hears sometimes? It sounds like a foghorn."

"If it sounds like a foghorn, I expect it *is* a foghorn," said Etta, and that was the end of that.

But what of Lambert?

Lambert went on screaming and kicking and wailing for his mobile telephone, and Art (who did not know his own strength) just put down his tray and ran for it whenever he brought him his food. They had locked him in a room above the boathouse; it had been the Captain's study, and the doors and windows were strong.

At mealtimes they tried to decide what to do with him. Coral thought they might set him adrift in a dinghy with enough food for a few days, and Fabio thought he should be dipped in boiling oil. But they never got very far because whenever they talked about Lambert, Aunt Myrtle always began to cry, because she blamed herself for having kidnapped such an awful boy and brought him to the Island.

Then, on the fourth day, as they came down to breakfast, Fabio and Minette found all the aunts looking at them with a pleased expression. Their teachers at school had looked like that when they had passed an exam.

"Your work has been satisfactory," said Etta.

"*And* your conduct," said Coral, flicking her beads out of the sugar bowl.

"So we have decided that you may work in the de-oiling shed today."

The children thought this was an odd kind of reward for being good; de-oiling seabirds is about the messiest job there is. But they kept quiet, and presently they were following Aunt Etta along the cliff path and down to the cove on the far side of the bay.

The de-oiling shed was a wooden building set back into the cliff. At high tide the water came almost to the walls, but now they could reach it by scrambling over low rocks covered in seaweed and pools full of anemones and shrimps and tiny scuttling crabs. The children would have liked to linger and explore, but Aunt Etta thrust them forward and knocked loudly on the door.

"Are you decent?" she called.

The children looked at each other. How could seabirds *not* be decent?

There was a scuttling noise, followed by a plopping sound—and then the door was opened from the inside.

The children had expected rough wooden walls, shelves, and perhaps a slatted floor. But the shed was more like the inside of a Turkish bath.

There were tiles on the walls; water gushed from taps into a large, blue-painted sink decorated with seashells and into two tubs set under the high windows. Hairbrushes lay on a low table, and hand mirrors, and there were more mirrors on the wall.

But it was what was inside the sink or lying on the wet floor that held them speechless. You can read about such things as often as you like, but seeing them is very different.

There were four mermaids in the shed. They wore knitted tops that Myrtle had made, but their tails, of course, were free—no one would have worn one of Myrtle's knitted tops on her tail. When Aunt Etta saw that the children, though pale, were not going to make a fuss, she introduced them.

"This is Ursula," she said, leading them up to a very old lady who sat in the sink nearest the door. Her hair was full of broken pieces of shell and sticks; the egg case of a dogfish hung over one ear, and she had only one tooth—a long one that came down over her lower lip.

But the girls who shared one of the tubs under the window were young. They were twins but were not at all alike. Queenie was very pretty, with golden ropes of hair and a pert look in her bright blue eyes; but Oona's hair was dark with a green sheen, and her gray eyes were sad.

And sprawled on the floor, trying to hide a piece of gum she had been chewing, was the girls' mother, Loreen. She was a fattish, blowsy person and looked as if she had given up on life. The knitted top she'd hastily put on was crooked, and the flowers in her hair were very dead.

Aunt Etta frowned at the chewing gum, which

Loreen had snuck from Art. "A disgusting habit," she said, glaring at the packet.

"It's my nerves," said Loreen. "I've got to have something for my nerves, with the state I'm in."

She was certainly in a state. As well as a bruise on her cheek and a black eye, Loreen was very badly oiled. All of them were oiled, but Loreen was really covered in the stuff.

"Have you been taking your tonic?" Etta asked.

"We've all been taking it. But we're not better. Oona's ears are still bad, and Queenie's itching all over. We can't go home yet," said Loreen firmly. "Not for a long time."

Etta ignored this. The way absolutely nobody wanted to go away even when they were healed was beginning to annoy her.

"They're not very big," complained the old crone, staring at Fabio and Minette. Everyone knew about the children and that they had been chosen and not kidnapped.

"We're strong, though," said Fabio, who was getting tired of this.

But there was one other person still to meet. In a dishpan on the floor floated something pale and smooth, which turned out to be a baby.

But not any baby. Probably the fattest baby in the universe. His wrists were lost in layers and layers of fat;

his neck was covered by a whole waterfall of chins; his small blue eyes were sunk in his swollen cheeks like currants in a pudding, and he was bald.

"My youngest," said Loreen. She looked tired rather than proud. "His name's Walter."

The children did not know what to say. Walter looked more like an overgrown maggot than a merbaby—but he was not oiled! When the oil slick came, his mother had held him aloft, and now Aunt Etta turned away from the dishpan with pursed lips, because Walter was exactly the kind of spoiled, pampered male of whom she particularly disapproved.

"Right," she said to the children. "Time to start work. The detergent's in that bottle—it gets diluted with three parts of water. And when you've finished, put them under the hose—all of them. Oona gets three of these drops in each ear, and remember, with anything fishy, scrub in the same direction as the scales, or you'll be in trouble."

The door closed behind her, and Queenie, the pretty, pert twin, pulled a face.

"What's the matter with you?" she said cheekily. "Cat got your tongue?"

"Now, Queenie," said her mother wearily. "Maybe they've never seen mermaids before."

"As a matter of fact, we haven't," said Minette.

She picked up the roughest of the scrubbing brushes

while Fabio poured out the detergent. Then they walked over to Queenie's tub, picked up her tail, and began to scrub.

The mermaids had not had an easy time even before they were caught in the oil slick. Loreen's husband was a bully—mermen are often bad-tempered—and the bruise on her cheek came from him.

Then a bad thing happened to Oona, the younger of the twins. She was caught in a fishing net and dragged aboard a fishing boat, but the person who unwrapped her wasn't an ordinary sensible fisherman; it was a chinless wonder called Lord Terence Brasenott who thought catching a mermaid was a terribly good joke.

"I say, what jolly fun," he kept saying. "What a pretty little thing. I'll take you back with me," he'd said, and pawed her with his horrible hands and tried to kiss her.

Oona spent three days in his cabin, weeping piteously, and by the time she managed to free herself and dive overboard, her voice had completely gone. This happens sometimes when people have had a serious shock; it is bad for anyone, but for mermaids, who are famous for singing, it is particularly bad. Even now, Oona could only manage a whisper or a croak.

No sooner had they got over this disaster than a French mermaid turned up from Calais and started making eyes at Loreen's husband. French mermaids have two tails, and the whole thing went to the silly man's head. He turned his wife and children out of their cave and set up home with his new love. He even turned out his grandmother, Old Ursula, which was particularly hard on Loreen as she had to take her along. Being burdened with your own grandmother can be difficult, but when it's your husband's grandmother, it can seem seriously unfair.

What happened next was Queenie's fault. She was pretty and she was headstrong, and though everyone had warned her what ships were like nowadays, she insisted on sitting on a rock and singing to the captain of a cargo boat coming from the Middle East.

"Arabia's in the Middle East," she said, "so they'll be carrying gold and treasure like in the *Arabian Nights;* you'll see."

Queenie had a good voice, and she'd kept up to date with tunes and didn't waste time on "Hey Nonny No" sort of songs, and it so happened that the captain was musical and a little drunk, and when he heard her, he got very excited and ran his ship onto the rocks.

But what came spilling out was not doubloons or pieces of silver that might have made the mermaids rich. What came out was . . . oil. Masses of thick, black, greasy oil straight from the oil wells of Saudi Arabia. It caught the whole family fair and square, half blinding them, weighing down their limbs. They just managed to reach the safety of the Island and land wearily on the shore—and there the aunts had found them.

The children learned all this while they cleaned them up. It was incredibly hard work. The girls' tails were slippery and surprisingly heavy—and Queenie was ticklish, so when they began to scrub, she started giggling and thrashing about. By the time Aunt Etta returned, the children were soaked through and dirty and tired, but she took no notice at all. They had to swill down the floor of the hut, and then the mermaids' tails were covered in plastic wrap so the family could be put into wheelbarrows and taken down to the bay without drying out. Only Old Ursula stayed where she was and admitted that though the children might be small, they knew how to work.

When they had finished in the mermaid shed, the children were taken to the house for a drink of fruit juice and a cookie, and then they were sent to help Aunt Coral clean out the chicken house. Fabio's family had kept chickens in South America, so he knew what to do. He and Coral had an interesting conversation about the tango, which she was fond of dancing under the light of the moon.

"You don't happen to know the steps?" she asked him.

Fabio looked doubtful. "I watched my mother when she danced in the cabaret."

"Good," said Aunt Coral. "I've always wanted a partner."

Fabio was not at all sure that he wanted to dance the tango with a very large aunt who had stuffed him in a tin trunk and kidnapped him. But he was too polite to refuse, and he had noticed the night before that the moon was far from full, so he could only hope she would forget.

Then, in the afternoon, things got strange again, because Aunt Myrtle took them down to the point to meet the seals.

They lay about by the edge of the water, the cows dozing while they waited for their pups to be born, the bulls jostling each other and shoving to test their strength.

But one seal was sitting quite alone on a rock. He had turned his back on the rough games of the other seals and was staring romantically out to sea. It was the seal who had come close to the shore on the first day; they would have known him anywhere.

"Herbert, I'd like you to meet Fabio and Minette," said Myrtle, just as if she were introducing someone in a drawing room.

Herbert opened his eyes very wide and looked at them. It was an extraordinary look for a seal; both children stepped back a pace; they felt as though they had been weighed up and examined by a great intelligence.

"He can't be an ordinary seal," said Fabio.

Aunt Myrtle looked at him gratefully. "No, dear, you're absolutely right. Herbert *is* a seal, but he's a very special kind of seal. He's a selkie."

"What's a selkie?" asked Fabio.

Myrtle sighed. "It's not easy to explain," she said, "because it's all to do with legends and beliefs. There aren't a lot of *facts.*"

"Tell us," begged Minette.

Aunt Myrtle sat down on an outcrop of rock, and the children came to sit beside her.

"All sorts of things are told about selkies," she began. "That they are the souls of drowned men . . . that they are a kind of faery, and if someone sticks a knife in them, they will turn back into humans."

"A *knife!*" Minette was horrified. "How could anyone do a thing like that?"

Aunt Myrtle shrugged. "I certainly couldn't." But she blushed, thinking of how she had sometimes wondered what would happen if she did get up the courage. Would Herbert really turn into a man, and if so, what *kind* of a man? Might he become a showing-off kind of man like a bullfighter, always trailing his cape about? Or a really boring person who thought about nothing except making money?

Herbert had come to the Island many years ago. His mother had brought him because he had a cough that wouldn't get better, and it had got about that the Island was safe even for seals who were not well. The aunts had healed his cough, and then Myrtle had played the cello to him and he had stayed.

They had known, of course, that he wasn't an ordinary seal. Herbert did not speak exactly, but he understood human speech, and sometimes when he and his mother talked together in the selkie language, which is halfway between human speech and the language of the seals, Myrtle could make out . . . not the words exactly, but the sense of what they said.

"He had a very famous grandmother," said Myrtle, dropping her voice. "At least, we think she was his grandmother. She was called the Selkie of Rossay, and there are stories told about her all over the islands."

"Tell us," begged Minette again. She could never get enough stories.

So Aunt Myrtle pushed her hair out of her eyes and began.

"The Selkie of Rossay was a female seal who lived about a hundred years ago. One night she came out of the sea and shed her sealskin and danced with nothing on by the light of the moon, and a fisherman came and fell passionately in love with her." Myrtle paused and gave a wistful sigh. "You know how it is," she said, "when people are dancing by the light of the moon."

The children nodded politely, though they didn't really.

"So he hid her sealskin and brought her some clothes and married her, and she stayed with him and had seven children, and they were perfectly happy. Though when they sat down, even on dry days and in completely dry clothes, the children left a damp patch. Not . . . you know . . . anything to do with accidents. Nothing nasty—it was an absolutely *fresh* damp patch—but it showed they had seal blood."

Herbert was listening most intently. He moved closer and cleared his throat.

"Then, one day, when she was rummaging in a trunk, the selkie found her old sealskin and put it on, and the sea called to her—it called to her so strongly there was nothing she could do—and she dived back into the sea. After a while she married a seal and had seven seal children. But for the rest of her life she was in a terrible muddle, calling her sea children by the names of her land children and her land children by the names of her sea children and never really knowing where she belonged. At least, that is the story."

Myrtle stopped, and Herbert gave an enormous sigh and rolled over onto his side. He might have forgotten how to speak like a human, but he had understood every word; the story Myrtle told was his own.

The Selkie of Rossay *had* been his grandmother. She had gone crazy in the end from not knowing whether it was better to be a woman or a seal, and Herbert's mother, the youngest of her seal children, had stayed with her until she died, seeing that she didn't starve even when her teeth fell out and her eyes filmed over.

Herbert's mother was still alive; she came ashore sometimes and nudged her son and tried to get him to make up his mind about what he wanted to be, because she knew it didn't matter whether one was a man or a seal so long as one stuck to it.

But Herbert took after his grandmother. He couldn't decide. When Myrtle played the cello to him, it seemed that being human was the best that he could hope for. But when he watched Art and saw what he would have to do if he was a man—wear trousers with suspenders or zippers, and shoelaces and all that kind of thing—he would dive back into the water and turn over and over in the waves and think: This is my world; it is here that I belong.

When the children got back to the house, they found Art with a cold compress on his forehead. He had tried to give Lambert some lunch, and Lambert had torn the plate out of his hand and hurled it across the room. Then he'd lain down on the floor, drummed his heels, and screamed for his father and his mobile telephone.

"I'd have thumped him," said Art now, "but I daren't. I don't know my own strength. I might have pulped him into a jelly."

Fabio didn't say anything, but he was beginning to

wonder about Art's great strength. Meanwhile Lambert was still in the room above the boathouse.

"But he can't stay there," said Coral. "The boy is a fiend. We've *got* to get rid of him."

But though they discussed it for the rest of the day, none of the aunts could see how this could be done short of killing the child—which they would very much have liked to do, but which was not the kind of thing that happened on the Island.

Chapter 5

WHEN THE CHILDREN came down to breakfast the next day, they saw at once that the aunts were worried. Etta's mustache stood out dark against her pale face, and her nose had sharpened to something you could have used to cut cheese.

"I really don't want to operate," they heard her say, "but it's serious. She's completely egg-bound."

"Who's egg-bound?" asked Fabio.

Aunt Etta ignored him.

"I've tried massage; I've tried Vaseline; I've tried a steam kettle," she said to her sisters.

"What about castor oil?" suggested Coral.

"It's worth a try, I suppose."

"Can we help?" asked Minette.

"No." Etta looked up briefly. "Well, perhaps you can carry the buckets. We're going up the hill. And kindly fold your napkins properly when you leave the table. You left them in a disgusting heap yesterday."

It was quite a procession that wound its way up the hill. Etta carried an enormous bottle of castor oil; Fabio lugged a footstool and a camp stove; Minette had two buckets and a bundle of rags.

The path was steep and the morning was warm, but Aunt Etta kept up a fast pace. She also chose to give them a lecture as she went.

"Now, I want to make it *absolutely* clear to you that I will *not* have favorites on this island. The unusual creatures you will be working with are *no more important* than the ordinary ones. A sick water flea needs just as much help as a mermaid. A flounder is *exactly* as important as a selkie. I hope you understand this because if you don't, you're not going to be any use doing your job."

The children said, yes, they had understood it, but when they reached the top of the hill, they were pleased they had been warned.

There were two hills, actually, with a dip in between that held a loch of dark, peaty water. On the far side of the loch was a great pile of brushwood and boulders and bracken. It looked like one of the stockades that the settlers in America used to build to protect themselves from the Indians.

But what stuck over the top of the stockade was not

an American settler. It was the head of an absolutely enormous bird.

The head was black, but its beak was a bright yellow and made the children think of those great machines—crunchers or diggers or shovelers—that one sees looming over building sites. Its eyes were yellow, too, huge and round and mad-looking, and as they stared, they were blasted backward by the deep honking noise they had heard on the first day.

"What is it?" stammered Fabio.

"It's a boobrie," said Aunt Etta, striding round the edge of the loch. "And I can tell you there aren't many of those left in the world. They're sort of a cousin of the dodo—people thought they were extinct, but they aren't. The sailors never discovered their island, so they just grew and grew and grew. But then people started doing atomic tests and that kind of nonsense nearby, and the ones that were left managed to fly away."

She led them round the other side of the stockade, and they saw a short ladder propped against the side of the nest. Aunt Etta climbed up it and beckoned to the children to follow, but they hung back, thinking of the huge yellow eyes, the dreadful beak.

"Hurry up!" said Etta, and when they still hesitated, she turned round, took a deep breath, and let them have it. "I have to tell you that kidnapping you was quite the most unpleasant experience any of us have had: that boardinghouse full of yakking women, and the London underground with all those fumes. If you think we'd have gone to all that trouble just to let you get eaten by some bird, you need to have your heads examined. Anyway, boobries are vegetarians; at least this kind are — more's the pity."

So the children followed her up the ladder and jumped down into the nest, which was trampled flat and lined with moss and feathers.

The boobrie was not really *so* enormous. She was smaller than an African elephant — more the size of an Indian one. It took a lot of courage to look up at her, but when they did, the children stopped being afraid. She *could* hurt you, of course — by stepping on your feet, for example — but they could see that she was a bird with serious troubles of her own.

The nest was ready for eggs, but there were no eggs to be seen. The boobrie's chest looked sadly naked, so they knew it was her own feathers she had plucked out to make a warm lining, but a lining for what? Where were the eggs and the chicks that would follow?

"I have to tell you that I am very worried about her," said Aunt Etta. "Being egg-bound is a most serious business."

"You mean her eggs are stuck inside of her? She can't get them out?" asked Minette.

"That's right. And she's too uncomfortable to go and look for something to eat."

"Doesn't she have a mate to bring her food?" asked Fabio.

Aunt Etta snorted. "She had, but she's lost him."

"You mean he's dead?"

"He may be, for all I know. Or he may have lost the way or forgotten all about her. You know how men are."

This annoyed Fabio. "I'm a man, or I will be, and I'll never leave my wife to starve in a nest. Never."

"Why did you say it's a pity she's a vegetarian?" Minette wanted to know.

"Because it makes it hard for us to feed her. We could have thrown her a frozen side of beef, but to dredge up all those sludgy sea lettuces and sea noodles and gut-weeds takes hours," said Etta. She was stamping round the boobrie, batting her with a stick, thumping her. "Get up, you stupid bird. I'm trying to help you."

At first the boobrie wouldn't move; she sat hunched and shivering, and from her throat came a single squawk, which seemed to be her way of saying "Ow!" But Etta was merciless. She thumped and scolded and prodded the bird until she struggled to her feet and stood there, swaying and honking.

Then Etta climbed onto the footstool and peered into the boobrie's back end and there, sure enough, was a glimmer of white speckled with blue.

"You can make seventy-two omelets from one boo-brie's egg," said Etta when the children had a look.

But of course she didn't want seventy-two omelets — she didn't care for omelets anyway — she wanted living chicks. "The next part is going to be messy," she warned.

But the children stayed to help, dipping rags into the hot castor oil and handing them to her as she dabbed and swabbed at the opening.

"We'll just have to wait and see," she said when she'd finished. "But if this doesn't work . . ."

"Could she . . . die . . . ?" asked Minette in a quavery voice.

"Anyone can die," said Etta snubbingly. "Including you and me."

But before she marched the children down again, she took them up the farther hill, which was the highest point of the Island.

The view was incredible. To the west, miles and miles of unbroken water with the sun making a golden path between the clouds, and to the east, a long way off but with their outlines sharp and clear, two islands — one hilly, one low and long.

And on a grassy ledge overhanging the wild northern shore was an ancient burial ground, with leaning and broken gravestones covered in lichen and battered by the rain.

"There's supposed to be a ghost here," said Etta. "But she only turns up every fifty years or so."

"What sort of a ghost?"

"A *good* ghost. A kind of hermit. She was called Ethelgonda, and she lived on the Island and looked after the creatures."

"Like you," said Minette.

"Not in the least like me," said Aunt Etta crushingly.

"I didn't think good people became ghosts," said Fabio.

"Well, a spirit then."

The children spent the rest of the day collecting the special seaweeds that the boobrie ate and wheelbarrowing them up to her nest. Each time they watched anxiously for a sign of an egg, but nothing seemed to be happening at all.

They were getting ready for bed that night when Myrtle came upstairs excitedly, her long hair flying.

"Come down for a minute," she said. "Herbert's mother has come, and she wants to meet you."

She hurried them down to the rocks, and there, sure enough, sitting beside Herbert was a smaller seal, a cow with the same whitish mark on her throat as her son. Herbert's mother was old—there was something weary about the way she held her head—but she lumbered up to them and snorted in a very welcoming way, while her son looked on proudly.

"This is a great honor, you know," said Myrtle, hopping about like a young girl. "She doesn't come out of the water often now; it tires her to be on land. Herbert will have told her about you."

Since it is difficult to shake hands with a seal, they bowed their heads politely, and Herbert's mother came closer and said something, speaking in a low voice and in the selkie language. The children thought she was asking them to help Herbert make up his mind about whether to be a person or a seal, and when they were back in their rooms, Fabio had an idea. "We could just cut him with a knife. Not hard. Just a nick — then he'd become human and that would be that."

"Oh, we couldn't!"

"I don't see why not. Then Myrtle would have a friend. He could learn the piano and they could play duets."

But when he thought about it, Fabio knew that Minette was right. He couldn't make even the smallest nick in that smooth and shining skin.

The next afternoon, the children had a shock. They had taken yet another load of seaweed to the boobrie and were shoveling it into the nest when the bird gave the loudest honk they had heard yet. For a moment, they thought it might be an egg, for the honk was a welcoming one.

But it wasn't. The boobrie was looking at the loch.

The children turned to follow her gaze—and gasped. A head had appeared in the middle of the lake.

But what a head! White and smooth and enormous . . . like the front end of a gigantic worm. After the head came a neck . . . also smooth . . . also white . . . a neck divided into rings of muscle and going on and on and on. It reared and waved above the surface of the water, and still more neck appeared . . . and more and more. Except that the neck was getting fatter, it couldn't all *be* neck—the bulgier part must be the body of the worm: a worm the length of a dozen boa constrictors.

The boobrie honked once more, and the children clutched each other, unable to move.

The creature was still rising up in the water, still getting longer, still pale and glistening and utterly strange. Then it turned its head toward them and opened its eyes, which were just two deep holes as black as its body was white.

"Whooo," it began to say. "Whooo"—and with every "oo" the air filled with such a stench of rottenness and decay and . . . *old*ness . . . that the children reeled backward. And then it began to slither out of the water. . . . It slithered and slithered and slithered, and still not all of it was out of the lake—and suddenly the children had had enough. Leaving their wheelbarrows where they were, they rushed down the hill to the house and almost fell into the sitting room, where the aunts were having tea.

"I didn't expect you to knock," said Aunt Etta, putting down her cup. "One knocks at the doors of bedrooms but not of sitting rooms when one is staying in a house. But I do expect you to come in quietly like human beings, and not like hooligans."

But the children were too frightened to be snubbed. "We saw a thing . . . a worm . . ."

"As long as a train . . . well, as long as a bus."

"All naked and white and smooth and slippery . . ."

"It said 'Whoo' and came at us, and its breath . . ." Minette shuddered, just remembering. "It came out of the lake and now it's coming after us, and it'll coil round and round us and smother us and—"

"Unlikely," said Aunt Etta. She passed the children a plate of scones and told them to sit down. "It seems to be very difficult to get you to listen," she said. "I'm sure that all three of us have told you how unpleasant we found the whole business of kidnapping you."

"Yes, indeed," said Coral. "That loathsome matron like a camel."

"So it is not very likely that we would go to all that trouble to feed you to a stoorworm," said Etta.

Being safe in the drawing room, eating a scone with strawberry jam, made Fabio feel very much braver.

"What *is* a stoorworm?"

"A wingless dragon. An Icelandic one; very unusual. Once the world was full of them, but you know how it is. Dragons with wings and fiery breaths in the skies. Dragons without wings and poisonous breaths in the water. The wingless ones were called worms. You must have heard of them: the Lambton Worm, the Laidly Worm, the Stoorworm."

But the children hadn't.

"If his breath is poisonous . . . he breathed on us quite hard," said Minette. "He said 'Whoooo' and blew at us. Does that mean we'll be ill or die?"

Aunt Coral shook her head. "He's only poisonous to greenfly and things like that. We use him to spray the fruit trees. And he probably wasn't saying 'Whoooo'; he was saying 'Who?'—meaning who are you? He talks like that—very slowly, because he comes from Iceland and they have more time over there."

But Minette was still alarmed. "Look," she said, staring through the window. "Oh look, he's slithering down the hill. . . . He's coming closer. . . . He's coming here!"

Aunt Myrtle came to stand beside her. "He'll be coming to visit Daddy," she said.

"They're good friends," explained Coral to the bewildered children. "They think alike about the world—you know, that the old days were better."

Standing by the open sitting-room door, they watched bravely as the stoorworm slithered into the hall, slithered up the first flight of stairs, along the landing, up the second flight. . . . In his bedroom they could hear the Captain shouting, "Come along, my dear fellow, come on in," and the front end of the worm went through into the Captain's bedroom while the back end was still in the hall, trying to lift its tail over the table.

Fabio had stopped feeling frightened, but he was becoming very suspicious. "Is there anything we have to do to the stoorworm?" he asked. If the mermaids needed scrubbing and the seals had to be given a bottle four times a day, and the boobrie's food had to wheelbarrowed up a steep hill, it seemed likely that the stoorworm too would mean hard work.

And he was quite right. "It's a question of seeing that he doesn't get tangled up," said Aunt Etta. "In the water he's all right, but you will see a few trees we've stripped of lower branches—those are stoorworm trees, and when he's on land we help him to coil himself round them neatly; otherwise he gets into knots. It's best to think of him as a kind of rope, or the cord of a Walkman."

Fabio didn't say anything. He had already gathered that when Aunt Etta said "we" she meant him and Minette—and she went on to explain that the worm was a person who liked to think about important things like *Where has yesterday gone?* or *Why hasn't God made sardines without bones?*

"The trouble is he's so long that his thoughts don't easily get to the other end, and that upsets him," said

Etta. "He wants to have an operation to make him shorter, but you must make it clear that we will *not* allow it," said Aunt Etta, fiercely tapping her nose. "Plastic surgery is something we could never permit on the Island."

"If you're bothered by his breath, you can always give him a peppermint," said Coral. "Though why everyone in the world should smell of toothpaste is something I have never understood. And now you'd better go and fetch the wheelbarrows from the hill."

Chapter 6

WE MUST START to think seriously about running away," said Fabio sleepily.

"Yes, we must," agreed Minette, yawning.

They had gone on saying this each night—it was almost like saying their prayers—but they hadn't got much further. It wasn't just that they would have to steal the *Peggoty* from the boathouse; they would also have to know in which direction to sail her. And of course running away has two parts to it. There is running away *from* somewhere and there is running away *to* somewhere.

"It's all right for you," Fabio said. "You've got two proper parents. All I've got in this country is an awful school and awful grandparents."

"Yes." But Minette was doubtful. If she ran away to her father, her mother would be cross, and if she ran away to her mother, her father would be cross. "I'd just like to wait until the boobrie's laid her egg."

And in the end, before they could make further plans, the children always fell asleep.

But as the days passed, there was one thing that really annoyed Fabio, and that was Lambert.

Fabio didn't mind working hard. All the same, he and Minette both had blisters on their hands from trundling the wheelbarrows up and down to the loch; Minette had strained her wrist trying to get a comb through the old mermaid's tangled hair; and both of them were bruised by the young seals bumping and flopping against them as they gave them their bottles. And there was Lambert doing nothing—absolutely nothing—except kicking and screaming and throwing his food about.

"Why doesn't someone thump him?" said Fabio crossly.

But nobody did. Aunt Myrtle wasn't a thumper, and the other aunts said that using force when training animals never worked. As for Art, he might have killed a man once, but that was as far as it got. So each day Lambert was brought his food on a tray, and each day he kicked and yelled for his father and his mobile telephone while Fabio and Minette did his share of the chores.

It was at the end of the first week that Fabio cracked, and it was because of the stoorworm.

The children had grown very fond of the worm. He ate the peppermints they gave him without fuss, and the questions he asked were interesting, like "Why don't we think with our stomachs?" or "Why are we back to front in the mirror but not upside down?"

But wrapping him round a tree was an awful job. It wasn't just his thoughts that got stuck halfway down his body, it was all the messages that told his lower end what was happening, and on a day when they had spent a whole hour disentangling him from a bramble thicket, Fabio suddenly snapped.

Art was just making his way down to the boathouse with Lambert's lunch on a tray.

"I'll take that for you, Art," said Fabio.

Art handed over the tray, and Fabio opened the door.

Lambert looked up. Then he did what he always did when someone came into the room. He picked up whatever was closest to him and threw it hard. This time it was a sawn-off log ready to go on the fire.

Fabio ducked neatly. Then he threw the tray at Lambert. The tray contained a plate of lentil soup, a slice of bread with butter, fried tomatoes on toast, and a banana milkshake. All of these landed on Lambert except for the bread and butter, which went slightly wide.

"Yow! Whee! Yuck!" Lambert spluttered and danced round the room, blinded by the tomatoes, which were the large splodgy kind with a great many seeds.

Fabio gave him a few moments to clean himself up. Then he said, "Right. You're not getting anything more to eat until you come and work. Minette and I are sick of doing the jobs you ought to be doing."

"I won't! I won't come and work!" Lambert tried to stamp his foot on the floor but stamped it into his soup bowl, which split in half and skidded across the room. "I won't stay here on this horrible island, and I won't stay with these creepy women, and I won't do anything. I want my father, and I want my mobile telephone, and I want to go home."

Fabio waited. "I don't care what you want," he said. "Minette and I want things too, but that doesn't mean we get them. From now on, you're going to do your share, and if you don't, I'm going to thump you."

Lambert had cleaned the tomato out of his eyes now. "You'd better not," he said. "I'm bigger than you."

This was true, but it didn't bother Fabio. "You may be bigger, but you're wimpier."

Lambert was a coward, but Fabio was very small and slight. Lambert put up his fists and danced forward. He had never boxed, but he had seen people do that on the telly.

Fabio, on the other hand, *had* boxed. He didn't care for it, but it was taught at Greymarsh Towers as part of making people into English gentlemen. He let fly with his right hand and landed a blow on Lambert's chin.

"Oow! Eeh! . . . You've busted my jaw. I'm going to tell my father. My father's rich and . . . Oowee . . ." Lambert was crouching down on the floor nursing his chin and moaning.

"Get up," said Fabio.

"I won't."

"Yes, you will. Get up or you'll be sorry."

Lambert got slowly to his feet. The bruise on his chin blended nicely with the color of the tomato smeared on his collar. Then suddenly he went for Fabio, tearing at his cheeks with his fingernails.

It hurt, but to Fabio it was a relief. He knew about fighting dirty. He had been doing it ever since he was three years old in the streets of Rio, and if that was what Lambert wanted, it was fine with him. Ignoring the blood streaming down his cheeks, he took hold of a handful of Lambert's hair and yanked the sniveling boy's head backward, knocking it against the wall. Then he kicked him extremely hard on the shins.

"Ow!" moaned Lambert. "Stop it!"

"I'll stop it as soon as you say you'll come and do your share of work."

"I don't want to. I want my father. I want my mobile tele—"

Fabio yanked his head forward, then pushed it back again hard against the wall and went on kicking.

"Are you going to come out and work or not?"

"No."

Fabio kicked again—and suddenly Lambert crumpled up and collapsed on the floor.

"All right," he blubbered. "I'll work, but stop it."

Fabio stopped at once. "Come on, then," he said. "You can help me muck out the chicken house."

The aunts saw the boys come. Fabio was carrying the remains of Lambert's lunch on the tray, including the broken soup bowl.

"You can take it out of my pocket money," he said, handing them the pieces.

"What pocket money?" asked Aunt Etta.

"Even kidnapped children have to have pocket money," said Fabio firmly.

So Lambert began to work. He worked badly and he worked slowly. He complained because the television was on the blink, and whenever he could, he crept off to look for his mobile telephone, which he was sure Myrtle had hidden somewhere. But when he stopped for too long, Fabio just looked at him, and he picked up his tools once more.

Everyone agreed that such a tiresome, blathering boy had to be kept away from the unusual creatures— the selkies and the boobrie and the stoorworm—so they gave him jobs to do in the house or with the animals on the farm. But a couple of days after Fabio had beaten him up, Lambert crept down to the shore with a lemonade bottle he had stolen from the larder. Inside the lemonade bottle was a message he had written to his father, telling him to come and rescue him. He was going to throw the bottle into the sea.

But he never got as far as doing that. Instead he dropped the bottle, which smashed on the stones, leaving a dangerous mess of broken glass, and came back to the house blubbering and screaming at the top of his voice.

"I saw a *thing!* I saw a horrible creepy thing!" His whole body shook with terror. He looked as if he was going to have a fit.

"What sort of a thing?" asked Fabio.

He and Minette were sitting at the kitchen table, shelling peas for supper.

"A girl . . . all queer and horrible. She didn't have any legs — not any!" He sobbed and gulped again, and a runnel of snot ran down from his nose.

Minette handed him her handkerchief. "What do you mean, Lambert?" she asked.

"The bottom end of her was a monster. She had a tail all covered in scales. It was growing from her body." Lambert retched and turned his head away. "I saw it. I *saw* it. I won't stay here, I won't!"

Minette and Fabio exchanged troubled glances.

"What was the top of her like?"

"I don't know . . . she had sort of green hair—and when I screamed, she flopped her tail—I *heard* it flop. . . ." He shuddered. "And then she dived into the water."

"It sounds like Oona," said Minette in a low voice. "Of course it would be her—she's been frightened enough already by that ridiculous Lord Brasenott. I'll go and comfort her. If only it had been Queenie, she'd have seen Lambert off."

She slipped out, and Fabio was left alone with the blubbering Lambert.

He had an idea.

"Lambert," he said. "Listen to this, because it's important. When Minette and I first came, we saw all sorts of strange creatures—mermaids like you've seen and a long slithery worm and a giant bird—oh, all sorts of things—but then we realized they weren't real. They couldn't be real because creatures like that don't exist. I mean, there aren't any such things as mermaids, are there?"

Lambert had stopped crying. He was actually listening.

"No," he said. "There aren't."

"So what has happened, Lambert, is that you're imagining them. It's like having a vision or a dream. And it's because of something that Art puts in the food. He uses a flour made of seaweed, and it has a drug in it that makes you see things. He doesn't mean to harm us, but it's the only kind of flour you can get here."

"They aren't really there?" asked Lambert, sniffing the snot back into his nose. "She wasn't there—that horrible girl and the awful tail that she flopped with—that wasn't there either?"

"No, it wasn't. And anything else you see like that will just be a dream. You've heard of drugs that give you visions, haven't you? They're called halluci—" But here Fabio gave up, not sure of how to pronounce *hallucinogenic* or even if that was the word he meant. "And it's best not to say anything to anyone—even if you think you see other things. Just don't take any notice, and if you get back to your father, don't tell him; he'd only laugh at you."

It worked. Lambert gave a few more gulps; he was still blotched, he was still hiccuping unpleasantly, but he was calm.

And from then on, if Lambert saw anything unusual, he was sure it was because of something in the food.

The aunts weren't happy about Fabio telling lies, but it seemed safer than letting Lambert go screaming all over the Island and hurting the feelings of the creatures that he came upon.

And so the days passed. Minette and Fabio still talked about getting away, but they always fell asleep before they could work out how to do it, and slowly the beauty of the place—the great wide skies, the flaming sunsets, and the never-ending sound of the sea—seemed to be becoming a part of them.

But meanwhile in London, all hell was breaking loose.

Chapter 7

EIGHT DAYS AFTER Minette ate her drugged cheese-and-tomato sandwich, Minette's mother, Mrs. Danby, rang Edinburgh to ask if Minette could stay with her father for an extra week. Minette's term had started, but that was not the kind of thing that bothered Mrs. Danby.

"I have the chance of a job filming in Paris," she said.

This wasn't strictly true. What she did have was yet another boyfriend, who said he'd take her to France for a bit of a "jolly."

Professor Danby, whom she'd interrupted as he was preparing for an important lecture on "The Use of the Semicolon," did not at first understand what she was saying.

"I can hardly keep Minette longer when I haven't got her," he said in his dry, irritable voice.

There was a pause at the other end while Mrs. Danby fought down the slight fluttering in her stomach.

"Don't be silly, Philip. I sent Minette to you more than a week ago. She's been with you since the fifteenth."

"No you didn't. I had a telephone message to say you were keeping her with you and taking her to the seaside. I remember it quite clearly."

The professor had in fact been rather pleased because the lecture he was giving was part of an important series—"The Use of the Semicolon," "The Use of the Comma," "The Use of the Paragraph," and so on— and he needed to get on with his work without being bothered by a child.

Now, though, he too began to feel as though his stomach was not quite where it should have been. But of course being the sort of people they were, the Danbys immediately began to blame each other.

"You must be mad, not letting me know she hadn't arrived."

"*I* must be mad?" hissed the professor. "*You* must be mad. Any normal mother would ring up to see that her daughter had arrived safely."

"Any normal father would ring and find out why she wasn't being sent."

"Are you accusing me of not being normal?" said the professor in a dangerously quiet voice. "A woman who stubbed out her cigarette on a poached egg."

"It wasn't a poached egg; it was a fried egg. And if you hadn't kept turning the lamps off because you were too cheap to pay the electricity bill, I'd have seen it wasn't an ashtray. And anyway, how a man who leaves a bath full of scum every time he —"

"Scum!" yelled the professor down the phone. "Are you accusing *me* of leaving scum? Why I couldn't even get *into* the bath without wading through a heap of your unspeakable toenail clippings."

They went on like this for some time, but then they remembered that their only daughter was missing and pulled themselves together.

"Can she have run away?" wondered Mrs. Danby.

"Why should she run away? She has two perfectly good homes."

"Yes. But she's been looking a bit peaked. And she sees tigers on the ceiling. Perhaps I should have let her have a night-light."

"If every child who sees tigers on the ceiling ran away, there'd be very few children left in their homes," said the professor.

But obviously the next thing to be done was to go to the police. So Professor Danby went to the police station in Edinburgh, and Mrs. Danby went to the police station in London. Then she rang her ex-husband and said that the police wanted them to come together and compare their stories exactly.

"You have to come down," said Mrs. Danby. "And quick. They say there's no time to waste."

So the professor took the train to London, and the next day both of Minette's parents sat side by side in a taxi on the way to the Metropolitan Police Station.

The officer they saw this time was a high-ranking one, a detective chief superintendent who had a secretary sitting beside him to take everything down.

"Now, I understand that you have heard nothing since your daughter disappeared ten days ago?" he asked. "No messages? No ransom demand?"

Both the Danbys shook their heads.

"I have very little money," said the professor. "I'm on the staff of the university, and they pay abominably. It's a disgrace how little —"

"And I'm on the dole," said Mrs. Danby, unusually honest. "So even if they asked us for money, it wouldn't help."

The detective wrote this down. "Now tell us, please, Mrs. Danby, exactly where and when you last saw your daughter."

"It was at two o'clock on the fifteenth of April. At King's Cross Station, Platform One. I handed her over to an aunt —"

"Wait a minute!" The superintendent's eyebrows drew together sharply. "You mean *your* aunt . . . or *her* aunt?"

97

"No. *An* aunt. An aunt from an agency. Minette always traveled with aunts."

The detective seemed to find this very interesting. "Go and get me the file on the Mountjoy case," he said to the secretary. "Sergeant Harris has it." He turned back to the Danbys. "Now tell me from what agency you hired this aunt. It's an extremely important point."

Mrs. Danby frowned. "Well, generally they came from an agency called *Useful Aunts.* I've used them for years—they're very reliable. But I think . . ." She rubbed her forehead. "I'm not sure . . . I think this one may have been labeled *Unusual Aunts.* Yes, I think so. And there was some writing above that which said *My name is Edna.* Or maybe it was *Etta.*"

"If you hadn't rotted your brain with tobacco, you might be able to remember," said the professor under his breath.

But at that moment the secretary came back with a blue folder. "Yes," said the detective as he opened it. "Yes. The two cases are extraordinarily similar." He looked up at the Danbys. "Another child disappeared on the same day as your daughter, and he too was put in the charge of an aunt. I think we're getting somewhere at last!"

The old Mountjoys were always pleased when Hubert-Henry went back to boarding school. They hated having children about, and they could never quite forgive their son for having married a foreign dancer in a night-club and producing such an unsuitable grandson.

Then, just a week after Hubert-Henry had left for Greymarsh Towers, a letter came from the headmaster that told Mr. Mountjoy that even though Hubert was not at school because of the Burry-Burry fever, the full fees for the term would still have to be paid.

That did it, of course. Mr. Mountjoy rang the headmaster and asked what nonsense was this about Burry-Burry fever and where was the boy who had been delivered to school on the first day of the term?

And the headmaster said, we don't have the boy, the aunt from the agency had told Matron that Hubert-Henry was ill.

So after the old Mountjoys had shouted down the telephone and threatened to sue the headmaster, they went to the police. They might not be fond of Hubert-Henry, but he was their grandson and their property, and if anyone had taken him, they wanted to know the reason why.

Which meant the police knew of two cases in which a child had vanished in the care of an aunt, and it was now that the Great London Aunt Hunt began.

The police only knew about two aunts because Lambert's father was still in America, so the boy had not yet been reported missing. But two aunts were enough to be going on with—and the newspapers and the police and the general public now went slightly mad.

AUNT PLAGUE MENACES THE CITY screamed the headlines, and MONSTER AUNTS ON KILLER SPREE!

Once people had been warned, they saw these murdering women everywhere.

An aunt was caught outside a supermarket trying to impale a sweet little baby with a giant knitting needle while his mother shopped inside.

"I was only trying to spear a wasp," she quavered. "I didn't want it to sting the child." But she was hauled off to the police station, and it was only when they found the back end of the squashed insect in her knitting bag that she was set free.

An even more sinister aunt was seen in Hyde Park, kicking in the head of a little boy who lay in the grass.

"I seen her clear as daylight," said a fat man who'd been walking his dog and sent for the police. "Kicking like a maniac she was!"

And, "Look how he's crying, the poor little fellow," said the other dog owners who had crowded round—and it was true that the boy, holding on to his soccer ball, *was* crying. Anyone would cry seeing their aunt bundled into a police van when she'd been showing them how to curl a penalty into the top right-hand corner of the goal. She'd been a striker for the Wolverhampton Under Eighteens soccer team, and he thought the world of her.

There was talk in Parliament of a curfew for aunts, forcing them to be in bed by eight o'clock; the *Daily Echo* said aunts should be electronically tagged like prisoners — and an elderly lady was arrested in the shoe department of a store for abusing her great-niece, who was trying on shoes for a party.

"She was shouting and screaming at the child, and her eyes were wild," said the woman who had turned her in — and the aunt would probably have gone to prison, but while she was in the cell, the shop assistants staged a walk-out and marched on the police station with banners, demanding that she be freed.

"I wouldn't just have shouted at the girl, I'd have wrung her neck," said a motherly shop assistant to the reporters standing round.

"The poisonous child had thirty-nine pairs of shoes out, and she was throwing them round the floor," said another shop girl. "If you ask me, that aunt had the patience of a saint not to scream at her earlier."

So the police let her go, and then the newspapers said they were too soft and that aunts should be flogged like in the good old days.

Meanwhile, posters of Etta and Coral were stuck up in police stations and public libraries and bus shelters everywhere. These pictures had been drawn by an artist from the descriptions he had been given by the people who had seen them last, and they were extremely odd.

Have You Seen These Women?

Aunt Etta had a nose like a pickax, a blob of hair like a jellyfish on top of her head, and a mustache she could have twirled, it was so big. Aunt Coral had a mad squint in one eye, seven pairs of earrings in each ear, and absolutely no neck.

Have You Seen These Women? it said at the bottom of the posters.

But of course no one had, because women like that do not exist. And so the days passed, and still the police had no clues to go on. The Unusual Aunts Agency had closed down, and it seemed as though the stolen children and their kidnappers had vanished off the face of the earth.

Chapter 8

AUNT ETTA WOKE and stretched and immediately felt very strange. Something had happened. And the something was important—perhaps the most important thing that had ever happened to her.

She got out of bed and went to the window. Her long gray braid hung down her back; her hairy legs and bony feet stuck out from under her flannel nightdress, but her mud-colored eyes were as excited as a young girl's.

Yet there was nothing unusual to be seen. A flock of gulls was out fishing; the sun was just beginning to come up behind the two islands to the east.

"All the same, there is something," thought Aunt Etta, and the excitement grew in her. "Only what?"

Then she realized that the excitement was coming from her feet. It was being sent through her toe bones and up her ankle bones and through her body.

For a moment she felt quite faint. Could it be? . . . But no . . . that would be a miracle; she had done nothing to deserve anything as tremendous as that.

The sound of heavy breathing made her turn. It was Coral. She too was in her nightdress, folds of it wrapped round her like a bell tent, she too was barefoot, and she too was panting with excitement.

"Oh Etta," she gasped. "I feel so strange."

Coral's long hair, which she dyed an interesting gold, hung down her back; she looked like a mad goddess. "I feel as though . . . only it can't be, can it? Not after a hundred years?"

"No . . . it can't."

But they clutched each other's hands, because it hadn't stopped, the extraordinary, amazing . . . feeling.

"We must wake Myrtle. She's musical."

But there was no need to wake Myrtle. Myrtle did not wear a nightdress; she wore pajamas because she often went out before dawn to talk to the seals, and she thought that pajamas were more respectable. They were made of gray flannel so that she did not show up too much in the dusk, and for a moment her sisters did not see her lying on the floor with her face pressed to the threadbare carpet.

"Myrtle, do you feel — " her sisters began.

But before she could answer, Myrtle lifted her head. They had never seen their sister look like that.

"Can it be?" began Coral.

"We must go up the hill," said Myrtle, and she spoke like someone in a dream. "We must turn our faces to the north."

"But dressed," said Etta, coming to her senses for a moment. "Not in our nightclothes. Not even if—"

But her sisters took no notice, and Etta herself only had time to put on her dressing gown before there was a thumping noise from next door. It was the Captain's walking stick banging on the wall, and it meant, "Come at once."

The sisters looked at each other anxiously. If he had heard it too, it could strain his heart. So much excitement is bad for old people.

And when they first saw the Captain, they were very worried. He was lying slumped on his pillows, his eyes shut, and he was trembling so much that the whole bed shook. But when they came up to him, they were amazed. Captain Harper was a hundred and three years old, but he looked for a moment like a boy.

"I've heard it," he murmured. "I've heard it and I've felt it. Even if that's all, even if there's no more than that, I'll die happy now."

"We're going on to the hill, Father," said Etta. "We'll tell you as soon as—"

The door burst open, and Fabio and Minette came running into the room. They had tumbled straight out of bed, bewildered and still half asleep, and followed the sound of voices.

"Something's happened," said Minette. She was wearing quite the silliest nightdress that even her mother could have bought, covered in patterns of dancing elephants and picnicking zebras, but with her dark hair wild about her shoulders and her bewildered eyes, she seemed to be listening to music from another land. "We were woken . . ."

"It's a feeling . . . only it isn't only a feeling." Fabio shook his head, trying to understand. "It's a sound, except it's all through us. We're not making it up."

The three aunts and the old Captain looked at the children and nodded. It was a pleased nod, and it meant that the children were all right; they were proper ones, without a touch of a Boo-Boo or a Little One. Lambert, they were sure, would have heard and felt nothing.

"You'd better come with us. Get your shoes on at least."

Outside the feeling was stronger. Minette and Fabio, struggling for words to describe it, were lost. They followed the aunts onto the turf path that led to the hill. Minette wore Myrtle's shawl round her shoulders—no one had taken time to dress properly.

The "feeling," whatever it was, was growing stronger.

It came through the soles of their feet, but also now from above, from everywhere. If they'd been doubtful whether it meant anything, the creatures would have put them right at once. In the dawn light, the birds wheeled round the cliff in a frenzy of agitation. The seals, usually drowsing on the point at this hour, were all in the water, swimming toward the northern strand — and in the lead was Herbert. Like all selkies, he slept with one eye open. He had been the first to know that something incredibly important was going to happen, and at once he had put aside his everyday worries. What did it matter now whether one was a man or a seal? He moved through the waves like a torpedo — and close behind Herbert came his mother.

The sky was changing. It was filled with strange colors that belonged neither to the dawn nor to the sunset, colors that the children had never seen and afterward could not describe.

On her great nest, the boobrie honked with all her power . . . honked and stirred . . . and flapped her wings, trying to fly off after the others, but she couldn't, with the eggs so heavy and stuck inside her . . . and she pushed her muscles together, pressing and pressing as she tried to become airborne. . . .

The stoorworm came out of the lake and slithered over the ground, following the aunts and the children. He was no longer the muddled creature who had lost control of his far end. He moved like a great serpent, controlled and lean and fast.

Down by the house, the goats butted their horns against the walls of their sty and broke free and went galloping along the shore like mad creatures.

The door of the mermaid shed opened, and Loreen and her daughters slithered across the rocks and plunged into the water.

"To the north," she shouted, holding Walter in the crook of her arm, and they set off for the wild strand beneath the hill.

"Wait for me, wait for me!" shouted Old Ursula, but they had gone, and she was left beating her tail furiously against the side of the sink.

The Sybil had come out of her cave. The mucky old prophetess was not talking about the weather now. She was writhing and moaning, her face had turned blue, and her hair was standing on end. "It's going to happen," she said. "It's going to happen."

But the aunts did not wait for her to tell them what. They raced panting up the hill with the children beside them, and all the time the feeling, which was getting stronger, was going through every cell in their bodies.

They reached the top of the hill—and then they were certain. From all sides it came now, like the breath of the universe. Below them the sea boiled against the northern shore; the mermaids, their troubles forgotten, trod water and stared toward the horizon; the seals made a semicircle, and those who were more than seals, who had been human once, could be seen bowing their heads.

And to make everything certain, from behind the largest of the tombstones with its strange carvings, there now rose a white, mysterious wraith, with rays of light coming from her face and outstretched hands.

"It's Ethelgonda," breathed Aunt Etta. "Ethelgonda the Good!" And everyone fell to their knees, for this was a ghost who had not appeared for well over fifty years.

The saintly hermit was smiling. She was totally happy; she enfolded them in her blessing.

"Yes," she said in a deep and beautiful voice. "You have not been mistaken. What you have heard is most truly the Great Hum."

Minette and Fabio, who had been spellbound by the apparition, heard the sound of the most heartfelt sobbing beside them and turned their heads. All three aunts were crying. Tears streamed down Aunt Etta's bony cheeks; tears made a path through Aunt Coral's nourishing night cream; tears dropped onto Aunt Myrtle's hands as she brought them to her face.

"It is the Hum," repeated Aunt Etta, in a choking voice.

"It is the Hum," nodded Aunt Coral.

And Myrtle too said, "It is the Hum."

"What is—" began Fabio, but Minette frowned him down. She felt that this was not the moment for questions.

"So does that mean . . . ?" faltered Aunt Etta, and the children looked at her, amazed. They did not know that this fierce woman could sound so shy and uncertain and humble.

The hermit nodded. "Yes, my dears," she said in her melodious voice. "It means that this place above all others has been chosen. You have been blessed."

The aunts rose slowly to their feet. They could still not quite believe what they had heard, yet the Hum now was everywhere, filling the sky, coming up from the earth.

"So *he* is really coming? After a hundred years?"

The holy woman nodded.

The aunts did not ask precisely *when* he was coming. They knew that one must not pry into mysteries but accept them gratefully, and they were right.

"I can say no more," said the saint. "You must hold yourself in readiness."

And then she vanished, and they were left alone with their miracle.

"You heard what Ethelgonda said. We must hold ourselves in readiness. Readiness means cleaning. Readiness means tidying. Readiness means cooking and scrubbing and fettling. It always has and it always will," said Aunt Etta.

She was almost her old, brisk bossy self as she sent the children to scour out the goat sty and swill down the floor of the mermaid shed and pick up the litter washed ashore.

Almost, but not quite. None of the aunts were quite the same. Etta still hung her navy blue knickers on the line each morning, but sometimes she patted her bun of hair like a young girl invited to a party. Coral's clothes got wilder and wilder; she was painting a great underwater mural on the back of the house in all the colors of the rainbow, and the tunes that Myrtle played on her cello had become very powerful and loud.

"If only Dorothy were here," said Etta, who missed her sister badly. Hitting people on the head with their own woks was nothing compared to the excitement of what was to come.

The Captain insisted on clean pajamas every day so he would not be caught short, and the old Sybil danced about in her cave in a frenzy of excitement. She still thought it was unwise to wash her face and hands, but she decided bravely to wash her feet. This took a long time (mold had grown between her toes, and mold can be interesting—the blue-green colors, the unusual shapes), but once one has heard the Great Hum, life is never the same.

The creatures, in their own way, were just as excited,

and now the aunts understood why it had been so difficult to get anyone to go away. They must have known
that something special was going to happen, even if they
did not know exactly what.

Even the animals that never talked, even the herrings
and the haddock and the flounders . . . even the lugworms buried in the sand seemed to be excited.

"How can a lugworm be excited?" Minette wanted to
know, but when Aunt Etta dug one up for her, she saw
that it might be.

As for Art, he baked buns—hundreds and hundreds
of buns, which overflowed his cake tins and had to be
stored in sealed bin bags in the larder. But the buns he
baked were not ordinary buns, and nor were the omelets
they had for lunch and tea and supper ordinary omelets.

Because something very wonderful had happened
out there on the hill after Ethelgonda vanished. They
were turning to go home when they heard a sound from
the boobrie's nest that stopped them in their tracks.

It wasn't the mournful honking they were used to. It
was a proud and cheerful clucking—a noise full of
motherhood and joy. Pressing and pressing her muscles
together to try to follow the others had not made the
boobrie airborne, but it had done something else. And
there it was—an enormous, blue-spotted, and totally
egg-shaped egg!

But the most touching thing happened the next day,

when they went up to congratulate the bird once more. For the egg she had laid when the Great Hum went through her body and she had pressed so hard had been followed by three more. Four gigantic spotted eggs had rolled together and were keeping warm beneath her body, but when she saw the aunts and the children, the boobrie moved aside, examined each egg very carefully—and then pushed one out toward them with her great yellow foot.

"Be careful, dear," said Myrtle. "It mustn't get cold."

With difficulty, for the egg was heavier than a cannonball, they rolled it back . . . and the boobrie pushed it out again with her enormous foot.

The same thing was repeated three times—and then they understood.

"It's a present," said Minette, awed. "She wants us to have it."

Minette was right. The boobrie wanted to *share*. There was nothing to be done except to fetch Art and load the egg onto a wheelbarrow—and since seventy-two omelets are an awful lot of omelets, the great bun bake began.

It was hard for the children to be patient during those days of waiting. They knew that when the time came, they would find out what the Great Hum meant and who was coming. But on a day when Fabio was sent out for the third time to make sure that not so much as half a cigarette carton or a spool of thread had been washed up on the north shore, he dug in his heels.

"I think you should tell us," he said. "Me and Minette, I mean. We can keep secrets."

"We will tell you when the time is ripe," said Aunt Etta, and they had to be content with that.

But what had been happening to Lambert?

The aunts were right. Lambert had slept through the beginning of the Hum and heard nothing.

When he did wake up at last, he realized that the house was empty. Doors stood open; there was no sign of Art in the kitchen. Everyone, though Lambert did not know it, was out on the hill.

"I want my breakfast," said Lambert crossly, but there was no one to hear him.

By the time he was dressed, he did hear a kind of thrumming noise, but to Lambert the magical sound seemed to be the kind of noise a generator might make, or some underground machinery.

But he was interested in the open bedroom doors. Since he had begun to work, Lambert had been allowed to come back into the house to sleep, but Myrtle and the others kept him firmly out of their rooms. Myrtle had not forgotten how he had frightened the ducklings when he first came.

Now, though, Myrtle's door stood open. Her bed

was unmade, and the ducklings had grown enough to manage outdoors.

Lambert crept in. His shifty eyes took in all of Myrtle's little treasures, and he sneered. Fancy bothering to pick up bits of driftwood and veined pebbles and arranging them on the bookcase as though they were ornaments, he thought. There wasn't a single thing in her room, as far as he could see, that was worth tuppence.

Then he stopped dead. Propped against the corner of the room was Myrtle's cello case. The cello wasn't inside it; he could see it leaning against another wall, half covered with a shawl, so the case would be empty.

Lambert crept closer. He knew he had been carried away in it, though he could remember nothing. He had overheard Myrtle talking about it to her sisters.

And that meant that anything he had been holding when he was snatched might still be there!

Lambert's face flushed with excitement, his thin lips were parted. If only the case wasn't locked!

And it wasn't! He tried the clasp, and it opened easily. The inside of the case was lined with blue velvet, faded and torn in places because it was so old.

At first there seemed to be nothing there except a crumpled silk scarf and a spare bow. Then as Lambert groped about in the back of the case, his hand found something dark and small that had been covered by the cloth.

Lambert's fingers closed round it with a cry. He had found it. He had found his mobile telephone!

He would get away now! He was safe. Hiding the telephone under his shirt, Lambert went back to his room and pulled the chest of drawers across the door. Then he crouched down like an animal with its prey and began to dial.

Three days after Lambert found his telephone, the children woke shortly after midnight to find Aunt Coral and Aunt Etta standing by their beds.

Fabio was so sleepy that he thought at first it was the full moon and he was expected to dance the tango with Aunt Coral, but it wasn't that.

"Put some clothes on," said Aunt Etta. "And clean your teeth."

"We cleaned them before we went to bed," said Minette.

"Well, clean them again. No one with gunge on their molars is worthy to hear what we have to tell."

Still half asleep, the children stumbled up the hill after the two aunts. At the top they found Aunt Myrtle sitting over a fire she had made, ringed by stones, and it was by the flicker of the flames and to the sound of the sea sighing against the rocks below that the children learned what they wanted to know.

"Mind you, what I'm going to say won't mean much

to you unless you know your history, and I doubt if you know a lot of that," said Aunt Etta. "So let me start by asking you a question. What does the word *kraken* mean to you?"

Fabio was silent, but Minette said shyly, "Is it a sea monster? A very big one?"

Etta nodded. "Yes. It is a sea monster, and it is bigger than anything you can imagine. But it has nothing to do with all the silly stories you hear. Nothing to do with rubbish about Giant Blobs or outsize cuttlefish or octopuses that pull people down to the ocean bed. No, the kraken is . . . or was . . . the Soul of the Sea. It is the greatest force for good the ocean has ever known."

Fabio and Minette looked at her, surprised. This wasn't at all the way Aunt Etta usually spoke.

So then she began to tell them the kraken's story. It took a long time to tell, and the fire had burned down and been rekindled many times before it was finished, but the children scarcely stirred.

"There was a time when everyone in the world knew about the kraken," Aunt Etta began. "They knew about his huge size and that when he rested with his back humped out of the water, he was taken for an island. They knew that when he reared up suddenly, the sea churned and boiled, and no ship that was near him had the slightest hope of avoiding shipwreck.

"But they knew too that for all his size, the kraken was a gentle creature. His eyes were full of soul, and when he opened his mouth, one could see that instead of teeth he had rows and rows of tendrils that were the greenish gold color of a mermaid's hair. Through this forest of tendrils, the sea poured in, and it was the sea that nourished him: the tiny invisible creatures that make up the plankton were all the kraken needed for food.

"They knew that the kraken came from the Far North and that the language he spoke best was Polar, though he understood other languages also. But mostly the kraken did not speak. The kraken sang. Or perhaps *singing* is not quite the right word. What the kraken did was to hum. It was a deep, slow sound, and it was like no other sound in the world, for what the kraken hummed was the Song of the Sea. It was a healing song. If you like, it was the Breath of the Universe. Whales can hum too . . . and Buddhist monks who spend their lives on high mountains trying to understand God . . . and small children when they are happy—but the sound they make is nothing compared to the sound made by the kraken.

"For many years the kraken swam quietly round the oceans of the world, humming his hum and singing his song and stopping sometimes to rest. And when he stopped, people who did not know much said: 'Goodness, surely there wasn't an island out in that bay before,' but people who were wise and in touch with the things that mattered smiled and felt honored and proud. Because when the kraken came, they remembered what a splendid thing the sea was: so clean and beautiful when it was calm, so mighty and exciting and awe-inspiring when it was rough. It was as though the great creature was guarding the sea for them, or even as though somehow he was showing them what a treasure-house it was.

"*Look!* the kraken seemed to be saying. *Behold . . . the sea!*

"In those days the kraken made it his business to circle the oceans of the world each year, and whenever he appeared, people started to behave themselves. Fishermen stopped catching more fish than they needed and threw the little ones back into the sea, and people who were dumping their rubbish into the water thought better of it, seeing the kraken's large and wondrous eyes fixed on them. And when he went on again, it was to leave the sea — and indeed the world — a better place.

"It was like a blessing, to have seen the kraken," said Aunt Etta now. "It brought you luck for the rest of your life."

"Did you ever see him?" asked Minette.

Aunt Etta shook her head. She looked very sad. "No one living now has seen him. He hasn't been seen for a hundred years or more. He was dreadfully hurt once, and he went into hiding."

The hurt that was done to the kraken was not to his body. The skin of a kraken is a meter deep, and no other animal can threaten him. No animal would want to—he traveled with a whole company of sharks and stingrays and killer whales who would have died rather than harm him.

But human beings are different. They always have been: interfering and bossy and mad for power. No one knew which whaling boat had shot a harpoon into the kraken's throat. Was it a Japanese ship or one belonging to the British or the Danes? Did the whalers mistake the kraken for a humpback whale, or were they just terrified, seeing a dark shape bigger than anything they had ever seen rear up in front of them?

Whatever the reason, they hurled the biggest of their harpoons and hit the kraken with terrible force in the softest part of his throat.

The kraken probably didn't believe it at first. No one had ever tried to harm him. Then he felt the pain and saw the dark dollops of his blood staining the sea.

When he understood what had happened, he began to thrash about, trying to rid himself of the harpoon— and the rope snapped. But the pain was still there and the kraken reared up, trying to dislodge the hooked horror in his neck. As he did so, the tidal wave made by his body tossed the whaling boat up and drew it under the sea, and every one of the men was drowned, which was just as well because the sea creatures who had traveled with the kraken would have torn them limb from limb.

And the kraken swam away to the north, the harpoon still in his throat. The pain died away, and presently an old sea nymph came with her brood of children and cut the hook out of the kraken's flesh with razor shells, and soon there was only a small scar left to show where it had been.

But the scar on the kraken's soul remained. He had traveled the world to sing the Song of the Sea and to heal the people who lived by it — and they had stabbed him in the throat. The kraken was two thousand years old, which is not old for a kraken, but now he felt tired, Let human beings look after themselves! He swam still farther north, and farther still to where the wildness of the sea and the large number of humped islands made him invisible, and he turned his back on the world and slept.

And while he slept, people forgot that there had been such a creature, and the stories about him got wilder and wilder until this healing monster was jumbled up in people's minds with Giant Blobs and vicious triffids and nonsense like that.

And the sea got muckier and muckier and more and more neglected.

But of course everyone did not forget. The sea creatures remembered — the seals and the selkies, the mermaids and the nixies, and the people who lived and worked on the islands and by the shore.

And the aunts remembered.

"Oh yes, we always remembered," said Etta now. "Our father told us about him, and our grandfather told our father. We have always known, but we never dreamed—"

She fell silent, overcome by her feelings, and the children gazed into the embers of the fire and thought about what they had heard.

Why am I not frightened? Minette wondered. Once she would have been terrified at the thought of a great sea monster swimming toward them, but now she felt only wonder. And something else: a longing to help and serve this creature she had never seen. She felt she would do anything for the kraken when he came. Which was silly, because how could an ordinary girl do anything for the mightiest monster in the world? But she didn't feel silly. She felt awed and uplifted, as though some amazing task awaited her.

Fabio didn't feel quite like that. Fabio felt that the story he had heard needed a celebration. So he did something rather noble. He turned to Coral, sitting in her cloak beside him, and said:

"Aunt Coral, the moon is full—or very nearly. Would you like to dance the tango?"

Chapter 9

STANLEY SPROTT, Lambert's father, had had a good time in America. He had bought three factories and a cinema and turned out a family living in a house next to the cinema so that he could bulldoze it and build a fast-food restaurant. There had been a court case and a fuss because the family had a handicapped child and a sick mother, but Mr. Sprott had won. He always did win because he knew how to hire the best lawyers, and now, as the chauffeur drove him in his Mercedes from the airport, he reckoned that his trip to the States would earn him a clear million dollars.

Beside him in the car sat his bodyguard, Des, a large man with small eyes and an even smaller brain. Des had only learned to read when he was twenty-five, and he liked to show that he could do it, so as they stopped for the traffic lights, he looked at the posters on the wall of the police station and said: "There's some mad aunts been on the rampage, kidnapping children. They're offering a thousand pounds reward if anyone's got any info."

Mr. Sprott thought this was very funny.

"Aunts!" he snorted as the car moved on, leaving the pictures of Aunt Coral and Aunt Etta flapping in the breeze. "Trust the police to be fooled by a bunch of aunts!"

Mr. Sprott had a very low opinion of the police, who had tried to interfere with some of his enterprises and been thoroughly foiled.

Arriving in his house, he stood for a moment in the hallway and looked about him. He had the feeling that somebody who should have been in his house was not.

But who? Who was it that was not there? While Des went to turn off the burglar alarms and look for letter bombs, Mr. Sprott thought about this.

Well, for one thing, his wife was not there. But there was nothing strange about that. His wife had faxed him from Paris to say that she was going to go and buy some more clothes in Rome, and she had faxed him from Rome to say she was going to buy some more clothes in Madrid.

So it wasn't Josette Sprott who should have been there and wasn't, and it wasn't the housekeeper, who always had two hours off in the afternoon.

Which meant that it was his son, Lambert.

"Lambert!" bellowed Mr. Sprott, standing in the middle of the hallway.

No answer.

"Get him on the intercom," Mr. Sprott told Des.

But though all the rooms were connected electronically, Lambert did not appear.

Mr. Sprott was not alarmed, but he was surprised. He had told Lambert when he was coming back, and the boy, though an awful sniveler, was fond of his father.

Mr. Sprott went to his study, sent out for a secretary, and was soon deep in his business affairs.

But when the housekeeper came back in the early evening, Mr. Sprott was reminded of his son once more.

"Didn't you bring Lambert, sir?" she asked him. Her voice was hopeful. She really hated the boy.

"How could I bring Lambert? I haven't got him. I never had him — he's staying here with you."

"No, he isn't. There was a message saying he was joining you in America. It was left by the aunt — she said there'd been a call."

"The aunt? What aunt?"

"The aunt from the agency. She took Lambert to the zoo, and when I got back, the boy was gone."

The flapping posters, the notice of the reward, ran through Mr. Sprott's mind. They didn't seem so funny now.

"I'm sorry, sir, but—"

"Be quiet." Mr. Sprott was scowling. "I'm going to the police. Tell Merton to bring the car round."

But at that moment, very faintly, a telephone rang upstairs.

It was his personal phone, or rather one of them. Mr. Sprott collected mobiles the way other people collected matches, and now he couldn't remember which one it was or where he might have left it. Under his bed? On the toilet tank? In the cocktail cabinet?

"Find it," he ordered, and the bodyguard and the secretary and the housekeeper ran all over the house trying to follow the sound.

It was Mr. Sprott who reached it just as it was about to stop ringing. It was under a pile of monogrammed underpants in his chest of drawers.

"Hello!" he shouted. He was a man who always shouted into telephones. There were some strange noises—a sort of gulping sound followed by a gabble. "Speak up, damn you. I can't hear you!"

"It's me, Daddy. It's Lambert. I've been kidnapped! You've got to come and get me!"

More gulping, more tears. What a crybaby the boy was!

"All right, Lambert, I'll come and get you, but where are you? Speak clearly."

"I'm on an island. It's an awful place—"

"What island? Where is it?"

"It's in the sea."

Stanley Sprott rolled his eyes. "Yes, Lambert, islands are usually in the sea. But where? Which sea?"

"I dunno—they won't tell me—but it's cold. There aren't any coconuts. I've been phoning and phoning you every day." He broke off, gulping again. "My batteries are running out."

"Lambert, please think. Are there any other islands nearby?"

"There are a couple on one side."

"What side? East? West? North? South?"

"I dunno. The sun comes up behind them, I think. It's awful here—it's weird. There are these aunts; they're mad and they give me drugged food. You've got to come, you've got to! There's one after me now!"

The line went dead. Mr. Sprott stood for a while, thinking. An isolated island with two islands to the east of it. And—unbelievably—a posse of aunts.

He gave his orders. "I want the *Hurricane* made ready. I'll pick her up at London docks. Get a couple of armed men aboard and see there's plenty of ammunition. Pick them carefully; this mission is secret!"

The *Hurricane* was his yacht—a converted patrol boat and his pride and joy.

It was only then that he went to the police. He would not trust them to find Lambert—that job he would do by himself without telling anybody—but he might as well find out if there were any other clues.

That evening a third picture appeared on the walls of the police station, and in bus shelters and public libraries. This was of Aunt Myrtle, as remembered by the housekeeper and the man who fed the seals in London Zoo. It was even more peculiar than the other two pictures. Aunt Myrtle seemed to be standing in a high wind with her mouth open, and once again no one came forward to say they had seen her.

But Stanley Sprott's team of researchers were already marking down all the islands in the North Sea and the Atlantic with two islands to the east of them. And the *Hurricane,* with a full complement of arms on board, lay ready at the docks.

Chapter 10

HE SEEMED TO BE swimming quite slowly and peacefully, though the swell he left as he moved through the water could be felt on shores a thousand miles away.

Above him, the air was filled with flocks of birds that circled him, and the sea creatures ringed him down below. The sky was a hazy gold, and the sunsets were glorious and lingering, as though the sun could not bear to go down on such a sight. The sea glittered and glistened.

As he swam, the kraken hummed, but not all the time. Sometimes he stopped and turned his head to speak to someone who was swimming close beside him, and when he did that, the birds in the air fell silent and the underwater creatures moved their fins and flippers carefully, so as not to make a splash. Because the some-one who was swimming beside the kraken was important, and they wanted to make sure that he understood what the kraken was telling him.

Strange things happened as the kraken moved south from his Arctic hideout. He came level with an oil rig where men were working the night shift. The lights of the rig were only distant specks to the kraken, but he paused and changed his Hum to a deeper one, and on the rig a man called Dave O'Hara said:

"I'm going to shut off the waste pipe."

His mates put down their beer mugs and stared at him.

"Why? What's got into you? It's always on at night."

This was true. The outlet pipe spilled its filthy sludge into the water night and day.

"I dunno," said Dave, "but I'm shutting it off."

And he did so . . . and the kraken swam on.

On the Island, Herbert was the first to know.

His mother had come out of the sea a few days before and had tried to nag him again.

"You must make up your mind, Herbert," she had said in the selkie language they spoke when they were alone. "You're not young anymore; and I won't be around forever. If you're going to stop being a seal and start being a man, you must do it now."

For a while, Herbert only looked at her. Then: "Listen!" he said in his quiet and serious voice.

She had listened, and she had heard it because

selkies are famous for the sharpness of their ears. Not the Great Hum with which the kraken sent out long-distance messages, but the quiet, thrumming noise he made when he was patrolling the ocean.

"This is not the time to be human, Mother. I shall greet him in the water, and proudly, as a seal."

It was because of Herbert that Myrtle understood more quickly than the other aunts how near the kraken was. She had tried to play Herbert one of his favorite pieces—a minuet by Mozart. Usually he listened to this with his eyes closed, absolutely enchanted; Mozart was his favorite composer. But now he was restless, eagerly looking out to sea, and then he shook his head once as if to excuse himself and dived into the waves.

Soon it wasn't only Myrtle who guessed. Aunt Etta saw three snow geese—birds she had never seen on the Island before—and Coral came back from a shell hunt, dancing with excitement.

"The sea is changing color," she said. "Only slightly, but it's changing."

Then suddenly it seemed as though everyone knew that the time was coming, and the last-minute preparations began.

In his bed, the old Captain sat with the telescope glued to his eyes and tried to be gloomy.

"Of course he won't be like the kraken was in the

olden days. He'll be smaller, like the seals are smaller and the sheep and the bosoms of the ladies. Maybe he won't be any bigger than a whale," said Captain Harper. But if anyone tried to take the telescope away from him, he became absolutely furious, and as the kraken came closer, he scarcely slept.

As for the aunts and the children, during those days they seemed to be welded together into one band of workers who thought of nothing except to make the best possible welcome for the kraken when he came. It was impossible to imagine that Fabio and Minette had been drugged and kidnapped against their will not three weeks before. There was no need to give them orders; they knew what needed doing almost as soon as the aunts, and they, like the aunts, never spared themselves.

Then one day, they too heard the Hum once more. It was the kraken's Daily Hum, his Working Hum, the Hum with which he cleaned and healed the sea, and it was getting closer, and closer. . . .

There was only one thing that puzzled the aunts. Every so often the Hum stopped, and they heard a low rumbling that might have been the kraken speaking. They couldn't understand the words from that great distance—and in any case none of the aunts spoke Polar—but they could understand the tone, and the feeling they had was that whoever the kraken was talking to was driving him a little mad.

But who could it be? The kraken had always been a loner.

They were soon to find out.

Chapter 11

THE GREAT LONDON Aunt Hunt was still going badly. The pictures of Etta and Coral and Myrtle went on flapping on the walls of the police stations everywhere, but the people who came to say they had seen one or another of them were obviously barmy. A man came and said a crossing guard who was helping schoolchildren across the road in Kensington had a mustache and was certainly Aunt Etta, but she wasn't. Another man said he had seen Aunt Myrtle busking outside a cinema, but he hadn't. And anyone weighing over two hundred pounds and wearing jewelry was apt to be hauled off by the police in case she was Coral.

"Don't call me 'aunt,'" terrified women were begging their nephews and nieces all over London's streets, and by the time the children had been gone three weeks, the word had almost disappeared.

Minette's mother, as the days passed with no news, smoked three packets of cigarettes a day, couldn't sleep without slurping a full tumbler of whiskey, and allowed her apartment to get into even more of a mess than before. Of course, in some ways it was easier without Minette, who kept trying to tidy up and open windows. All the same, Mrs. Danby couldn't help wishing she had let her have a night-light.

"And I should have taken her to the seaside—she always wanted to go," she said to her latest boyfriend.

"You can take her when she comes back," he said, dropping his empty beer can over the side of the sofa. "Though I've never seen much point to the seaside myself. The water comes in, the water goes out—what's the sense in that?"

Professor Danby too wished he had done some things and hadn't done others. He had promised every time she came to take Minette to the ice rink and there'd never been time, and he'd known really that she didn't want an encyclopedia without pictures for her birthday.

But when they telephoned each other for news of Minette, the Danbys quarreled as much as ever. They had decided that she had run away, and of course they blamed each other.

"I'm surprised she lasted so long in that pigsty you live in," the professor said.

"Well, really," Mrs. Danby would reply. "Considering that your place would make an underground tomb on a rainy Sunday look like Disneyland, you've got a nerve!"

The Mountjoys were not sorry about anything they had done. They were sure that Fabio had had everything he needed in their house and that in sending him to Greymarsh Towers—and *paying* for it—they had treated him better than any poor child from the back of beyond had a right to expect. But they did wonder whether they should tell Fabio's mother that he had disappeared, and his other grandparents in South America.

"I really can't face the thought of having a lot of foreigners coming here and waving their arms," said Mrs. Mountjoy. "They probably paint their faces and don't wear shoes."

Old Mr. Mountjoy agreed. "Still, she is the boy's mother. We'll give it a few more days, and then if there's no news, we'll have to let them know."

Both the Mountjoys and the Danbys were angry with the police. "You've gone cold on the case," Mrs. Danby accused the superintendent.

But she was very wrong. Discovering the third kidnap and the third aunt had given the police a new and important lead. Two days after Stanley Sprott came to report that this son was missing, an "Aunt Myrtle" was seen in the Putney swimming baths. She had long grayish hair and an open mouth, which is a silly thing to have in a swimming bath, so it had to be her.

The police wearily pulled her in and sent an officer to Mr. Sprott's house to ask the housekeeper to come and identify her—and learned that Mr. Sprott wasn't there.

So where was he? they wanted to know. He was supposed to be standing by in case there was news of Lambert.

At first no one would tell him, but when the policeman threatened to get a search warrant, Mr. Sprott's secretary admitted that he had gone away in his yacht.

"That'll be the *Hurricane*," said the superintendent thoughtfully when the officer got back to the station.

They knew a bit about Mr. Sprott's activities and his yacht.

"I think we'll see what he's up to. He may have got a lead on the boy."

"What about the other parents? It's likely the children are all together. Should we tell them?"

"Not yet. If we find them, we'll bring the parents out by helicopter. But we won't say anything yet."

The team that Stanley Sprott had sent to the chart room at the British Museum, to look for the lonely islands with two islands to the east of them, had found an ancient map with three that seemed likely.

Now the *Hurricane* was steaming to the first of these—

a place called Dooneray off the west coast of Scotland. It was a small island and there were no houses marked on it, but it seemed quite likely that the mad aunts who held his son were keeping him imprisoned in a cave.

As he paced the deck, Stanley Sprott was wondering about the ransom. Why had no one asked him for money in exchange for Lambert? Not that he'd have paid it — he'd have blown the kidnappers to hell before he wasted money like that — but it was odd. Everything was odd about this child snatch.

Though Mr. Sprott was wearing a uniform — a navy-cut reefer and a cap covered in gold braid — he never did any real work on the boat. He had a captain who sailed it and two crew members to whom he kept shouting orders, which they ignored. If they hadn't, they would have run aground many a time, because Mr. Sprott had no real knowledge or understanding of boats.

The *Hurricane* had all the silly things on board that one finds on boats that are rich men's toys: a Jacuzzi with gold taps, a vast bed covered with a leopard skin, and a lounge with a built-in cocktail bar.

But the boat itself wasn't silly. She'd been a patrol boat belonging to naval intelligence, and she had all the latest electronic aids to help her find her position. She also had something unusual: an outsize hold with reinforced sides in which Mr. Sprott carried things he didn't want people to see.

And she was armed. A heavy-caliber machine gun was fitted on the stern deck, which Mr. Sprott said he needed in case of robbers in the Indian Ocean. And though sometimes his passengers were pretty girls who sunbathed and did nothing except giggle and drink cocktails, sometimes his passengers were not silly at all, like the two men who were now playing cards below-decks. Their names were Boris and Casimir, and they came from a country where a boy who didn't know how to use a gun by the time he was six years old wasn't too likely to grow up.

And always, whether the *Hurricane* was on a pleasure cruise or on serious business, Stanley Sprott took along his bodyguard, Des.

"There it is," said the captain, pointing to a low shape in the sea in front of them. "That's Dooneray now."

It was true that the island had no houses, but it had a whole rash of huts—new-looking wooden ones. And moving round between the huts and down on the shore were people. Quite a lot of people.

"They're a funny color," said Des, screwing up his eyes.

Des was right. The people were . . . pink. Quite a bright pink that caught the light and glistened a little.

The *Hurricane* shut down her engines. There was no pier; they would have to drop anchor and go ashore in the dinghy.

Some of the pink people looked up and waved.

"I'm not going ashore," said the first mate. "I'm not going if it costs me my job. Someone else can take the dinghy."

"Nor me neither," said Des. "I'll do anything for you, boss, but I'm not going to land among that lot."

"You'll do exactly what I tell you," said Stanley Sprott. But he didn't speak with quite his usual venom. To tell the truth, he too was looking a little sick.

No one could have been nicer than the leader of the pink people. He had a friendly smile, and he introduced his wife, who was called Mabel, and his cousin, whose name was James.

But he wouldn't put on any clothes. None of them would put on any clothes.

"I'm afraid you must take us as you find us. This is a nudist colony; we believe most strongly that our Creator wants us to keep our bodies open to the air and light. In fact, we would be grateful if you too would take off your clothes. It is a rule of the island that no one who comes here keeps his skin muffled in unhealthy garments."

Behind him, in the dinghy, Casimir giggled, and Mr. Sprott turned to glare at him. Then: "Rubbish!" he said. "Now listen carefully: I've got you all covered." He pointed to the two gunmen in the boat. "And I want every man, woman, and child to line up over there. I'm looking for a missing boy, and I'm going to search every nook and cranny, so don't try to hide anything or I'll blow you all to hell."

"We wouldn't dream of it," said the leader politely. "But can't we offer you some lunch?"

Mr. Sprott shuddered. On a patch of grass a group of people with nothing on were frying sausages over an open-air grill. He had never seen anything so dangerous.

A terrible hour followed. The pink people went on being polite and friendly, but they still wouldn't put on any clothes. They let him go where he liked—into their sleeping huts, their communal dining room, their gym. . . . Though he knew really that if Lambert had been held by mad aunts who were nudists, he would have mentioned it on the telephone, Mr. Sprott felt obliged to search every inch of the island, and he made Des search with him.

When they left, the leader presented them with a bunch of sea thrift and an oyster.

"Go in peace, friends," he said.

As they set a course for the second island on their list, Mr. Sprott was not in a good temper. Mr. Sprott, in fact, boiled and snorted and raged and swore that he would get the pink people arrested and deported and imprisoned, which was silly of him, since the nudists had every right to be where they were. As for the police manning the fishing boat that was following the *Hurricane,* they laughed so much that they could hardly keep a straight course. They had watched Mr. Sprott's landing through their binoculars and thought it was the funniest thing they had ever seen.

Chapter 12

MINETTE WOKE EARLY and immediately decided that she had to wash her hair. She didn't usually wash it before breakfast, but on this particular morning she knew it had to be done.

When she'd finished, she draped a towel round her head and went to see Fabio. He was polishing his shoes. Not the sneakers he'd worn ever since he came to the Island, but his smart shoes—the ones he'd been wearing when he was kidnapped.

He said nothing about her hair and she said nothing about his shoes, and they went down to breakfast. Minette half expected Aunt Etta to be cross with her—Minette's long hair took ages to dry, and when it was at all windy, the aunts made her stay indoors until it was done. But Aunt Etta, sitting as usual behind the porridge pot, only said "Good morning"—and then both children found themselves staring at her in a way that was undoubtedly rude.

She was wearing her usual navy blue jersey and her usual long, navy blue skirt, and they were sure that underneath it she wore her usual navy blue knickers. But pinned to her jersey was a bow. The bow was made of pink velvet with white spots, and after this amazing sight they knew that what they had felt when they got up was real.

What happened next was that Myrtle came in, looking windblown and agitated, and said, "Herbert's gone."

Aunt Etta merely nodded. If it was true that the time had come, Herbert would have gone out to meet him at sea.

Then Coral appeared, wearing almost all her jewelry and a wreath of dried thong-weed in her hair.

"There's a naak in the loch," she said. "A funny, stern sort of fellow. The stoorworm won't be pleased."

Naaks are Estonian; they are the ghosts of people who have drowned and are apt to be silent and grim. This one, Coral said, was the ghost of a schoolteacher.

"One of those strict ones with a cane, I should imagine," she said, "though it's not easy to tell underwater."

The arrival of the naak all the way from Estonia made it certain. If the ghost of a drowned schoolteacher with a cane had come nearly a thousand miles to welcome the kraken, he must be coming very soon.

It was the strangest of days. Everyone was violently excited, but they didn't dare to say aloud what they believed.

The stoorworm insisted on being wound round a tree by the north shore so that he could get a good view, and just when Fabio had fixed him up, he decided that the kraken would come straight into the bay by the house and asked to be unwound again.

"Wait for me, wait for me," shouted Old Ursula to the other mermaids, and this time they did wait for the poor old thing and swam out to the rock they had chosen, holding Walter aloft, and sat there practicing a song that Myrtle had taught them. It was a Lapp reindeer-herding song and not particularly suitable, but it was the most northern song that Myrtle had been able to find.

In Art's kitchen, the iced buns he'd made from the boobrie's egg overflowed the larder, were stuffed into flour bins . . . and still they came from his oven.

The Sybil's face turned from blue to purple; her washed feet glistened in the light.

The Captain had pushed his bed right against the window and wouldn't take time off even to eat.

Only Lambert felt nothing and noticed nothing and spent the day crouched over his telephone, trying to get through to his father, even though his batteries were now completely flat.

By late afternoon the shore was packed with creatures of every sort. Like people lining the route of a royal wedding or a funeral, they had come early to get a good place from which they could see. There were sea otters and jellyfish; there were anemones and starfish peering out of their pools; there were shoals of haddock and flounders and codlings. . . . Some of the animals lined the north shore, others waited in the bay by the house; the birds and rabbits and mice and voles watched from the hill. The children could hardly get down their tea, and the aunts did not nag them. They too were having trouble with Art's boobrie buns.

The sun began to dip behind the horizon. The Hum, which had been steady all day, began to change its rhythm, and every so often there was this strange gap filled with a kind of exasperated rumbling.

"Please don't make us go to bed," begged Minette, and Fabio said he wasn't *going* to bed and if they tried to make him, there'd be trouble.

But when darkness came and the old clock in the kitchen struck nine, and ten, and eleven, everyone lost hope. At midnight the children went to bed of their own accord; the lugworms and the water fleas and the starfish crawled back into the sand or burrowed under stones. On their rock, the mermaids stopped singing, and the boobrie fell silent on her nest.

"We must have been mistaken," said the aunts bleakly — and they too went to bed.

But when they woke in the morning, there was a new island out in the bay.

The island slept. It slept the sleep of the dead after the long journey—and round it and on it and under it, the creatures who had come with it slept too.

The Hum had stopped. Only a slight sighing, a soft soughing, could be heard as he drew breath and let it out.

For the watchers on the shore, this second welcome was different from the first. It seemed to have nothing to do with velvet bows and polished shoes. It came from somewhere deeper down.

Fabio and Minette stood side by side, half hidden by an old bent alder that grew by the brook where it ran into the sea. They couldn't find any words. There weren't any to find. The aunts, down on the shore, were holding hands like children.

On their rock, the mermaids were not singing, and when Walter began to grizzle, Loreen shushed him angrily. For the kraken slept, and the excited welcome they had planned had become a vigil. No one would wake the great beast: not the naak with his cane, nor the boobrie on her nest; no one.

They waited for one hour, for two. . . . The sunshine grew stronger. The sea was turning the most amazing colors, as if a rainbow were hidden underneath the waves, and the air as they breathed in tasted like gorgeous fruit.

"It's like the beginning of the world," whispered Minette.

And then the kraken sneezed!

Everything changed after that. The moles and the mice and the rabbits on the hill were blown backward and righted themselves again; Aunt Etta's bun flew from its mooring of hairpins; the boobrie let out a startled squeal . . . and everybody laughed.

And the kraken lifted his head out of the water and began to swim very slowly, very carefully, so as not to swamp the shore, toward the bay.

He was facing the house now, facing the aunts and the children.

Minette, and Fabio beside her, made exactly the same noise: a gasp of wonder and surprise. For in spite of all they had been told about the kraken—about his goodness, about his effect on the sea, about his healing powers—they had not been able to imagine anything very different from a gigantic whale.

But the kraken's eyes were not in the least like the eyes of a whale. They were huge and round and golden: to gaze into them was like looking into a lamp that did not burn or dazzle but warmed and comforted. His nostrils were small and deep, but his mouth was large and generous, curving across his face like a bow, tilted upward at the corners.

As he moved toward them, the mermaids started to sing, croakily at first, then more strongly. Herbert swam beside the kraken's head, solemn and proud.

And now they saw that his body was not black as they had imagined but dappled in soft colors—the chestnut of a chaffinch's breast, the rose of a stippled trout, the blue-gray of a moonstone—all were in his skin as it caught the light.

But he had stopped. He was looking at the aunts. He began to speak.

Unfortunately, he spoke in Polar. It sounded like the rumbling and clashing of icebergs, and no one understood a word.

Aunt Etta hurried into the house and fetched a megaphone. "I'm sorry, we don't understand," she shouted.

But the kraken had already gathered that. He tried again. This time he spoke Norwegian because Norway is farther south than the Pole, and he tried only one word, but still nobody understood.

"Could you try English?" shouted Aunt Etta through the megaphone.

There was a long pause while the kraken thought about this. Then he took a deep breath and said:

"Children?"

His accent was strange, but they understood him perfectly, and the relief was tremendous,

"What about the children?" yelled Aunt Etta through her megaphone.

The kraken repeated the word.

"Children?" he asked. "Are there . . . here . . . children?"

The aunts talked excitedly among themselves. Did that mean that the kraken wanted children, or that he didn't?

But, anyway, none of them were able to tell a lie. They moved over to the alder tree, pulled out Fabio and Minette, and led them down to the sand. They didn't even think about Lambert, who was still shut in his room. Lambert wasn't a child; he was a stunted adult.

There was a pause while the kraken looked at Fabio and Minette. Have we got it wrong? the children wondered. Are we going to be eaten after all?

Then the kraken smiled. It was the most amazing smile; his great mouth curved up and up, and his eyes glowed with warmth.

And then he sank, and the birds that had been resting on him flew upward like a white cloud.

He was gone for a few minutes—and when he surfaced again, there was someone on his back.

The someone was very small compared to the kraken, not much bigger than a minicar or a dolphin—

but it was absolutely clear who it was. He had the same round eyes, the same wide mouth, the same rainbow-colored skin. . . .

But he was worried.

"Will I be all right, Father?" said the kraken's son, as he had said again and again on the journey.

"You will be all right," said the kraken, as he had said a hundred times. And then: "Look—there are children to play with and care for you."

They spoke in Polar, but what they said was perfectly clear to everyone. In particular, what was clear was the look the infant kraken gave to Fabio and Minette as they stood quietly on the shore.

And to the aunts there came a great thunderclap of understanding. When they had kidnapped the children, they had done it because they wanted help, but even at the time it felt strange to find themselves behaving like criminals. Now they realized that there had been a Higher Purpose, as there so often is.

For they understood that the kraken was bringing his child to the Island to be cared for while he circled the oceans of the world, and that he wanted him to be with people of his own age, not elderly aunts.

"We are most truly blessed," said Aunt Etta. She still had her megaphone to her mouth, and the word *blessed* echoed over the whole Island and was taken up by all the watchers on the shore.

"Blessed," nodded the stoorworm. "Blessed," said the naak (but in Estonian). "Blessed," cried the mermaids from the rocks.

Only Minette and Fabio were silent. Minette was remembering how she had wanted to serve the great beast when first she heard of him. Fabio, on the other hand, was wondering what infant krakens *ate*.

Chapter 13

THE KRAKEN STAYED for several days, resting after his long journey from the Arctic. Mostly he lay quietly in the bay, keeping an eye on his child, but just having him there made everything flourish.

The children would run down to the shore barefoot every morning.

"It isn't just that the sand is more yellow," said Minette. "It's as if it feels more like itself. Like sand is meant to be."

It was the same with everything while the kraken guarded them. The turf was greener and springier, the wheeling birds were whiter, and the patterns they made in the sky were lovelier.

Everybody on the Island felt it—everyone except Lambert, who stayed huddled in his room.

"Imagine if we hadn't been kidnapped," said Fabio.

"Imagine if we'd never known there was such a thing as a kraken!"

If the kraken had been anyone else—if he'd been one of those saints whose feet people wanted to touch because they were so holy, or a pop star from whose head silly people tried to cut bits of hair—the aunts would have been worried, because absolutely everyone wanted to be where he was. Art rowed out in the little dinghy very early one morning, and they could see him talking earnestly to the kraken's head, and when he came back, he was different.

"I told him," he said to the aunts. "I never told no one else and I didn't tell you neither, but, well . . . when he opened those great eyes of his, I saw it didn't matter, so I'll tell you now. All those years it's been on my mind, but I was afraid to come clean."

And then he told them that he hadn't killed a man at all. He'd been in prison for shoplifting, but that didn't seem very exciting, so he'd told the lie because he thought the aunts would think him more manly.

"But when I was with him, I reckoned you'd forgive me," he said—and of course they did and said that telling the truth was far more manly than killing people, which any creep could do if he set his mind to it and had the right tools.

The stoorworm swam out every day and slithered onto the kraken's back, and they could hear the clatter and boom as the pair spoke together in Icelandic. No one knew what the kraken said to him, but when he came back, the worm was always calmer and never said anything about being too long for his ideas and needing to be made shorter by plastic surgery.

The mermaids too became different. They left the de-oiling shed and swam round the wonderful beast and sang—and though Oona was still croaky, her voice came back slowly as she laid her head against the kraken's hide and the memory of the chinless Lord Brasenott became fainter and fainter.

As for the boobrie, she did something extraordinary. She plucked Aunt Coral's cloak from her shoulders and spread it over the eggs with her beak, and then she flapped down to the bay and sat on the kraken's back and honked at him.

She honked for a whole hour, and it was hard to believe that he understood her, but he did. She was telling him how sad she was without her husband and asking the kraken to look out for him when he swam on again in case he had lost the way.

"He was always a forgetful bird," she said.

Herbert hardly came out of the water; he was always close to the kraken in the bay. He had a new strength and dignity now that he knew he would spend his life as a seal, because there is nothing more calming than making up one's mind. Myrtle missed playing the cello to him very much, but she understood. As for Herbert's mother, who was very old now and very frail, she stopped nagging him altogether, for she realized that if Herbert had decided to become a man with trousers and a zipper, he would only have been able to get up to the kraken in a boat and speak to him through a megaphone, and that would hardly be the same.

But it wasn't just the special creatures, those with a touch of magic in them, who wanted to see and talk to the kraken. Everything that moved or crawled or swam wanted to be with him. Processions of sludge worms, schools of pilchards and puffer fish, platoons of lobsters, and countless moon snails all made their way toward him.

"Is he getting enough rest?" Aunt Etta wondered.

But when she asked the kraken, he only turned his marvelous eyes toward her and said (at least she thought he said—his English was rather strange) that there was no living thing he did not welcome.

There were three people, though, who did *not* row out to the kraken and tell him their troubles. Lambert, of course, wasn't interested in anyone he couldn't get on his mobile telephone. And, anyway, he thought the kraken was a hallucination. But Minette and Fabio, who understood the kraken's powers, didn't approach either. Minette did not ask him how to make her parents kind to each other, and Fabio did not ask him how to blow up the headmaster of Greymarsh Towers. This was partly because their past lives now seemed quite unreal to the children, but it was mostly because they were busier than they had ever been in their lives.

For the kraken wasn't just resting. He was watching. And what he was watching was his son. Or rather, he was watching how Fabio and Minette *coped* with his son.

It had been difficult for the kraken, deciding what to do with his child. At first he thought he would put off his healing journey round the world until his son was older. But baby krakens grow very slowly—he would have had to wait for more than a hundred years for the child to grow up, and when he realized what a mess the world was in, he knew he couldn't risk it.

Then he thought maybe he could leave his motherless infant in the Arctic among the walruses and polar bears and narwhals he was used to. But this plan had gone down badly with his son, who wanted to travel with his father.

"You can't. It's too far," the kraken had said.

It takes a year and a day to circle the oceans of the world, and it was much too far. The baby swam slowly and often needed lifts on his father's back, and no one can really give himself to healing the world when he is worried about his child.

The kraken had heard about the Island and the caring

aunts as he heard about everything, and at last he had decided to see if it was a good place to leave his son. But he had not been quite happy. Aunts were fine things, but these were aunts without children, and the baby kraken needed people of his own age. Or rather, people who were a bit older but could remember the troubles and the games and the tantrums of being very young.

Which was why the first word he said when he arrived was "children" and why now he watched Fabio and Minette most carefully out of his golden eyes. If they were not suitable as child-minders, he meant to give up his journey and go home. Once you have children, nothing matters more than their safekeeping. Every parent in the world knows that.

The baby kraken was not at all like his father. He was still soft and blobby, as though his body hadn't quite decided what was going to happen to it. Bulges came out of him sometimes that were almost arms and legs, but not the kind of arms you could do very much with and not the kind of legs that were much use for walking. He would lose these later and become streamlined and suited to the sea, but at the moment he was rather like a large beanbag, and one never knew what kind of shape he would decide to be.

And yet one could see that he was the mighty kraken's son. He had the same large wondrous eyes, the same wide mouth that smiled easily, the same interested nostrils that seemed to suck up the scents of land and sea.

Like his father, he too could make the creatures of the sea come to him, and when he rested in a rock pool, the barnacles and whelks and brittle stars all seemed to glow with happiness and health.

But there was one thing he could not do.

"Can he *hum?*" Fabio asked on the first day.

They were having lunch. Lambert had bolted his food and rushed back to his room, where he lay on his bed with the curtains drawn. He still believed that he was being drugged and that the strange creatures he was seeing were not really there, but seeing a whole *island* that wasn't really there was driving him a little crazy.

Aunt Etta shook her head. "He's too young. A kraken humming is a bit like a boy's voice breaking; it just happens when he's ready. It's a pity, because that's how krakens speak to each other across distances."

"Is there any way of teaching him to do it sooner?" asked Minette. "Could his father . . . ?"

But Aunt Etta said no—it would just happen when the time was right. She didn't add that his father was worried, knowing that there was no way his child could call him once he went away.

But if he couldn't hum, the kraken was beginning to speak. The trouble for Fabio and Minette was *what* he spoke. With his father he spoke Polar, but other languages got mixed up with it, and when he started off in English, he quickly wandered off into Norwegian or Swedish or even Finnish, which the children did not understand at all.

But Fabio himself had needed to learn English not so long ago, and he remembered that what he had learned first was the names of things to eat.

After that it was easy. For the young kraken did not just feed on the plankton in the seawater like his father—he was still growing and needed solid food, which he ground up with his gums rather like an old man with no teeth.

"This is a sausage," Fabio would say, holding up one of Art's bangers, and the kraken would repeat "soss," or "spag" when it was spaghetti, of which he was very fond, and of course he soon learned to say "More" or "*No!*" which all young creatures learn to say very early.

By now he was letting the children play with him in the water, throwing a ball or pretending to hide behind a rock. He would even follow them in the dinghy—but always after a short time he went back to his father and stayed very close to his side, for the bond between these two was very, very strong. And though the great kraken was more certain with every day that passed that he had found the right place to leave his son, his heart was heavy at the thought of the parting that must soon come.

Chapter 14

THE NEXT ISLAND on which Stanley Sprott landed did not have any naked people on it. It did not have any people on it at all. What it had on it was sheep.

The *Hurricane* came to it through driving sheets of rain. It was the wettest rain they had ever come across, and it looked as though it must stop soon because the sky would have emptied itself, but it didn't. And on the low-lying, sodden island were hundreds — no, thousands — of soaking sheep.

"There's nowhere to land," said the skipper.

But when they'd circled the island twice, they found a narrow inlet and, chugging up it, saw a shingle bay where the dinghy could be beached.

No one had wanted to land among the pink nudists, and no one wanted to land among the wet sheep.

"The boy won't be there," said Des. "No one could last on this dump."

But Mr. Sprott had a bee in his bonnet about a honeycomb of underground caves and tunnels full of mad aunts who were holding Lambert.

"They might have brought the sheep to put people off," he said, "or they might come up and shoot them for meat"—and he ordered the *Hurricane* to put down her anchor.

Leaving Casimir to guard the boat, they rowed to the island and went ashore.

It was not a pleasant place. Sheep are not often cheerful once they are grown up, and these sheep were the wettest, gloomiest sheep you could imagine. They stood pressed together, the water running down their noses, giving off a smell of wet wool and lanolin. Some of them had foot rot. And though sheep-pats are not as squelchy as cow-pats, they are not agreeable to walk on in the rain.

"We must go round and round the island in smaller and smaller circles; that way we won't miss any openings. It's like looking for a ball in a field," said Stanley Sprott.

So they trudged round and round, the water dripping down their necks, slipping and sliding on the wet grass and on the wet other things, while the sheep huddled together, too miserable even to lift their heads, and occasionally made a gloomy bleating noise that did not sound much like *Baa* but more like the crying of doomed spirits in hell. If the mad aunts had brought them to put people off, they hadn't done so badly.

"There won't be any caves," said Des. "The soil's wrong for caves."

But Stanley Sprott only told him to keep his mouth shut.

Then, almost in the middle of the island, they did find an opening that led underground.

"Down you go," said Mr. Sprott, very excited. "Make sure they know you're armed. We'll keep you covered."

So Des went down into the hole and came back almost at once, looking very sick.

"Well? What's down there?"

"More sheep," said Des, rubbing his behind. "Rams. Two of them and as mad as hatters." He turned round so that Mr. Sprott could see the jagged holes in his trousers. "Lucky they didn't get through to the flesh. It can give you rabies, being butted by rams."

While Stanley Sprott had been pursuing his son among nudists and sheep, the police had been following in a fishing boat. Now, though, they ran into bad weather; fog came rolling in from the west, and the skipper of the fishing boat found that his radar was jammed. He insisted on turning into the next port to get it fixed, and this meant that the *Hurricane* steamed on without being tailed.

There was only one island left that fitted Lambert's description. It was a long way away, but it had to be the right one; it had to!

"Full steam ahead!" barked Mr. Sprott to the skipper, who only raised an eyebrow. He'd had the *Hurricane* doing over twelve knots ever since they'd seen the last sheep, and he wasn't going any faster until the weather cleared.

Meanwhile, in London, Minette's parents and Fabio's grandparents had called a meeting to complain about the police and the feeble way they were handling their case. The superintendent had told the Danbys and the Mountjoys that there was a possible lead on the children's whereabouts, and having some hope again brought out all their disagreeableness.

The meeting took place in the Mountjoys' cold house with the brass gong in the hall and the portraits of dead Mountjoys on the wall. The Mountjoys didn't like the look of Mrs. Danby, who was, as usual, chain-smoking and wearing a blouse that showed more than they thought was right. They liked Professor Danby a bit better because he was stern and gloomy like themselves. But the main point of the meeting wasn't to make friends; it was to complain.

"If you ask me, the police are too busy finding homes for dirty tramps and mollycoddling the unemployed to do their job properly," said old Mr. Mountjoy.

He had decided not to send for Hubert-Henry's family after all. His wife had been having nightmares about Indians with poisoned arrows ambushing her in her bed, and her heart was not strong.

Professor Danby agreed. "Even when they find the kidnappers, I expect they'll just send them to prison. In the old days they'd have been hung, and rightly so."

The Mountjoys nodded their heads. "It is absolutely shocking the way this case has been dealt with. Outrageous."

They decided to complain to their member of Parliament, and Professor Danby said he would insist on a full inquiry.

Mr. Mountjoy approved of that. "And I shall write to the minister for law and order. God knows what the country is coming to when three children can vanish off the face of the earth without anything being done about it!"

Mrs. Danby stubbed out her cigarette and lit another one. "I'm thinking we might sue the police," she said thoughtfully. "Get some money out of them. We might as well have something for the anxiety we've been through."

Professor Danby was about to disagree with her. He always disagreed with his wife—but this time he didn't.

"It's an idea," he admitted.

"We could give the kids a good time with the money we get," said Mrs. Danby. She'd buy Minette lots of new dresses, and if there was any money left over, she could do with some new clothes herself. There was a lovely pink georgette with a black underskirt she'd seen at Adrienne's Boutique . . . and the sitting-room carpet was getting really shabby.

Professor Danby too was thinking of how he could help Minette with some extra money to spend; her bedroom at his house could do with a proper writing desk so she could do her homework, and if there was any money to spare, he needed the new three-hundred-volume *Grammar Scholastica*. He'd had his eyes on it for months, but the cost was absurd.

Even the old Mountjoys thought that suing the police was a good idea. Hubert-Henry's fees at Greymarsh Towers were ridiculously high; any help would be welcome.

They were working out how best to do this when the parlormaid came in with the tea things on a silver tray. She was the only one who had been fond of Fabio, and now she asked whether there had been any news of him.

"No, there hasn't," snapped Mrs. Mountjoy, and told her to bring some more hot water. What were servants coming to, sticking their noses into family business?

While the Danbys and the Mountjoys met to complain in London, something sad and serious happened in the city of Newcastle upon Tyne. The mother of Boo-Boo and the Little One tripped on a cracked paving stone and broke her hip.

Breaking a hip is a bad business. An ambulance came and rushed her off to the hospital, where they put a pin into the joint and told her she had to stay for a week and be careful for a long time after that.

This left her husband, the tax inspector, with a problem. Being a tax inspector is very hard work. You have to go to an office every day and fill in lots and lots of forms and send rude letters to people who are trying not to pay their taxes, and do a great many math problems. Betty's husband, whose name was Ronald, was a very good tax inspector, and he did not feel he could look after Boo-Boo and the Little One as well as do his job.

But now something amazing happened. He was just wondering what on earth to do with his children when a tall, fierce-looking lady came striding up the path, carrying a suitcase and the kind of saucepan that people use to stir-fry things in. The tax inspector had never owned one because his wife, Betty, did not cook foreign foods, but he knew it was a wok, and once he had realized this, he knew who the lady was. It was Betty's sister Dorothy, who had been imprisoned in Hong Kong for hitting a restaurant owner on the head because he was serving pangolin steaks in his restaurant. She must have kept the wok as a memento, and as she came closer he saw that he was right, because there was a dent in the side that might well have been made by the restaurant owner's head.

"Where's Betty?" said Dorothy, putting down her case. She did not like her sister Betty, who shaved her legs and had three kinds of toilet freshener in her loo, but families are families, and on her way home to the Island she had decided to call on her and see how she was.

She soon realized her mistake. Visiting Betty in the hospital was one thing, but being asked to look after Boo-Boo and the Little One was quite another.

"I can't stand children, you know that," said Dorothy. She could have said, "I can't stand *your* children," but she didn't because of Betty being "family."

Betty began to cry. Her leg was in plaster and hitched up to something, and she had a bruise on her face where she had fallen, so when she cried she looked very pathetic indeed.

"Please, Dotty—oh, please. Poor Ronald works so hard, and he can't give up his job."

Dorothy didn't like being called Dotty, and she didn't like Ronald, and she really loathed Betty's house, where everything was covered in little crocheted hats or frilly embroidered cloths or sprayed with some gooey scent that climbed into your nostrils and stayed there. Betty's chairs had chair covers, and the chair covers had more covers to keep the covers clean, as though sitting down was a dangerous act, and the whole thing drove Dorothy round the bend. Also she was homesick for the Island and for Myrtle and Coral and in particular for Etta, who was next to her in age and her closest friend.

But there was Betty looking absolutely miserable — and after all, it wasn't her fault that she was an idiot and had two ridiculous children. Life isn't fair and never has been.

"I'll stay for a week," Dorothy said. "Until you're over the worst. But that's all."

But after a few days Dorothy cracked. Boo-Boo (who was a boy) and the Little One (who was a girl) were the daftest children she had ever seen. They cried if their pajama cases got mixed up, so that Boo-Boo's striped pj's ended up in the skirts of the fairy doll and the Little One's ruffled nightdress was zipped into the stomach of a fluffy poodle. They cried if she handed them the wrong bath towel, so that Boo-Boo had to dry himself on the Teletubbies while the Little One was rubbed down in roller-skating Yogi Bears. They threw a tantrum if she brought the cereal packet to the table without its frilly cereal packet container, and they complained because she hadn't combed out the tassels on the lampshades.

"Right, this is it," said Dorothy on the fifth day. "I'm going home."

But when she told Betty, who was still in the hospital, her sister cried once more.

"What am I going to do?" she sobbed. "None of my neighbors seem to want to look after my children."

Dorothy opened her mouth to tell her why and closed it again. After all, Betty was ill and she was her sister, and she wouldn't be able to shave her legs for weeks because of the plaster. On the other hand, nothing now could stop Dorothy from going back to the Island.

"I suppose I could take the children with me. Just until you're better."

As soon as she said it, she wished she hadn't, but it was too late. Betty looked at her gratefully. Usually she would have done anything to keep her darlings from that rough place where the animals wandered in and out of the house and nothing was done *nicely*, but now it was her only hope.

"Thank you, Dorothy," she said. "Perhaps the sea air will do them good."

So the following week Dorothy took the train to catch the steamer to catch the second steamer to catch the ferry that would in the end get her to her home. She did not have a chance to let her sisters know whom she was bringing, which was just as well. Even if they had been very badly oiled, Boo-Boo and the Little One would not have been welcome on the Island.

Chapter 15

MINETTE SAT on her bed beside the open window, trying to brush her hair. Aunt Etta insisted on a hundred strokes each night, but now she put her brush down and sighed.

"I'm never going to have children. *Never.* It's awful."

"Oh come on," said Fabio, wandering in from the bathroom. "It isn't as bad as that."

But it had been very bad.

They had woken early and at once known what had happened. Even before they went to the window, they had felt the emptiness and the silence.

Downstairs the three aunts sat stiffly at the breakfast table. Coral looked thinner, and Myrtle's blouse was on back to front.

"Go to him," said Aunt Etta as soon as the children had finished. "You're excused from all your other duties."

Outside it really hit them. Yet the kraken had only been here just over a week. How could the bay seem so empty, so wrong? And how could such a great beast slip away so silently?

It was all very well for Aunt Etta to say, "Go to him," but where was he? Not by the shore, not in his favorite rock pool. The mermaids were guarding the entrance to the bay, but the children knew he would not have tried to follow his father. He might be small, but he knew what it was to keep a promise.

They found him in the end, half hidden under an overhanging rock. He was almost submerged, but his head came up out of the water, and he was staring at the open sea. When he saw them, he made the most pitiful sound they had ever heard, a heartbroken moan that ended in a whimper. Like a puppy told to "stay" when its master leaves the room, the baby kraken waited . . . and looked as though he would wait to the end of time for his father to return.

"Come on," said Fabio, leaning down from the rock. "It's time for breakfast. We'll go and see what Art has for you."

But the kraken only looked at him, and then two tears welled out of his golden eyes and rolled into the sea.

He wouldn't eat and he wouldn't play.

"No ball," he said when they fetched the beach ball

and "No hide an' see." He wouldn't follow them in the boat, though when they moved away, he moaned and shivered even more. In the end they got into the water with him and swam round him, rubbing his back and telling him again and again that his father would be back, that they loved him, that he was the last of a great and mighty line of krakens and must try to be brave.

Everyone helped. The mermaids came and sang to him, but he only closed his eyes and juddered with sighs. The stoorworm swam out and spoke into his ear.

"To go is to come," said the worm in his solemn voice.

What he meant was that the earth was round, so that the great kraken was on his way back as soon as he set off. But thoughts about the earth being round were too difficult for the kraken's son, whose tears went on flowing and making the seaweed and the little fish look larger and brighter wherever they fell.

"Do you think if Myrtle played the cello to him, it would help?" asked Minette, but it didn't. Although Myrtle had just said good-bye to Herbert, who had gone off with the great kraken, she came at once, but you never know where you are with music. It can make you happy, but it can also make you very, very sad.

The children did not dare to leave him alone; whenever they moved away, he moaned even more pitifully. Art brought their lunch to the shore and they tried to share it with him, but he only turned his head away.

"No soss," he said when they offered him a sausage roll, and "No cheeps" when they handed him the potato chips that had been his favorites.

By the end of the day the children were getting frantic.

"What if he just fades away and dies?" said Minette, close to tears.

"He won't," said Fabio.

But his eyes were even blacker than usual. People *did* turn their faces to the wall and die; he had seen it in Brazil.

When he had been on his way for a few hours, the great kraken began his Healing Hum once more. Everything was as it had been when he was on the way to the Island. The sky was blue, the air was soft; above him flew his escort of birds, below him the dolphins and seals circled.

He drew level with a fishing boat a hundred miles away. The crew had pulled in three tons of tuna and were casting their nets once more to add to the pile of bloodied, thrashing creatures on the deck when the captain straightened himself and rubbed his forehead.

"Enough," he said suddenly. "We've caught enough."

His crew stared at him. He was the greediest fisherman in that part of the world; he'd been fined again and again for exceeding the quota.

"You heard me," he said, and the nets were pulled in and the boat turned and headed for home.

But though the kraken went on putting the sea to rights, as he had done before, his heart was heavy. There was an awful emptiness on his left side where his son had swum beside him, and at night his back felt strange without the small bump that had slept on it.

"You're to promise to stay and be good," he had said to his son, and the child had understood, but it was best not to remember the look in his eyes.

After they had traveled for a day and a night, Herbert came to the front of the kraken's head and said good-bye. It was hard for him to leave the kraken and return to the Island, but his mother was getting very weak and he felt it was his duty.

It was even lonelier after Herbert left. Other seals swam with the kraken, but they were ordinary seals, not selkies; they did not know his thoughts as Herbert had done.

On a great rock, after another day of swimming, the kraken saw something he had been looking out for: a huge black bird with a yellow beak and yellow feet, huddled up and muddled-looking. He paused and looked directly at the unfortunate bird, and as the kraken's eyes pierced his sadness, the boobrie came to himself again. He remembered that he had a wife who had been expecting eggs and that he had gone to look for food and got lost and had forgotten who he was and where he was going.

Now, as clear as daylight, the boobrie saw the Island and the nest by the loch and his partner waiting and waiting. Why, he might be a father by now . . . and he flapped his wings once and twice and a third time, and then managed to lift himself off and fly away.

And the kraken swam on.

By the third day, Fabio and Minette were beginning to lose hope. They had tried everything they could think of to cheer up the little kraken. They used up all Art's dish-washing liquid to blow bubbles for him, they invented underwater games, they sang to him and told him stories, but nothing helped. The only thing you could say was that when they left him even for a moment, he was worse, moaning more pitifully and watering the sea with his tears.

What worried them most was that he wouldn't eat.

It wasn't just "No soss," it was "No spag," though he had loved spaghetti, and "No burgs," even when Art soused the hamburgers with rich tomato sauce. They watched carefully to see if he was feeding himself from the seaweed and plants by the shore, but he wasn't.

"I can just see him getting thinner every minute,"

said Minette, who wasn't looking exactly fat herself.

At teatime Aunt Etta came down to the shore and said enough was enough.

"You're to go up to the house and have hot baths and have your tea in the dining room. You look like something the cat's brought in, both of you."

"No, please. We can't leave him," said Minette. "We want to bring a tent down and spend the night on the beach."

"Better not keep Art waiting," was all Aunt Etta said.

So the children had their hot baths and went into the dining room. Art had laid out all their favorite things: sardines and cheese straws and chunks of pineapple on sticks.

And the cake tin was on the sideboard. Poor Art always put the cake tin on the sideboard. He put it out for breakfast and for lunch and for tea, hoping and hoping that someone would manage to eat another bun.

For if one can make seventy-two omelets from a boobrie egg, it is quite amazing how many buns one can make. Art had made the buns look very beautiful: there were buns with pink icing and a cherry on top, and buns with white icing and sprinkles on top, and buns with brown icing and chocolate drops on top—but one by one the aunts and the children had stopped eating them. Boobrie buns are very filling, and they just couldn't get them down anymore.

Now, as Fabio picked up the tin, Minette said, "No! Absolutely not. I couldn't!"

"I know," said Fabio. "I couldn't, either. But I wonder . . ."

When they got back to the shore, the children took no notice at all of the kraken. They sat down very close to the water's edge and opened the cake tin. Fabio held up a white bun and Minette held up a pink bun. They pretended to eat them, making loud chewing noises.

"Buns," said Fabio, rubbing his stomach.

And: *"Buns,"* said Minette, sighing with pleasure.

The kraken came closer and watched them.

The children went on pretending to eat buns.

The kraken edged closer still.

"No buns for you," said Fabio. "You don't like buns."

An offended look spread over the kraken's face. He was not used to being left out. He was half out of the water now, his head on the sand.

"Buns?" said the kraken, trying out the word.

Fabio shrugged. "Well, you can try one, I suppose, but you won't like it." He picked out a white bun with a big cherry on top and held it up. The kraken studied it . . . opened his mouth . . . shut it. For a moment, nothing happened. Then a glow came into his golden eyes.

"Buns," said the baby kraken. "Ah, *buns!*" and opened his mouth once more. . . .

When the little kraken had eaten seven buns, Fabio

turned to see Minette crouching on the sand. Her hands covered her face, but he could see the tears squeezing out between her fingers.

"Well, really," he said crossly. "You'd better *not* have children of your own if you're going to be as wet as that."

182

Chapter 16

I
F YOU COULD go back now—if your parents came to fetch you away, what would you do?" asked Fabio the next day.

Minette felt the familiar crunching in her stomach. Only what was the crunching about? Was it about whether her parents loved her and loved each other, or was it about something else? . . . Was it about going away from the Island?

"How could we leave him?" she said. "We'd have to stay until his father came back. It's only a year and a day—less now. We'd have to stay that long, wouldn't we?"

Fabio nodded. "That's what I think. But if they find us . . ."

They had been playing ball with the little kraken in a rock pool, keeping a close watch because Walter was nearby and sometimes the kraken became muddled and thought the fat merbaby with his round bald head was a beach ball, too.

"I'm not ever going back to my grandparents," Fabio went on. "The ones in London, I mean. Not ever. If I have to leave the Island, I'm going back to South America. I don't know how, but I'm going."

Minette nodded. He looked very small, sitting on a boulder with his hands round his knees, but she believed him. Both the children had changed since they came to the Island; they were stronger, and sunburned, their hair thick and glossy with health.

"Isn't everything beautiful?" said Minette, looking out across the bay. "Of course, it was even before he came, but now . . ."

This was true. It was early summer now; the grass was studded with clover and oxeye daisies; the rowan that sheltered the house was covered in new green leaves—but it was more than that. It was as though the great kraken's blessing stayed with them, and would stay, even though he himself was gone.

Everyone felt it—and even fewer people went away! The naak did not go back to Estonia; the mermaids, though they had lost all traces of oil, stayed where they were—and the Sybil went on washing her feet.

After the kraken left, the Captain had sent for his daughters.

"I can die happy now," he said, "because I've seen him. So you can measure me up for my coffin."

But when the aunts had gone away to cry and came back with a tape measure, they found him and the stoorworm taking tea together.

"If my head is upstairs and my tail is downstairs, where is *me?*" the stoorworm was asking, and it was clear that the old man had changed his mind about dying.

But down on the point, Herbert's mother really was coming to the end of her life.

"I'm ready to go, Herbert," she said. "I'm ready to give myself to the waves."

And Herbert said: "The time will come, Mother. Don't hurry it." But he knew it would not be long now and that when the great kraken returned for his son, Herbert would be free to go away with him.

It was during one of these peaceful days that they were woken by a sound that was new to the Islanders: a proud and joyful squawking that sent the aunts and children running up the hill.

And there they were! Three chicks the size of bull terriers, their feathers still moist from the egg, their yellow beaks already open as they cheeped and wriggled for food.

"More wheelbarrowing," was all Aunt Etta said, because with the male boobrie still away the mother would never manage to feed her chicks alone, but the aunts were almost as proud as the bird herself. Boobries have not bred where there are humans for hundreds of years.

Even Lambert had suddenly become almost nice, and this was the most extraordinary thing of all. He did his work without grumbling, he ate his food—sometimes he even smiled.

"He too has been touched by the spirit of the great kraken," said Myrtle, but Fabio disagreed.

"If that creep is being nice, there'll be a reason," he said.

And he was absolutely right.

The battery of Lambert's mobile phone had suddenly given a spurt of life, and he had dialed his father's number. The *Hurricane* was now steaming toward the Island, and it so happened that Stanley Sprott heard his phone ringing down in the cabin and answered it.

Mr. Sprott knew better than to ask his son anything sensible, like "What latitude and longitude are you on?" or "Are there any submerged rocks near the entrance to the bay?"—but there was one question he did ask.

"Those women who are holding you prisoner—are they nudists?"

"Eh?" said Lambert, who did not know what nudists were.

"Are they wearing clothes?" Mr. Sprott wanted to know.

Lambert thought about this. "Yes," he said. "They're wearing clothes."

"And sheep? Are there a lot of sheep?"

Lambert said he didn't think so. "Just a few on the hill." Then his battery began to play up again, and he said frantically: "But you're coming, aren't you? You're coming to fetch me?"

"Yes, Lambert, I'm coming," said Mr. Sprott.

It was after he talked to his father that Lambert changed. Soon now the *Hurricane* would come and his father would blow everyone to hell: the creepy aunts, the horrible children, and the foul monsters who weren't really there. When Lambert smiled now, it was because that was what he was thinking about: all the people he hated lying dead in their own blood.

"I feel sick," said Boo-Boo, leaning over the rail of the steamer.

"I feel sick too," said the Little One. "I feel sicker than you."

Aunt Dorothy looked at them with loathing. What she really wanted to do was throw them into the sea and make her own way to the Island. Doing good is all right when you are beating up restaurant owners or thumping people who are trapping rare animals for their skins, but doing good by taking on your sister's horrible children is just stupid.

The steamer was hardly going up and down, but now first Boo-Boo and then the Little One were sick, and as soon as they'd finished, they started worrying about whether they had messed up their clothes.

"Etta is going to kill me when she sees them," thought Dorothy.

But though she would very much have liked to throw them both overboard, she realized it could not be done, so she took them down into the cabin and dabbed at the Little One's velvet coat collar and Boo-Boo's silly blazer, and told them to lie down until they landed.

But landing was only the beginning. After that they had to take a ferry to a smaller island, and then they had to wait until the one fisherman who could be trusted not to gape or gawk or give away the secrets of the Island could take them across at night. There was no one else the aunts ever used—and just how sick these idiotic children would be in an open boat at night was anybody's guess.

The *Hurricane* came in quietly at noon. She anchored to the south of the Island, hidden from the house by a copse of windblown trees, and Mr. Sprott took Des and one of the gunmen with him in the dinghy for a reconnaissance.

But even if she had come into the bay by the house, no one would have seen her. Fabio and Minette had taken the kraken to the north shore for a picnic, and the aunts were visiting the Sybil, which they did once a week to see that she was eating properly. Even the Captain was not looking through his telescope but dozing quietly in his bed.

Mr. Sprott had at first meant to come in with his cannon firing, but then he had thought better of it. After all, Lambert had to be got out safely first.

As the dinghy rounded the spur of rocks, with its row of slumbering seals, he saw a boy standing alone on the edge of the sea.

"It's Lambert!" said Des.

And it was!

Whatever plans Mr. Sprott might have made were set aside as his son waded toward him and threw himself, weeping, into his arms.

"Take me away, quick. Take me to the *Hurricane*. Oh hurry, please, Dad."

Mr. Sprott pulled himself out of Lambert's clinging arms and looked at his son. He looked well. In fact, he looked better than Mr. Sprott had ever seen him look; but that was neither here nor there. The boy was obviously terrified.

"It's an awful place. They feed you poisoned food, and then you see things," sobbed Lambert.

"What sort of things, Lambert?"

"Creepy-crawly things . . . things that slither, and freaks with tails—only they're not really there."

There was a sudden yell from Des. The bodyguard knew that it was as much as his life was worth to yell when they were trying to get into a place unseen, but now he stood up in the dinghy and pointed with staring eyes at a rock sticking out of the water.

"My God," he shouted. "Look, guv'nor! It's a bloomin' mermaid!"

"No, it isn't," cried Lambert. "She isn't really there. It's because of what you've eaten. None of them are there; the other one isn't there, and the old one isn't there, and the long white worm isn't there. They're all because of what Art put in the—"

"Be quiet, Lambert," said his father. Then to Des, "Catch her."

Des didn't need to be told twice. He slipped off his holster and dived into the sea.

The girl was Queenie, and she thought the whole thing very funny. She waited until the clumsy man was almost up to her—then she gave her silvery laugh and vanished underneath the waves.

"She isn't there, she isn't there," Lambert went on yelling. "It's what you've eaten—it's Art's seaweed flour."

"Don't be silly, Lambert," said his father. "I haven't eaten any seaweed flour, and I saw her quite clearly.

Unless it was a trick. It must have been a trick, but if so, it was a good one."

Des was still thrashing about in the icy water. Now suddenly he dived down, grabbed at something—and missed. But when he swam back to the boat, he had two things clutched in his hand: a silver fish scale and a golden hair.

Mr. Sprott examined them. Then he turned to his son.

"Now then, Lambert," he said. "Just tell us what else you've seen on the Island."

"I haven't seen it—it isn't—"

"All right, boy. Tell us what you *haven't* seen, then. Tell us carefully."

By the time Lambert had finished babbling about old mermaids with no teeth and long white worms that sucked peppermints and outsize birds the size of elephants—all of which *weren't there*—Mr. Sprott's face wore a look of eager cunning. Of course it was probably all rubbish, but if it wasn't, the money one could make! And those trees with the branches stripped off—the ones that Lambert called stoorworm trees—they were there, all right.

"Go on, what else?" he prompted, digging his son roughly in the ribs.

But Lambert had said all he could. The sight of that island in the bay that hadn't been there at night and then *really* hadn't been there in the morning had frightened him so much that he couldn't say another word, or anything about the small island that had broken off from the big one and was around somewhere.

"Please, Daddy, take me home," he whined. "Look, there they are; they're coming for me!"

Stanley Sprott looked up. The three dreaded women whose pictures were on the wall of every police station in London were coming toward them.

Aunt Myrtle was in the lead, which was unusual for her. She was carrying a brown paper parcel, and she was very nervous—but in a way Lambert was *hers*, just as Fabio was Aunt Coral's, and Minette belonged to Etta, and she felt she had to hand him back herself.

"Good morning," she said, bracing herself. "I see you have come to fetch Lambert—he will be pleased to go home. I'm afraid he never quite fitted in."

Mr. Sprott stared at her. The cheek of the woman was unbelievable!

"I've washed and ironed his underclothes and his pajamas. I wasn't able to take many of his clothes in the cello case, but you'll find everything is there."

Myrtle now felt she had done all she could and stepped back, leaving her sisters to take charge, which they did by asking Mr. Sprott if he would care to stay to lunch.

As she spoke, Etta was looking warily over the bay.

She had told everyone to stay out of sight as soon as the dinghy had rounded the point, but one could never be sure, she thought, not realizing that it was already too late.

"No, don't," begged Lambert. "Don't eat anything in there—you'll think you see creepy-crawlies."

"Be quiet, Lambert," said his father—and told the aunts he would be delighted.

It was a strange lunch. The aunts had been well brought up, and though they thought that Mr. Sprott was just as nasty as one would expect of someone who was Lambert's father, they were most polite, passing him the salt and pepper and filling up his plate.

"Won't you try a brandy snap?" asked Aunt Coral. "They were freshly made this morning."

Mr. Sprott took one and decided it was time to come to the point.

"Now, ladies," he said, smiling his oily smile, "I have a suggestion to make to you." He leaned forward, folding his hands on the tablecloth. "I am getting on in years and I need somewhere to end my days—so I want you to sell me this island."

There was a gasp from Myrtle, and Aunt Etta stared at him in amazement.

"Sell the Island?" said Coral.

"Sell the Island?" said Myrtle.

"*Sell* it!" thundered Aunt Etta.

"I take it it belongs to you, does it not? And Captain Harper?"

The sisters looked at each other. They had never thought of *owning* the Island. It was just there, and they looked after it. But now they remembered that their father had in fact bought it from an old couple who could no longer do the work.

"I suppose it does," said Etta now. "But there's absolutely no question of selling it."

"No question at all," said Coral.

"Oh no, we couldn't do that," said Myrtle bravely.

Mr. Sprott leaned back in his chair and smiled. They did not seem to realize that they were completely in his power.

"I'm prepared to offer ten thousand pounds," he said. "And that's generous for a miserable little island. . . . I mean for a simple unspoiled island with only one house on it."

He'd get the money back in a month, charging two hundred pounds for helicopter rides to the Island of Freaks. The pretty mermaid was worth a fortune on her own; he'd put her in an aquarium, and people would have to pay extra to hear her sing and comb her hair. As for that creepy worm, he could just see the visitors clutching each other and screaming. He'd have to keep him in a cage with electric wire. It would be a cross between a zoo, a carnival, and Disneyland.

"Very well, ladies. Twelve thousand pounds, and that's my last word absolutely!"

But Etta had had enough of this unpleasant game. "I'm afraid we wouldn't sell the island for a hundred million pounds," she said. "We regard it as a Sacred Trust. Now if you would care to take Lambert back with you, I will tell Art that he can clear the table."

"Oh no you won't!"

Mr. Sprott's voice had changed. He had become the dangerous bully that he was before. "I think you have forgotten something, dear ladies. You have kidnapped three children. Abducted them by force. My son and two others. The penalty for kidnapping is life imprisonment — and it might even be hanging. They're thinking of bringing back the death penalty, I've heard. So I really think you'd better sell me the Island — or would you rather I turned you over to the police?"

There was a sudden scuffle at the door.

"You can't! You can't turn them over to the police, because they didn't kidnap us." Minette had run all the way from the north shore. Her hair was tousled, her clothes were in a mess, but what was strange was that she wasn't at all frightened. "I *asked* if I could come. I asked Aunt Etta if there was a third place, and she brought me here."

Fabio, who had followed her into the room, caught on at once. "And I wasn't kidnapped either! Aunt Coral saved me from a vile school where they tie you to pillars and try to set fire to your clothes. If anybody says I was kidnapped, I'll thump them!"

"And Lambert wasn't really kidnapped either." Minette, who never lied, seemed to have gone crazy. "He tried to steal Aunt Myrtle's chloroform, and the fumes knocked him out, and Aunt Myrtle brought him along because there was no one at home to look after him."

Both children stood and glared at him like angry tigers.

What they were saying was rubbish, Mr. Sprott knew that—the police would get the truth out of them in no time—but he had changed his mind. It had seemed worth a try to do everything the easy way—buy the Island and then do what he wanted with it when they'd all gone. But there were other ways of getting what he wanted.

"Very well, it looks as though I was mistaken. Come along, Lambert, I'll take you home."

He took the brown paper parcel with Lambert's pajamas, shook hands politely, and left with his son.

Oh yes, there were other ways of getting his hands on those weird beasts, thought Stanley Sprott. Before he'd finished, they would wish they *had* sold him the Island, because what was going to happen now would not be pleasant at all!

Chapter 17

MEANWHILE, IN LONDON, Minette's parents had found a better way of making money than suing the police.

Mrs. Danby thought of it first, and Professor Danby didn't hear about it until he saw a newspaper that the tea lady had brought into the university common room.

On the front page was a picture of Minette as a baby in her mother's arms. HEARTBROKEN MOTHER MOURNS LOST DAUGHTER said the headline, and underneath the picture were some terribly sad things that Minette's mother had said, like there was no second of the day when she did not feel the pain of being without her daughter like a wound in her side. "She was a little angel," Mrs. Danby had told the reporter, and she went on to say that a candle burned night and day by

Minette's bed and would go on burning until she was safely returned.

As soon as he saw the newspaper, Professor Danby rang his wife.

"How much did they pay you for that?" he wanted to know.

"Twenty thousand," said Minette's mother, "and no more than I deserve with what I've been through."

"I don't know how you can bring yourself to talk to a filthy rag like the *Daily Screech*," said the professor, and slammed down the phone.

But all day he was furious. Twenty thousand pounds! It wasn't as though he wasn't suffering just as much over his lost daughter. He didn't light candles by her bed because of the fire risk, but the housekeeper, who was fond of Minette, had bought a bunch of flowers and put them in her room. Of course the *Daily Screech* was out of the question—he wouldn't be seen dead with his photograph in a rag like that—but if the *Morning Gazette* was interested, he might say a few words about his sorrow and his loss. There was a photograph somewhere that the housekeeper had taken outside the university in which he was standing beside his daughter, wearing his gown and hood. It had come out rather well and made it clear the kind of background that she came from.

Fabio's grandparents were too snobby to talk to any

kind of newspaper, but they appeared on a late-night television panel to bleat about the lack of discipline in modern life and the feebleness of the police, who still hadn't returned their grandson.

And even as Minette's parents were getting rich and Fabio's grandparents were complaining, a helicopter was getting ready to take off from the Metropolitan Police pad outside London. It was a small machine manned only by one policeman and a policewoman—and their orders were clear.

"Remember, if you get a chance to land, it's the two children we want. The aunts can wait. And don't pick a fight with Sprott. We're after the boy and the girl right now, and nothing else."

As soon as they opened the door of the mermaid shed, Fabio and Minette realized that something serious had happened.

Loreen lay on the tiled floor, chewing mouthfuls of gum and weeping. In her sink in the corner, Oona looked stricken and pale. Old Ursula was shaking her head and muttering.

"It's my fault," Loreen wailed. "I've been a rotten mother and I deserve all I get."

"What is it?" the children asked. "What's happened?"

Loreen hiccuped and tried to speak, but what with her gum and her sorrow, no one could make out what she was saying, and it was Old Ursula who said: "Queenie's eloped. She's swum off with that muscleman who came yesterday and tried to catch her."

"What muscleman?"

"He came in the dinghy with Lambert's father, and Queenie went up to sing to him. We didn't think she fancied him, but she's gone."

A low croak came from Oona as she tried to speak. "She . . . *didn't* . . . fancy him. She . . . said his biceps were silly."

But the other mermaids took no notice of Oona, who was trying to make out that Queenie hadn't gone of her own free will. Twins always stuck together, and what had happened with Lord Brasenott made Oona think that all men were evil, which was silly.

"I spoiled her," wailed Loreen. "She always had the best shells and the prettiest pearls for her hair."

"Now don't carry on so," said Ursula. "It isn't your fault Queenie turned out so flighty."

"She didn't—" began Oona, but Loreen only put another piece of gum in her mouth and went on wailing. "I've been a rotten mother, and it's all my fault," she said again, and she picked Walter out of the dishpan and slapped his tail, though he hadn't done anything except grizzle and whine in his usual way.

"We must tell the aunts," said Fabio.

"Oh dear, must we?" cried Loreen.

But Old Ursula said yes, it was best to own up. "Get some wheelbarrows and we'll go up to the house," she said. Flopping about over land made the mermaids' tails sore.

So the children came back with three wheelbarrows and Art to push the third one. No one took any notice of Oona, who went on croaking that her sister had not *liked* the muscleman.

The aunts were very much upset. Not because Queenie was flighty, which they'd known all along, but because it meant that Mr. Sprott now knew that there were mermaids on the Island—and maybe other things too.

"I wonder if he knew before he came to lunch," said Coral. "Do you think that was why he wanted to buy the Island?"

"Perhaps he'll come back with photographers?" faltered Myrtle.

Fabio and Minette looked at each other. They had lived in the world outside long enough to know that Mr. Sprott might come back with something much more serious than that.

A day passed, and half a night, and then they heard the sound they had been dreading: the noise of a boat coming into the bay. So Sprott was back already!

In an instant the aunts were out of bed. Etta ran for

the Captain's blunderbuss, Coral fetched Art's catapult, and Myrtle grabbed the long-handled brush she used to scrub her back.

Outside, the night was black and moonless, but they could make out the boat nosing in beside the jetty. The engine died . . . the cargo was unloaded . . . and almost instantly the boat went into reverse and moved away.

The aunts, clutching their weapons, peered into the darkness. Then suddenly Etta broke the silence with a great shout and ran toward the jetty. And there, standing tall among her suitcases, was a woman in a long raincoat, holding what seemed to be a frying pan.

"Dorothy! Oh my dear, how wonderful to see you!" She hugged her sister, unable to keep back her tears of happiness and relief.

It was only then, as the other aunts came forward, that Etta could make out two small figures standing behind the luggage.

"Good heavens, Dorothy, what have you got there?" she asked, shining her flashlight.

"You may well ask," said Dorothy, and pushed Boo-Boo and the Little One forward into the light.

Having Betty's children to stay would have been bad at any time. Now with Queenie gone and everyone so jittery, it was a nightmare.

They were awful children. Not awful like Lambert,

but awful all the same. It wasn't their fault; they'd been brought up to behave like idiots. Boo-Boo (who was a boy called Alfred) wore a bow tie and kept asking Art for shoe polish.

"It's got to be *tan*, not brown," he said to poor Art, who was trying to prepare mash for the boobrie chicks and take the Captain his meals and cope with the extra people to feed.

The Little One (who was a girl called Griselda) began to cry straightaway because Dorothy had forgotten to pack the hankie with a picture of a flower fairy on it that she kept under her pillow, and both the children were terrified of germs. Fortunately, they were so wrapped up in their silly fusses about which pajama case was which that they didn't even notice the strange animals or the danger they might be in. They just went on dusting the chairs before they sat down in them and looking at themselves in mirrors and complaining because their underclothes hadn't been ironed, exactly as if they were still in Newcastle upon Tyne. If Fabio hadn't been so busy with the kraken, his temper would certainly have got the better of him, but as it was he hardly saw them.

But having Dorothy made up for everything.

Dorothy knew that there was evil in the world. She had met people like Stanley Sprott, and she had seen some dreadful things abroad—"monsters" that were supposed to be mermaids kept pickled in jars, or deformed beasts put in cages for people to gawk at—but she was not afraid. It was Dorothy who filled the Captain's blunderbuss with carpet tacks and set up tripwires behind the house and showed them how to make a cosh—a heavy sticklike weapon.

But when, at the end of the first day, Etta took her sister down to see the young kraken, the tough, hard-faced woman changed into someone very different.

"Oh, Etta," she breathed, looking down at the little creature as he slept, "that I should live to see this day!"

Queenie sat in Mr. Sprott's bathroom on the *Hurricane* up to her neck in scented water. The bath was a Jacuzzi, with water bubbling up from all sorts of places. The taps were gold and so were the shower fittings, and on shelves all round were cut-glass bottles full of wonderful things: colored crystals and glittering hair sprays and creams for making the body firm, and more creams for making it soft once it was firm, and more creams still for making it not just soft and firm but also pink.

The creams belonged to Mrs. Sprott, but she wasn't there, so Queenie had the bathroom to herself. It was exactly the kind of bathroom she had dreamed of when she heard stories about mermaids marrying princes and going to live in palaces, but as she splashed more water over her tail, the tears kept welling out of her eyes, and she was shaken by terrible sobs. She had never in all her life been so unhappy and afraid.

For Oona had been right. Queenie had not swum away to be with the muscleman. Queenie had been most cruelly caught by Mr. Sprott's henchmen, and this bathroom was as much her prison as any cell in a cold and dirty dungeon.

She had gone out for a moonlight swim, and when she got to the end of the bay, she found a net under the water stretched between two rocks. At first she thought the net had been put there by fishermen, but as she tried to free herself, it was pulled tighter and tighter still, and she was towed away behind the dinghy and hauled aboard the *Hurricane* like a slab of dead meat.

"Oh, why didn't I listen?" cried poor Queenie. "My mother told me to stay out of the way of men."

She would have given anything now to see Loreen chewing her gum or Old Ursula with her toothless smile; she even missed Walter. But the person she longed for most was Oona. She understood now how Oona had felt on board Lord Brasenott's yacht; no wonder the poor girl had lost her voice. The round window of the bathroom had a curtain, but Des and the two horrible men who guarded the boat had pulled it aside, and every so often their faces leered in at her.

"Oh, what is to become of me!" cried poor Queenie, and felt so sad that she wanted to die.

And while Queenie wept in the bath, Lambert sniveled in his father's cabin.

"I don't want a mermaid for a stepmother," he whined. "I don't want a mermaid for a stepmother *anyway,* and I certainly don't want a mermaid for a stepmother who isn't really there."

"Don't be silly, Lambert," said Mr. Sprott. "One doesn't marry mermaids, and anyway your mother is still alive."

But he sighed deeply as he said it, for Queenie was much prettier than Mrs. Sprott with her purple hair and her clawlike fingernails and her greedy eyes. Mrs. Sprott was a kind of dung beetle, only instead of collecting balls of nice soft manure, she collected clothes and shoes and jewels and furs and dumped them in his house before going out for more.

"They'll laugh at me at school if I have a mermaid for a stepmother, and I don't like fish. Even half a fish I don't like . . . even a fish that isn't really there," moaned Lambert.

"Oh, be quiet, Lambert," said Mr. Sprott. "No one's going to marry her. We're going to show her off in a tank and make a fortune off of her. But first she'll have to tell us where the other creepy-crawlies are to be found. I'm going to catch the lot of them and then—"

But he didn't finish what he was going to say. Lambert couldn't be trusted not to blab. Not until the weird beasts were on board and tied up and on their way across the Atlantic would he say anything. He had decided to set up his carnival on an island off the coast of Florida that belonged to a friend. Or rather to a business partner. A man like Stanley Sprott did not have friends.

But first he had to cross-examine Queenie and see how much of his son's babble was true. He found Des ogling the mermaid through the bathroom window, while Casimir and Boris grumbled that it was their turn.

"I found her," Des was saying. "So I get the longest turn. She's mine, really, and the old man ought to—"

He turned to see Mr. Sprott standing behind him. "If any of you lay a finger on this mermaid, you'll go straight overboard," he said, and told Des to board up the window. Then he opened the door and drew up a stool beside the bath.

"Now dear," he said, "I've got a few questions to ask you. It's about your family. You're not alone, are you? You've got a mummy and a daddy."

"I haven't got a daddy," said Queenie, pulling Aunt Myrtle's bodice tighter round her top.

"But a mummy . . . and little brothers and sisters?"

"Only one of each and my great-grandmother."

Queenie was too frightened to realize that she was being trapped.

"And of course there are the other . . . unusual creatures on the Island. Lambert told me about a worm. White, isn't he?"

Queenie nodded. "He's very clever," she said.

"And what else is there on the Island?"

Now at last the mermaid saw where this was leading. "Nothing," she faltered. "Just the aunts."

"Oh, I think there are," said Mr. Sprott. "Perhaps if I take the plug out of the bath, it will help you to think."

"No! Oh please, no!"

To take water from a mermaid is the most terrible thing you can do. But Mr. Sprott had already pulled it out; the water was draining away. Now he picked up the electric hair dryer.

"No!" she cried again, trying to protect her tail from the terrifying heat.

Mr. Sprott turned it off.

"You've remembered something else?"

"There's a big bird . . . a boobrie." Surely he wouldn't want the boobrie? What use would she be to him?

"And where is it to be found? Is there a nest?"

"No . . . I don't know. . . . It's up on the hill. Oh, please put the water back."

But Mr. Sprott did not put the water back—and now he put on the dryer again and let the ghastly heat play over her tail until the freshness of the silver became dull and dead. . . . Queenie's tail had been her pride and joy,

and now it looked as though it had been on a fishmonger's slab for a week.

She held out as long as she could. Then she said pitifully: "There are some selkies. They're just seals, really. There's nothing to them."

But Mr. Sprott wasn't to be fobbed off so easily.

"What sort of seals?" He had dropped the hair dryer. Instead, he had taken a pair of scissors and was holding a hank of her golden hair, ready to chop it off. "Go on — answer. Don't keep me waiting. I don't like to be kept waiting."

"I don't know," whispered poor Queenie. "It's just stories. People say they can turn into humans if someone drops seven tears into the water or if they're touched with cold steel."

Mr. Sprott's eyes glittered. He saw the circus ring . . . a seal on a tub . . . then a sharp pronged fork in its backside and lo, a woman jumps down. A transformation scene, better than a pantomime.

"Go on — what else is there? What else?"

But though he threatened her again with the hair dryer, Queenie kept silent about the little kraken. For she knew that the end of the kraken meant the end of the sea as she knew it — and thus the end of her world — and Mr. Sprott did not dare to hurt her anymore, or she wouldn't be worth putting on show.

"I'll speak to you again tomorrow," he said, turning

the water on again. "Don't think I've finished with you, because I haven't."

But as he gave his orders — the hold to be cleared, reinforced nets and lifting gear to be got ready, and harpoon guns to stun the beasts before they were hauled aboard — he did not realize that the greatest prize on the Island was still unknown to him. Neither Queenie nor Lambert had mentioned the kraken's son.

Chapter 18

THE GREAT KRAKEN had reached the warmer southern seas. The fishes that joined him were brilliantly colored, with fan tails and exotic spikes, and from the islands flashing birds with crests of crimson and orange came to welcome him and perch on his back. The water was clear and calm, and the corals on the seabed were of every color under the sun.

As he swam, the great kraken hummed his Healing Hum, and the turtles who had lumbered out of the sea to lay their eggs on the sandbanks were left in peace, and the rich men who had come to slaughter the porpoises pulled in their harpoons as the swell made by the kraken's passing reached their boats.

Yet the kraken was not happy. The dolphins and seals that swam round him felt this and were puzzled.

He was smiling less; his golden eyes sometimes had a clouded look.

But why? He did not know—only that somehow he felt uneasy. He was missing his son, of course, but there could have been no safer place to leave him than the Island of the Aunts.

"I must pull myself together," thought the kraken. "I do not belong to myself; I belong to the sea."

And he put aside his vague and troubled thoughts and swam on.

Two days after Boo-Boo and the Little One came to the Island, Old Ursula disappeared. She had swum out to say good-bye to Herbert's mother and never come back.

The other mermaids were frantic.

"I should have been nicer to her," wailed Loreen. "I shouldn't have said her tail smelled. It did smell, but I shouldn't have said it." And Oona wept because time and again she'd left the old creature flapping in the sink instead of helping her.

As for the aunts, they now knew once and for all how great was the danger they were in. Great-grandmothers do fall in love, but they aren't often silly about it when they do. Old Ursula could not have eloped; she must have been snatched—and that meant that Queenie too had been taken by force. And sure enough, when they searched the bay, they found a net stretched between two rocks.

"We must have a Council of War," said Etta, and made everybody do thirty press-ups so as to make the blood go to their heads and help them to think.

But even with all the blood in their heads, they knew that fighting off Sprott and his men would be almost impossible and that their only hope would be to get the animals to hide.

"The stoorworm must stay at the bottom of the loch—no coming up for chats," said Coral.

"And Herbert and his mother should come closer to the house," said Myrtle. "They could have the pond in the vegetable garden."

Art offered to guard the mermaid shed with the Captain's blunderbuss—secretly he still hoped he might have a chance to kill someone after all—and they decided that the Sybil must be brought indoors; she was far too loopy to be left on her own.

But it was easier to decide what should be done about the creatures than to get them to do it. The stoorworm pointed out that he was after all a wingless *dragon* and should be helping to guard the Island, not skulking about in the bottom of lakes, and Herbert wouldn't bring his mother any closer because she wanted to die in the sea and not in somebody's brussels sprouts.

But of course it was the kraken that they worried about most of all, and it was now that the aunts wished from the bottom of their hearts that they had never kidnapped Fabio and Minette.

They knew exactly where the little beast could be hidden: in a large underwater cave, a kind of grotto on the north shore with only the smallest opening onto the strand. It was a beautiful place, with a pool of clear, deep water surrounded by gently shelving rock, and at the back of the grotto was an opening to the cliff that gave enough light to see by. The opening came out by Ethelgonda's burial ground, and the naak had promised to keep watch up there.

But to keep the kraken in a cave when he was used to the freedom of the sea would not be easy. He would need people all the time. And people, to the kraken, were Fabio and Minette.

"There is no question of your staying along with him through the night," said Etta firmly. "My sisters and I will take shifts."

"Yes, there is. We'll take a blanket and lots of food — but we're going to do it. It's our job," said Minette.

"It's not your job to risk that kind of danger."

But something odd was happening to Fabio and Minette. Perhaps it was from living on the Island among creatures that did not need to speak very much, but they seemed to know each other's thoughts.

"If you didn't want us to do our work, you shouldn't have kidnapped us," said Minette.

And Fabio, between gritted teeth, said, "Nothing is going to stop us being with the kraken. Nothing."

By nightfall, they were all at their posts: Art guarding the mermaids, Coral crouched by the boobrie's nest, which they had ringed with barbed wire; the Sybil zooming round the house muttering about windchill factors and burning the Captain's semolina.

And the kraken was hidden in his secret place beneath the cliff.

The children had lit candles and put them on the ledges, and the flames flickering on the stone lit up the colors of the rock.

"It's like Merlin's crystal cave," said Minette dreamily, and she was right. Because the kraken was his father's son, all sorts of creatures came to be near him in the water: crimson crabs and clusters of pipefish and families of sea mice. . . . But if it was beautiful in the cave, keeping the kraken quiet and happy was hard work. Fortunately, he was learning English so fast that they could sing to him and tell him stories.

"More *Snow White*," he would command, or "More *Puss in Boots*."

But the stories he liked best were the ones they made up about his father—about the great kraken and his adventures as he swam through the oceans of the world.

Where the sides of the grotto sloped to the water there was one place that was almost flat, and it was there that the children had made a kind of camp. They had brought sleeping bags and plenty of food and, of course, the tin of boobrie buns. If the kraken got restless and swam too near the opening of the cave, they only had to bang with a wooden spoon on the tin and he would hurry back, his mouth already open for his treat.

Even so, the aunts were worried about them, and sometime in the small hours, Etta and Dorothy stopped patrolling the Island and went down to the grotto again, determined to make the children come up to the house and go to bed.

The kraken was asleep, his head just out of the water. And on either side of him, curled up on the ledge so that their arms were almost touching him, slept Fabio and Minette.

And the aunts turned back and said nothing, for it was clear that these three lived in a circle of friendship that nothing now could break.

There was no attack from Sprott's people that night, but just before dawn something did happen.

Down on the point, Herbert's mother slipped quietly from life. Her eyes filmed over; she sighed deeply, her whiskers trembled. . . . Then she spoke her son's name once—not in the selkie language, but in proper human speech so that Myrtle too could understand.

"*Herbert,*" said Herbert's mother. She didn't say anything more, but from the way she said it they knew that she thought Herbert had been a good son and she was thanking him. Then she hoisted herself slowly to the very edge of the rock, lifted her head once toward the sky—and gave herself to the sea.

It was a beautiful death—exactly the kind of death the old seal had chosen—but of course for Herbert it was a moment of great sadness, and when it was over, Myrtle would not leave him even to get her meals.

Her sisters were worried about this. Myrtle had always felt things too much. When she was small, she had tried to bring a tin of sardines back to life by floating the headless fishes in a washbasin, and they did not think she should be out on the point on a night when there might be danger.

But Myrtle in her own way was obstinate.

"I can't leave Herbert alone with his sorrow," she said—and she wrapped her legs in an old gray blanket and settled down beside her friend.

There was a time when Queenie would have hated sharing a bath with Old Ursula, but now she was touchingly glad of her company. The old mermaid was as tough as old boots, and she didn't give a fig for Mr. Sprott's threats.

"He can't do anything to me. I'm old and I don't care," she said.

Mr. Sprott hated her. She spat at him and cursed him and tried to bite him with her single tooth, and when Des came anywhere near, she screeched at him.

"Don't you dare ogle my great-granddaughter, you plug-ugly," she yelled.

"You can't put that old horror on show," said Des. "Nobody'll pay to see the likes of her!"

Mr. Sprott shrugged. "Maybe I'll sell her to medical science to be cut up," he said. "No one knows how a mermaid's tail is joined to her body."

Seeing Ursula so angry and unafraid did Queenie good. But of course they both knew what danger they were in. And sure enough, later that evening, Boris, Casimir, and Des came in with blindfolds, which they tied roughly round the mermaids' eyes. Then they were wrapped in coarse sacking and felt themselves raised up, swaying on steel hooks, and then lowered, still swaying horribly, into some deep cold place.

When they could see again, they found that they were sitting in a crude, rusty tank filled with water. The tank was in the corner of a large, dark, empty space, stuffy and evil-smelling. There were no windows and no lamps, and all they could hear was the slap of the water against the ship's sides.

They were in the hold of the *Hurricane*, which Sprott

had prepared, like a slave ship of old, for his prisoners.

"Don't worry, you won't be by yourselves much longer," jeered Des. "Lots of your little friends will be along soon."

Then he climbed up the steel ladder, pulled it up after him, and shut the trapdoor, leaving them alone in the foul-smelling darkness.

There were five men in the launch: Stanley Sprott himself, Boris, Casimir, the ship's mate, and Des. Lambert had been left behind with the skipper—the poor boy was definitely going crazy—but Sprott had forced the mate of the *Hurricane* to come too.

The launch was towing two large inflatable rafts loaded with equipment with which to net the creatures and stun them before they were floated out to the *Hurricane*.

All the men had guns and knives and whistles to blow if they wanted extra help, and their orders were clear.

"Now remember, if you have to shoot, shoot the aunts, not the creatures. You can't get money for aunts. But don't shoot at all if you can help it. We want silence and we want speed."

The launch slid onto the sand. The men got out.

Boris and Casimir set off up the hill; they were going for the boobrie and the stoorworm. Sprott himself and the mate made their way to the mermaid shed: Sprott liked the idea of carrying the wriggling, struggling mermaids over his shoulder.

And Des was to capture the selkies.

Des had grumbled about this. "What do you want a couple of old seals for?" he asked Mr. Sprott.

Sprott had not told anyone what Queenie had said about selkies; it was probably rubbish anyway. "They're supposed to be able to sing," was all he said.

So Des was not in a good mood as he climbed up the rocks toward the sleeping seals. Even if they could sing, it didn't seem very exciting—lots of animals made noises in their throats—and how the devil was he supposed to pick out the selkies from the others?

"There're two of them, lying apart from the rest," Lambert had said. "They've got funny eyes." And then he'd started to snivel and go on again about how they weren't really there.

But as he got closer, Des saw that Lambert was right. There *were* two seals lying apart from the rest. A big bull seal and a smaller one; a cow probably. He'd tackle the smaller one first, and if things went wrong, he could always skin the brutes. Sealskins fetched a good price.

Des crept closer. The big seal opened his eyes, and even in the dim moonlight, Des could see that his eyes were not quite like those of an ordinary seal.

But it was the smaller one he was after. She'd been asleep, but now she stirred. . . .

Really, it was uncanny how human she looked. Her body was just a gray splodge and he couldn't see her flippers, but as she yawned and opened her eyes, you could almost forget she was a seal.

Des shook himself. He was getting fanciful. Better get her netted and dragged away. It shouldn't be a problem; she was only half grown—he probably wouldn't even need the stunner.

He crept the last ten feet, stood up . . . and threw the net.

And the selkie screamed. He had never heard such a scream coming from the throat of an animal. It was a completely human scream, and it was all Des could do not to drop the net and run back to the ship.

But he didn't. He cursed and tried to tighten the net while the seal struggled and kicked—and then suddenly the screams had words to them! Proper human words.

"Leave me alone," shrieked the selkie in her high-pitched voice. "Let me go at once, you brute. Help! Oh, help!"

Up by the boobrie's nest, Coral got to her feet, vaulted over the barbed wire—all two hundred and twenty-five pounds of her—and began to run toward the point. Etta, who had been helping Art to guard the mermaid shed, seized the blunderbuss and did the same. Going to rescue Myrtle was something they did as naturally as they breathed.

But someone else was coming to Myrtle's rescue.

As Des straightened himself to pull the net tighter, something came at him: an enormous wet wall of gray muscle . . . a tank of solid blubber that sent him sprawling. He tried to get to his feet, but the bull seal threw back his head and roared, and then he opened his mouth and Des saw the evil-looking teeth and felt his hot breath. The creature was going for his throat . . . in a moment it would be all up with him.

Choking, struggling, Des tried to reach his knife, but every time it was in his grasp, the seal charged again. Helpless, sprawled on the ground, he tried to cover his face, but the awful teeth were closing on his flesh. . . .

Then, when he thought his last moment had come, he found the knife and lunged. The seal reared back, and Des almost missed . . . almost but not quite. He'd made a nick in the animal's shoulder, nothing more . . . but, my God, what was happening now? It wasn't teeth that were fastening round his throat, it was hands, it was fingers. . . .

With a bloodcurdling shriek, Des managed to struggle to his feet—and then he ran . . . ran and ran, almost mad with horror . . . ran, with the spittle running out of his mouth, away and away across the Island, trying to escape from what he'd seen. Ran until he stumbled over a gorse bush, and found himself falling . . . falling down toward a pool of dark water far below.

Chapter 19

THE STOORWORM had always been worried about his thoughts getting stuck halfway down his body.

Now he didn't worry anymore. The terrible sadness he felt as he lay curled up in the hold of the *Hurricane* had not got stuck anywhere. It went right down through every single segment to the tip of his tail. He was just a long tube of wretchedness and despair and shame.

It had all happened in a moment. He had heard the boobrie squawk in terror and come up from the bottom of the lake to see if he could help, and a man had shot something into his throat—a red-hot needle, it felt like . . . and then he remembered nothing more until he woke in a kind of snake pit in this ghastly place.

"I have failed my friends," he thought, "and I have failed myself." And he felt so sad that he wanted to die.

From the rusty tank in the corner where the mermaids sat came the sound of sobbing. Oona was sobbing because *men* kept coming down below to peer and pry—men that were worse even than Lord Brasenott—and she was terribly afraid. But the noisiest and most terrible tears came from Loreen.

"My baby!" she kept hiccuping. "My little darling, where is he?"

When Sprott had overcome Art and broken open the door of the mermaid shed, Walter had been asleep in his dishpan, and there had been no time for Loreen to grab him before she was thrown over Sprott's shoulder and carried toward the boat.

"Will someone find him?" gulped Loreen. And Old Ursula said of course they would—but the trouble was, no one knew what was happening on the Island and who was left.

Perhaps the most heartrending sight in that ghastly place were the boobrie chicks, penned in a wire cage, their yellow beaks bruised and bloodstained . . . and lying down, with her great yellow legs in the air like an outsize chicken ready for the pot, their mother. Lowering the struggling giant bird through the trapdoor had been so difficult that they had given her another injection, and now the chicks climbed over her, peeping in bewilderment, not understanding why their mother was so still.

But Sprott's greatest prize was not in the hold. The kraken lay on the deck, tethered by ropes that bit so hard he could not even turn his head, and every few minutes Sprott came up to look at him and rub his hands and gloat. He had no idea what it was that he had caught, only that it would make him very, very rich. For it could speak, this thing that they had caught when Des fell into its cave. It had said "Father" once, when they nailed it down onto the deck, but now its eyes were closed and it spoke no more.

"Hurry up down there," Sprott shouted to the crew who were fixing the starboard engine. They would have been gone long before but for the engine playing up. It was high time they got away across the Atlantic. He'd given orders to have the thing on the deck hosed down every ten minutes, but it wasn't eating. None of the creatures were eating . . . they needed to be in proper cages.

For a moment he wondered if the little boy was dead—the one who'd tried to stop them in the cave. Probably not—the skulls of children were tougher than you'd think. All the same, he'd be glad to be gone.

"I thought I told you to hurry," Sprott shouted once again.

But still the *Hurricane* lay unmoving on the gray sea—and on the deck, the little kraken, his heart broken, prepared for death.

Minette sat on the floor of Fabio's little room, her hands round her knees, and waited for him to wake.

She had been there for several hours, and she would not move, however much the aunts complained.

"You're not helping him," said Etta. "He'll come round when he's ready."

But she did not speak in her usual brisk voice, and Minette took no notice. All the aunts were like wraiths since the kraken had gone.

So Minette watched and waited by her friend. Outside, in the bathroom, she could hear the high, stupid voices of Betty's children.

"There's something nasty in the washbasin. It smells fishy. You can't clean your teeth," whined Boo-Boo.

"It's eaten my Tinkerbell toothpaste. I don't like it here. I want to go home!"

"I want to go home too. I want to go home *now*."

Minette sighed. She could never get used to the awfulness of Boo-Boo and the Little One. What was in the washbasin was the merbaby, Walter. He was missing his mother and chewed anything he could reach.

Fabio lay without moving on the bed; the bandage round his head stood out very white in the darkened room. What if he didn't come round at all?

But that was stupid. He was breathing. He had a concussion, that was all.

Minette shut her eyes, remembering. They'd been in the cave, telling the kraken a story . . . trying to stop him going too near the entrance. Then suddenly, something

227

had hurtled down from the opening in the cliff above them and landed in the water. A man they had never seen before, gasping and struggling for breath.

They hadn't been frightened at first—not until he clambered out and stared at the kraken . . . stared and stared. . . . Then he felt in his sodden clothes, and from an oilskin pouch he took out a whistle and blew three sharp, shrill blasts.

They had understood then. Fabio charged at the man, trying to wrench the whistle away, but it was too late. More men came from the sea, and the cave filled up with shouting and flashlights and the glint of weapons. Minette had gone to the kraken's head, slipping into the water with him, trying to calm him, but the net came down over them both. . . . He'd thought it was a game at first—cruelty was something he couldn't understand— and she'd half hoped they'd take her with him so that she could comfort him. But they had pulled her out roughly and thrown her back into the pool.

And as she climbed out, she'd seen Fabio lying on the ledge of rock . . . and the blood seeping from his head.

Out in the corridor the Little One was whimpering again. "They've given me the wrong sweeties. I've got blue sweeties and I'm a girl. Girls ought to have *pink* sweeties."

It was another hour before Fabio stirred, but then he was awake at once.

"Have they got him? Has he gone?"

"Yes."

Fabio put a hand to his head. "Did they knock me out?"

"They kept thumping your head against the stone." Minette's voice broke as she remembered Fabio's courage and the cruelty of the men.

"And the others? The stoorworm . . . the mermaids?"

"They've got everyone except Walter."

Fabio had managed to sit up.

"Is the *Hurricane* still there?"

"Yes. We don't know why, but she is."

"Then we must board her. We must rescue *him*. We must rescue everybody."

Minette stared at him. "You're mad. How could we? We've only got the *Peggoty*. And the aunts won't let us out of their sight. We're really prisoners now because they blame themselves for you being hurt and because they left the creatures unguarded to help Myrtle. You've no idea what it's like down there. And Dorothy broke one of the thugs' noses with her wok; they dragged him back to the boat, but there's blood everywhere."

Fabio took no notice. "We have to. We have to get to him."

"Even if we did, what could we —" began Minette, and broke off. She felt like Fabio underneath. They had to try and help.

Fabio had pushed back the bedclothes. The room spun round, then steadied. He was just trying his feet on the floor when the unspeakable Boo-Boo came in.

"That's my teddy you've got in there. I put him to sleep in your bed when you were in the cave, and I want him because we're going to play mummies and daddies in the yard and he's my little boy."

Fabio threw the stuffed animal across the room.

"Get out," he said. And then: "There must be someone who could help."

Minette looked at him. He had had an awful blow to his head — would he be able to cope with any more strangeness?

But that was silly. Fabio could cope with anything.

"There is somebody," she said.

Herbert sat quietly on the point and looked out to the sea, which until yesterday had been his home. He wore a pair of Art's trousers, stripy socks, and a sweater of the Captain's. The clothes felt prickly on his skin, and his soul felt prickly too. The tears of Myrtle, the despair of the aunts, buzzed round his head. It had been so quiet in the sea.

But what was done was done. He was a man now, not a seal, and it was as a man that he must try to help the kraken's son.

The *Peggoty* was in the boathouse. She was only an

old fishing boat, not a tenth the size of the *Hurricane*, but if he could get alongside and get a grappling hook onto the deck, he could climb up the rope and board her. Some selkies, when they changed shape, had trouble with their arms and legs, but his were strong.

He was checking the *Peggoty's* oars when Fabio and Minette appeared in the doorway of the shed. Fabio had pulled a woolen cap over his bandage.

"We want to go with you," said Minette.

Fabio was silent. He had expected to find it a shock meeting someone who not twenty-four hours ago had been a seal, but now nothing mattered except to get to the *Hurricane*. Herbert had been a handsome seal, and he was a handsome man, but what was important was that he looked trustworthy and reliable—and strong. Some people who listen to music on the cello can be a little arty and vague, but not Herbert.

"Have you asked the aunts?" said Herbert, coiling a rope.

The children did not answer. Then:

"We have to go. The kraken was our job. We have to help him, and the others too. We have to try."

Herbert straightened himself and looked at them. He was a man now, but he was not a man like other men. He had a sense of all nature being one . . . of children being part of the universe and not creatures set apart. He knew that if the kraken died, the sea would never be

231

the same again, and he remembered that the kraken had trusted these two as he had trusted no one.

All the same, knowing the danger, he hesitated.

But it looked as though the matter would be taken out of his hands. For before he could speak, all three of them heard the unmistakable drone of a helicopter coming toward the Island. The noise grew louder, the helicopter circled the Island once . . . then began the descent onto the level patch of grass behind the house.

Tears sprang to Minette's eyes, and Fabio drew in a hissing breath. Now, just when they had a chance of reaching the kraken, they had been found and would be dragged back.

Frantically they looked about for somewhere to hide. But it was too late. A policeman was climbing out of the machine and hurrying toward the house; a policewoman followed.

The adventure was over.

Chapter 20

KING'S CROSS STATION had not looked so smart since the Queen had arrived there at the time of her silver jubilee.

There were streamers all over the station saying "Welcome back!" and on Platform One, where the train bringing the kidnapped children was due to arrive, was a party of schoolchildren carrying banners. The banners said things like YOU ARE SAFE NOW and YOUR TROUBLES ARE ENDED, and the children who carried them had learned a welcoming song that they would sing as soon as the snatched children stepped out of the train.

A chocolate firm had sent a bumper pack of sweets, and their prettiest salesgirl, dressed like a chocolate bar, was waiting to present it. A famous clothes shop had made up parcels of T-shirts, and a bicycle manufacturer had brought two mountain bikes to present to the children who had been snatched so cruelly by the kidnapping aunts. Everyone knew about the miracle that had made it possible for the police helicopter to swoop down and gather up the missing boy and girl in a single daring raid.

Mrs. Danby, Minette's mother, was in the place of honor, standing on the strip of red carpet that had been put out for the children to walk on when they stepped out of their first-class carriage. She wore a dazzling new outfit that she had bought with the money from the *Daily Screech:* a shocking-pink suit and a little pillbox hat with a veil. When she ran forward to hug Minette, she would push the veil up so that people could see her tears. Professor Danby stood beside her, looking solemn. Whenever his wife took a step forward so as to be nearer to where the train would stop, he took one too. He wasn't going to be upstaged by that show-off he'd been fool enough to marry!

The old Mountjoys had been given special chairs so that they could wait for their grandson in comfort. They were, of course, very pleased that Fabio had been found, but they couldn't help wondering if all the work they had put into making him into an English gentleman had been wasted. The children had been discovered on some rough island in the middle of the Atlantic Ocean, and that could hardly be a good thing. Maybe they would come off the train with straw in their hair and mud on their shoes—if they wore shoes at all.

And, of course, as well the schoolchildren and the relatives and the Lady Mayoress with her golden chain, the platform was full of photographers and journalists and television crews with all their gear. The moment when the poor, snatched little children got down from the train and ran into the arms of their loved ones would be shown not just all over England but all over the world. Even now the commentators were setting the scene, babbling excitedly into their microphones.

"Only five minutes to go before the train bringing those frightened, wretched youngsters to safety will draw up just fifty feet from where I stand," said the lady from ITV. "Mrs. Danby can hardly hold back her excitement — she has just run forward so as to get even closer to her missing daughter. . . ."

This was true — Mrs. Danby *had* run forward, but this was because her husband was up to his tricks again, trying to upstage her so that the camera picked him up as well as her, and she wasn't having that.

"And the grandparents of the wild little boy who found shelter and kindliness in their home — what a touching couple they make, in the autumn of their years, waiting with joy for this great moment," the commentator went on.

Up in Edinburgh, Professor Danby's housekeeper was glued to the telly. There'd be a row about which of the parents was to have the girl first, she thought, and hoped it would be the professor, because she'd put flowers in Minette's room and polished her new writing desk.

Minette's mother's boyfriend was watching too, lying as usual with a can of beer on the sofa. He too hoped Minette would go to her father first. Not that he had anything against the kid, but the apartment was cramped, and he'd got the sack again and needed somewhere to flake out in the day.

And in the hospital in Newcastle upon Tyne, Betty sat in the dayroom and watched, surrounded by other patients and those nurses who could spare a moment. She needed the treat because her hip was mending very slowly; she should have been out of the hospital a week ago, and there she still was.

"Only three more minutes now," said one of the newscasters, looking at the station clock, which was a silly thing to say. Since when have trains coming down from the north been on time, even trains full of police officers bringing kidnapped children back to safety?

The commentator described Mrs. Danby's hat once more and told the viewers that old Mrs. Mountjoy's face was full of longing.

The schoolchildren holding their banners shuffled their feet and cleared their throats, ready for their welcoming song.

The station clock ticked on.

And then at last they saw the train coming, curving round into the station, and a great cheer went up. The Lady Mayoress straightened her chain, the crowd that had gathered outside the platform gates waved, the television cameras whirred. . . .

The train slowed down . . . stopped.

The door opened. A policewoman got down, and another, then they turned and held out their hands to the two children.

The girl was the first to come out. She was lifted down from the carriage and stood for a moment looking about her, smoothing down the velvet collar and patting her curls.

Then the boy was lifted down; he straightened his cap and dusted down his blazer.

"Where's my mummy?" said the little girl in a cross and whining voice. "I want my mummy. You said you'd take us to her."

"I want her too," wailed the little boy. "I want my mummy *now*."

Mrs. Danby's mouth fell open. The professor glared. "Is this a joke?" snapped Mr. Mountjoy.

And in the dayroom of the hospital in Newcastle upon Tyne, poor Betty gave a single high-pitched cry and fell back senseless in her chair.

Chapter 21

HERBERT WAS MAGNIFICENT. In spite of the darkness and the choppy sea, he sent the *Peggoty* sailing steadily toward the single light burning on the *Hurricane*. His hands on the tiller never faltered; he seemed to understand the old boat as he understood the sea.

Fabio and Minette sat very close together in the stern, not daring to speak. When the helicopter took off again and they realized what a wonderful mistake had been made, they had wasted no more time. While Herbert was filling gas cans by the jetty, they had climbed aboard and down into the little cabin full of fishing hooks and ropes and tackle and pulled a tarpaulin over their heads. With luck, by the time they were found, they would be too far out to turn back.

But it wasn't Herbert who found them—it was Aunt Etta and Aunt Coral. It had never occurred to the children that the aunts would be part of the boarding party. Dorothy was staying behind because she had sprained her wrist when she bashed Casimir with her wok, and Herbert had forbidden Myrtle to come.

"You have had a shock, Myrtle, and you must rest," Herbert had said, and that was that. But not even Herbert had been able to stop Etta and Coral.

They had never seen the aunts so angry.

"Turn back at *once!*" commanded Etta. "These children will *not* face any more danger! I forbid it!" And Coral tried to get hold of the tiller and force the boat to change course.

But Herbert stood firm. He had sensed the change in the sea and knew what would happen to the ocean if the kraken's son perished. Even the children did not matter compared to that.

They glided silently alongside the *Hurricane.* No lights were burning in the cabins; no one expected an attack. With unbelievable strength Herbert threw the knotted rope, and they heard the grappling iron fasten on the wooden boards.

Within seconds, Herbert had climbed the rope and was on deck. Etta and the children followed. Coral with her bulk took longer, but she did it.

They stood in silence, listening. Herbert had his knife ready. If they could cut the kraken free and push him overboard, he could swim to safety.

They had almost reached him when it happened.

The door from below opened, a beam of light was thrown onto the deck—and Lambert stood there in his pajamas, blinking.

The poor boy was definitely going crazy. Since the *Hurricane* had filled up with creepy-crawlies that weren't really there, Lambert had been plagued by dreadful dreams. In this one he'd dreamed that Old Ursula had come to his school, sliding on her tail, and said she was his grandmother, and all the boys had jeered at him and thrown him buckets of fish.

Now he came onto the deck, too afraid to wake his father, and saw a huddle of shapes creeping toward the tarpaulin where that thing that didn't exist was lying.

He gave a cry of terror, and as Herbert turned, the knife in his hand, the Klaxon began to blare and search-lights raked the deck.

Ten minutes later, the rescuers had joined the prisoners in the stench and darkness of the hold.

You couldn't really blame the police. When the helicopter landed on the Island, two little children had run straight out into the arms of the policewoman and begged to be taken home.

"Take us away," they had lisped pathetically. "We hate it here. Take us home to our mummy."

It was clear that the poor little scraps had been abominably treated. They had not been allowed to clean their teeth and had been given sweets that tasted nasty—drugged ones, the policewoman was sure. All the way they had whimpered and complained, and it was clear that the aunts who had held them were as evil and dangerous as everyone imagined.

But of course the muddle took some time to sort out. The tax inspector had to come from Newcastle upon Tyne to fetch his children, and no one knew whether the T-shirts and the chocolate bars should be given to them or kept for when the other children came. And the whole business of capturing the vile kidnappers and the children that they were holding had to be done still.

But it couldn't be done at once, because a great fog had come down, covering the western coast and making it impossible for helicopters to take off or ships to move.

The prisoners had been in the hold of the *Hurricane* for several hours when they heard the engine judder into life.

Soon they would be off, and then . . . Nobody put into words what would happen once they were out in the Atlantic, but all of them knew. Why should Sprott let them live to tell the world what he had done?

In a corner, Minette was talking quietly to Fabio.

"If I could get to the kraken . . . just for a few minutes."

Fabio shrugged. "How would it help? We've nothing to cut him free with."

"I've got an idea. It might not work, but we've got nothing to lose."

"What sort of an idea?"

Minette looked round. The aunts were dozing, their backs against the wall; the worm was curled round himself like a piece of worn-out hosepipe. . . .

She moved closer to Fabio and whispered in his ear.

Fabio looked doubtful. "Remember what Aunt Etta said—that they can't do it until they're ready."

"Yes, I know—but once or twice when he's been learning a song, I thought . . . And anything's better than nothing."

"All right," said Fabio. "Let me think."

He sat for a while with his head in his hands. Then he went over to speak to Herbert, who nodded and went over to the mermaids' tank.

"I can't," they heard poor Queenie say. "I haven't the heart."

But Herbert was firm: "I'm afraid you must," he said in his sensible voice.

An hour later Des came down the ladder with some bread and a bucketful of drinking water, and as he did so, Queenie called to him.

"Des," she trilled. "Could you come here a minute?"

He put down his bucket and sidled past Herbert. He

could never be sure whether this was or wasn't the man who had tried to strangle him on the point—it had been too dark to see his face—but Herbert gave him the creeps.

"I've got ever such a painful place here in my back," Queenie went on. "Would you come and look, please?"

Des bent over her, and Queenie tossed her hair so that it fell over his face.

"No, not there," she fluted. "You show him, Oona."

It was only thinking of the kraken that gave Oona the courage to come closer to the man with his horrible hot breath, but she did it, and she too tossed her long thick hair so that Des was completely covered in the mermaids' tresses.

"Where?" he kept saying. "Where does it hurt?"

Only Boris was guarding the hatch—Casimir wasn't good for much since Dorothy had broken his nose—and Fabio now climbed up the ladder. "Help," he shouted. "The mermaids are being pestered. Send someone down!"

Sprott heard him and was furious. He had forbidden the men to go near the twins.

"What's going on there?" he yelled, and as Boris turned, Fabio dodged round behind him, running toward the deckhouse, while down below the mermaids began to scream.

The chase did not last long—Boris caught Fabio and

almost threw him down into the hold. But Minette had been behind Fabio and managed to slip out unseen in the muddle and the fog, and she made her way to where the captured kraken lay.

The kraken lay tethered and dangerously still. He still breathed but only just; his eyes were closed.

She tiptoed forward and laid her cheek against his head, and her tears fell on his face.

But Minette had not escaped from belowdecks to cry. She had only a few minutes to do what she had set herself to do.

"You mustn't give in like this," she said into his ear. "It's wrong. You're a brave and important person. You have to fight back."

The kraken tried to turn his head, but the ropes bit into his throat. She saw the look in his golden eyes, and her heart sank. But she wouldn't seem to be sorry for him; that was not the way.

"You must remember who you are," she said sternly.

The little kraken sniffed and was silent.

"You must think of your father," she went on.

"Father," said the kraken. He seemed a little stronger when he said that, and she could see he was thinking of the mighty creature who had given him life.

"That's right." Minette followed this up. "What does your father do?"

The little kraken sighed. It was a heartbreaking sound, as though all the sorrow in the world was coming out of his throat.

"Go on. Think," prompted Minette.

The kraken sighed again. He was not good at simply thinking. Then:

"Smiles," he said.

"Yes. He smiles. He's got a lovely smile." Minette saw the curve of the great beast's mouth as he swam into the bay. "And what else does he do?"

There was another pause. Then: "Swims," said the little kraken. "He swims."

"That's right. He swims." Minette nodded hard, giving encouragement. "And what does he do when he swims?"

No answer.

"What does he do when he swims round the oceans of the world making everything better? Think."

The little kraken thought. You could see him trying, but the ropes were beginning to cut into his flesh. He was too young to think through pain.

"Don't know," he moaned.

But Minette would give him no chance to go under. "Yes, you do. When he swims he does something else. What is it?"

Another sigh. Then: "He hums," said the little kraken.

"That's right." She rubbed his head to give him encouragement. "He hums, doesn't he? Humming is what krakens *do.*"

He tried to turn his head. His eyes were still bewildered.

"Humming is what krakens do," repeated Minette. "Isn't it?"

"Yes." His voice was very weak, but he was following her.

"And you're a kraken," she insisted. "Aren't you? A kraken is what you are."

It didn't seem as though the poor exhausted creature could speak again, but he took a weary breath and tried once more.

"I'm a kraken," he repeated obediently. "A kraken is what I *am.*"

At first she'd thought it was going to work. There had been a flash of pride in his eyes as he spoke, but almost at once he fell silent and turned away—and then Boris came and pushed her roughly down the ladder.

Now she sat beside Fabio, her head in her hands, and knew that it was over. She had done all she could, and she had failed.

In the darkness, the wan faces of the captives showed a wretchedness that was beyond tears. The two aunts sat with closed eyes, trying to bear what they had done. Facing their own deaths was not so hard, but what they had done to Fabio and Minette was not to be endured. Only Herbert was still upright, listening to the sound of the water against the sides of the ship.

Another hour passed . . . and another. . . . The *Hurricane*'s engine had been turned off while they waited for the fog to lift, but now they heard it start up again.

Unsteady at first, fainter than before . . . wavering . . . but gradually settling into a kind of thrumming rhythm.

Except that the engine hadn't sounded quite like that. . . .

Fabio, who had been dozing, sat up suddenly and dug Minette in the ribs.

Then slowly, wonderingly, the wretched prisoners looked at each other with a dawning hope.

The great kraken had reached the islands of the southern reef. The turquoise water, the coral strands, were staggeringly beautiful.

There was little to do in this paradise. The people who lived there respected the sea and the creatures in it, and they came out to pay their respects to the great kraken, standing with bowed heads. They did not gawk or gape or stare; the legend of the kraken who healed the sea was in their stories and had been for generations.

"He does not smile," said the old chief, whose great-grandmother had seen the kraken when he came before and told him about the healer's mouth curving in a bow that made everyone joyous to watch.

"He is troubled," said the chief's wife, who was a magic woman.

"How strangely his hum is sounding," said a child. "There are two hums, aren't there? A big hum and a little hum."

"It must be an echo."

But the kraken had stopped swimming. He was quite still in the water, resting. His head was tilted. Like the islanders, he was listening . . . listening. . . .

What was going on? His own hum was being interfered with. It was being disturbed. This had never happened before. Sometimes there had been an echo from his hum when he swam in a fjord between mountains, and sometimes the whales joined in, but this was different. What he could hear was his own hum, but it was smaller.

He fell silent, and all the creatures under the water came up to look at him and wonder what was happening.

But the silence was not complete. The small hum, the *underneath* hum, was still there. It was unsteady, quavery . . . but it was growing now in strength.

A great judder went through the kraken, sending the resting birds up in a flutter from his back. He made himself absolutely quiet once more, but it was still there —

this other, fainter hum that wasn't his own hum . . . and yet was just exactly that.

Then the people on the barrier reef saw a most extra-ordinary sight. The great kraken reared up out of the water — and now he did not hum. Instead he roared.

And then he turned.

Chapter 22

I DON'T WANT to watch! I don't *want* to!" shrieked Lambert. He tried to hold on to the cabin door, but his father dragged him out so roughly that he fell forward onto the deck.

"You *will* watch, you namby-pamby little shrieker. You'll watch them go overboard and you'll like it. It's time you learned that you don't get something for nothing."

Pushing and pulling, kicking Lambert's shins, Mr. Sprott forced his son toward the rail.

He felt mistreated. If the aunts had sold him the Island as he wanted, he wouldn't have to drown them now, and the children too. It was their own fault, really. There was no way he could get his moneymaking schemes under way with people blathering and giving the game away. He was going to say that he'd found the creatures wild at sea and rescued them.

"Right, go and get them," he ordered Des. And then, furiously, "I thought I told you to stop the thing making that blasted noise!"

Des looked at the kraken, still tethered to the deck.

"I've tried, boss. I've kicked him and I've thumped him, but you said I wasn't to do him in."

Evil people cannot bear the sound of the hum. They feel it as a threat to all they stand for, and the kraken had been humming now for many hours.

Boris meanwhile had opened the latch.

"Out," he said. "Up! Only the peoples."

One by one they came out. Fabio, Minette, the aunts . . . Herbert.

On deck it was cold but marvelously fresh after the stuffiness of the hold. Gulls were flying above them; it all looked so normal—except for the look in Sprott's eyes.

"I don't want to see them drown, I don't want to," yelled Lambert, twisting in his father's grasp.

The children moved closer together. It was going to happen, then—and almost straightaway.

Boris and Des had fetched the weights they were going to tie to their victims' ankles; not that there was much chance that they would be able to swim to safety. The *Hurricane* had been steaming steadily away from the Island.

The aunts had come to stand behind the children;

Etta behind Minette, Coral behind Fabio, as though by some miracle they could still protect them.

Fabio and Minette had linked hands. Everything inside them seemed to have turned to stone.

Don't let me make a fuss, Fabio was praying. *Don't let me be like Lambert.*

"We'll start with the fat one," ordered Sprott. "Take her to the rails and get the weights on."

Des went over to Aunt Coral.

"Move," he said, prodding her with the butt of his gun — and as he did so, Fabio went mad.

"How dare you!" he shouted, and tried to attack the bodyguard with his fists.

Sprott thought this was very funny. "All right, you can go first then if you're so full of beans," he said, and the two thugs pinned Fabio's arms behind his back and started to carry him to the side.

They were trying to fix the weights onto his thrashing legs when the skipper put his head out of the wheelhouse.

"Better hurry," he said. "I don't like the look of the sky."

There was nothing to like the look of. Not the sea, not the sky, not the surface of the water, not the clouds. Some dreadful weather was on the way.

The waves darkened, the water boiled; the sun vanished behind a mushroom cloud.

The gulls flew up, screeching.

And on the deck of the *Hurricane*—someone began to scream.

"Hold on to me," Fabio had shouted to Minette, but they were torn apart at once by the mountainous icy waves.

Minette had thought of herself as a good swimmer, but this was nothing to do with swimming—she was being hurled up, then sucked down, rolled over. . . .

And the cold was beyond belief.

All round her were broken planks and debris from the *Hurricane*. The ship had split in two the instant the great kraken had rammed her. She saw the roof of the boobrie's splintered cage bobbing close by; two of the chicks were clinging to the top of it—but where was the third?

A wave broke over her head and she went under again; the weight of the water pressed her down and down; her lungs were bursting. "I'm going to die," she thought, as far as she could think at all.

Then, with a last thrust of her legs, she reached the surface. And as she did so, she saw someone quite close to her, swimming as masterfully and strongly as if he were in a millpond rather than the raging sea.

"Wait, I'm coming," called Herbert, and she reached out for him, but then another wave took her and she went under yet again and was sure she was lost. Then she felt herself pulled up and up by her hair . . . and found that she was clinging to Herbert's back and able to breathe once more.

"Hold on tight, but don't choke me," called Herbert—and set off through the waves as calmly as he had done when he was still a seal.

"Fabio?" she managed to ask.

But Herbert had not seen Fabio.

They passed the stoorworm and saw something large gripped tightly in the coils of his tail. The worm's ancestors had come from the sea, and Herbert wasted no time on him. He would get Aunt Coral to safety if anybody could.

A mattress swam past them, then the galley table with the third boobrie chick clinging on by his yellow feet.

"Keep still, Aunt Etta," came Queenie's high-pitched voice above the sound of the waves. "You mustn't wriggle."

The twins were holding Aunt Etta up between them as she spluttered and kicked her feet.

Hanging on to Herbert's back took all Minette's strength, but she was still searching desperately for Fabio.

"Please, Herbert, we must find him."

After he and Minette were torn apart, Fabio had

sighted the lifeboat that had been thrown clear when the *Hurricane* sank. He managed to swim toward it . . . to get a hand on the gunnel. . . . If the people inside it would help him, he could pull himself up.

But the people inside it were Stanley Sprott and his crew.

Sprott looked over the side and saw the struggling boy. "Get rid of him," he said.

And as the small hand came up, Boris hit it with an oar and pushed the boy back into the water.

There was not much hope for Fabio after that. He was going down for the last time when Herbert found him.

"Hold on to my shoulder," he ordered. "And don't talk."

Herbert was an amazing swimmer, but he knew that to support two children all the long way back to the Island might be beyond his strength. Even a seal would not try to swim with two pups on his back.

Everyone was in difficulties. The raft on which the boobrie chicks balanced was sinking, and above them the boobrie mother squawked in anguish, not knowing which of the two to pick up in her beak. The worm's tail muscles had gone into cramp from holding up the waterlogged Aunt Coral. . . .

Herbert measured the long way to the Island and set his teeth.

"Come on, everybody, follow me," he called manfully. One could only do one's best.

The kraken had found his son. He cared for nothing else. He swam away from the shipwreck with the child on his back. Anger still coursed through his body. He was not the Healer of the Sea now. He was a father whose child had been hurt. Let everyone else beware, for he and his son were on their way!

But after the first joy of being safe, the little kraken wriggled forward so that his mouth was right against his father's ear, and he began to talk very fast in Polar. He was explaining what had happened and how the people on the Island had tried to keep him safe.

And then he said the word that the great kraken had spoken when he first swam into the bay.

"Children?" said the little kraken. And again, looking back at the wreckage: "Children?"

But it was not really a question. It was an order. The little kraken was growing up.

And the great kraken sighed, because he wanted above all to be away from the shrieks and the splintered wood of the wreckage and be in the quietness of the sea. But he heeded his son. He turned and swam back to the wreck and to the struggling creatures trying to hold each other up in the water.

Then Minette and Fabio felt something below

them — the strong living island of muscle that was the kraken's back — and felt it rise and rise until everyone was safely gathered on it: the aunts and the creatures, the boobries in their cage . . . and they themselves, sliding off Herbert's weary shoulders to feel firm ground beneath their feet.

It was an incredible, magic journey that they took after the panic and terror they had been through, floating secure and safe on the great creature's back, until the Island was in sight, and there was no more danger and no more fear.

But the kraken had not saved everybody.

Stanley Sprott lay sprawled across the bottom of the battered, leaking lifeboat. Boris, only half conscious, was clinging to the gunnel. Des was hanging over the side, trying to be sick; he had been drinking seawater. Lambert was curled up like a baby between the skipper and the mate.

Casimir had drowned in the struggle to reach the lifeboat after the *Hurricane* was rammed.

They had been drifting for a long time. The sea was still strange; slate color one minute, the color of blood the next. No rescue ships were setting out in this awesome ocean.

In the lifeboat there was no more water and no more food. The men's lips were blistered. Their swollen tongues stuck to the roofs of their mouths. Befuddled as they were, they tried to make sense of what had happened.

Only they couldn't. No one could make sense of it.

"An island?" muttered Sprott. He could see it, bigger than anyone could believe, moving toward them with the speed of a comet.

But how could it? How could an island move?

"It wasn't there," said Lambert suddenly. Weakened by hunger and thirst, those were the only words he could still say.

Sprott's head was a jumble of pictures.

A mermaid holding up . . . an aunt. But had there really been mermaids? And a great bird the size of an elephant flapping over the wreckage. . . .

No, it was ridiculous. It was impossible. He fingered the bruise on his forehead. He must have a concussion.

"Not . . . really there . . ." murmured Lambert. He wouldn't last much longer unless they were rescued soon.

"I'm going mad," thought Sprott. "I'll have to be careful. We'll all have to be careful, or they'll put us in a loony bin if we're rescued. All that happened was a storm came up and the *Hurricane* was wrecked. Everything else is nonsense."

"Not . . . there . . ." said Lambert faintly.

Sprott looked at his son. He had always despised

Lambert, but he was sorry now. Lambert was right. He had said all along that the . . . things . . . weren't really there, and they weren't. How could they have been?

"Quite right, Lambert," said Stanley Sprott, and leaned back and closed his eyes.

If they were rescued, he'd say nothing—and see that the others said nothing too. He wasn't going to be locked up as a loony, that was for sure. . . .

The last days on the Island were strangely happy. The children knew they would soon be fetched away, but they were able to enjoy each moment as it came, and being in an adventure seemed to have done everybody good.

The stoorworm no longer complained about being too long for his thoughts.

"If I'd been any shorter, I couldn't have held up Aunt Coral in the sea," he said, and stopped talking about plastic surgery once and for all.

As for Loreen, when Aunt Myrtle fetched Walter out of the washbasin and put him in his mother's arms, she let out a shriek of joy.

"He's grown hair!" she cried.

"He's grown *a* hair," said Queenie, who was giving herself airs because she had saved Aunt Etta.

But the most exciting thing happened to the boobrie.

After she waddled up to her nest with her three bedraggled chicks, she found somebody sitting in it.

The boobrie paused, hissed, stretched out her neck. Who was it who *dared* to sit in *her* nest? Hooting, honking, and complaining, she flapped her wings and prepared to attack.

Then, suddenly, she stopped. She lay down in front of the stranger, she clapped her beak against his . . . her eyes rolled with welcome and with love.

"My goodness," said Fabio. "It's her husband. He's come back!"

And he had. He didn't seem to be a very intelligent bird, but knowing that there were two boobries now to look after the chicks was a great relief to everybody.

Herbert was, of course, a hero, but not at all conceited. He began straightaway to tidy up the aunt's house and to label Art's storage jars and to show him how to cut the heads off fish.

But it was Myrtle who had been his special friend, and he did everything he could to help her. He told her when her skirt was on back to front, and he corrected her when she played a tune too fast on the cello, and he insisted that she have swimming lessons twice a day.

"Oh, Herbert, the water is so cold!" Myrtle would cry.

But Herbert said it was dangerous to live so close to the sea and not be able to swim, and every morning and every evening Myrtle had to get her rubber ring and put on her chill-proof vest and Aunt Etta's navy blue bloomers and go into the sea.

But the important thing—the thing that was on everybody's mind—was what was going to happen to the kraken.

After he had brought them safely to the shore, the great kraken had moved a little bit away to the mouth of the bay. He stayed submerged most of the time and out of sight, and his son stayed with him.

"He's thinking," said Aunt Etta, and she was right.

He was thinking about what to do next. Should he give up his healing journey around the world and go back to the Arctic? Or should he find somewhere else to leave his son? For he knew without being told that things were going to be different on the Island.

Then one morning Ethelgonda appeared, shimmering above her tombstone, so they knew that it would be an important day.

And sure enough, by noon the great kraken swam slowly into the bay with his son on his back. It was a most anxious moment. No one could blame the kraken if he turned his back on human beings once again and left the sea to spoil, and it was as though all those who waited by the shore were holding their breath.

Then he began to talk. He talked in Polar, and it was his son who translated.

"Although people deserve that I should leave them to their mess and their wickedness, I have decided to go on with my journey around the oceans of the world. But I shall not take one year and one day to make the journey. I shall take two years and two days . . . or even three years and three days, so that my son, who has been restored to me, can come also and be with me at my side."

When he said that, a great cheer went up, and Fabio and Minette hugged each other, because it was the closest to a happy ending they could hope for.

That evening, when it was quiet, the little kraken came and said good-bye all by himself to the children who had cared for him. There was just one bun left in the boobrie tin, but when Fabio gave it to the kraken, he did not at once open his mouth. He said: "*Share!*"

So the children broke the bun into three parts, and everybody had a piece. It was a most squashed and sorry-looking bun, with cracked icing and a wizened cherry clinging to the top . . . but afterward the children remembered it as tasting like a bun in Paradise.

The next morning the kraken and his son had gone.

And only a few hours later the noise they had been expecting was heard over the Island: the sound of a helicopter. But not one . . . three . . . and coming from them was a whole posse of policemen with guns and handcuffs and body armor, come to fetch back the children and arrest the aunts.

Chapter 23

AUNT ETTA AND Aunt Coral had been in prison for several weeks before their trial for kidnapping came to the courts. The children were not allowed to visit them, and so the first time they saw them was in the dock at the Old Bailey, handcuffed to the policewomen who brought them up from the cells.

For Minette and Fabio, seeing them like that was like being kicked very hard in the stomach, and Minette gave a gasp of distress, which the people in the court-room heard.

"Poor little thing—look how frightened she is," they whispered. And it was true. Minette was very fright-ened, and so was Fabio—frightened for the aunts and what might happen to them; very frightened indeed.

Etta had always been thin, but now she was all bone, and Coral's bulk had gone so that her skin hung in folds.

It wasn't the prison food or the other prisoners that had worn them down; it was waking up day after day to gray walls that closed them in. It was their loss of freedom.

The courtroom was very dark and very old. The judge sat high above everyone else like God, and below him were men in gowns and wigs: a ferrety-looking man who was the prosecuting counsel and had to prove that the aunts were guilty, and a man with a round face like a Christmas pudding who was the defense counsel and had to try and show that the aunts were innocent. The jury—three women and nine men, sat on the judge's right. One of them, a lady with a large bosom and orange hair, kept fanning herself with a piece of paper. Minette's parents sat on benches facing the judge, as far away from each other as possible, and the old Mount-joys were in the back row.

It was only Aunt Etta and Aunt Coral who were being tried. Myrtle had been allowed to return to the Island because Mr. Sprott was in a clinic in America and too muddled to accuse anyone of kidnapping his son. Etta and Coral were glad of that. They thought that Myrtle would probably have died in prison.

The case had attracted a lot of attention. KILLER AUNTS BROUGHT TO JUSTICE screamed the newspaper headlines, and the strange pictures of Etta and Coral that had been on the walls of the police station were printed again, making everyone certain that these were the most evil women in the world.

"Will the prisoner stand," said the clerk of the court—and the children drew in their breath, for the prisoner was Etta.

The charge was read out.

"Do you plead guilty or not guilty?" she was asked.

"Not guilty," said Etta, holding her head high.

Then the witnesses were called. Minette's mother came first, tripping toward the witness box and patting her hair. She was sorry the trial wasn't shown on the telly, because her hat was exactly right—serious and dark but flattering—and because she had been an actress, she swore to tell the whole truth and nothing but the truth in a very dramatic way.

"Is this the woman who met you at King's Cross Station?" asked the prosecuting counsel, who looked like a ferret, pointing at Etta.

"Yes, it is."

"And did you think she was a fit person to have charge of your daughter?"

"Yes, I did, because she came from an agency. But I thought she had a sinister face."

"Could you tell us what you mean by *sinister?*"

Minette's father was called next, and he described the false message that said Minette would not be traveling to Edinburgh.

Then it was Minette's turn.

There had been a lot of argument about whether Fabio and Minette were old enough to give evidence, but in the end it was decided that they could. So Minette too swore to tell the whole truth and nothing but the truth, and then a footstool was fetched so that her head came over the edge of the witness box, and the ferrety man began.

"Now, Minette, you will tell us what happened when you traveled with this person to Edinburgh," he said. "Just take your time," he said, speaking very carefully, as though Minette were three years old.

"We talked about things," said Minette.

"What sort of things?"

"Seals . . . and whether there were ghosts or not . . . and then I asked her if there was a third place."

"Could you tell us what you mean by that?"

Minette bent her head, thinking. "All my life I've kept going back and forth between my parents . . . and when I got there they were always horrible about each other, so I got . . . tired. And sad. And I asked Aunt Etta if there was a third place. A place that wasn't *either* or *or*—and she said there was; there was one for everybody. Only they had to be brave and want it."

"And what happened then?"

"I fell asleep. And when I woke up, I was there. In the third place."

"I see. You woke up in a completely strange place. And were you frightened?"

Minette smiled—a slow, very sweet smile that lit up the dark courtroom like a beacon. "No. Not for long. I had a night-light, you see. I was frightened in London and in Edinburgh because of the dark and the cracks in the ceiling. I used to think I saw tigers . . . and my parents both thought I was silly. But there, when I woke, the first thing I saw was this light."

The ferrety man in the wig didn't like her answer. His job was to prove how wicked the aunts were, and she wasn't helping. "Are you telling me that you woke up in a completely strange place, *having been kidnapped,* and you weren't frightened?"

Minette lifted her chin.

"I wasn't kidnapped," she said clearly. "I was *chosen.*"

That evening the newspapers quoted her words. "I WASN'T KIDNAPPED, I WAS CHOSEN," SAYS CHILD SNATCH VICTIM, and they all carried pictures of Minette.

The next morning it was Aunt Coral's turn, and it was Fabio who went into the witness box and climbed onto the footstool. Again it was the ferrety prosecutor who asked the first questions.

"Now, my boy, will you tell us what happened on the way to Greymarsh Towers."

"I was sick," said Fabio.

"Is that because you were frightened?"

"Yes."

"You were frightened of that lady there?" he asked, pointing to Aunt Coral.

"No. I was frightened of going back to school. It was a horrible place. They put my head down the toilet and kicked me and hung me out of the top-floor windows by my ankles because I came from Brazil and wasn't like them."

There was a sympathetic murmur from the public gallery, and the lady with orange hair stopped fanning herself and made a clucking noise.

"I don't think we need to hear about your school," said the ferret, but the judge leaned down and said Fabio should tell his story in his own way.

"So Aunt Coral went to talk to the matron, and then she came back and said I couldn't go to school because they were in quarantine, and I was terribly pleased. But then I realized it meant going back to my grandparents, and that was almost as bad. They made me kneel on dried peas, and they kept saying how vulgar my mother was. And then I realized that Aunt Coral knew how I felt because she was rather a magic person, and I knew I could trust her."

"So you were drugged and kidnapped," the prosecutor went on.

Minette at this point had smiled, but Fabio didn't. He glared, but the words he said were the same.

"I wasn't kidnapped," he said. "I was *chosen*."

By the next day the newspapers were writing rather differently about the trial, and some strange things were happening. Those children who were old enough to hear about the trial began to ask their parents for different bedtime stories: stories about magical aunts who came and took children away to islands where they didn't have to go to school.

Of course, the aunts were guilty; everyone knew that. They would go to prison, probably for the rest of their lives, but there wasn't so much glee about, and the people who stood outside the courtroom holding up banners saying HANGING IS TOO GOOD FOR THEM stopped yelling and went home.

The third day of the trial was the last, and the ferret started his questions again.

"What exactly did you do on the Island?" he wanted to know.

"We worked," said the children. "We helped to clean the animals and milk the goats and feed the baby seals."

"Exactly. You worked all the time? From dawn to dusk."

"Yes."

"And didn't you get tired?"

"Of course we got tired." Fabio scowled at him. "What's wrong with being tired? Working like that was *good*. Everybody ought to do it instead of messing about at school trying to solve math problems that don't have anything to do with real life and writing silly essays about people who are dead."

When he found he couldn't drive the children into a corner, the ferret started on the aunts, and it seemed as though there really couldn't be any hope. They *had* taken the children without their parents' knowledge; they didn't try to deny that. Neither Coral nor Etta was any good at telling lies.

And now it came to the end, to the summing-up, when the judge had to make the jury understand exactly what the case was about. Everyone in the courtroom was silent; everyone knew the verdict would be "guilty," but even those people who had wanted it at the beginning weren't so certain now.

Then Etta beckoned to the Christmas-pudding man who was supposed to be defending them and whispered something, and he went over to the judge and whispered to him, and the judge nodded. No one knew what had been said, but after a few minutes a clerk came in carrying two big dictionaries.

"Your Honor," said the pudding. "I ask for leave to read out the two most up-to-date definitions of kidnapping. The first comes from the London Dictionary and it says: *Kidnap: To hold a person against his will.*" He turned to Minette. "May I ask you to step into the box again?"

She did so.

"Would you say that you had been held against your will?"

"*No,*" said Minette.

The question was repeated to Fabio.

"*No,*" shouted the boy.

The pudding picked up the second book. "The definition of kidnapping given here is: *To hold a person for ransom. To demand money to secure the victim's release.*"

He looked at the benches where Minette's parents and Fabio's grandparents were sitting. Then he called them out one by one, and to each of them he asked: "Have you ever been asked for a single penny by either of these ladies?"

And crossly, peevishly, they admitted that they had not.

"In that case, Your Honor, it is my opinion that no kidnap took place."

The jury was out for six hours, and during the whole of this time Fabio and Minette absolutely refused to leave the building.

"We're staying until they bring in the verdict," said Fabio—and nothing the police or the social workers or anyone else could say would move them.

So they sat on hard chairs in an office behind the courtroom and waited. They were so tired they could hardly stop themselves from slipping to the ground, but they did it. It was like keeping watch when someone was ill or dying; it had to be done.

It was after midnight before the jury returned, and everybody filed back into the courtroom.

"Have you reached a verdict?" asked the judge, leaning down from his box.

"We have, my lord," replied the foreman in a solemn voice.

"And do you find the defendants guilty or not guilty?"

There had never been such silence. Not a breath was heard in the court; not a rustle . . .

The foreman raised his head.

"Not guilty."

Oddly, it was not Minette but Fabio who burst into tears.

Chapter 24

THE ISLAND HAD NEVER looked more beautiful. The sea sparkled and danced, the sun shone through the green crests on the waves; and on the hill the blossoming gorse was a mass of gold.

The children had been allowed to come up for a week to say good-bye. Minette had to go back to her parents, but Fabio's mother was taking him back to South America. She had read about the trial and about Fabio's school, and she no longer thought that her son needed to grow up as an English gentleman.

So it should have been a really sad farewell, but it wasn't because the aunts had called them into the dining room the day they came and shown them an important-looking document covered in red seals.

"It's our will," they said.

The children started to read it, but they couldn't

make head or tail of it, and in the end Etta said: "What it says is that we have left you the Island. To both of you jointly. When we die, the Island will be yours."

They had stood round them; all the aunts—Etta and Coral and Myrtle and Dorothy—and nodded in a pleased way.

"We know that you will regard it as a Sacred Trust," they said.

The children could hardly believe it at first. It was too big to take in: the thought that the Island would one day be theirs, and they could live on it and care for it and be together. It made the years in between seem unimportant. Minette was not so frightened now of her parents' moods—and they were trying to behave better. Time would go quickly. Very soon now, she and Fabio would return and their real lives would begin.

"Will you manage the work until we come back?" Fabio asked, and they said, yes, they would because Dorothy had decided to stay. She thought it was time to hang up her wok, and she had decided to breed piranha fish in a tank so that if any more Sprotts came to the Island, she could see them off.

As for Herbert, he went on making himself useful, as he had done ever since they escaped from the *Hurricane*. He polished the napkin rings and tidied Art's cutlery drawer and ordered some bedroom slippers for the Sybil from a catalog.

But most of all, he went on helping Myrtle. He showed her how to keep her hair tidy in a net, he stuck her loose sheet music together with tape, and every single morning and every single evening he saw that she put on Aunt Etta's bloomers and her rubber ring and had her swimming lesson in the sea.

All the same, Fabio and Minette, who had not seen him since before the trial, felt that Herbert had changed. He seemed to be working too hard, as though he was afraid of what might happen if he did not keep busy, and sometimes they caught him gazing out the window with a strange look in his large brown eyes.

"He's homesick," Myrtle whispered to the children. "He misses the sea."

The children were very upset. Herbert, after all, had saved their lives.

"Isn't there anything that can be done?" asked Fabio.

Aunt Myrtle sighed. "He *could* be turned back into a seal," she said slowly. "There is a way."

"Not a knife?" said Minette, horrified.

"No. That might work but . . ." She shook her head. "The mermaids say that if one weeps seven tears over a selkie when the moon is rising . . . seven human tears . . ."

"But could you bear it?" asked Minette. "I mean, he's your friend."

Myrtle looked down at her Wellington boots. "I could . . . bear it," she said, biting her lip, "if it is the right thing to do. One can always bear what is right."

So they went to the other aunts and had a meeting, and then they went to find Herbert, who was cleaning the windows of the sitting room.

"Herbert, we want you to tell us the truth," said Aunt Etta. "Were you happier as a seal? Do you want to return?"

Herbert spun round, the polishing cloth in his hand. There was no need for him to answer. They only had to look into his eyes.

"He has reached the Rock of the Farnes," Herbert said in a dreamy voice. "But he swims slowly. I could catch up with him."

So they realized that Herbert's thoughts all this time had been with the great kraken and that he longed to swim with him and be his escort in the work of cleaning the sea.

But when they told Herbert what the mermaids had said and that he could be turned into a seal again if someone wept seven human tears over him, he shook his head.

"Myrtle stayed by my side when my mother died; she played music to me in all weathers. I couldn't leave her now."

So then Myrtle stepped forward, and now she was not a vague and dippy woman whose hair fell down. She was a heroine.

"If it is right for you to swim with the great kraken,

you must do so, Herbert," she said, and though there was a sob in her throat, she held her head high.

They decided to do the turning in the crystal cave, and of course everyone wanted to come. The Captain couldn't leave his bed, but the stoorworm promised to tell him about it and the mermaids insisted on being there, and the naak and even the boobries, though it wasn't at all certain that they knew what was going on.

They had to wait until the moon broke out of its covering of cloud, but when Herbert threw off his dressing gown and stood there only in Art's boxer shorts, everyone sighed because it was all so dignified and beautiful, like a ceremony in ancient Greece.

It was Myrtle, of course, who was to do the actual crying, and because the tears had to fall directly on his head, Herbert knelt before her . . . and then she began.

She remembered all the good times—the music on Seal Point, the silent evenings beside her friend watching the sunset. . . .

One tear fell on Herbert's head . . . then two . . . then three . . . four . . . five . . . six . . .

Only one more.

But just when everyone was clutching everyone else, ready for the great moment, the tears stopped.

It was most embarrassing. Myrtle sniffed. She blinked. She blushed. She had shed six tears, and she couldn't shed a seventh.

For the truth was (though she never told anyone) that at that moment she had suddenly realized that she need never again go into the cold sea in her chill-proof vest and her sister's navy bloomers. She still minded terribly losing Herbert, but the relief had blocked her tear ducts as thoroughly as if they had been plugged with cement.

It was a dreadful moment, but of course help was at hand. Minette only had to think of saying good-bye to the man who had saved her life and she was off.

She took Myrtle's place—and as the seventh tear fell onto Herbert's head, there was a flash of blinding, jagged light.

And when they looked again, they knew they had done right. On the ledge of the rock was a pair of crumpled boxer shorts—but streaking out of the cave into the open sea was a silver hunk of streamlined muscle that thrust through the waves like an arrow.

The next morning was the children's last on the Island. They got up early and walked along the strand, as they had done on the first day, when they woke up to find they had been kidnapped.

"You will come back, won't you?" Minette asked. "You won't stay and become prime minister of Brazil?"

She wanted to make him swear; to have a kind of ceremony—but then she saw his face as he looked out over the Island and saw that he loved it as she did, and she knew for certain that they would both be back. And the ache of parting became sort of a different ache—an ache of happiness—and they turned and went back toward the house, where the aunts were waiting.